PRAISE FOR CYNTHIA EDEN
AND HER NOVELS . . .

BROKEN

"Cynthia Eden's *Broken* is what romantic suspense is supposed to be—fast, furious, and very sexy!"
Karen Rose, *New York Times* bestselling author

"Sexy, mysterious, and full of heart-pounding suspense!"
Laura Kaye, *New York Times* bestselling author

"I dare you not to love a Cynthia Eden book!"
Larissa Ione, *New York Times* bestselling author

"Fast-paced, smart, sexy and emotionally wrenching—everything I love about a Cynthia Eden book!"
HelenKay Dimon

"Cynthia Eden's on my must-buy list."
Angie Fox, *New York Times* bestselling author

By Cynthia Eden

The LOST Series
WRECKED
TAKEN
TORN
SHATTERED
TWISTED
BROKEN

CYNTHIA EDEN

WRECKED

AVONBOOKS

An Imprint of HarperCollinsPublishers

WRECKED. Copyright © 2017 by Cindy Roussos. All rights reserved. Printed in the United States of America. No part of this book may be used or reproduced in any manner whatsoever without written permission except in the case of brief quotations embodied in critical articles and reviews. For information, address HarperCollins Publishers, 195 Broadway, New York, NY 10007.

First Avon Books mass market printing: June 2017

ISBN 978-0-06-243748-8

Avon, Avon & logo, and Avon Books & logo are registered trademarks of HarperCollins Publishers in the United States of America and other countries.

HarperCollins is a registered trademark of HarperCollins Publishers in the United States of America and other countries.

17 18 19 20 21   QGM   10 9 8 7 6 5 4 3 2 1

For the readers. For the dreamers. For all of those who understand the true pleasure that can be found . . . in a book.

ACKNOWLEDGMENTS

I'VE HAD SUCH AN INCREDIBLE TIME WRITING MY LOST books. I want to thank the awesome staff at Avon for all of their help and insight. I want to thank my readers for following this series and reading the twists and turns in the books. To put it simply, thank you for getting LOST with me.

CHAPTER ONE

THE KNIFE SLICED INTO HER SKIN. IT CUT DEEP, and the pain was white-hot. Ana Young locked her teeth together and stared straight ahead . . . straight into her brother's horrified eyes. He was tied in the chair across from her, yanking and twisting against his ropes as he tried to break free.

But he couldn't escape. Neither could she.

But she could stay silent.

Asher . . . her twin wasn't silent. He was screaming, *"Let my sister go! Stop it! Stop, please! Don't hurt her!"*

Asher didn't get it. The man with the knife . . . he enjoyed hurting her.

Another slice. Even deeper this time. Ana licked her lip and tasted blood. The first slice had been to her face. Only her attacker had paused after that.

"Let's save her pretty face for later."

And the knife had gone into her body, again and again. She tried to keep her eyes open. Tried to keep looking at Asher. When the end came, she wanted his face to be the last thing that she saw. She wanted Asher to know that she hadn't been afraid. That she was strong.

Another slice of that knife and she could feel tears sliding down her cheeks. The pain was wrecking her. Destroying the girl she'd been. Leaving someone else—some*thing* else in her place.

Don't fear the pain. Don't tense when the knife sinks into you. Look at Asher. Look at him.

"Let my sister go, you fucking bastard! You want to hurt someone? Hurt me, not Ana! Let her go!"

Ana's eyes were sagging shut. Asher's voice was fading. It suddenly seemed so distant. Odd, since he was just a few feet away. They'd put them close together so Asher would be able to see every cut perfectly.

Was she dying? Ana didn't want to go out like this. Tied up, trapped. Some sick bastard's toy.

She didn't want to go out like this . . .

Her eyes closed.

And part of her died.

The good part.

"Ana?" A hard hand closed over her shoulder. Ana jerked at the touch, and the dream—more like twisted memory—vanished in an instant. She jumped to her feet, whirling around, and Ana found her boss, Gabe Spencer, frowning at her.

Way to make a killer impression on the big boss, Ana.

She shoved back her hair, lifted her chin, and straightened her spine. Not that straightening her spine did much. When you were all of five feet, two inches, it was often hard to look intimidating. She wasn't the kind of woman who wore high heels—they just slowed her down when she was chasing criminals—so Ana had long grown accustomed to tipping back her chin and staring at the world with her go-to-hell gaze.

Only it wasn't exactly appropriate to use that gaze on the big boss.

Like it's appropriate to be caught sleeping at the office by him.

Ana cleared her throat. "Hi, Gabe. I was . . . brainstorming on the new case." She smiled at him. The smile was one of her secret weapons. Slow and disarming, that smile had saved her ass more times than she could count. In her line of work, some people erroneously thought that looking delicate was a weakness. Not so . . . Ana used her deceptively delicate appearance every single chance that she had.

But Gabe—former SEAL and now big, bad man in charge of LOST—well, he didn't exactly look disarmed. His bright blue stare swept over her, and a faint furrow appeared between his brows. "Did you pull another all-nighter?"

Maybe.

"Ana . . ." He sighed out her name. "I hired you because I *know* you're good. Your track record speaks for itself. You don't have to burn yourself out because you're trying to tear through the old case files at LOST in order to prove something to me."

Gabe was a good guy. He wasn't chewing her ass out for the on-the-job nap. He understood exactly what she'd been doing.

So Ana let her guard drop, just a bit, with him. After all, she'd known Gabe for years. They'd been friends long before she'd finally let him lure her into joining the LOST team. Gabe knew her secrets. Well, most of them. There were some secrets that even Ana's twin brother, Asher, didn't know.

And I plan to keep things that way.

"There are just so many of them," Ana said, glancing over at her desk and the files that were spread out there. "All those people . . . still missing. All those families . . . just hoping that their kids will come home. Husbands, looking for wives. Mothers, looking for their daughters. Friends, looking for—" She broke off, her lips pressing together. "I just want to help them."

And that was why she'd finally given in and joined LOST.

The Last Option Search Team was Gabe's baby. Years ago, his sister had vanished, and when the local authorities hadn't been able to find her, Gabe had joined the search. Unfortunately, he'd found his sister too late. He'd buried her instead of returning her home, and after that terrible tragedy, Gabe had made it his mission to help other families. The agents who worked at LOST were truly the last option for so many. People turned to LOST when their hope was gone. When the FBI and the cops and everyone else said the case was dead . . . LOST kept looking.

And the agents at LOST had been showing amazing results. Hell, within the last year, they'd even stopped two serial killers. They'd saved victims, not just found bodies. They were making a huge difference in the world.

And I want to be part of that difference.

So maybe she'd been burning the midnight oil as she reviewed case files. One in particular kept nagging at her. Cathy Wise. The girl had been just thirteen when she vanished.

And I was fourteen when I was abducted. Only Ana had gotten to go home again.

Cathy . . . hadn't. Not yet.

"I get personally involved," Ana confessed. "I know I should probably hold back but . . ." *But I can see myself in these cases. We have to help the victims.*

"No." Gabe's voice was soft. "We need to be involved, Ana. We need to care. It motivates us to get the job done." He inclined his head toward the files. "But you can't let the job consume you. As hard as we try, there will always be other cases out there. Others who go missing."

Her stomach twisted because she knew he was right. Every day, someone new vanished. Every day, a life was destroyed.

"That's why I'm in your office now," Gabe added. A faint smile curved his lips and his eyes glinted. "Not just because I wanted to interrupt your nap time."

Trust me, with the dream I was having . . . I'm glad you did interrupt.

"We have a new case."

Ana took a quick step toward him.

But Gabe lifted a hand. "Before you get too excited, this case comes with some strings."

Strings? What was that supposed to mean? She was over her probationary period at LOST. She'd been handling cases on her own for weeks now.

"You'll have a partner on this one."

Well, yes, that was standard LOST procedure. *Always have someone watching your ass.* That was a Gabe Spencer directive that had come down on day one.

"He's . . . not with LOST."

Okay, now she was curious. "Then who is he with?"

"The FBI."

She tensed. A natural reaction for her. She didn't tend to like the Feds. With her past, with the way she'd seen the Feds tear into people's lives . . . *I don't exactly play nicely with them.*

"He's the one who brought us the case, Ana. Come in, talk with him, and just listen to what he has to say." Gabe paused. "And you should know that the agent asked to work with you, specifically."

Oh, hell, no. She did *not* like where this was going. Her inner alarms were definitely ringing. "What's this FBI agent's name?" The knot in her stomach twisted tighter even as she started a mental chant of *Don't be Cash Knox. Don't be Cash Knox. Don't be—*

"FBI Agent Cash Knox."

Of course. Because she truly did have some of the worst luck in the world.

"There a problem?" Gabe asked, squinting a bit at her.

Oh, jeez. Ana hoped she hadn't flinched or made some kind of horrible, pained face when he mentioned the FBI agent's name. "No, no problem at all." She pasted a big smile on her face.

"Agent Knox said that he'd worked with you before."

Worked with me. Had sex with me. Let's not go over all the gory details right now.

"But," Gabe continued carefully, as he inclined his dark head toward her, "this case . . . it's not going to be an easy one."

Fine with her. "I don't like easy."

He nodded, looking pleased, and Ana knew she'd given the right answer. "Then come into my office,"

Gabe said, "and I'll tell you everything. Agent Knox is waiting for us."

Right. She rolled back her shoulders. "Lead the way." *While I get my shit together.* Because she hadn't seen Cash in years . . . two years and a month, to be exact. She hadn't laid eyes on the guy since she'd left him sleeping after a night of great sex. She'd slipped away and hadn't looked back.

Because Cash is like Gabe . . . one of the "good" guys. And good guys weren't meant for her. Ana shoved a lock of hair behind her ear, grabbed her rather beat-up jacket from the back of her chair, and she hurriedly followed Gabe out of her office and down the hallway.

As they walked down that hallway, she glanced out of the bank of windows to her right. The bustling city of Atlanta was definitely alive and well . . . even though it was only a little after eight a.m. Gabe had been right about her all-nighter. She'd pulled another one because staying at home, having her demons torment her—well, it wasn't an option she wanted. So she'd escaped into work.

I thought if I couldn't help myself, maybe I could help someone else. Someone like Cathy Wise.

They passed Gabe's assistant and Melody gave Ana a quick, friendly wave. Ana waved back even as her gaze darted to Gabe's closed door. Cash was in there. How was she supposed to handle this?

Act as if nothing ever happened. She could do that. Cash would be all business, and so would she. Besides, it wasn't as if a good guy like Cash would cause trouble. Maybe he didn't even remember their night together. They'd both been drinking, thanks to the big celebration. Ana had brought in one of the FBI's ten most wanted, a sadistic asshole named Bernie Tate who'd enjoyed kidnapping and murdering women in their early twenties. He'd taken three victims by the time he was stopped.

And I was the one who stopped him.

She was still proud of that fact.

Gabe opened the door to his office and held it, waiting for her to walk inside. Ana schooled her features, made sure her steps were slow and steady, and she marched in to face her past.

FBI Special Agent Cash Knox was turned away from her. He stood in front of the large windows in Gabe's office, and Cash's stare was on the city below. But, as soon as she crossed the threshold into the office, his body stiffened and his head turned in her direction.

Cash's gaze met hers. She'd forgotten just how intense his green eyes were. Forgotten that his face wasn't exactly handsome. Instead, it was rugged, a face with an edge that had made her think of danger the first time she'd seen him. Cash's jaw was hard, square, and currently clenched. His cheekbones were high, and a faint dimple notched the middle of his chin. A line of stubble coated his jaw, dark stubble to match his hair. Cash kept his hair cut almost ruthlessly short—that style hadn't changed in the last two years. The guy's hair was so thick that if he let it grow, she was sure it would be something to see . . . sexy.

But that wasn't his style. An FBI agent who toed the line didn't have too-long hair. *And I'm guessing that stubble isn't his normal style, either.* It looked as if she wasn't the only one who'd pulled an all-nighter.

Cash stalked toward her. He had on a suit—a well-cut coat and basic black pants. She thought of that suit as FBI business time. His badge gleamed on his hip and when he shifted his arm, she saw the bulk of his holster.

Gabe followed Ana into the office and shut the door behind him.

"Ana Young," Cash said, his voice as deep as she remembered. "It's been a long time." He offered his hand to her.

And she was a professional, so she just gave him a small smile and took that hand. "Has it?" She released her hold after touching him for what she figured was a good-manners length of time. Maybe her fingers tingled from the contact. Maybe she just imagined the tingle.

"It has," Cash agreed, dipping his head toward her. "Two years, to be exact."

No, it's been two years and one month. Not that either of us should know that.

Cash lowered his hand back to his side. "The last time I saw you . . ." Cash began.

Do not finish that sentence. The last time he'd seen her, she'd been naked. And on top of him.

"The last time I saw you," Cash repeated, his jaw hardening, "you'd just done the job that several dozen FBI agents hadn't been able to accomplish. You'd found Bernie Tate and you'd brought him into federal custody."

Her eyelids flickered. "It was my job. I was a bounty

hunter." Actually, she could admit with pride that she'd been the best freaking bounty hunter in the whole United States. "And there was quite a reward on his head." But the reward hadn't mattered to her—it never did. She'd wanted to get that monster off the streets so that he wouldn't hurt anyone else.

And she had. Bernie was currently rotting in a maximum security hold in Virginia, Wingate Penitentiary. A place reputed to be a real hell on earth.

"I need you to do that job again," Cash said.

Now she blinked in surprise. "Excuse me?"

Gabe walked around her and headed toward his desk. "Seems there was an . . . incident late last night." He eased into his chair and the leather gave a long groan beneath him. "Since you were pulling an all-nighter at the office, I'm guessing you missed the news."

Ana glanced between Gabe and Cash. "What news?"

"Bernie Tate was being transferred," Cash explained grimly. "But during that transfer, the prison van broke down. Bernie Tate escaped."

"You are kidding me." He'd better be kidding.

"I wish that were the case," Cash told her. "Trust me, I do, but he's gone. And I need you to find him."

"Before he kills again." She started to pace. She did that—when she was pissed, when she was scared, when she was trying to figure out what the hell to do next. "I can't believe this! The guy should have been locked away for the rest of his life! He shouldn't be out! How the hell did this happen?" She thought of his victims . . .

She still remembered them all.

Brenda George, twenty-two, a nursing student who'd

been stabbed twenty-two times . . . the perfect number to match her age.

Kennedy Crenshaw, twenty-four, a young mother who'd still been alive when the cops found her . . . only she'd died an hour later, her body littered with stab wounds.

Janice Burrell, twenty-eight, a divorcee who'd made the mistake of hooking up with Bernie at a bar. He'd stabbed her so many times that her blood had covered the walls of her motel room.

"He said there were more victims," Cash murmured. "So the FBI worked out a deal to have him moved to a different prison, provided the guy talked and told us where those bodies were hidden."

Her eyes squeezed together. "You got played. Bernie isn't the kind of guy who hides his kills. He wanted everyone to know what he was doing. He was *proud* of his crimes."

"I agree," Cash said, surprising her.

Her eyes opened and locked on him.

"But my boss didn't listen to me." The faint lines on either side of his mouth deepened. "Now we're in a serious clusterfuck situation. The media is in a frenzy. We've got manhunts going in the area, and we need to get Bernie Tate back into custody, freaking yesterday."

Gabe tapped his fingers on the top of his desk. "I explained to the agent here that LOST doesn't normally hunt down criminals." His expression tightened as he studied Cash. "Our goal is to help the victims."

Cash raked a hand over his hair. "And I told your boss that if we don't stop Bernie, there *will* be more victims. It's only a matter of time."

Ana swiped her tongue over her top lip, feeling the old scar that raised the skin there. "Agent Knox is right. Bernie Tate isn't going to just disappear quietly into the sunset. He *will* start hunting again, and he'll take down as many innocent people as he can." She strode toward the windows. "Especially since he's been in prison," Ana mused. "He's been away from the blood for too long. He liked the blood, liked the thrill he got from hurting women." She could see people walking down on the street below. Men and women, going about their normal lives. Having no idea . . .

Danger is everywhere.

"You caught him before, Ana," Cash said, his voice roughening with intensity. "I think you can do it again. I got the all-clear from my boss to pull you in on this. The FBI wants Bernie back in custody, as quickly and as quietly as possible." There was a pause. "I need you, Ana."

She spun around. Her gaze jerked toward him. There was something in his eyes . . .

Cash exhaled on a long breath. "As I told your boss, the FBI is willing to offer certain incentives for your cooperation on this case."

"What kind of incentives?"

Gabe gave a low laugh. "The 'you scratch my back, and I'll scratch yours' variety."

"The FBI is promising help on future LOST cases," Cash elaborated. "The FBI and LOST have crossed paths plenty of times, and sometimes that intersection has proven . . . painful."

That's an understatement.

"We're offering support to LOST, we're offering

whatever damn deal it takes," Cash added grimly. "We just need you on board in the hunt for Bernie."

"The FBI certainly seems desperate," Gabe said.

Yes, Ana had just been thinking the same thing.

"Don't have much faith in your ability to bring the guy in, huh?" Gabe asked as he cocked his head to study Cash.

Anger flashed in Cash's eyes. "Let's cut the bullshit, shall we?"

Let's do that. She'd never had a lot of patience for bullshit.

Cash pointed at Ana. "She's the best tracker there is. I still don't know how the hell she found him before, but time is of the essence. Bernie Tate is missing, and the FBI wants him brought back in. If Ana does the job, the FBI will owe LOST."

Definitely the "I'll scratch yours" variety of favor.

"What do you think, Ana?" Gabe asked, drawing her gaze once more. "You joined LOST to find the victims, not to clean up messes left by the FBI. So if you don't want to take the case, you don't have to do it."

Cash growled.

Goose bumps rose on her arms.

Gabe rose to his feet. "Ana's choice," he said simply. "I told you I'd give you the chance to lay out the case for her, and I have. What happens next is completely up to Ana."

Her heartbeat drummed steadily in her chest. She thought of the files on her desk. The *victims* that needed her help.

And she thought of the women who could die if Bernie Tate was left to run free.

"May I talk to Ana alone?" Cash asked, his voice still rough.

Surprise flashed on Gabe's face. "Don't really know why you'd need to do that. Whatever you have to say to Ana can certainly be said to me, too." Now he slid from around his desk and walked to Ana's side. His arm brushed her shoulder. "I've known Ana for a very long time, and like I told you before, she has my utmost respect. That's why the choice is hers. If she wants this case, LOST will fully support her, if not . . ."

Cash's gaze slid between her and Gabe. His green stare hardened. He opened his mouth to speak—

"I'd like a moment with him," Ana said quickly. *Because I'm not sure what Cash may say next.*

Gabe's eyes slowly slid over her face. Whatever he saw there . . . well, it had him nodding. "Getting kicked out of my own office, huh?" A rueful smile curved his lips. "That's a new one."

She was so not winning points with him today. "Gabe . . ."

His hand brushed over her shoulder. "I'll be outside. I need to talk with my assistant, anyway. And . . . Ana . . ."

"Yes?"

"*You* make the choice."

He nodded toward Cash and slowly exited the room. Ana didn't realize she'd been holding her breath, not until the door closed behind him.

Then . . .

She became aware of just how thick and heavy the silence was in that office. She could also feel the weight of Cash's stare. She made herself look back at him.

"You seem . . . close to your boss."

Her eyes narrowed. *You'd better watch your step, Special Agent.* "Gabe is a good man. He wants to help the victims out there."

Cash swore. "And Bernie Tate isn't a victim."

"No, he isn't." Her hands twisted together. "But if Bernie isn't brought back into custody, there *will* be more dead women left in his wake. We both know that's true."

He stepped toward her. "Then you're going to help me? You could have just said so—"

"There are conditions." And she hadn't wanted to discuss these conditions in front of Gabe.

"Name them."

"One . . . I want honesty from you."

His eyelids flickered. "Are you saying I've lied to you before?"

"I'm saying that the FBI doesn't always play by the rules. If I'm working with you, if you're my partner on this, then I need to know I can trust you. I need to know that you'll have my back."

"I will." He sounded so sincere.

She wanted to believe him. "I'll need access to every bit of intel you have on Bernie, even the confidential material, so don't think of holding back."

He nodded. "Done."

Okay, so far, so good. Time for the last condition. "You don't mention our past."

A muscle flexed along his jaw. "Want to run that by me again?"

"I don't think I need to do that." She lifted a brow. "I'm absolutely certain you know what I'm talking about. There will *not* be a repeat performance. If we're hunting Bernie, that's all we're doing. We'll stay professional, and the past will stay exactly where it belongs . . . dead and buried."

His gaze slid toward the closed office door. "You don't want the boss knowing about us."

"I don't want *anyone* knowing my personal business. If you have a problem with that—"

"Easy, Ana," he said, his voice going a bit soft when he said her name. Soft . . . raspy . . . the way he'd said it that long-ago night. "Despite what you think, I've never been the type to kiss and tell. Our past is our business, no one else's."

"Good." She gave a brisk nod. "Then it should stay that way." Ana offered her hand to him. "I think we have a deal."

Once more, his hand closed around hers.

And, dammit, his touch *did* make her skin tingle. She'd offered her hand to him again just so she could see and unfortunately . . .

The attraction is still there. I touch him and my body reacts. I look at him and I need.

But sometimes, Ana's needs could become very, very dark.

Cash doesn't know about that part of me. He won't ever know. Because this case was strictly business. And now they had a deal.

Time to hunt a killer . . . before he took another life.

BERNIE TATE GROANED as his eyes opened. He expected to see the old, sagging cot above him, his cellmate's ass would be dragging low over him but . . .

No, I'm not in that hellhole. Not anymore.

His memory came rushing back to him. He'd been on that transport bus, the only prisoner. The guard had cuffed his hands but left his feet loose. Stupid mistake.

Bernie had waited for the perfect opportunity. Waited for his chance at freedom . . .

He smiled. *That chance had come.*

There was no sagging cot above him. There was just the rough wood of a cabin. He could smell the scent of a fire burning somewhere close by, probably in the other room. His partner had sure done one real fine job of getting his ass to freedom.

Bernie sat up and swung his legs off the narrow bed. He shot to his feet, his stomach growling to remind him that he hadn't eaten since before he'd boarded that transport bus. Maybe his partner had a meal waiting in the cabin for him. Bernie smiled as he took a few fast steps toward the door.

Then Bernie tripped and he slammed, face-first, into the wooden floor.

"What the hell?" Bernie snarled as he shoved himself up. He was in good shape—he'd made a damn point of staying in shape. Trapped in that prison, all he'd been able to do was work out. Exercise had kept him sane. Exercise . . . and his plans.

He had so many fine plans.

Goal one . . . find the bitch who got me locked up. Make her pay. Make her bleed. Make her scream.

But . . .

Bernie grabbed for his ankle. There was some kind of shackle on him. A cuff that locked around his left ankle and trailed back to the narrow bed. He grabbed the chain and yanked it and the whole bed jerked toward him because the other side of that chain was locked around the foot of the bed.

The door squeaked behind him. His head jerked and his body twisted as he glared at the asshole in the doorway. "Is this some kind of joke?" Bernie shouted. "Get this thing off me!"

Then . . . then Bernie saw the knife. Glinting.

"No joke, Bernie." His partner stepped closer. The knife lifted. "It's time for you to pay."

What? No, no, this wasn't happening. He was free! He'd gotten away from that rat-hole prison. Away from the guards. He was free—

The knife sliced down toward him. Bernie lifted his hands, trying to shield his face.

The blade drove straight through his left hand and Bernie screamed.

"See?" his partner whispered. "Payback."

CHAPTER TWO

YOUR BOSS GAVE YOU THE COMPANY JET," CASH murmured as he sat across from Ana—*in one very plush company jet*. "You must have a lot of pull with him." And, yeah, that was jealousy twisting his guts up but he couldn't help it.

When it came to Ana Young—Ana *Break-My-Heart* Young—his emotions were always raw.

At his words, Ana stopped looking at the clouds outside of her window and her head turned toward him. When she locked her dark gaze on him, Cash felt that stare like a punch straight to his gut. Ana wasn't the kind of woman that a guy forgot, though Cash had sure as hell tried to put their night behind him.

Ana was different.

She was the kind of woman who could wreck a man.

"If you have a question about my relationship with Gabe," Ana said, her voice clear and easy, "then ask. But don't make snide-ass comments that are only going to piss me off, okay?"

That was Ana. Straight to the point. A woman who didn't play games. He could sure respect that. "Are you involved with him?"

"Am I sleeping with my boss? No. He's married, actually. Quite happily." Her lips kicked up into a quick smile. "To a former client."

His gaze darted to her lips. Her lips were truly incredible—red and full. And her scar *shouldn't* have been sexy. Cash hated that Ana had been hurt. Hated that she was scarred in any way. If he'd had his way, she would have never known a moment of pain or fear.

Ana had a habit of lightly licking the faint line of her scar when she was in deep thought. A quick swipe of her pink tongue across her top lip.

Drives me insane.

Not that she knew it. Not that he'd tell her. It had been two years, for fuck's sake. He'd moved the hell on. And even if Ana wasn't sleeping with her boss, a woman like her would sure be sleeping with *someone*.

Whoever the guy was . . . he was one lucky bastard.

"What about you, Agent Knox?"

His brows rose. Since when was he *Agent Knox?*

"You involved with someone?" Her gaze dipped to his left hand. "I don't see a ring, but that doesn't mean anything. You certainly strike me as the marrying kind."

He flexed his fingers. "Not involved. Definitely not married." But her words were nagging. "What do you mean about me being the marrying kind?"

She waved her hand toward him. "Oh, you know."

He had no clue.

"You're the true-blue type. The white knight. So I just figured you'd have a white picket fence and an adoring family waiting for you by now." Sadness flickered in her eyes, just for a moment. "I rather wanted that for you."

Wait, *what?* "Ana Young," he said, rasping out her name. "You confuse the hell out of me."

Her long lashes fell, casting shadows against her cheeks.

"So . . . are we going to talk about it at all?" Cash drawled, aware that his Texas accent had just slipped out. Ana had grown up in Texas, too, though she'd certainly never talked to him about her life. Not that they'd done a whole lot of talking when they'd known each other before.

They'd met. Ignited. Burned up the sheets.

Then she'd vanished.

Her lashes slowly lifted. Her gaze swept over his face. "You look the same." Her head tilted a bit as she studied him. "Though the stubble is new. Kind of gives you a rough edge." She paused. "I like it."

Ana.

"As far as talking about 'it' . . . I'm assuming you mean the case? Because we really don't have anything else to talk about."

That was cold and clear. And Cash found himself smiling. "You seem the same, too." Direct. Sexy as all hell. But . . . "Prettier, though. How is that possible? How do you get better with time?"

She stared back at him. Her eyes were so dark, but he could see the gold hidden in their depths. That gold had ignited when he'd been inside of her and she'd been coming for him.

Focus on the case, man!

Because he wasn't there for a walk down memory lane. He was with Ana because she truly was the best. And . . .

So maybe I lied to Ana a bit. He lied to people all the time, and they had no clue. Ana had just said he was the white knight type.

That was hilarious. He was as far from a white knight as it was possible to be. His eyes narrowed as he stared at her. Ana didn't understand exactly what was happening with this case, but he did.

After all, he'd been the one there when Bernie Tate was sentenced to life in prison. He'd heard the convicted man's screams. His demands to "See the bitch who did this to me! Bring her to me! I'll make her sorry!" Ana hadn't been around then. She'd moved on, another case, another killer. So she hadn't realized just how much hate was focused on her.

Perhaps time should have made that hatred dim. It hadn't. As soon as Cash had learned of Bernie's disappearance, Cash had gone to Wingate Penitentiary. He'd seen Bernie's cell, talked to the guy's cellmate, and heard all about how Bernie still blamed the "beautiful lying bitch" who'd tossed him in jail.

Bernie hadn't forgiven and he hadn't forgotten. Now that he was free, Cash was betting the guy would be hell-bent on his vengeance. And that vengeance? It would be focused on the gorgeous, ex–bounty hunter who was currently seated across from Cash.

Bernie wanted to make Ana pay.

Not happening.

So, yeah, Cash had flown straight to Ana. He *did* want her to help him track Bernie. He hadn't been lying when he said the woman had skills. But Cash also wanted to keep Ana close because . . .

The escaped killer wanted her. If Ana and Cash didn't find Bernie soon, then Cash had no doubt that Bernie would be finding them. Or rather . . . *Ana*.

And when the killer came calling, Cash would make damn sure he was ready. Bernie wouldn't be cutting into Ana's soft skin with one of his knives. Bernie the Butcher would never claim her as a victim.

Hell, no.

"Okay, you've been glaring at me for a few minutes," Ana murmured. "Something you want to share?"

Cash cleared his throat. "Just thinking what I said was true. You are even more beautiful now." That part wasn't a lie. The woman was absolutely gorgeous. Heart-shaped face. That dark, thick tumble of hair that skimmed over her shoulders. Her dark and deep eyes . . .

Men looked at Ana. Then they looked again—and couldn't look away.

He knew she'd used her looks to her advantage a time or twenty during her bounty hunting days. Hell, if a woman like her came after you . . . what man ran?

"And I see you can be as charming as you were before." Her smile flashed, then vanished. "Though you really don't need to waste your charm on me. This is business. Just a case, and then we walk away."

Cash nodded. "I'm clear on the plan. Don't worry." He glanced at his watch. "We'll be landing soon." And their first stop would be the prison. Ana wanted to talk to Bernie's cellmate. Cash had told her that he'd already interviewed the guy, but she still wanted her turn at him. And Cash had to admit to being curious because he'd love to see Ana in action. The woman truly was the stuff of legend.

He'd been in a Virginia field office two years ago when she'd come strolling in, as pretty as you please, with a man in front of her. She'd stood in the waiting area, then delicately cleared her throat and said that she was there to collect the reward.

Every jaw in the building had dropped when the agents got a look at Bernie. Bernie "the Butcher" Tate.

One of the FBI's ten most wanted . . . taken down by a woman who seemed to barely skim past five feet in height. Power did come in small packages.

"I'll want to talk to the guy who was driving the transport, too," Ana said.

"He doesn't remember anything. Said the engine stopped, he got out of the bus to check under the hood, then he got hit from behind."

"And when he woke up, the prisoner was gone." Ana shook her head. "That's a convenient story. Have you checked to make sure that an extra ten or twenty grand wasn't *conveniently* dropped into his bank account, too?"

He had. "So far, the guy is clear."

"On the surface, anyone can look good. You have to dig deep to see the dark spots." Her hands tightened on the hand rests on either side of her body. "Bernie obviously has a friend nearby, someone who helped him vanish."

Yeah, Cash knew a partner had to be involved.

"Bernie has been away from his prey for too long," Ana said, worry edging into her voice. "He'll hunt at the first opportunity."

"How did you find Bernie before?" It was the question that had plagued him too many times. "Everyone else was looking for him, no one found him but you. How did you do it?"

Her smile flashed again. "I did it the same way I'll do it this time."

"How?"

She gave a light laugh, husky, oddly sweet. "If I tell you my trade secret, what good will I be to you then?"

"Plenty of good," Cash growled back.

She seemed to consider it. "Fine . . . you have me all wrong, you see."

He did?

"You think it's all about me being the hunter, stalking, finding these men—these criminals." She shook her head. "That's wrong. I'm not finding them. I'm understanding them."

"Like . . . profiling them?" Because he'd studied profiling plenty during his time at Quantico.

"Something like that. But . . ." Her gaze skittered away from him. "I understand the prey that they want. I become that prey."

She—*what?*

"I look at their victims. I see what the killers see. I become what I need to be in order to lure them in."

Bait.

That soft laughter of hers came again. "You think I don't understand *you,* too, Agent Knox?"

He couldn't look away from her, but Ana's gaze wasn't on him.

"You think I don't know why you came all the way to Atlanta in order to get me for this case?"

"Ana . . ."

"White knight," she whispered. "You don't need to protect me."

"You have me wrong."

"I don't think so. I told you. I'm very, very good at reading people. Actually . . ." Her index finger rose to tap against her lip. Or rather, against the scar that slid across her top lip. "Actually, I'm very good at reading monsters."

He tensed. Cash knew Ana's story. It would have been impossible to grow up in Texas and *not* know about what happened to Ana Young and her twin brother, Asher.

Her finger paused a moment longer, then fell away from her lip. "I'm surprised the FBI gave you the go-ahead to use me."

Use me. Those words made him want to squirm. Guilt was riding him hard. But . . . *I'm protecting her, too. I won't let Bernie get his hands on Ana.* "With a situation of this magnitude, my boss was willing to bend his normal rules."

"Your boss." She still wasn't looking at him. "Darius Vail, right? Isn't he the executive assistant director for the Criminal, Cyber, Response and Services Branch?"

"Yes, it's Vail."

"And you're right below him on the totem pole. The agent in charge of the Criminal Investigative Division." Now her dark stare cut toward him. "You've certainly moved up the ranks at the Bureau quickly, haven't you?"

"I'm good at what I do." Had she been keeping tabs on him? *Careful, Ana, you'll make me think you care.*

"I have no doubt about that." She shrugged. "Just as I'm very good at what I do."

He held her gaze. "Then I suppose we'll be perfect partners, won't we?"

Ana smiled at him. It was a smile that didn't warm her dark eyes. "I guess we'll see . . ."

WINGATE FEDERAL PENITENTIARY.

Ana stared up at the imposing structure. The high, stone walls . . . the barbed wire that covered the top of those walls. And the armed guards that she could see patrolling in the towers.

Intimidating.

"This place is supposed to be escape-proof," Cash murmured as they climbed out of the rented SUV and started walking toward the gates. "It's been open for over fifty years, and this is the first escape."

"Hardly the press the folks in charge would want."

"The warden is pissed," he added.

Ana shifted her attention to the gates. She could see a man in a brown suit pacing there, moving with short, angry strides. *Guessing that's the warden.*

"Of course, Warden Phelps is saying the escape didn't happen *at* his facility, so he's not responsible."

"A blame game isn't going to help us find Bernie any faster." The warden could point his fingers at the transport driver as long as he wanted. "Only thing that matters to me right now . . . does the warden know he's supposed to stay out of my way?"

Cash gave a choked laugh. "Um, no, but I'm sure he'll be understanding that real fast."

And the warden rushed toward them. He was a tall,

thin man, with red cheeks and light blue eyes. His gaze swept over Ana, and confusion flashed on his face, then he looked over at Cash.

"Agent Knox." The warden grabbed Cash's hand. Pumped it hard. "Do you have news? Have your agents found Tate?"

His agents. Right. Because Cash was in charge of a whole team of agents. Gabe had been the one to do the research on Cash and send his intel to Ana's smart phone. It wasn't as if she'd been keeping up with Cash's rock star progress at the FBI over the last two years . . . But, yeah, he'd sure jumped to the top of the FBI agent hierarchy fast. His case closure rate was impressive to behold. And the criminals he'd taken down?

She had to admire his work. He'd certainly made his mark in the Criminal Investigative Division.

"He isn't back into custody yet," Cash said.

The warden's expression immediately turned crestfallen.

"This is Ana Young." Cash put his hand at the small of Ana's back. She made herself not tense, but she still felt that odd current that zipped through her when he was near. "She's working as a liaison with the FBI. Ana, this is Warden Hayden Phelps."

"Warden." She gave him a brisk nod.

"Ms. Young." He said her name quickly, then looked at Cash. "I don't understand why you're back here. You've already seen his cell. Talked to his cellmate and—"

"*I* haven't done those things," Ana interjected, keeping her voice smooth. "That's why we're here.

Sometimes, a second pair of eyes can make all the difference."

The warden's stare came back to her. And his eyes narrowed as he stared at her face. Then his blue eyes were widening—with recognition.

Ana was used to that shocked stare. When she'd been a teen, she'd gotten it all the time. As soon as folks recognized her—boom. *Hello, shock and sadness.*

As she'd aged, she'd stopped getting the stare quite so much. But it still happened. Certain true-crime buffs would always recognize her face or her name.

Judging by the way the warden was currently staring at her, Phelps definitely recognized her. It stood to reason, though, that a prison warden would know plenty about true crime.

"It's you," he said.

Right. Me. The girl who got away. The scarred victim. The—

"Are you his girlfriend?"

"What?" Ana demanded, the question shocking her.

"Tate." Phelps rubbed his chin. "He had all of those sketches of you . . ." He took an aggressive step toward Cash. *"Why did you bring his girlfriend to the prison?"*

Cash opened his mouth to reply.

But Ana stepped in front of him. "Hey, warden, settle down." She put her hands on her hips. "Let's get a few things straight. First of all, I'm not anyone's girlfriend, and I sure as hell am not involved with a piece of shit like Bernie Tate."

The warden blinked.

"Next"—Ana's voice sharpened—"Agent Knox clearly told you I was working as a liaison with the FBI—so that means I have clearance from him to be here. That clearance means you don't get to act like a jerk when you talk to me. It means you follow orders, and the current order that Agent Knox and I have is for you to stop wasting our time and let us into the prison. We want to see Bernie's cell and we want to talk to his cellmate."

The warden licked his lips. "She . . . doesn't know?"

He was about to piss her off. She was right in front of him and the guy was still talking to Cash.

But then the warden spun on his heel and hurried back toward the gate. "You'll both need to leave your weapons at the gate."

She hadn't brought a weapon to this fun little tour. Not like it was her first prison visit. She knew the drill. Before she followed the warden, Ana glanced back at Cash. "There something you need to tell me before we go in?" Because the warden's words . . . *She . . . doesn't know?* were nagging at her.

Cash hesitated.

"Aw, Agent Knox," she murmured. "You've been holding back. Hardly the way for our partnership to start." Then she headed toward the gate and the warden.

But Cash quickly caught up to her. "Tate may have . . . a fixation on you."

She walked through the screening area, making sure to lift up her arms while she was searched.

Cash got a patdown near her.

"A fixation, huh?" Ana asked. "So that's how the

warden recognized me." *And not because of my own past.* Oddly, she was relieved. She hated for everyone to know about her private hell. Why did her soul have to be bared for the masses? "The guy has a picture of me in his cell?"

The guards motioned for her to move beyond the security check. Nodding, she headed deeper into the prison. The warden was steps ahead of her.

"Not just one picture," Cash said, his voice rumbling behind her.

They passed the general population area. All of the cells were locked, but the inmates rushed forward when they caught a glimpse of Ana. There were plenty of catcalls, plenty of shouts, plenty of fucking twisted offers.

Ana ignored them all. Replying in any way would have just encouraged the men there, and she wasn't in the mood for their shit.

But . . . Cash moved closer to her. She could feel the heat of his body against hers. She looked back and saw that his green eyes were glinting with fury and his jaw was clenched tightly.

"I could screw you so hard, baby!" one prisoner called out. *"You'd be screaming for me to—"*

Cash stopped walking.

Ana sighed. "Don't."

But he was already turning toward the prisoner.

Ana grabbed Cash's arm. "We do not have time for this crap. He doesn't matter. He's just a dumbass locked in a cell. We have a job to do."

She could feel the rough tension in his body. Cash wanted to attack. Too bad, he didn't exactly have that luxury. He was the FBI agent. He had to play by the rules.

"That's right, asshole," the prisoner laughed. *"Listen to the cunt. You listen—"*

Cash lunged toward the bars. The prisoner let out a yell and jerked back.

A cold smile curved Cash's lips. A smile that changed his face. He wasn't handsome any longer. He was dangerous. Dark. Cruel?

The prisoner had gone dead silent.

Everyone had.

"You think I can't get your ass tossed into solitary confinement?" Cash curled his fingers around the bars. "You think I can't make you wish for hell?"

The prisoner—a too-pale redheaded man with tattoos covering his arms—gave a ragged laugh. "This is hell."

"No." Cash shook his head. "But keep talking to her like that, and I *will* show you hell."

She grabbed his arm again. "Come on, Cash."

This time, he let her pull him away. The redhead didn't say another word. Whispers and rumbles filled the air. But then the warden was leading them down a different corridor, directing them toward a separate area.

Quieter but . . .

Ana glanced to the right. There were still plenty of prisoners in this area, but these prisoners were different. Not wild and loud.

Goose bumps rose on her arms when she met the cold stare of another too-pale inmate. *Guess these guys don't get out too much at all.* His gaze was unblinking, and he stood just behind his bars. *Watching her.*

He smiled and that smile chilled Ana to her core.

They passed another cell. A tall man was in this cell. His arms were wrapped around his body and he was rocking back and forth and . . . humming. A low, ghostly hum.

"These prisoners require more intense supervision," the warden explained. He pointed to the humming prisoner. "That's James Duman. You might've heard about him. James—"

"Killed his family and stayed in the house with their remains for a week," Cash said, cutting through the warden's words.

Yes, she did remember that story. At the time, she'd thought the guy had to be insane but James Duman had refused to offer an insanity plea at his trial. He'd just pled guilty, and said that he had to be locked up, tight.

So he wouldn't kill again.

They finally reached the last cell, and when Ana looked into that cell, her breath caught in her throat. Now she understood just what Cash had been holding back and, yes, she could even see why the warden had asked if she was Tate's girlfriend.

The guy didn't have just one picture of her on his wall.

She *was* the whole fucking wall. Sketched pictures of her, one right after the other, littered that wall. Some of the sketches were of her whole face. Some were just close-ups of her eyes, of her nose. Of her mouth.

Of the scar that sliced across her upper lip.

Warden Phelps cleared his throat. "Prison psychiatrist said it was good for the inmates to . . . express themselves artistically."

Ana turned her head and stared at the warden. Just stared.

His cheeks reddened even more.

And soft laughter came from deep inside the cell.

"Man had an obsession," a low voice called out. "And I can see why."

Ana exhaled slowly and turned back toward that voice. She could see the speaker, a man who was lying on the bottom bunk in the cell. As she watched him, he slowly uncurled his body and headed toward her. He was an average-looking fellow, medium height, medium build. Dark brown hair, hazy green eyes. He had the kind of face that wouldn't stand out in a person's mind, probably exactly the sort of face that a criminal wanted. *Easy to forget.*

"This is Ray Laker," Phelps said gruffly. "He's been Tate's cellmate from day one."

Ray smiled at her.

"Put your hands through the bars, Ray," Phelps barked. Ray complied and the guard who'd been leading their little march through the prison hurriedly stepped up and cuffed Ray Laker's hands, effectively pinning him in place next to the bars.

"Let them in," Phelps directed the guard. The young guard bustled forward and pulled out his key ring. A few moments later, the cell door creaked open. Ana walked into the cell first, making sure to take her time and not tense her body. She headed toward the back wall—and all of the images of herself.

Cash marched to her side. "I . . . didn't want to worry you on the way here." His voice was low, probably meant just for her ears.

Ana laughed. "Liar." She glanced at him from the corner of her eye. "You were afraid if you told me about all of this . . ." Ana waved toward the wall. "I wouldn't help you." Now she turned to fully face him. "What did you think? That I'd be afraid?"

"Yes." Again, his voice was low.

"This doesn't scare me. It pisses me off." Bernie had been in this cell, and he'd been staring at her image all this time? Her words were tough and fierce, but inside . . . deep inside . . .

Cash stepped closer to her. "It's okay to be afraid."

"Screw off, Agent Knox." She turned on her heel. "And don't keep any more secrets from me." She stalked toward the cuffed man. "So your cellmate . . . he wanted to make me pay, huh?"

It stood to reason that was the case, considering that in a few of the images . . . her eyes had been scratched out.

Ray sagged against the bars, but his head turned in her direction. "You're Ana."

She tapped her foot on the cell floor.

"Had to listen to him rage about you plenty of nights. You tricked him. Lied to him. Made him think you were weak . . ." Ray laughed. "Got to say, it sure is a pleasure to meet you. I *hated* that asshole Tate. Everyone else here acted like he was the big bad, but I knew he was nothing but a piece of shit. And to think . . . someone as small as you took him down . . ." More laughter.

Ana's hands fisted at her sides. "Yes, meeting me is a pleasure. A real thrill." Her head cocked to the side. "Know what else would be a thrill? If *you* were responsible for bringing that jerk back to jail."

Ray's eyes turned to slits.

She hadn't been lying to Cash earlier. She really did understand monsters. She sized up Ray and knew exactly what he wanted. *Power. Control.* "Tate bossed your ass around the entire time you were here. Now he's gone, and I know you don't want him to be living the high life on the outside. You want him dragged back here, then tossed into solitary confinement. After this escape crap, you know the guards will give him hell every single day. Won't you enjoy watching that? His hell, where *you're* in charge?"

Ray swallowed. He didn't speak, but then again, he didn't have to say a word. His gleaming eyes told Ana that she was right.

The warden just watched them. The guard shifted nervously from foot to foot, and Cash . . . he was still by the wall of her images.

"No visitors came to see Tate," Ana said. Cash had told her that during the plane ride there. "And I'm sure the FBI is already going through all his mail, but what I want to know right now is . . . did Tate ever mention anyone to *you?* Anyone out there that he considered to be a friend?"

Ray shook his head. "Bastard had no friends."

When you were a psychopath, it was hard to have lasting friendships. She huffed out a hard breath. "Was he excited a few days before the escape? Did his behavior change?"

Ray's gaze cut toward the warden. "Wouldn't know about that . . ."

Okay, that answer was a *yes*. "When did he get excited? When did he know he was getting out of here?"

Now Ray eased back from the bars, as much as he could ease back, anyway. His gaze slid toward the wall of images. *I should probably call it the Wall of Ana.*

But he didn't speak.

"In prison," Ana said, considering things, "you don't want to be a snitch."

Ray's lips were closed tightly. The prisoners in the other cells would be able to hear this conversation. The warden should have tried to give them more privacy but . . .

Sometimes, it isn't about what you say.

She'd read Ray right, Ana knew she had. The guy hated Tate and wanted him to suffer, but Ray also didn't want word to spread that he'd been the one to turn on his cellmate.

So he was telling her what had happened, without words.

Ana spun on her heel and hurried toward the wall. She stared at all of the pictures of herself. Her lips, her eyes—her nose. Most of the pictures were of her face. The sketches appeared to have been drawn with the same heavy hand, lots of dark shading. Lines drawn in the paper so deep, again and again.

Deep, like a knife slicing deep into skin. So very deep.

Most of the pictures were like that, except the image in the very middle of the wall. Ana's hand reached out to touch the picture.

"I told you to take all of the images down, Phelps," Cash snapped out.

Her hand stilled. *Ah, so Cash didn't expect me to see these. He thought I wouldn't find out about lie number one.*

Tricky agent.

"I didn't have time," Phelps replied, voice tight. "I have a prison to run and—"

"Doesn't matter," Ana cut in. "I'm glad you left them right here." It made things so much easier. She caught the edge of the paper for that center picture. Ana yanked the paper down, staring at the image.

It was her, but a drawing of her whole body, not just of her face or some of her features. A rustic cabin was in the background. She was wearing jeans—and her battered jacket. The same jacket she was wearing right then.

Bernie wouldn't have known about my jacket. My brother gave it to me a year ago.

"Better artist," Ana murmured. "The lines are different. Softer." They didn't cut into the paper with angry slashes. The lines flowed and circled. Ana lifted the paper toward Cash. "Someone has been watching me." But . . . "I've never been to that cabin." She studied that cabin—single story, old-fashioned log-style with a lake to the left. She looked back at Ray. He gave the faintest of nods. "Right, we're done here." She pushed the paper at Cash. "Let's get the hell out of this prison."

He blinked. "Ana?"

"I hate prisons, have I ever told you that?" Her steps were quick as she headed for the cell door. Cash followed on her heels. "Can't stand the idea of being confined." *Because when I was a kid, some sick assholes tied me to a chair and played a game of torture the girl.* Since then, Ana hadn't been able to stomach any sort of confinement. Even seat belts made her tense. Being in the plane, having to put that belt across her lap? Her whole body had stiffened.

The warden led them back through the prison. There were catcalls, shouts, but Ana didn't even glance at any of the prisoners, and Cash didn't flip out on her and go into his überprotective mode, either.

Then they were outside. The sunlight was bright, making her squint. Ana kept marching forward until she reached their rented SUV. Only then did she glance back. Cash was having a quiet, intense conversation with the warden. They kept glancing at her, then away.

She just waited.

A few moments later, Cash was heading toward her with the sketch secured in an evidence bag that he carried. She leaned back against the side of the SUV, watching him approach. The walls of the prison were so big, looming behind him.

"If I had to spend the rest of my life in a place like that," Ana said as his boots crunched the gravel in the parking lot, "I know I'd go mad."

"No, not you. You're too strong for something like that."

"You have no clue." She studied that prison. The heavy stones. The armed guards. The barbed wire. "I made it through hell once. I wouldn't again." Her mind would shatter long before that happened.

"Ana?"

She cleared her throat. What had she been thinking? She didn't *share* with people—not with anyone but her twin. And she didn't have to tell him stuff like that because Asher understood her so completely.

Her head inclined toward the sketch he held. "Get the lab guys at the FBI to run every possible scan and test imaginable on that paper. Maybe you'll get lucky and find a fingerprint. Some DNA. *Something.* Because the person who drew that image? That would be Tate's partner."

A furrow appeared between his brows.

"The cabin is his hiding spot," Ana continued. "We should get some maps of the area, look for property that fits the image there. A small log cabin nestled near a lake. Close to the prison, but not too close. I mean, he'd want to vanish fast but not be in an immediate search area."

"How can you be sure?" He was just inches away from her.

Too close. Caging me in.

Ana turned around and grabbed for the door handle. "Because like I said, someone has been watching me."

The lock disengaged. She knew he'd pressed the key remote in his pocket. She jumped inside but . . .

Cash didn't move. He stepped closer to her. "Explain."

"My jacket. It was a gift on my birthday. I know it looks old as hell . . ." Now her rusty laughter came out in a weak laugh. "But it's supposed to look that way. It's vintage, a special order gift for me." Asher had given her the jacket and teased, *See, Ana, it already looks all hard-core. Perfect for you.* "Tate had someone watching me. Someone who saw me in the jacket. He didn't draw that picture, his partner did." She eased out a slow breath. "Ray told us his behavior changed—"

"Ray wasn't saying jack."

He'd said plenty. Just not always with words. "Tate was excited after he got the image. He knew he was going to that cabin. We find the cabin, we find him." She stared into Cash's eyes. Then, not even sure why she was doing it, Ana's hand rose and her fingers pressed to the shadowy line of stubble on his jaw. "Don't be mad," she whispered, "because I figured it out before you."

His eyes widened.

She smiled at him.

"Ana Fucking Young." Cash shook his head. "I saw those pictures of you—and I wanted to attack."

Her smile faltered. This wasn't Cash bullshitting her. This wasn't any one-upmanship game. This was . . .

Something more.

Her fingers started to slide away from his jaw, but his hand rose and locked around hers, holding her fingers in place.

Confinement, I can't—

"It pissed me off to see those pictures of you. I ordered Phelps to have them removed." His head turned and she felt the quick press of his lips against her palm.

Her heart thundered in her chest.

But Cash took a step back.

"If he'd done that, if he'd followed my orders, then we'd be screwed." He shook his head. "How the fuck did I miss this?" He started to spin away.

Ana grabbed his hand. "Stop."

Cash looked up at her.

"Get your team to check the paper. Get the warden to see if he can find the record of who sent this to Tate." She should have talked more to the warden when they were inside, but she'd started to suffocate in there. Too much confinement. Too many bars.

Too many nightmares.

"And while they're doing that," Ana continued doggedly, "you and I will hunt for that cabin. Partners, right? Let's go find that sonofabitch." *Because he isn't going to get me. I won't be his prey.*

Tate thought that he would kill her?

No. She'd find him, then she'd toss his ass back into that prison so that Warden Phelps could make Bernie Tate's life a living hell.

CHAPTER THREE

THE LOG CABIN WAITED, NESTLED BENEATH pine trees and sitting on the edge of the lake. A perfect, picturesque scene.

It was the third cabin that Cash had visited that day. The third that matched up, based on topographical maps, with the image from the sketch that had been in Bernie Tate's cell. They were deep in the heart of Virginia's Blue Ridge Mountains, a beautiful area, but one that hid too many isolated spots.

"Fresh tire tracks," Ana said softly, her body brushing against his as they stood on the driver's side of the SUV. They'd gone out there with two local deputies, two nervous-looking young guys who were currently gripping their weapons as tightly as possible.

Cash had wanted backup for the cabin search, but the deputies weren't exactly inspiring confidence in him.

His gaze dipped toward the tire tracks that Ana had noticed and he nodded. They were fresh, but there was no sign of a vehicle at that cabin right then. The place was a rental, and according to the rental property management company, it *should* have been empty.

He had the keys to the place in his pocket and he

also had the all-clear from the owners to search the cabin. "Stay here," he told Ana.

Her expression hardened. "Come on, Cash, let me cover your ass. Not those guys." She jerked her thumb toward the deputies. "Wouldn't you feel *safer* with me at your back?"

He'd feel safer knowing she wasn't anywhere within Tate's firing range. Not that the guy had ever used bullets on his prey. A knife had been his weapon of choice because he liked the intimate kills.

Slow.

Bloody.

"Stay here," he told Ana, and he put his backup gun in her hand. "If you see Bernie Tate run out of that cabin . . ."

"Don't worry, I won't hesitate to take him down." But worry flashed in her eyes. "Be careful, okay?"

"Always." He motioned to the deputy. One deputy would go inside with him, one would stay with Ana. That had been the method they used at the last two cabins. And they'd turned up jack shit at those places but . . .

This place could be different.

He wanted it to be different. He wanted to find Bernie Tate and eliminate the threat the man posed to Ana. He approached the cabin quickly, his gaze scanning the area for any danger. Cash wasn't about to be caught off guard. When he reached the cabin, Cash flattened his body against the wood near the entrance. The young deputy followed suit, but the deputy's breathing was loud, heaving in and out in deep bursts.

Cash reached for the doorknob. His fingers brushed against it, and he stilled.

Unlocked.

He looked back at the deputy, then Cash's gaze slid toward the parked SUV. He couldn't see Ana over there. She was supposed to be crouching down, staying covered. It *looked* as if she were following orders, but with Ana . . . well, a guy could never be too sure.

Cash nodded once, grimly, to the deputy. Then he rushed inside the cabin, with his gun ready and his grip dead steady.

The smell hit him first. Thick, coppery, cloying.

Blood.

Waste.

Human waste.

The deputy started gagging. Cash didn't have that luxury. He ran forward, following the stench, terrified that they'd arrived too late. Had Bernie Tate taken another victim? Ana had said that the killer would be itching to use his knife again.

Sonofabitch, I don't want to be too late.

He flew down the small hallway. Saw the door. Halfway open . . .

With his left hand, Cash pushed that door open fully, and with his right hand, he kept his steady grip on the gun, ready for a threat from Tate. Ready—

"OhmyGod!" The shocked cry came from the deputy who'd followed Cash into the back room.

Cash didn't make a sound.

His gaze was on the victim. A victim who'd been stabbed, again and again and again. Blood spatter filled the walls. A thick pool of blood had congealed beneath the victim.

"It's like a damn slaughter," the deputy gasped, and then Cash heard the deputy vomiting.

Contaminating their crime scene.

Cash shoved the guy back. "Go outside, hurry!"

The deputy stumbled out.

And Cash looked at the horror show around him.

Sonofabitch.

WHEN THE DEPUTY came flying out of the cabin, his face bleached of color and his hands waving frantically in the air, Ana knew they'd hit pay dirt.

Bernie Tate, you bastard. We've got you.

But the deputy was panicked. Terrified.

And where is Cash? Ana didn't hesitate. She jumped up from her safe spot and ran straight toward the cabin. Cash's backup weapon was held securely in her hand.

The young deputy who'd fled the cabin fell to his knees and started vomiting.

Ana still didn't stop. *Cash. Where is Cash?*

She burst into the cabin and the smell hit her. Nausea rose in her throat, but she choked it right back down. "Cash!" His name tore from her as she ran down the hallway. Then he was lunging toward her, appearing to jump right from the room at the end of that narrow hall.

"No, Ana, *stop!*"

She staggered to a stop. Her breath heaved, but her gun didn't so much as tremble. "What happened? Are you all right?" Her frantic gaze flew over him. Cash seemed fine. No wounds that she could see.

"I'm okay." He didn't holster his gun. "I need to check the perimeter and make sure the perp isn't still nearby."

"Tate?" She glanced over her shoulder. There weren't many places the guy could hide inside the cabin. And that smell . . .

Who did the bastard kill? Another victim . . . Ana knew another victim waited in the room behind Cash. Her stomach knotted. *I was too late. I didn't stop him.*

"Not Tate." Cash shook his head. "He won't be hurting anyone else."

He sounded so certain. It took a moment for her to realize exactly *how* he could know that truth and then she was shoving against him and stumbling forward.

"No, Ana." He grabbed her, wrapping his arm around her and pulling her against him. "You don't need to see that."

Her head turned. Their faces were separated by inches. "It's not my first dead body." No, her first dead body had come when she was fourteen. She'd watched the bastards who'd taken her die before her eyes. The first abductor's blood had splattered onto her.

But I didn't scream.

"Ana . . ."

"Let me go, Cash."

"It's a crime scene. You can't touch anything. You—"

"Let. Me. Go." She wasn't going to screw up the crime scene, but she was going to look into that room.

His mouth brushed against her temple. "Some things stay with you. No matter how hard you try to banish the memory, you can't forget." His breath teased her cheek. "You don't want this memory."

A memory that had driven a deputy to run from the house. And the guy was probably still vomiting outside.

Cash slowly slid his arm away from her. "I'm going to check the rest of the cabin." He hesitated. "Go back outside, Ana. Go back out with the deputies."

He eased away from her.

Ana looked toward the bedroom. The door was slightly ajar and she could just see the blood on the floor. She took a slow, gliding step forward.

"Ana . . ." A warning was in Cash's voice.

"My picture was on his wall. Me. Over and over again. He was coming after *me*." She looked back at Cash. "I have to see what's in that room."

He swallowed, his Adam's apple bobbing. Then instead of backing away from her, he moved closer. Ana squared her shoulders and headed for that door. Such a thin, old door. The floor groaned beneath her feet.

She crept closer. Slipped into that little room. The stench was stronger. Blood and urine and . . .

He was on the floor.

Bernie Tate.

Bernie the Butcher. That had been the name the media gave him. A monster who'd used his knife to carve up women. But . . .

This time, Bernie was the one who'd been carved up. Stabbed so many times that his body was a gory mass. Nausea rose within her again, sharp and twisting and she didn't even realize that she'd reached out—

Until her left hand grabbed tight to Cash. Her fingers curled around his arm as Ana held on to him.

"Let's get out of here," Cash said.

Her stricken gaze was on Bernie's face. *Someone butchered the butcher. Someone butchered the . . .*

She backed out of that room. Every breath she took . . . it was like she was inhaling death. But as soon as she was in that hallway, Ana shook her head once. Twice. She was *not* going to lose her control in that place.

"You okay? Ana?"

She tipped back her head and stared up at Cash. She was still holding on to him. "His partner . . . did that?" Such a brutal kill. So much rage. So much hate. Ana shook her head. "Not his partner." No, Bernie might have *thought* he was working with someone he trusted, but it had been a trick.

I know monsters.

The killer hadn't been able to get to Bernie while he was in prison. He'd wanted payback. The kind that could only be given with a pound of flesh.

Wound for wound. A life for a life.

So the killer had waited for the perfect opportunity. During Bernie's transfer, that opportunity had presented itself. He'd gotten Bernie. He'd made sure that transfer van broke down. And then . . .

Someone butchered the butcher.

BLUE AND RED police lights lit up the small cabin. Ana sat huddled in the back of a patrol car. More FBI agents were on scene, and the local sheriff was out, too, barking orders as teams searched the area.

She'd done her part. She'd helped to find Bernie.

Her gaze slid to the left. A black body bag was being loaded into the coroner's van. *Another one of the missing . . . found.*

Now that her job had ended, the Feds were taking over again. She was supposed to stay in the background. Cash had given that order, only he'd phrased it in his *nice* way.

Just sit tight, Ana. We'll search the scene. It has to be handled the right way. Officially. The press is going to be all over this thing.

More of his teammates had come rushing in. All nice, friendly agents—but stiff in the typical FBI way. The agent she'd liked the most was Faye Comwell, a direct woman who'd said exactly what she thought and hadn't played any sort of pissing-match game with the local authorities.

"Uh, ma'am?"

She turned her head and saw the poor deputy who'd vomited earlier. The guy was still a little too pale.

"Is there anything you need, ma'am?"

"Deputy . . . Welch, wasn't it?" Ana asked.

He nodded.

"I need a ride back to town, deputy. As fun as it is to hang out at a murder scene . . ." *Not fun, not fun at all.* "I want to get into a motel room and crash." Pulling that all-nighter hadn't helped her any, but she'd hardly expected to find herself on *this* case. She was bone tired, and the adrenaline rush she'd felt before— *before* she'd seen the body—had bottomed out. She just wanted to escape the chaos of that scene.

And the press? She knew Cash was right. They would be closing in. And Ana had no intention of being present when they arrived.

"I—I can take you back," he said quickly. "As long as you don't mind riding in the patrol car."

"Not my first time back here." She gave him a tired smile. "Just get me the hell away from this place."

"Right, I will—"

"Ana!" Cash's voice—strong, a bit worried.

So much for an easy escape.

"She's here!" Deputy Welch called out. Her eyebrows beetled at the guy, but he totally missed her angry stare because he'd whirled around and was waving to Cash. "I've been keeping a close watch on her, just like I promised."

As if she needed watching. Ana knew perfectly well how to protect herself—and the green deputy, if necessary—but it had quickly become apparent that the killer was long gone. The tire tracks showed that he'd driven away long before they arrived. And the way the blood had congealed . . . *Tate's death occurred hours before.*

"Give me a moment with her, will you, deputy?" Cash murmured.

The deputy nodded and quickly made himself scarce.

Sighing, Ana slipped from the car. She wasn't exactly sure why she'd been hoping to vanish without facing Cash again. Maybe because that was her MO? Slip away . . . don't look back.

"Are you all right?" Cash asked her, concern evident in his eyes.

Ana pushed back a lock of hair that wanted to tumble into her face. "I'm fine, Cash. Like I told you, that wasn't my first dead body. With my line of work, it won't be my last, either."

He stepped closer to her. "You don't have to bullshit with me."

"I'm not. I've seen—"

"That kill was particularly brutal, and we both know it. Hell, you think I wasn't flinching in there? I was. The guy was carved up, Ana. I didn't want you to have that image stuck in your head. I didn't want you to have the nightmares that come from seeing shit like that."

You think that's bad? Try watching your brother kill two men before your eyes. Even better, watch your mother die right in front of you as she screams for help. Try being the one who gets carved up by a sadistic, stoned-out-of-his-mind bastard. Ana cleared her throat. "I already have nightmares, and I manage them just fine." She managed them by having as many late nights as she could. By working herself into exhaustion so that when she slept, it would be like falling into a deep, black void. She'd be too tired for the nightmares to plague her—that was the general plan, anyway.

Only it didn't always work out for her.

She glanced over his shoulder, peering at the chaos that still reigned around the cabin. "What happens now?"

"Now . . . we tell the public that Bernie Tate is dead. We reassure people that he is no longer a threat."

"And the person who killed him? You don't think that perp is a threat?"

His head dipped toward her. "I think the same thing you do, Ana. That this kill was personal. That it involved a whole lot of rage and hate. A very smart individual went to a whole lot of trouble to get Bernie Tate out of that prison, to get him to this cabin, to *kill* him.

The attack was focused totally on Bernie, not any innocent civilians. Hell, even the transport driver was left alive."

Yes, he did think the same thing she did. "I guess my job is done then." Bernie had been found and the Feds would be taking over the hunt for the Butcher's killer. "It was . . . good to see you again, Cash."

"You don't mean that."

"Actually, I do." And maybe that truth surprised her. "Not the best of circumstances but . . ." She let that sentence trail away because Ana wasn't sure what to say. She floundered a moment, then managed, "I'm glad you're doing well. And I wish you luck catching this killer."

He stared down at her.

She tried not to fidget.

"Over again, huh?" Cash murmured. His hand rose and the back of his knuckles feathered over her cheek. "At least this time, you're telling me good-bye."

She flinched.

"Ana, shit, I didn't mean—"

"Yes, you did." Her chin lifted. "Good-bye, Cash. I'll get the deputy to take me back to town, and come morning . . ." Because the sky was already beginning to darken again. "I'll fly home. If you need me to hunt down anyone else for you, well, you know where I am."

"I know." His expression softened. "Good-bye, Ana."

He turned away. Headed back toward the pack of agents and deputies. Ana climbed into the patrol car. A few moments later, Deputy Welch was driving her toward the small town of Heather, Virginia.

NO REPEAT PERFORMANCE.

When Cash had approached Ana about working together, she'd been clear regarding her list of conditions.

Condition one . . . honesty. She'd wanted total honesty from him.

He hadn't given it to her. She'd found that shit out fast and her eyes had flashed with fire at him.

Condition two . . . she'd wanted their past kept secret. He'd done that part—hadn't breathed a word to anyone about their night together. Mostly because that night was *his*. Just as she'd been his, for a few precious hours.

No repeat performance. Ana had used those exact words with him. She'd said they would be professional, partners only.

But the case was over and . . .

Cash's gaze slid to the thin motel room wall. He was back in town. Night had fallen. The press had been appeased, for the moment, and he should be crashing.

He wasn't. Adrenaline hummed just beneath his skin, and that fucking thin wall . . . it separated him from Ana. She was in the room next door to him, by his request. He'd slipped the desk clerk an extra twenty to be near her.

Why?

Because he still had the urge to protect her, even with Bernie gone? Yeah, that fucking urge was there.

But also . . . he'd just wanted to be close to her. Ana Young was a mystery to him, and he'd always enjoyed solving mysteries. Smart, sexy, dangerous . . . that was his Ana. But there was so much more to her than what met the eye.

He wanted Ana. The desire he felt for her should have vanished over the last two years. It hadn't. If anything, it had just grown stronger. When he'd seen her walk into Gabe's office at LOST, he'd felt as if he'd been punched. The desire he'd felt for her had come raging back to the surface and it had taken all of his self-control to stand there, to act normal . . . when he'd wanted to grab Ana and pull her close.

Not the way I'm supposed to be. I'm the agent on the fast track. I have my control in place, always. Except with Ana.

He whirled away from the wall. He needed a shower, a cold one. To wash away the day and to—

A door squeaked. A faint sound, but one he could hear because of the thin wall he'd been cursing just moments before. His gaze shot to the clock on the small bedside table. Close to midnight. But . . .

He hurried toward the blinds near his room door. He cracked those blinds and peered outside.

But Ana is leaving.

Where was she going? And why?

None of my business. I should go get in the shower. Ana doesn't want a repeat performance.

It had been one hell of a day. Maybe she didn't want a repeat performance, but maybe she wanted a friend. He could do that for her, couldn't he? He could *be* that for her.

Cash grabbed his coat and hurried outside. Ana was already walking through the parking lot, her battered jacket over her delicate shoulders, but when she heard his feet pounding on the pavement behind her, Ana swung around, her body tensing.

Cash put up his hands. "Easy. It's just me."

The tension didn't leave her body. "Like seeing you is supposed to make me relax."

His gaze swept over her. "I heard you leave. I just wanted to . . . to check on you."

Her soft laughter floated in the night. "There you go again. Being the good guy. Do you ever get tired of that role?"

Cash took another step toward her. "You have me all wrong, Ana."

"No, I don't." She rolled back her shoulders. "I am absolutely fine. You don't have to worry about me. I'm a big girl."

"Ana—"

"I'm going out for a drink. There's a bar around the corner." She pointed to the left. "I saw it when Deputy Welch dropped me off. I couldn't sleep, so grabbing a drink seemed like a good idea."

He nodded. "It does seem like a good idea. I think I'll grab one, too."

Ana didn't speak.

His gaze sharpened on her. "Unless that's a problem?" The moon was full, hanging low and heavy in the sky, and there were plenty of lights shining in the parking lot. It was easy for him to see Ana's face.

And the flash of anger that just appeared.

"No problem," she said, but her voice was tight. "It's a free country. You get to do what you want." She turned to the left and started walking toward the bar.

"You don't get to do everything you want," Cash said, sliding closer to her and automatically shortening his strides to match hers. "No one gets that option. We can't hurt others. Can't attack, can't kill without reason."

"Oh, Cash, you sound like such an FBI agent." There was the faintest thread of laughter in her voice. "Maybe shut that off, just for tonight?"

It wasn't possible for him to do that. He knew Ana had plenty of secrets from her past, but he did, too. Secrets he'd worked hard to bury.

Secrets that could hurt innocent people.

People . . . like Ana.

He should have stayed away from her. *Always.* But Ana drew him in. Even then, he was stepping closer to her. Her scent—light, sweet, feminine—teased him.

Cash could hear the music from the bar—a rock song that was beating out in a powerful rhythm that filled the night. As they neared the small, flat building, he saw a bouncer sitting beside the entrance. The guy just waved them inside, and when they stepped in, Cash saw why.

Obviously, a slow night.

A small crowd stood in front of the band, maybe fifteen people. A few stragglers sat at the bar. The place was dim, the music loud, and no one seemed to be giving them so much as a second glance as they stood inside the doorway.

"My kind of place," Ana murmured, then she headed for the bar. She tapped her fingers in time with the music. When the bartender appeared, Ana leaned toward him and said, "Give me a beer."

"Make it two," Cash told him, lifting two fingers as he slid onto the stool beside her.

A moment later, the bartender pushed two foaming mugs toward them.

Ana lifted her mug and gave Cash a little salute. "Shall we drink to our good-bye?"

He didn't want a good-bye from her. He wanted one hell of a lot more.

But she was already tipping back her mug and taking a quick drink. When she was done, a small dollop of foam clung to her upper lip. As he watched, her tongue slid out and licked away that foam, sliding over the slight edge of her scar.

He grabbed his mug and drank fast, hard.

Her eyebrows rose. "Guess you enjoy the beer."

No, I'm just trying to keep my hands off you.

She hopped onto the stool. Her fingers kept tapping on the bar. She turned so that her eyes were on the band and on the small group of dancers out there. "I like places like this," Ana mused, taking another sip from her beer. "Dark, with loud music. No one knows who you are and they don't give a shit about your past in dives like this."

He lowered his mug to the bar. "You enjoy being anonymous."

"Nothing wrong with that." Her body was swaying now, and she was still staring at the dance floor. Her gaze cut toward him. "Don't suppose you want to dance?"

Good thing he wasn't drinking the beer. If he had been, Cash would have choked. Had Ana really asked him to dance? "I don't . . . dancing isn't . . ." Dammit, he was screwing this up.

She laughed. "Don't worry. I'll find another partner." Then Ana hopped off the bar stool and headed straight for the dance floor.

I'll find another partner.

"Buddy," the bartender muttered from behind him, "you are one dumb sonofabitch."

As he saw another man approach Ana, Cash realized the bartender was right. He grabbed his mug and drained the rest of the beer in one long gulp.

THE FBI AGENT was in the bar.

Shit, shit, shit.

Going out for a drink had seemed like a good idea, until now. Until FBI Special Agent Cash Knox had appeared with Ana Young in tow.

Ana, I know all about you.

Sinking back into the shadows at the bar seemed like the best plan. No, getting the hell out of there was the best plan.

No one knows it was me. No one has any clue about me and Bernie. The FBI agent wasn't there to search for a killer. He was just there to drink. While Ana Young . . . she was dancing. Laughing with some blond guy.

They had no clue.

I thought they would still be at the cabin. Looking for clues.

But maybe they didn't care. Maybe they realized the truth. Bernie Tate had gotten exactly what he deserved.

A fast trip to hell.

Ana was laughing. Would she have been laughing if Bernie hadn't died? Would she have been laughing when Bernie came for her?

No. She's glad he's dead. She's celebrating.

A slow smile spread on the killer's face.

And I'll celebrate, too. Celebrate tonight . . . and then get to work again tomorrow.

CHAPTER FOUR

MATT QUADE WAS HER TYPE. TALL, MUSCLED, with a rough edge. He danced easily, his smile was wicked, and she could see the edge of a tribal tattoo sliding up the side of his neck.

His hands were around her waist, and he had her pulled close to his body. Not *too* close, not yet. After all, they'd just met.

But Matt's dark gaze promised her a definite escape.

"I have got to say," Matt told her, his words a rumble as he leaned in close to her ear. "That scar on your lip is the sexiest thing I've ever seen. I am dying to—"

"Back away, buddy."

Cash's voice. Cash's very *cold* voice.

"It's my turn to dance," Cash said.

Matt stiffened against her, and he turned toward the guy who'd just interrupted his moment, a snarl curling his lips.

Ana wasn't in the mood for any macho bullshit, so she just shoved against Matt's chest. "Thanks for the dance."

Matt's brows pulled low.

"He's the guy I came here with," Ana stated, her voice low, easy. "He's the one I'll be leaving with."

"Huh. Like that, is it?" Matt's fingers fell away from her waist. "My mistake." He gave a little nod to Cash and headed toward the bar.

No, it isn't like that. But she hadn't wanted to get caught in some kind of pissing match. Ana turned to face Cash. "I thought you didn't dance."

"You're leaving with me?"

She smiled at him. "In your dreams."

"Only every damn night." He caught her hand and pulled her against him. "To warn you, I can't dance for shit."

A quick laugh tumbled from her.

"But I couldn't stand the sight of you being so close to him." Cash's fingers slid down to curve over her waist. "Of him touching you."

Alarms flashed. "You sound jealous."

"Because I *am* fucking jealous."

The band had slowed down. Their bodies swayed and brushed and an electric thrill surged through her. "You're not supposed to be." She shook her head. "You have no reason to be. We weren't fucking, Cash. We were dancing in a public bar. Nothing wrong with that."

"I wanted to be the one with you."

She looked up at him through her lashes.

He growled. "I'm . . . sorry. Okay? I know I'm being an ass."

She shrugged and slipped a little closer to him. "You are, but I wanted to dance with you, so I'm glad you're here. This once, I'll forgive you for being an ass." *Because Matt said the wrong thing . . . he pushed . . .*

"I saw your face," Cash murmured, "when he mentioned your scar. He hurt you."

She didn't speak. Ana had thought she'd been more careful. She usually guarded her expression much better.

"I wanted to drive my fist into him."

Shocked, she pulled back. Stopped dancing. "That . . . isn't you."

"Isn't it?" He pulled her back against him. "How many times do I have to say that you've got me all wrong, Ana Young?"

She could feel the leashed power of his body against her.

"You think I'm the good guy because I have the badge, but you don't know who I was before I joined the FBI."

"I know you pretty well." Intimately well. He was the kind of lover who took exquisite care of his partner. The kind always in control.

The kind who didn't understand that sometimes, she needed something darker.

Rougher.

Because I'm not a good girl, Cash. I haven't been for a very long time. When a woman only felt alive when she was hunting down some of the worst criminals out there, yes, that was a problem. One that a shrink would have a field day solving. Too bad Ana wasn't the sharing sort. She'd been forced to see a few shrinks when she'd been a teenager. She'd bullshitted them, told them exactly what she knew they *needed* to hear, and then she'd left their offices with their carefully muted colors. She'd gone back to her home, a home with a father who was slowly drinking himself to death because he couldn't bear the guilt tearing him apart.

And she'd broken down.

Even Asher didn't know about the pain she carried. She hadn't been able to tell her twin. He already shouldered far too much guilt.

"No repeat performance."

She missed a dance step and her foot pressed down on his.

"I get the rules," Cash said, "but if you want to change those rules at any point, I'm here."

Tomorrow, I won't be here. I'll be back in Atlanta. Cash will be hunting for Tate's killer. Different paths, different lives.

"I'm not in this bar tonight because I'm looking for sex," Ana told him. Maybe they should be clear about that. "I don't run out and hook up with strangers." She kept dancing as she stared up at him, her eyes narrowed, her heart racing. "Is that really what you think I do?"

"Ana, no, I—"

"Dancing, Cash, not fucking. Because, you want to hear a funny story?" She laughed and the sound was bitter to her own ears. "Once upon a time, I knew this girl . . . she spent every single waking minute dancing. She started ballet when she was three. She danced and she danced and she had this amazing future waiting for her." Her voice was low, grim. "She was already being recruited by scouts. She was supposed to go to New York when she finished high school. She was going to be a prima ballerina. She was going to spend her life on a stage, spinning around and around." Ana stopped dancing, going still on the small, wooden floor. *Just as that dream stopped.* "But then bad men came into her life. They killed her mother. They killed a part of her. She couldn't dance the same way, not anymore. She started shaking any time she went on a stage because people would whisper about her, they'd talk about what happened *to* her. She wasn't the same."

"Ana . . ." His voice was so rough.

"One thing stayed the same, though. That girl always loved to dance. Dancing made her feel free. It made her forget everything else, if only for a little while." She brushed past him, her shoulder hitting his arm.

"Ana, *stop.*" He grabbed her and spun her back to face him. "I am an asshole, and I'm sorry."

She considered that. "I'm very sorry that you're an asshole, too." Her gaze held his. "Now let go of me."

She thought he was going to argue. She could see the frustration in his eyes, but he let her go. *Smart move, Agent Knox.* But she didn't storm away, not yet. Because there was still one more thing to say. "If you thought . . . all this time . . . that you were just another random guy for me . . ." *That hurt.* "Then I'm so incredibly glad I left you that morning." Just as she was leaving him then.

Ana kept her head up as she left the bar.

And Cash didn't follow her. A good thing because she didn't want him to realize there were tears in her eyes.

HE WAS STARING at the motel wall again.

Cash knew he should get in bed. He should sleep. He should move the hell on but . . .

I hurt Ana. That was the last thing he'd ever meant to do. She would leave come morning. He wouldn't see her again. He . . . he didn't want her to remember him this way.

But staring at the wall wasn't going to change anything.

Cash yanked a hand through his hair and he marched for the door. When he opened it, he saw sheets of rain falling in the motel parking lot. He hadn't even realized it was raining, he'd been too focused on Ana.

On how he just kept screwing up with her.

Determined now, he walked toward her door. Cash lifted his hand and knocked lightly.

Maybe she was asleep. Maybe he was being an even bigger ass. Maybe—

Ana opened the door. Her dark hair was tousled. Her eyes so big and deep and dark. He stared at her, and there were so many things that Cash wanted.

But the one thing he wanted most? To take her pain away. "I'm sorry."

Ana stared at him.

"I was jealous and I was a dick and if I could take back the things I said, believe me, I would."

The rain kept falling.

"I think about you," Cash confessed. "Too fucking much. You slip into my dreams. You creep into my thoughts during the day. I know I should move the hell on, but there is something about you . . . you got beneath my skin." So deep. Deeper than she knew.

And the need he felt for her had started long before he was lucky enough to have Ana Young in his bed.

Another secret. For another time.

Or maybe, maybe it would be best if she never knew that secret.

"You're getting wet," Ana murmured.

He was. The rain was slanting down, hitting him beneath the small overhang of the motel roof.

"Come inside." She stepped back.

He headed in, aware that water was dripping down his back.

She closed the door behind him.

And Cash tried to figure out what he was supposed to say next.

But Ana was the one to do the talking. "You want to know why I slept with you two years ago."

Uh, yeah, he did.

Ana walked past him and sat on the edge of her bed. She wore a pair of jogging shorts and a loose NAVY sweatshirt. He wondered who'd given her the sweatshirt—and why she'd kept it.

"I was riding a high after bringing in Tate. He was my first big capture, and I felt incredible after I dropped him off to the FBI agents." Her hands pressed into the bedding. "And I'd met you. You were different from the guys I generally encountered in my work. Not constantly trying to prove you were a badass. You were quiet. Deep. Still waters and all that."

He stalked closer to her.

Ana lifted her hand and stared down at her fingers. "Do you feel it, when we touch?"

His hands had fisted.

"A little spark. A charge that flares between us." Her

lips curved in a slow smile. Ana had the sexiest smile. "I liked that charge. I liked the attraction. It was easy. Uncomplicated. And . . . not dark."

Not dark?

"Not twisted. Not scary. You see, I do have a type, Cash." Her voice softened when she said his name. "My type isn't by-the-book agents. It's not men who always follow the rules. I tend to gravitate toward danger. Toward men who understand—too well—about the darkness in life." Her head tilted back as she stared up at him. "Not strangers that I pick up in bars. Just so we're real clear on that."

"Ana . . ."

"*You* were the only one-night stand I've ever had. And you were totally the wrong kind of guy for me to be with. You just . . . you don't get me, Cash."

Yes, he did.

"I think I broke my last rule," she murmured. "I told you we wouldn't talk about the past."

"Why did you leave? Without a word?"

She sighed. "Because you were a mistake I didn't want to repeat."

That was pretty damn brutal. It was—

Her eyes searched his. "Why didn't you try to find me?" Ana asked.

He hadn't gone after Ana because . . .

The secrets I carry will hurt her too much.

"You aren't the only one who has made mistakes," Cash said quietly. "There are plenty of things about my past that I wish I could take back. Things I wish I could change."

"Oh, really?" She tilted her head back and studied him. "Tell me."

She'd bared her soul to him. Only fair that he do the same to her. "When I was growing up, I had this older half-brother . . . a real fucking asshole."

Her brows climbed.

"He was on drugs. I knew it. My mom knew it. She just couldn't stop him. His father had been out of the picture for years and my old man . . . well, I guess he was loser number two for my mom. Talk about another worthless bastard." His laughter was bitter, as bitter as the memories that plagued him. "My name? It was a joke to my father. Said he hadn't wanted a son, that he'd just wanted cash. He barely hung around after I was born. He left us all."

She stiffened.

"My mom tried to take care of us, but my older brother made it clear he never liked me. I was a pain in his ass. The guy was always out for himself. Never caring who else he hurt. And he hurt my mom—every time she refused to give him money. Every time she told him that he'd have to get clean, he'd hit her." Cash could still remember that horror. His mother's cries. The thud of fists.

"A real fucking asshole," Cash said again. "But I was just a little kid. Didn't think I could do jack shit. I had to watch him. Just watch . . . until one day, one day, I got tired of watching."

He'd been thirteen. Scrawny but finally taller. Muscles just starting to come in. "There was no money in the house. He had already hit Mom once, and he was going in to hit her again. I grabbed his fist. He was so surprised. He whirled around, laughing and I just . . . I lost it."

She pushed off the bed, rising to her feet.

"I hit him. Again and again and again. I hit him until my knuckles were bleeding and raw. I hit him until he was just lying on the ground, limp. I hit him until I realized my mom had her arms around me. She was crying and begging me to stop. Telling me that I was about to kill him."

Ana reached out to him. "Cash, I—I didn't . . ."

She was staring at him with compassion. With sympathy. His stomach knotted. Ana just didn't get it. "I wanted to kill him."

Her lips parted.

"To this day, I wish . . ." His hand rose and he touched her lips. Those beautiful, perfect lips, with the faint scar. "To this day, I wish that I had killed him."

"Your own brother?" There was shock there. Right. Because Ana was close to her twin. The twin who'd saved her life.

Yes, he knew Ana's story well. Too well.

"I told him to get out. To never come near me or my mom again. Told him if he did, he was a dead man." His own lips twisted as his hand slid away from her silken lips. "Years passed, and I didn't hear anything else from him. I never gave a damn thought to where he was or what he was doing. I was just glad the bastard wasn't near me. My life got better. My life. My mom's life. Everything was better." *For me.*

Her lashes flickered. "What happened to him? Where is your brother now?"

"Dead." *In hell*.

"I'm sorry."

That was it—too much. She shouldn't be sorry. She shouldn't stare at him with compassion. She shouldn't call him the good guy.

White knight—what a sick joke.

His hands closed around her shoulders. "I'm not sorry. I just wish I'd been the one to kill him, back when I was a thirteen-year-old kid. I wish I hadn't stopped."

"Cash?"

"You think I joined the FBI because I've got some hero complex, don't you? You think you have me figured out."

Ana swallowed. "Why did you join?"

"I joined because I know what kind of darkness people really hide inside themselves. I've been hiding my own darkness for most of my life." Hiding it. Fighting it. Vowing to *never, fucking never* be like his brother.

"You think you're one of the monsters?" Ana asked, shaking her head.

Yeah, baby, I do. And if you knew all my secrets, you would, too.

"You're wrong." Ana seemed so certain.

He bent his head. His mouth brushed across hers. He felt her sudden start of surprise. She jerked back.

"No, Ana," Cash told her simply. "This time, you are. You're wrong."

And he knew he would be leaving her. Just like this. Half of his past exposed. Half still hidden because he didn't want to destroy the light in Ana's eyes. Because he didn't want to ever hurt her.

Ana had been hurt enough.

He turned away. Headed for the door. Then he stopped. "I'm sorry you didn't get to dance longer tonight. I didn't know that part about you." He looked back at her. "It fits, though. You kind of even look like a dancer."

Sadness flashed on her beautiful face.

"Maybe we'll dance together again one day." He gave her a little salute. "You're a good partner, Ana Young." And he meant that, in so many ways.

He looked away from her. *Keep moving, Knox. Keep moving.* He was at the door now. His hand reached out and curled around the knob. Ana was silent behind him.

This time, he'd be the one to walk away.

He opened the door.

And Ana's hand slammed down on the wood. She'd moved so silently. Surprised, he turned his head, looking at her. She stared up at him, her gaze sharp, searching. As if she didn't know him.

You don't, Ana. Not really.

"That wasn't a very good kiss, Cash."

He blinked.

"I know you can do better."

He turned to fully face her.

"I've seen you do better," Ana whispered. She rose onto her tiptoes in front of him. "I've felt you do better." Her hands pressed to his chest.

He lowered his head and his mouth touched hers. He was careful at first because this was Ana, and she mattered—more than any other woman ever had. He stroked her lips. But—

"I want everything," Ana whispered.

So did he.

The kiss became rougher. He pulled her closer. Her lips parted and his tongue thrust inside. She tasted just like he remembered. Sweet candy. Rich wine. Every dream he'd ever had.

She gave a little moan. He loved that sound. Loved the feel of her lips and her tongue and her body. Her breasts were pressed to his chest. She was kissing him back with a wild passion—the same passion he remembered feeling with her before.

She'd talk about a spark between them. A flare.

But the truth was that when Cash touched Ana, it felt as if he ignited.

"That is so much better," she said.

His hands were on her waist. And Cash knew he was holding Ana too tightly. He should let her go.

But that's the problem. I never want to let Ana go.

He lifted her up, holding her easily, and he caged her between his body and the motel room door. Ana's legs wrapped around his hips. He pressed to her, his cock heavy and swollen with arousal. To be *inside* Ana . . .

Hell the fuck yes.

But . . .

He caught her lower lip between his teeth. Sucked. Licked. Then his tongue slid into her mouth once more. The kiss was hot and wet. Open. Deep.

It shook him to his core.

A kiss.

Just a kiss.

His head lifted. He stared into Ana's eyes. *It is so easy to get lost in her gaze.*

Her legs slowly slid away from his hips. He lowered

her down until her feet touched the floor. Ana's breath whispered out as she stared up at him. "Now that," Ana said, her voice husky, "is the kind of kiss that a woman won't forget."

Cash swallowed. "Glad you'll remember me."

"Oh, Cash, trust me, you aren't an easy man to forget."

His fingers brushed over her cheek. "Good night, Ana Young."

She smiled at him. "Good night, Cash Knox." Then Ana slipped away from the door. He opened it, saw the hail of rain falling outside, and he walked away.

Just . . . walked.

Because he wasn't going to make any other mistakes with Ana.

No mistakes . . .

ANA SHUT THE door behind Cash. Her hand lifted to her lips, but she wasn't touching her scar. Not this time.

She was remembering the feel of his mouth against hers. She could still taste him.

She liked Cash's taste.

But she wasn't going to make another mistake with him. Not tonight. Walking away from him two years ago had been hard enough. She'd wanted to stay in his bed. Wanted to stay with him.

If she gave in to their attraction again . . .

What would happen? Would I be able to walk away?

She wasn't sure.

And the fact that the guy had layers she hadn't fully expected . . .

"Take a cold shower, Ana," she whispered to herself. "Very, very cold."

She'd take her shower, she'd go to bed, and then, when morning came, she'd fly away from Cash.

End of story.

The *end*.

THE PHONE RANG in the middle of the night. It was a jarring cry, and it pulled Ana from her sleep. Her hand flew out, fumbling, and she hit the nightstand. It took her two swipes to grab her phone and yank it toward her ear.

Middle of the night. Is it Asher? Is everything okay?

Because her twin was the only one who normally called her in the middle of the night. The last time he'd done that, Asher's world had been imploding. And—

"Asher?" His name was the first word she spoke as she put the phone to her ear, but then Ana realized . . . *no, it can't be Asher. The ringtone was wrong.*

She heard the harsh sound of a sharply indrawn breath.

Ana sat up in bed, wakefulness coming in a rush. "Who is this?" The clock on the nightstand said it was nearing three a.m.

"Wasn't it beautiful?" The voice was distorted. Robotic?

"What?" Ana snapped. *"Who is this?"* she demanded again.

"All of his blood . . . wasn't it beautiful?"

Chill bumps rose on Ana's arms.

"He got what he deserved." The voice was just wrong—high, definitely robotic sounding. Too sharp in her ears.

"Are you talking about Bernie Tate?" Ana demanded. She jumped from the bed and slammed her hand onto the wall between her and Cash. She needed his attention. She needed him. *Wake the hell up, Cash.* "Did you kill him?"

Again, that robotic voice filled the line. "Punishment."

Her hand flattened on the wall. "How did you get my number?"

She could hear Cash scrambling around in the other room, the heavy thread of his footsteps, the squeak of his door—

"You understand me, Ana."

She whirled away from the wall and hurried toward her motel room door. "I don't." Her eye pressed to the small peep hole. A moment later, Cash was there, the fluorescent light shining too brightly on him.

The robotic voice told her, "I'll make them all pay."

"What?" Her fingers fumbled with the lock. She turned it, grabbed the knob, and yanked the door open.

"They will all pay, I promise."

And the call ended.

Cash rushed into her room. He grabbed her arms. "Ana? What's happening? What's wrong?" His gaze swept around the small motel room, as if he were looking for a threat.

She lifted her phone. "The killer . . . I think he just called me."

His hold tightened on her. "What?"

"And if he wasn't bullshitting, if that really was our guy . . ." Ana swallowed. "Cash, there are going to be more dead bodies."

CHAPTER FIVE

THE PILE OF MISSING PERSONS' FOLDERS FILLED her desk. Ana sat, slumped in her chair, her gaze on those files. Cathy Wise's case was at the top of that pile. Cathy's file was open, revealing the age progression photo that Gabe had recently commissioned.

A woman with blond hair, high cheekbones, and pale blue eyes stared at Ana. A faint dimple was in the middle of the woman's chin. A small mole near her left eye.

Age progression photos always made her a bit sad. *This is what your child would've looked like . . . if she hadn't been taken.*

Ana slammed the file shut, making her pile tremble.

She'd flown back to Atlanta first thing that morning. Been in the office by noon. And . . .

I still hear that freaking robotic voice in my head.

She knew the caller had used a voice distorter, obviously. It was ridiculously easy to come by those now. Dozens of voice distorting apps were available online. Most of them were even free. The call had come from an "Unknown Caller"—maybe from a burner phone.

Cash had said his guys at the FBI would try to track down her caller, but he hadn't seemed overly hopeful.

But he *had* been adamant that Ana leave town. That she get on the plane.

"Leaving in the middle of a freaking case," she growled under her breath as she leaned back in her chair and closed her eyes. "That sucked."

"What sucked?"

Ana's eyes flew open. That voice was familiar and just hearing it caused a surge of warmth and affection to fill her. She pushed out of her chair and hurried toward the door—and toward her brother.

Asher Young was her twin, but he was definitely not built along the same delicate lines that she was—the guy was big, strong. Rather like a tank. Way over six feet and with shoulders that stretched far and wide.

But his dark hair was like hers. And he had her dark eyes.

And he has his own scars.

A faint white scar slipped under his strong chin.

She wrapped her arms around him and held on tight for a big hug. "I didn't realize you were back in town. I thought you were still working that case in Florida."

He hugged her back, his powerful grip lifting her off her feet for a moment. "Just got back," he said.

She felt safe with Asher. Always had. Always would. They'd been through absolute hell together, and that pain had just made their bond stronger.

He eased her to her feet and she stared up at him, seeing the pain reflected in his eyes. "You found your lost girl, didn't you?" Because she knew he'd been working to find a missing twelve-year-old girl. Calley

Shawton. Little Calley had been missing for five years now.

So she wouldn't be twelve any longer. She'd be seventeen. In high school. Getting ready to go to her prom or—

"Found her remains." Anger and pain thickened his voice. "Buried in a neighbor's backyard. The sick bastard had volunteered for years in the search for her. *Years.* Cops never even looked his way."

She hugged him again, harder. "I'm sorry." Because she hated it when cases ended this way.

"Gave her parents closure." His voice was grim. Asher shook his head. "Closure? Is that really the word I'm supposed to use? Like getting her bones is supposed to make them feel better." He slipped from Ana's embrace and walked toward her window. "No," he said as he rolled back his shoulders, "the only *closure* that will help is when that sick sonofabitch is sent to prison for the rest of his life." He looked back at her. "But Florida is a state that has the death penalty, so maybe that will be the punishment he gets."

Punishment.

"Closure comes when the bastards who hurt others are stopped," Asher continued. She saw him clench his fists, then flex his wrists. "Sometimes, death is the only way to do that."

I'll make them all pay. For an instant, she could hear that distorted, robotic voice filling her head again.

"Dammit, I'm sorry." He blew out a frustrated breath. "Don't mean to dump on you like this."

She shut her office door. "If you can't dump on me, then what kind of sister would I be?"

He turned to face her. His eyes were narrowed. "Something's wrong."

She shrugged. "Nothing I can't handle."

"Ana, what is it?"

Secrets. So many of them. "I had a field assignment, too."

He swore. "That's what you were talking about when I came in. You lost your victim, too?"

She started to nod, but stopped. This was Asher. She didn't need to pretend with him. "It was Bernie Tate."

Shock flashed on his face. "Bernie the Butcher?"

Ana nodded. "He escaped from prison, or, at least, that was what it looked like. I found him—Cash and I . . . I mean, Agent Knox and I—but Bernie was dead. He'd been stabbed, again and again." *And again.*

Asher took a step toward her. "You okay?"

Her chin notched up. "Of course."

His eyes gleamed. "Ana, you say 'of course' even when you're about to collapse."

Her gaze slid away from his. "I got a call last night. I think it was from Bernie's killer."

"What the actual fuck?" He rushed toward her. "Ana, you *lead* with that shit when you're talking to me. A killer called you? And you didn't contact me? Why the—"

"Stop." She kept her voice flat and calm with an extreme effort. "You're doing it again, Asher." Trying to protect her. Trying to shield her from everything.

An impossible task.

"I'm safe. I'm okay."

A muscle flexed in his jaw. Poor Asher. No matter what she said or did, Ana knew he kept blaming himself. She wanted to take that burden off his shoulders. She wished so much that she could.

"I worry about you, Ana."

Asher was the one person in the world that she loved, completely. Totally. She would lie for her brother. Fight for him.

Kill for him.

Just as he'd killed for her.

"I know," Ana said, clearing her throat, "but I'm okay. Agent Knox was right there. I was never in any danger." *And I know how to take care of myself. I'm not some defenseless fourteen-year-old girl any longer.*

"Agent Knox?" Asher seemed to test the name. "Don't think I've ever met him."

"No, you haven't." Her shoulders straightened. "He thinks the caller . . . well, the way the caller talked, Bernie had gotten some kind of payback." Her gaze held his. "Punishment. That was what the caller said to me. Cash—Agent Knox figured the perp had to be related to one of Bernie's victims. The FBI was going to start running down all known victim connections to see if they could track down the killer." She headed toward her desk. Her fingers fluttered over Cathy's file.

"You don't agree with the agent's assessment?"

She opened the file. Cathy's blue gaze stared up at her. "Ana?"

Just as quickly, she closed the file. "The caller said something else that's been bothering me." She turned around, propping her hip on the edge of her desk. "'They will all pay.' Those were the exact words. If this was just about Bernie, about his crimes, why say that?" She let her words sink in a moment. "It . . . to me, it seemed like the caller was planning to kill more people."

He nodded. "Seems like the same shit to me, too."

She bit her lower lip. "I got shut out. Sent away from the investigation and back here. I have all these suspicions, and I don't know what the hell I'm supposed to do next."

"That sucks."

A quick laugh broke from her. "Yes that's what I was saying." She pushed back her hair. "The FBI closed rank on me. I got shipped away. They took over the case."

"What did your Agent Knox say before you left?"

He's not my Agent Knox. "He thanked me for finding Bernie. Then he walked away." And it hurt. Because . . .

Because I wasn't ready to leave Cash.

"The killer called you," Asher said. His brows were pulled low. "You're *sure* the guy was legit?"

"He certainly seemed that way to me."

"Then maybe it's not over. No reason you can't conduct your own investigation without the FBI's assistance. After all, you've got me. I can help you."

But, once more, her gaze slid to the files on her desk. So many cases. "But they're waiting," Ana whispered. "Do I make them wait longer because I'm trying to get justice for Bernie Tate? Bernie Freaking Tate?" She shook her head and focused on her brother. "How twisted is that?"

Asher glanced down at his watch. "Let's go grab lunch and we can talk this out. Sound like a plan?"

"Yes, yes, let's do that." Because staying there, waiting like that . . . thinking in circles . . . she was about to drive herself crazy.

"WE HAVE ANOTHER one."

Cash stiffened as his fingers curled around his phone. His boss had just called him a few moments ago, and Cash had stepped away from the crime scene at the cabin so that he could take the call.

Bernie Tate's blood still stained the cabin floor. The place still reeked of death and human waste. It was like the pit of hell. And his boss was seriously telling him . . .

"You remember Forrest Hutchins?" Darius asked.

Forrest Hutchins. Forrest . . . The name clicked. "Yeah, I remember him." He'd studied the guy at Quantico. "He took homeless men from the streets of Richmond about ten years ago. Kept them imprisoned for weeks, slowly starved them to death." A slow, painful way to go. And the bastard had said he'd done it in the name of *science*. Because he'd wanted to see how long it took the human body to turn on itself. How desperate would an individual become? How far would a person go to stay alive?

Forrest Hutchins had been a psychology grad student at the time of his heinous crimes. He'd been captured, been put on trial, but . . . instead of being locked in a maximum security prison, the guy had been sent to a psychiatric hospital. The judge and jury had decided the guy was insane. *Not legally responsible for his crimes.*

"I don't know why it took so long for the FBI to get this notification," his boss continued, his voice grim and angry. "But Forrest went missing from his hospital two weeks ago. *Two damn weeks.* The staff there is saying they alerted the authorities, that they sent faxes out and other bullshit . . ." His voice trailed away. "The blame game is in full effect right now. The governor is about to rip the director of that hospital a new one, and with the press in a frenzy over Tate's death, we are all in serious *cover-our-asses* mode."

A dull ache built behind Cash's left eye. "The psychiatric hospital that Forrest was in . . ."

"River View Psychiatric. It's about two hours away from your current location."

Shit. So when the director had said, "We have another one . . ." had the guy meant that they had another missing criminal on their hands?

Or another potential victim? Both?

"Two infamous killers," Darius snapped. "Both go missing from the same state, within two weeks of each other? This looks so damn bad."

Cash glanced back at the cabin. Yellow police tape fluttered in the breeze. "One of them isn't missing any longer."

"Yeah, well, I want both of them found. Leave a team of agents at the crime scene and get to tracking Forrest. That sick sonofabitch shouldn't be out there—"

"Just how did he escape?" Cash asked, cutting through Darius's words.

A stark pause.

"Executive Assistant Director? How did he get away from the hospital?"

"No one knows. All I've got from the hospital is that he was in his room one day and gone the next.

Bullshit. Now, before the public goes into even more of a panic, I need you to lock this down, understand?"

Cash understood plenty. After Ana had told him about her mysterious caller, he'd been pissed. *The bastard had called Ana? Had targeted her?* Cash hadn't been able to get Ana on the plane fast enough. He'd wanted her out of the killer's line of sight. He'd wanted her as far away as possible.

He'd wanted her safe.

But he'd also had the same fear she did . . .

There will be others. There could already be others.

So he'd contacted his boss. Told him to watch out . . . that they could have one serious clusterfuck on their hands. *The killer went to a whole lot of trouble to get to Bernie Tate. The crime was so violent. We aren't looking at a one-and-done attack here.*

"Get a handle on this case," the executive assistant director urged. "Before it blows up in all of our faces."

ASHER SAT ACROSS from Ana, a faint smile on his face. "We both know you aren't going to drop the Tate case."

She fiddled with her salad. "When the FBI kicks you out, what are you supposed to do?"

He laughed. "Find a way to kick yourself back inside." He leaned toward her. The noise of the restaurant seemed to fade into the background as he said, "If you want to work this case, do it."

But what about the other victims who are waiting? Ana shook her head. "We found Tate. That was my job. To find him. Not to stop his killer."

"Why are you even trying to bullshit with me?"

She looked away from his gaze. For a moment, she just studied the other diners. They were talking. Laughing. Some had their noses shoved into their phones. "They're all safe," she murmured.

"What?"

Ana put down her fork. "The people here, they're safe. Or at least, they *think* they're safe. They don't get how dangerous life is. How fragile. They don't know that they could walk out of here and just vanish. Their families wouldn't know what happened to them. Their employers wouldn't know." She snapped her fingers. "That fast, and it's over. That fast, and you become just a file on someone's desk."

"Ana . . ."

"That fast," she whispered. "And it's over."

He caught her hand in his. "Is LOST too much for you?"

Her breath seemed to chill her lungs.

"I signed on because of you, only you. You wanted to join LOST to make a difference. To give families hope."

Ana nodded. He was right. She had. Being a bounty hunter—it had all been about criminals. She'd wanted to help the victims. To find *them*. And Asher, well, he was an ex-SEAL. Gabe had been more than ready to bring him on board, too. Extra force, more strength. The backup the team needed.

Together, she and Asher were supposed to be a perfect package.

So why do I feel like I am cracking apart on the inside?

"I'm sorry you didn't find your victim alive," she said, aware that her voice was too ragged.

"Ana . . ." A muscle jerked in his jaw. "I got the bastard who hurt her. He's going to pay."

They're all going to pay. Her gaze fell.

"If being at LOST isn't what you want, say the word." His fingers squeezed hers. "You know I have your back. Always."

She did. She . . .

Ana's phone rang. She hesitated, goose bumps rising on her arms. It was her generic ringtone, the one she set for callers she *didn't* know. Ana pulled her hand away from Asher. She reached into her bag, pulled out her phone . . .

Not an unknown caller. But she still didn't recognize the number. Heart racing, Ana put the phone to her ear. "Hello?"

"Ana."

Cash's voice.

Her gaze flew to her brother's face. She gave him a weak smile. "Sorry, I have to take this." She hurried away from the table, trying to find a quiet spot in the restaurant, nearly an impossibility. She ducked into an alcove. "Cash, what's wrong? Did you find the killer?"

"No. I just . . . I wanted to make sure you'd gotten home safely."

"Um, yes, yes, I'm fine." She could see Asher from her position. His shoulders were stiff.

"There might be another one, Ana."

Her heart jerked.

"I'm checking on the situation right now, but if you get any other phone calls from that SOB, you notify me right away, got it?"

"You are so good at giving orders."

"Ana . . ." He growled her name.

"Don't worry. If I get another phone call, you'll hear about it immediately." She eased back another step. "Who's the victim this time?"

Silence.

"Cash, I can help, you know."

"Yeah, yeah, I know it." A pause. "The victim is Forrest Hutchins."

The name was familiar, nagging at the back of her mind but . . .

Hutchins, Hutchins, Hutchins . . .

"He was in the River View Psychiatric Hospital," Cash said. "After he abducted and starved five homeless men to death, the court decided the guy was insane. He's been locked up in this place for the last three years."

Her eyes squeezed shut. Now she remembered the name.

"Seems he vanished two weeks ago. I'm heading to the facility to try to figure out what the hell happened."

She wanted to be there. "Do you need me?"

"I need you to stay safe." His words were tight. "I don't like that the killer called you. A call is personal. It means he could be targeting you."

Her eyes opened. The noise of the restaurant seemed so distant.

"I'll contact you once I know more," Cash assured her. "And if you get any more late night calls from the SOB, notify me. Immediately."

"I will."

"Sorry to wreck your day."

"You didn't," she said quickly. "I was just having lunch."

And she saw that her brother was heading toward her. Asher's face was tense, worried, as he closed in.

"I can handle any danger that comes my way," Ana said, her words rushing out. "You don't need to worry about protecting me."

"That's the thing, though. I do worry. I think about you far too much, Ana Young. You're in my head, and I can't get you out."

I was out for two years.

"The last thing I want," Cash said, voice deepening even more, "is for you to be hurt again."

Asher was in front of her. "Ana, is there a problem?"

She gave a hard shake of her head toward her brother.

Cash had gone silent.

"Cash?" she pressed.

"I'll talk to you again soon, Ana. Until then, try to stay away from killers."

Easier said than done. Ana ended the call and stared at her brother—a man who'd killed.

For me.

ASHER YOUNG DIDN'T love easily. He wasn't a gentle man, and he knew the darkness in him would never go away.

He loved his fiancée, Bailey Jones. Loved her so much that the emotion sometimes scared him. He'd come close to losing Bailey recently, and for a moment, he'd worried that he might lose his sanity.

He loved Bailey . . . and he loved his sister. There was literally nothing he would not do for Ana. Years ago, she'd suffered because of him. That grief still cut him up, still had him waking at night, bellowing his rage.

Ana didn't blame him, he knew that. But he blamed himself. And he'd made it his mission to be sure that his twin never suffered again.

So after Asher took Ana back to her office at LOST, he headed in for a little one-on-one time with his boss—and former SEAL buddy, Gabe Spencer. Asher closed Gabe's fancy office door behind him with a soft click.

Gabe glanced up, his brows rising. "Hey, Asher, what's up?"

Asher leaned back against the door, considering things. "Agent Cash Knox." Ana had kept slipping up when she talked about the agent. *Cash*. Her voice had softened. Ana didn't do that—her voice didn't soften for anyone, especially not some FBI agent. "I need to know about him."

Surprise flickered over Gabe's face as he leaned back in his chair. "Agent Knox? He's the special agent who knows Ana. He came in, ready to make any kind of deal to get her on the Bernie Tate case." He rubbed his jaw. "They'd worked together before, and I think Ana made quite the impression on him."

Asher didn't move. "Ana didn't mention that she'd worked with him before."

"No?" Gabe didn't look concerned. "Well, I'm sure during her bounty hunting days, Ana worked with so many law enforcement personnel that she didn't make a list for you." Amusement coated the words. "Too many people to keep track of."

This wasn't just a professional relationship. He'd heard that truth in Ana's voice. "When did they work together?"

"Bernie Tate," Gabe said, sighing. "That's how they met. Cash was with the FBI when Ana turned over Tate. So when Tate went missing again, well, it made sense for the agent to come looking for Ana."

On the surface, yeah, he might be able to buy that story. But . . .

Ana had secrets in her eyes. "You know anything else about the guy?" Asher pushed.

"Only that he's been rocketing up the ranks at the FBI." Now Gabe's voice was measured. "When I checked him out through my contacts, the guy had the highest recs possible. He's supposed to be a good agent, damn dedicated, with an eye for bringing down the worst criminals out there." Gabe stared knowingly at Asher. "Kind of sounds like your potential new best friend."

Asher just glared at him. "I'm not in the market for a best friend. I've got your sorry ass."

Gabe laughed. "That is so no way to talk to your boss."

Asher started to speak, then he stopped.

Gabe's laughter faded away. "Is there a problem I need to know about? Something with Agent Knox?"

Maybe the problem was just that Asher was an overprotective sonofabitch. Ana knew how to take care of herself. He was worrying for nothing. But . . .

Let my sister go! Stop it! Stop, please! Don't hurt her!

Asher heard his voice, echoing in his mind. Ana was his family. "I think I want to do a little digging on the guy myself."

Gabe rose. "Look, I know your last case was a hard one. And that it probably hit a little too close to home." Gabe stalked toward him, sympathy flashing in his eyes. "I hesitated on assigning it to you because every sign I had pointed to that girl being dead. But I knew, I *knew* you could find her killer. You did. You stopped him. Just like you stopped the men who were hurting you and Ana so long ago."

Oh, buddy, you don't know the whole story. So few did. He'd told Bailey the truth, when he'd been desperate for her to see him as he really was. Surprisingly, Bailey hadn't kicked his ass to the curb. She'd stayed with him, dark spots and all.

"Not every person in the world is a monster," Gabe added. "Sometimes, there are good people out there. Agent Knox? He's one of the good guys." Gabe's hand curled around his shoulder. "Now why don't you just take the afternoon off? I know Bailey is still settling in to the new house you two bought. Go spend some time with that beautiful woman."

Being with Bailey—yeah, that was what he needed. Her smile wiped away his pain. His rage. She made him feel better.

Cleaner. Like the past doesn't mark me.

But it did. He'd always be marked by his past. Just as Ana was marked. Scars on the outside. And on the inside.

It was the scars on the inside that were the worst. Those scars twisted a person up. Destroyed a soul.

Turned a *good* man . . .

Into a monster.

CHAPTER SIX

THE PRETTY BLONDE BEHIND THE DESK WAS stonewalling her.

Ana dug deep and managed to produce a bright smile. She showed her ID one more time and kept her voice as sugary sweet as possible when she said, "But I'm sure FBI Agent Knox is waiting for me inside your facility. I'm working as a liaison with the FBI on this investigation." She glanced around, trying to look perfectly confused. "He told me to meet him at River View Psychiatric, so here I am." Her gaze returned to the blonde. "He's going to be incredibly upset if you delay our investigation."

The blonde hesitated.

Ana's smile stretched just a wee bit more. She was lying to the pretty receptionist. Totally lying. But, well, she'd decided after her lunch with Asher that she wasn't going to be cut out of this investigation. She didn't need to be protected.

She needed to be a partner in this investigation.

She'd talked to Gabe, briefed him on the situation, and in true "I am the best boss ever" fashion, he'd even given her the company plane to use for her trip back to Virginia. Now she was at the psychiatric hospital, trying to weasel her way inside. An armed guard was giving her the squint eye, so she really needed for the blonde receptionist to get things moving.

"You're not on our check-in list," the receptionist said, her lips tugging down in a frown. "Agent Knox went inside just an hour ago, but he didn't tell me anything about you being here."

That's because I didn't call in advance. If I had, he would have just told me not to come. "He was probably distracted," Ana said easily. "Mind on the case. I mean, when a man like Forrest Hutchins goes missing . . . well, that situation is certainly cause for alarm."

The receptionist's hand rose to her throat. "I can't believe he escaped," she whispered. "He was supposed to be locked up in the quiet room. No one in or out."

"The quiet room?"

The blonde leaned toward Ana and her voice dropped conspiratorially. "We're not supposed to call it solitary confinement, but that's what it is."

Thank God for the chatty receptionist.

"Forrest had an incident with one of the other patients," the receptionist continued, her expression tightening. "He was put in the quiet room so that he could calm himself back down."

"Did Forrest often have *incidents* while he was here?"

The blonde's gaze flickered toward the guard. "He was a very violent man."

Was. Not is. Interesting.

The blonde reached for her phone. "I'll just call the head of the hospital. Dr. Summers will be able to vouch for you, I'm sure. I mean, Agent Knox must have told her that you were coming."

Or not. Ana kept her smile in place.

But then, over the blonde's shoulder, she caught sight of a familiar figure.

Tall, wide shoulders, determined gait, thick hair, stubble covered jaw, and an expression that said . . .

Ana Young, what the hell are you doing here?

"Don't worry about the call," Ana said dismissively. "There's Agent Knox. He'll vouch for me." Or he'd haul her ass out of there. Though she was really hoping more for option A.

Cash quickened his stride as he cleared the guard's screening area. "Ana." He snarled her name. "What in the hell—"

"Don't be mad at her," Ana cut through his words, hurrying toward Cash even as she motioned her hand vaguely to the gaping receptionist. "She was just following orders. She didn't realize you expected me to follow you into the hospital."

His eyes glittered at her. "I expected you to follow me?"

"Right, yes, of course." Ana glanced back at the receptionist, nodding. "I told her that I was working as your liaison, but in your rush this morning, you must have forgotten to properly inform all the staff members." She exhaled and shook her head. "No matter. I'm here now. I'm ready to help."

"Well, thank Christ for that," he drawled loudly. Then he snagged her wrist in a grip that was a bit *too* tight. "Before you *help,* how about we have a quick, private conversation?"

"Sounds like a great plan." She kept her expression bright and attentive as he pretty much dragged her *out* of that reception area, out of the main entrance and into the facility's parking lot. As soon as they were away from prying eyes, she jerked her hand free of his.

"Ana." Once more, her name was a snarl. He needed to watch that snarling tendency. The guy was becoming way too animal-like. "What in the hell are you doing here?"

"Helping you." Wasn't that obvious?

"Ana . . ."

"Would you lower your voice?" Because she'd just spotted another guard patrolling the parking lot. From what she could tell, the facility had some pretty good security. But maybe all those guards had been put in place *after* Forrest vanished. "Stop causing a scene with your partner."

He just stared at her. Then he muttered, "You're going to drive me to drink."

"Probably." But they didn't have time for his issues right then. "Look, we both know you called me because you wanted my help. You wanted me here with you."

Cash shook his head. "No! I wanted you far away. *Safe.* That's why I put you on the plane in the first place! The killer contacted you—"

"Exactly," Ana cut in, nodding.

His cheeks tinted red. "You were supposed to stay in Atlanta."

"I'm supposed to finish my case." Now she crossed her arms over her chest and studied him. "I think you have the wrong idea about me."

His brows shot up.

"I don't give up easily."

"You didn't give up! You *found* Tate. You did your job."

"But I didn't find his killer. And the fact that the guy is talking to me—or *did* talk to me—that means I'm involved. Killers don't just randomly pick up the phone and start dialing folks for fun. They pick their victims for a reason."

His jaw locked. "I don't want you to be a victim."

His words were so gruff. She softened as she said, "I know. But I don't . . . I don't know what I am to this perp." *Not yet.* "I do know that I'm not going to hide. I won't turn my back on what's happening. I can't. That's just not who I am."

"Because you don't walk away."

"I don't." She offered him a small smile. "Instead, I butt in. I come in with the force of a battering ram, and I get my job done."

His grim expression didn't change. "I don't want a target on your back."

"So far, I have nothing in common with your victims." She'd been over this, again and again, during her flight. "The two men—Bernie and Forrest—they were both killers. Criminals. They have that trait in common. I'm not like them." She knew it was too early to speculate about what was happening with these crimes but . . . . "The caller talked about making them pay. It was almost as if he was trying to reassure me."

Cash stiffened.

"I don't think I'm in danger. I'm not a target. I'm someone who can help you." Okay, she'd said her part. She wasn't going to beg. "But if the FBI thinks that a lowly ex–bounty hunter can't be of assistance—"

"Cut the bull, Ana. There is nothing lowly about you and we both know it."

Her smile became real.

He blinked at her. Then he held up his hand. "Don't go getting all cocky yet." She heard the twang of Texas dip into his voice. "Doesn't mean I like your methods. You were just trying to sneak into a psychiatric facility. You were *lying* about an FBI agent's orders."

She winced. "I know. I am so bad."

"Ana . . ."

"Bad," she murmured, "but very, very good at my job. So how about you read me the riot act later, and we go investigate the quiet room together now?"

His eyelids flickered. "You already know about the quiet room?"

She looped her arm through his. "You would not believe how chatty that receptionist was . . ."

HE DIDN'T LIKE the quiet room.

Cash stood in the middle of the dark room. No windows. One bed. Such a small space, maybe eight feet long, four feet wide.

The walls were blue. A light blue. Cash was sure the color had been chosen because it was supposed to be peaceful. Serene.

But he didn't feel serene in that little cage. *And that's what this room is. A cage.*

Behind him, Dr. Ellen Summers cleared her throat. He looked back at her, and she pointed to the security camera that was positioned in the corner of the room. "Unfortunately, the patient disabled the camera."

"Disabled?" Ana repeated. "How'd he do that?"

"He ripped it down and smashed it with his bare hands. Smashed it until he bled and two of his fingers broke." Dr. Summers kept a serene expression on her face. She inclined her head toward Cash. "Forrest is a profoundly disturbed individual. His outbursts were quite strong. Though, I am happy to say, they were occurring less frequently as a result of the therapy he had been receiving."

Ana slowly circled around the room. "Therapy, right." She toed the edge of the bed. "What kind of therapy would that be?"

Dr. Summers drew herself up to her full height. The doctor was tall, slim, with blond hair that fell to her chin in a perfectly cut bob. "I'm not at liberty to tell *you* that."

"You can tell me," Cash said, voice hard. "In light of what happened at this facility, you *will* tell me that."

The doctor's lips thinned.

"This isn't some game," Cash told her bluntly. "This is the kind of screwup that closes down a facility. A *killer* escaped under your watch. He walked away and it took you two weeks to notify the FBI."

Dr. Summers took a step back. "I followed all the proper channels. I contacted local authorities. I sent faxes, emails. I didn't know the FBI would be involved—"

"Forrest Hutchins kidnapped and murdered five men. Trust me, the FBI is very interested in every single thing that happens to him."

She nodded quickly. "Right. I—I just thought that once the local authorities started searching, they'd find him quickly. Our facility is very isolated. The nearest town is forty miles away. He would have needed to walk for hours in order to just reach the gas station on County Road—"

"He didn't have to walk if he had a ride waiting for him," Ana cut in.

Cash had been thinking the same thing.

But Dr. Summers shook her head. "Forrest Hutchins had no visitors. His family didn't even come to see him."

No, they'd just paid a shitload to make sure he got into the facility, an experimental facility that had opened just before his sentencing. *For both criminals and the general population.* Although those two patient groups were supposed to always be kept separate. Always.

"He received no mail. He had no computer access. As soon as he stepped through the doors at my facility, he had no additional contact with the outside world."

"That part of his therapy?" Ana asked, cocking her head as she studied the other woman.

"Partially. But Forrest wasn't exactly big on human interaction. He saw most people as being beneath him. Test subjects, if you will. You don't *talk* to your experiments. You don't send them letters. You don't communicate on the phone with them. You just . . . you use them." For the first time, sadness flickered in her gaze. "He didn't connect with anyone, not on an emotional level. That was his problem. The judge saw that—the judge knew that he had problems. I work with people like Forrest every day. I *help* them." She glanced around the empty quiet room, seemingly lost for a moment. "I think I could have helped him, too. No, no, I *was* helping him."

"Right up to the moment when he vanished." Ana paced closer to Cash.

Dr. Summers clutched her clipboard a little tighter. "There are guards on the perimeter of this facility. There are cameras situated along the exterior of our hospital. He couldn't have just walked away. Forrest would have been seen. He would have—"

"Is *that* why you delayed reporting?" Cash cut in to ask because he'd seen the faxes she sent to the local authorities. They'd been sent at least four days *after* Forrest's disappearance. "Because you thought the guy was hiding out somewhere inside your facility?"

"We were conducting an in-house investigation," Dr. Summer began, voice tight.

"No," Cash fired back. "You were trying to cover your own ass. You didn't want word leaking to the media that your facility wasn't secure because when that happened, you knew you'd come under investigation. Judges wouldn't be sending you new patients. Families would be panicking. So you thought you could make this problem go away on your own, but that shit didn't work. And now I'm here to try and clean up the mess."

Silence.

"Nothing like this has ever happened before." The doctor's words were very quiet. "An escape like this—of someone of Forrest's fame—it will ruin us. My facility is needed. Not just for the patients that the court sends to us . . . but we help the poor, the destitute. We give them treatment." Her eyes were bright with emotion. "We are needed."

"Trust me, I get that." And he did. "But what you need to get is this . . . Forrest Hutchins killed five men. Now he's gone, with at least a two-week head start. What in the hell do you think will happen to anyone unfortunate enough to be in the guy's path?" Cash asked her.

The doctor didn't reply.

"We want full access to your facility." Cash rubbed his jaw. "And I'll be interviewing all of your staff members. People don't just vanish, not without a trace. Someone always sees *something*. Someone knows *something*. We just have to pose the right questions to the right people." And he intended to keep asking those questions until he got answers.

"Dr. Summers?" A woman with blond hair stood in the doorway. Her blue eyes danced nervously around the room. "You have a call. It's the governor." Her voice cracked a bit on that last part.

Dr. Summers winced.

"You take that call, Dr. Summers," Cash told her. "We'll start our search."

She hurried away.

The blonde woman lingered a moment.

Ana crept closer to Cash. "The chatty receptionist," she whispered to him, then she hurried toward the younger woman. "I'm sorry, I didn't get your name before." She offered her hand to the blonde.

"Megan. Megan Thomas." The blonde quickly shook Ana's hand, then backed away.

"Thanks for your assistance before, Megan," Ana said smoothly. "And if you happen to know anything about Forrest Hutchins that you think can help Agent Knox and me . . ." She let the sentence trail away.

And Cash caught the faint flicker of Megan's eyelashes.

"*Is* there something that you'd like to tell us?" Ana asked.

"He seemed . . . kind to me."

Now that was a surprise. "Excuse me?"

"I assist Dr. Summers sometimes." Megan toyed with a lock of her hair. "I'm working on a graduate degree in counseling, so she lets me assist her. I saw her working with Forrest. After all the stories, I expected him to be a monster."

He is a monster.

"But he was always nice to me. Soft spoken with all the guards." Her gaze fell to the floor. "It was hard for me to see him as a killer."

Cash advanced toward the blonde. "Tell that to the five men he murdered."

Megan staggered back a step. "He . . . he was only agitated when Dr. Summers was around."

Agitated? Cash thought that was a nice word to describe a rage that had resulted in a camera being smashed to hell and back. "Any idea why he responded so strongly to her?"

Megan's lashes lifted. "He said he didn't like being her experiment." She started to say more, then shook her head. "I have to get back to my post. My relief cover can only stay a short time." Then she turned on her heel and strode away.

Ana stared after the blonde a moment, then she glanced over at Cash. "An experiment, huh?" she mused. "So the guy could dish out the punishment, but not take it."

"Seems that way." His stare swept over the room once more. "There's nothing to see here."

"Yes, well, because unlike our not-so-friendly prison warden, Dr. Summers cleaned up." She waved her hand. "No personal effects in here, though I'm thinking there never *were* any."

No, he didn't think so, either.

"How would he have gotten out of this place?" Ana asked, her lips tightening. "I saw the security outside the facility. A guard was on constant patrol. And just to get back here to the quiet room, we had to go through three different checkpoints. Someone should have *seen* the guy."

"Bernie had help vanishing," Cash reminded her. "Maybe Forrest did, too." Only with the layout of this facility, he was wondering . . .

Had the guy gotten inside help?

Forrest Hutchins was a blond, blue-eyed man. Most news reports had even called the bastard "Hollywood handsome." He'd been a charmer. Smart, cold. Sadistic. Rich.

"Megan liked him," Ana murmured. "Maybe she wasn't the only one who had a soft spot for this particular killer."

Maybe. Megan's words had already set off alarm bells in Cash's head. He'd be investigating that woman—

hell, yes. A woman like her, with such open access to the facility . . . *she'd make a perfect accomplice.* If Forrest had left on his own. *If.*

"Let's start searching," Cash said, rolling back his shoulders. "It's a big facility, and we've got four floors to cover."

And dozens of staff members to interview.

It was going to be a fucking long day.

ANA YOUNG WAS interesting.

A victim, but not broken. Not trapped in the pain of her past.

She'd been tortured, nearly killed. Humiliated. Degraded.

And the men who'd taken her had been murdered. Sliced apart with brutal efficiency. Their deaths were cloaked in mystery. Suspicions. Had Ana been the one to kill them? Her brother had claimed he'd done the work, but . . .

But Ana's eyes were the eyes of a killer.

She'd become a hunter. A bounty hunter. She'd tracked down the worst scum in the United States. She'd never backed down from a case. She'd deliberately sought out the most twisted prey.

Not a victim, not anymore.

Now she worked for LOST. How intriguing. The Last Option Search Team was still fairly new, but most people had heard the news stories about them. They found the missing. They didn't give up hope.

How noble.

How . . .

Sad.

Sometimes, you have to give up hope. The victims die. They never come home. The families are left in wreckage. And the bad guys . . .

They don't get the punishment they deserve.

Did Ana understand that truth? It would seem that she did. It would seem that she certainly understood that sometimes, the only way to give justice was to go Old Testament.

An eye for an eye.

A life for a life.

Did Ana understand? Perhaps it was time to find out . . .

THE GRAVEL CRUNCHED beneath Ana's feet. She turned to stare up at River View Psychiatric Hospital, shielding her eyes from the glare of the setting sun. "How in the hell did you get out of here?" she asked.

But, of course, there was no answer. It wasn't as if Forrest Hutchins was going to appear and tell her how he'd slipped away.

Her gaze slid over the building. Guards. Cameras. Isolated location, nestled deep in the Blue Ridge Mountains.

River View Psychiatric was a historic facility. She'd done Internet research on the place during her trip over. A massive, nine-thousand-square-foot facility, it had once been a home for orphaned girls in the early 1950s. Later, it had been a veterans' hospital before finally being transformed into a psychiatric facility a few years ago.

The place wasn't the easiest to access. And she just

wasn't getting how Forrest could have slipped out on his own. *Someone must have helped you.*

A partner . . . one who'd turned on Forrest the same way that Bernie's mystery friend had? Was she searching frantically for a man who was already dead? Two weeks . . . Forrest had been gone so long. Bernie hadn't made it twenty-four hours, much less two whole weeks.

Her focus shifted to the left. The place was called River View for a reason—the Langmire River stretched for miles, sweeping away from the facility and heading toward the small town of Langmire, Virginia, about forty miles away. If the guy was a good swimmer, *if,* then maybe he could have escaped that way. But those rapids there were a beast, and he'd seriously need to be nearly Olympic caliber to handle a swim like that.

If we don't find him soon, I bet Cash will start a search in the water. Because maybe the guy's body washed away.

She stared at that river for a moment. Life was sure strange. She'd been reading about Langmire just days before . . . the missing person's case that had gripped her attention—little Cathy Wise—she'd vanished from Langmire.

And now I'm here. Back on her old turf.

But she wasn't there to find Cathy, not yet.

Gravel crunched—not from her steps this time—but from his. Her gaze cut back toward the prison entrance, and she saw Cash striding toward her. His face was hard, tense, pretty much just as it had been when she first arrived. *But at least he didn't kick my ass out. I'm working with him. That's a start.*

Because there was something about this case . . .

Her phone rang, vibrating in her pocket. At the sound of that ringtone, Ana tensed.

She knew that Cash had heard the ring because his steps quickened.

Ana lifted her hand. She put the phone to her ear. "Asher, this isn't really a good time for me."

Cash stilled. *Yeah, it's my brother. Not the killer we are after.*

"You left town without telling me, Ana," Asher snapped. "That shit is not cool."

"Yes, well, since you're my brother, not my keeper, I figured I was good." Asher never tried to tell her what to do—because he knew she'd tell him to stick those orders right back up his ass. He was overprotective, sure, but—

"Is he with you?"

"He?" Ana asked carefully, her gaze on Cash.

"Agent Knox," Asher gritted out.

Talking to him about Cash was a mistake. "Gabe told you I'm pursuing this case."

"Gabe told me he gave you the jet and you hauled ass to get up to Virginia." Worry thickened his voice. "Another killer has gone missing, and you're trying to find him."

"*I* told you," Ana said clearly, "that I didn't feel like the case was over. I couldn't just leave it."

"You went back to Knox."

Why did he keep harping on that? On Cash?

"Ana, be careful with him."

Cash was staring straight at her.

"Asher, I love you, but I've got this. Trust me." Then

she hung up the phone, aware of a slight sting in her cheeks. She didn't know what Asher's deal was. The guy could be an overprotective pain but . . .

This had been different.

He'd been different.

"Problem?" Cash asked her quietly.

"Nothing I can't handle." That was the absolute truth. If she hadn't been aware of her audience, she would have ripped right into her brother.

"Asher." He repeated the name and gave a little nod. "That's your brother, right?"

She turned away from him and headed toward her rental car. "I guess everyone knows our story." Asher and Ana. The tortured twins. Tormented. Terrified.

Only . . .

She stopped at her car, her fingers pressed to the driver's side door. "The news stories all made me the victim. The girl with all the slices, all the stab wounds. Poor little Ana Young."

Once more, the gravel crunched. She saw his reflection appear in her window. He stood right behind her, his face tense. "Are you saying the stories are wrong?"

"The press turned my brother into a killer. All he did was save me. He wasn't a killer. He was a hero." His screams still haunted her. She shook her head. "Forget it. We aren't here to drag up my past." She turned and found that he was close enough to touch. But she didn't touch him because maybe . . . maybe it was too dangerous when they touched.

Maybe I want him too much when we touch. And she'd been the one to set up the rules.

She'd also been the one to race back to his side.

So I have issues. Lots of them. No big surprise.

Ana licked her upper lip. "How do you think Forrest got out? Maybe he bribed a guard? Or the cute blonde receptionist-slash-counselor got a little too friendly with him—"

"His family certainly has enough money to pay for guards to look the other way." He leaned forward, propping his hand on the car behind her, caging Ana with his body. "After all, it was their money that got him in this place instead of in a prison cell."

Her eyes widened. "You're saying his parents *bribed*—"

"I'm saying money talks, even though most people don't want to admit that."

His scent was around her. Strong, woodsy. Sexy.

"I've got my team tearing through his family's financials *and* the financials of the employees here. If someone got a payoff recently, we'll know."

"You think it was an inside job."

"No."

She blinked, surprised.

"I don't think his family got Forrest out of here. I don't think they bribed some guard to help him. I don't even think Megan Thomas was seduced by him and agreed to help the guy with an escape."

He sounded so very certain.

"I don't believe," Cash continued darkly, "that Forrest Hutchins is relaxing on some deserted island right now. But I have to check all the options. I have to be very, very thorough."

A shiver slid over Ana. "What do you think happened?"

His head inclined toward her. "You're the one who came rushing up here, Ana. You're the one who said that she understood monsters. What do *you* think happened to Forrest Hutchins?"

The drumming of her heartbeat suddenly seemed very loud as it echoed in her ears.

"Come on, Ana. You came all this way—rushed up here for one reason—and we both know it." His gaze held hers.

"I think Forrest is the victim." She barely breathed the words. "I don't think there was ever any grand escape attempt. I think he was taken from here, I just don't know how. I think he's just like Bernie. I think payback is coming and—"

And her phone was ringing again. But this time, the ringtone was different. Not the familiar hard rock beat that she'd assigned to her brother.

Cash tensed.

She fumbled and lifted her phone. "Hello?"

"You aren't in Atlanta." The robotic voice blasted in her ear. "Don't you have a job to do, Ana Young?"

She lowered the phone a few precious inches and swiped her finger over the screen, turning on the speaker so that Cash could hear the caller.

"I'm doing my job," Ana said curtly. "I'm not calling some stranger and hiding behind a fake voice so I can—"

"You aren't a stranger to me. I know you so well. Inside and out."

Cash's eyes blazed.

"Forrest Hutchins isn't worth your time. He's not lost."

"Did you do something to him?"

Laughter came then, so high and sharp with that robotic distortion that Ana flinched. "Didn't do a thing. He did it to himself."

Cash swore.

And silence beat on the phone.

Frantically, Ana shook her head at Cash. *Don't make another sound.* She mouthed her words to him, but it was too late.

His curse had been picked up by the caller.

"Ana, you're with the FBI agent, aren't you?" The robotic voice questioned. Before she could speak, the caller said, "You can't trust him. Don't make that mistake."

What?

Cash pulled the phone from her fingers. "This is Agent Cash Knox—"

"I know who you are. Ana doesn't."

Fury flashed on Cash's face. "Did you have anything to do with the escape of Forrest Hutchins?"

"He didn't escape anything. Not this time. Justice came for him. Just as it will come for the others."

Her thundering heartbeat shook Ana's chest.

"Who the hell is this?" Cash demanded.

But the line had gone dead.

CHAPTER SEVEN

THE FBI COULDN'T TRACK THE CALL." CASH hated delivering that bit of news. "The guy is good, Ana. I'll give the bastard that much."

They'd traveled to Langmire and were currently in Cash's motel room. The motel's parking lot had been filled with big rigs when they pulled up. Langmire wasn't any kind of vacation spot. The town was a tiny little dot on the map, one that time seemed to have forgotten. The main strip consisted of a diner, a bar, and a gas station. The only people who stopped at the motel were the ones who had to pull off the road for the night.

Another broken-down motel.

Another case that wasn't going to end well.

"Is this the part where you try to shove me on a plane again?" Ana asked curiously. "You know, for my own good and all of that."

"Ana, the bastard is *calling* you."

"That's right. He is. That means he wants contact, and we can use that contact. You and your FBI buddies are monitoring my calls—"

"But this joker knows what the fuck he is doing—he

had his signal pinging all over the damn eastern half of the U.S. The guy is smart. And smart criminals are the most dangerous ones out there."

She sat on the edge of his bed, her dark gaze solemn. "I don't think he wants to hurt me."

"He's *calling*—"

"I think he believes I understand him." A faint line appeared between her brows. "You know, I get that the FBI has plenty of its own profilers on hand, but I really think we need to bring in Sarah Jacobs."

Cash had been pacing in that small room, but at her words, he stopped.

"Ah," Ana murmured. "I see you've heard of Sarah."

He'd actually worked with her before, back in the days before she'd joined LOST. Sarah Jacobs was a force to be reckoned with when it came to the criminal mind. LOST's star profiler had made headlines just a few months before . . .

"Her father is a serial killer," Cash said, aware that his words were stilted. "How do you . . . it doesn't make you nervous, Ana? Working with her? Knowing that she's . . ." But he stopped because he wasn't sure what to say.

"Knowing that she's what?" Ana rose. "Like him? Like Murphy the Monster?"

Because that was the name the press had given Sarah's father. "Yes," he said, nearly biting off the words.

"She's not like him. Sarah is nothing like him." Ana stalked closer. Her eyes gleamed. "She's a good person. She just had the shitty luck of having a psycho for a father."

His chest tightened. "Ana . . ." *There's something*

I need to say. Something I should tell you. Right the fuck now.

"Sarah can help us. The guy on the phone—he's targeting killers. She can build us a profile that we can use to track him down. Say the word, and I'll contact LOST. When I left Atlanta, Sarah was working a case in Colorado, but I know she will help—"

He shook his head. "The FBI has profilers already working on the case."

Her lips tightened. "You don't have Sarah Jacobs."

No, no, they didn't. He turned away from her and raked a hand through his hair. "Something isn't right."

"Uh, yes, a killer is calling me. We're in another no-tell motel and—"

Cash shook his head. "I mean that I'm missing something." Something that was nagging at him. *The caller said Forrest didn't escape. That the guy hadn't escaped anything.*

"I know what you mean," Ana said. The floor creaked beneath her feet as she moved closer to him. "Why did he say I can't trust you?"

Cash spun around. And—Ana was right there. Close enough to touch. To kiss.

Keep your hands off her.

But Ana had come back to him. He'd put her on the plane. He'd done the right thing.

She'd come back. Now what in the hell was he supposed to do? His control was too thin with her. Always had been.

He'd known about Ana Young for years. Growing up in Texas, he'd seen her photographs in the paper. Watched videos of her on TV.

And he'd hated the pain she'd endured.

His hand lifted and his fingers brushed across her silken cheek before cupping her delicate jaw.

It was her eyes that had gotten to him. He'd been eighteen when he'd first looked up at the news and seen Ana's dark gaze staring back at him. So much pain had been in her eyes. Pain and horror. He'd wanted to take all of that pain away.

She'd been a stranger. Surrounded by cops. A survivor. And he'd been . . .

Wrong. Wrong for her.

"Cash?"

Fate had brought her into his life again when she'd come parading Bernie Tate into the FBI field office. He'd looked up and once again, he'd gotten lost in Ana's dark gaze. Only this time, her eyes had been different. No pain, only determination. Strength.

Then she'd smiled at him and his whole world had shifted.

Now she's back again.

"Either kiss me or talk to me, but do *something*."

He blinked. "You want me to kiss you?" No, he'd misheard. There was no way Ana had just said that to him. "Your rules. Hands off, remember? You said—"

"Fine. I'll do it." She rose onto her toes. Her hands curled around his shoulders and she pulled him down toward her, and Ana's lips—her sweet, sensual lips—took his.

He stiffened when her mouth touched his. That thin control of his? It was shredding with every soft touch of her lips. When her tongue pressed to his mouth, when she gave that soft little moan . . .

Ana, I tried to do the right thing.

But he couldn't hold back, not when the one woman he wanted more than any other was in his arms. When she was kissing him. When her body was against his . . .

He locked his arms around her and pulled her closer. *Still not close enough.* He lifted Ana up, held her easily and pinned her against the nearest wall.

She gave a light, husky laugh, one that slid over his body like a caress. "That's what I was hoping for." Desire filled her gaze. "Let go of that control. I don't want it. I want you—every single bit of you. Wild and rough, no stopping. Just like before. *That's* what I want."

When she'd left him before—after the one night that had changed everything for him—Cash had worried that he'd been too rough with her. But having Ana in his arms . . .

He kissed her again. He thrust his tongue past her lips and savored her. She tasted so good. Sweet but rich . . . and the things that woman could do with her tongue.

She's starred in a hundred wet dreams since that night.

If she had any idea just how obsessed he'd become, Ana wouldn't be letting him touch her. She'd be sticking to her rules. She'd be getting the hell away from him.

But he couldn't let her go. Not again. He'd already tried that good-guy role before. Now, he was taking what he wanted. He was taking Ana.

Her nails dug into his shoulders, and he loved that bite. Stinging and hard. He tore his mouth from hers and kissed his way down her neck. He knew just where to put his mouth on her, knew where to suck and lick and let her feel the faint edge of his teeth.

She moaned and her body quaked against his.

That's right, Ana. I know exactly what you like. I remember everything.

His cock shoved against the zipper of his jeans. He was fully erect, aching and hard for her. Cash wanted to drive deep and take them both to oblivion. He wanted to forget the damn case. Forget the past. Forget everything but the pleasure they could give to each other.

Ana's hands slid down his chest. Her touch seemed to singe him. For an instant, he worried that she was about to push him away. That she'd say she only wanted a kiss. Nothing more.

He clawed for his control, ready to pull back—

But her fingers went to his waistband. She fumbled with his belt.

"Ana." Her name ripped from him. "Be fucking sure."

Her long lashes lifted as she stared up at him. "How's this for sure?" Her voice was pure sex. "I want you inside me, Cash. Right now."

Sonofa—

He kept a tight grip on her as he whirled away from that wall.

"Cash!"

He carried her to the bed. Dropped her on the mattress then backed the hell up.

She tossed back her hair. "That was . . . interesting."

He ditched his coat. Removed his holster. Then he stared at her. Stared and tried to think past the haze of lust that was about to blind him.

Her eyes swept slowly over him. "Turn off the lights, Cash."

She'd done that before. When he'd had her in his bed, she'd made sure all of the lights were off. He'd been so frantic for her, insanely desperate, and that same desperation was already rising in him again but . . .

Cash shook his head.

She tensed. "Cash? You don't want me?" Her expression had gone blank.

He stripped off his shirt and tossed it aside. "There's something we should be clear about right now."

She was sitting up on the bed, hunching her shoulders.

"I *always* want you. I look at you, and I get hard. That's just a fact of life for me."

Her shoulders rolled back. She flashed him the slow smile that was like a punch to his gut. "Then just turn off—"

"I'm seeing you this time, Ana. Every single inch of you. You were the one who did the exploring last time." Her mouth had been all over him. *That tongue . . .* "This time, I get to call the shots."

For just a moment, her guarded expression changed. Fear flashed on her face, but was gone in the next instant. He leaned over her, putting his hands on either side of her body so that his palms sank down into the mattress. "I will know every single inch of you tonight, Ana."

"No."

A dull ringing filled his ears.

Ana pushed her hand against his chest. "No, that's not how it works." Her expression was blank but her voice was tight.

Afraid. Ana is afraid of me.

He didn't want that. Not ever.

"I like the dark, Cash. I need it."

No, she didn't. He caught her right hand. Lifted it to his mouth and pressed a hot kiss to her wrist.

"Don't do this," Ana said. "Don't make me leave you."

His heart jerked in his chest. There hadn't just been fear in Ana's voice right then—there had been pain.

He pressed another kiss to her wrist.

"I have a lot of scars, Cash."

His heart wasn't just jerking in his chest. It was breaking.

"I get that—for some really weird-ass reason—some guys think the scar on my lip is sexy."

He remembered the dumbass who'd been dancing with her at the bar. Cash had overheard the guy talking about her scar and Ana's shoulders had tensed at his words. Pain had flashed on her face, and he'd wanted to pound the jerk.

"I know about your scars." With an effort, he kept his voice gentle. His lust had to wait. In that moment, Ana needed his reassurance. "And I don't give a damn about them."

Her dark eyes held his. "They aren't pretty, Cash. I was sliced . . . Stabbed . . ." She swallowed. "Let's just turn the lights off, okay?" Her voice was pleading. He'd never seen strong Ana plead for anything.

And he never wanted her to plead again. "Do you always turn off the lights with your lovers?"

"Yes."

His eyes closed. "Ana, you are the most beautiful woman I've ever seen." He swallowed and opened his eyes, focusing on her again. "Your scars don't matter to me. I want to kiss you, stroke every inch of you. *I want you to see yourself the way I see you.*"

But Ana was shaking her head.

The trust isn't there. Not yet. Ana wants me, but not enough to lower this shield. Not enough to let me have her the way no other lover ever has.

"Don't make me leave," Ana said again.

And he wouldn't. He couldn't. He lowered her hand back to the bed. Cash stood fully, then turned as he made his way to the light switch near the door. He hit the button, killing the overhead lights, but a faint glow still came from the lamp on the bedside, a glow that pooled around Ana.

"Thank you," she whispered.

He stalked toward that lamp. "One day," he said, his voice low and deep, "you'll let me have all of you. It won't matter if the lights are on. It won't matter if we're out in broad daylight. You'll want me so much that nothing will matter but being skin to skin." His fingers curled around the switch on the lamp. "That's a promise, Ana."

He plunged them into darkness.

Cash heard the quick rasp of Ana's breathing as she exhaled on a relieved sigh. He stood there a moment, waiting for his eyes to adjust to the darkness. A thin crack of light slipped through the old curtains that covered the window. Just a crack.

The bed squeaked and he heard the rustle of clothing. Now that the darkness covered her, Ana was confident again.

You don't need to hide from me. Not ever.

He stepped toward her, toward the bed. His hand reached out and he touched her shoulder. Bare now. She'd slipped off her shirt. His fingers slid over the soft curve and he felt the strap of her bra. "Just because it's dark, that doesn't mean I can't explore you." His finger eased beneath that strap and he pushed it down her arm. "It doesn't mean I can't learn every inch of your body."

"Cash . . ."

"Stretch out on the bed, Ana." His voice was firm. His hands were rock steady on her, and his dick—it wanted in her.

But first, he *would* explore. He'd savor. He'd touch and taste until she was begging for him. And until he was lost without her.

The bed groaned again as she slipped away from him. Cash ditched his shoes and his socks, but he kept his jeans on—the better to keep himself in check. His dick was locked behind the zipper, and he intended to enjoy her body.

He climbed onto the bed with her. Ana had positioned herself so that she was centered on the mattress. When he touched her leg, he realized she'd removed her jeans. His fingers slid up her silken skin. She shivered. He felt that little tremble all the way through his body.

Let's see if I can make you do more than just shiver, my Ana.

His fingers touched her panties. A soft scrap of silk. He wanted to rip those panties away and put his mouth on her. Would her sex be as sweet as her lips?

Wait. Explore. Wait . . .

His fingers feathered up her side. Raised skin told him that he'd just touched one of her scars. A scar that Ana was so determined to hide. His head bent and he pressed a kiss to that mark.

"Cash . . . don't . . ." She reached for him.

He caught her wrist. Held it tight. And kissed the scar again.

Her breath heaved out on a low gasp.

He began to kiss his way toward her breasts. He let her hand go and . . .

Felt raised skin, just beneath his lips. He kissed that mark, softly, carefully. This line was longer, slicing across her torso. His fingers caressed her. He moved up—

Another scar. His eyes squeezed shut in the darkness. He wished that he could take her pain away. His hands were sliding over her, and he felt them all—the stab wounds were small lines, while the slices that had cut her beautiful body open were longer, stretching for several inches.

"Now you see why I don't like the light." Her hands reached for him again. "Just stop, Cash. Let me touch *you.*"

He caught her hands. Locked both of her wrists in his left hand and held her tight. "You are fucking perfect." It was time she understood that.

"Cash . . ."

He pushed forward, sliding between her spread legs, shoving his cock against the entrance of her body even as he stretched her arms above her head, pushing them toward the old, scarred headboard. "Do you feel how much I want you?"

"Y-yes . . ." His normally confident Ana was so different tonight, in the dark.

"You. Are. Perfect." He kissed her. A deep, hard kiss. One that left no doubt as to what he wanted.

Her. All of her.

"Keep your hands up here," he ordered against her lips. "Don't stop me." Because he was just getting started. Slowly, his hand slipped away from her wrists.

She didn't move.

Good.

He took off her bra. Bent to kiss her breast and—

A scar. Small, curving, right over her heart.

I want to take all of her pain away.

He kissed that scar.

Her fingers fluttered over his shoulder. "Cash—"

"Hands up, Ana." His voice was thick.

Her hands went back up.

He kissed her nipple. Licked the tight peak. She gave the little gasp that he found sexy as all hell, so he licked her again. His hand reached for her other breast. He stroked it as he licked, wanting to push her past her fear and her embarrassment, wanting her to need him more than she needed anything else.

Ana shouldn't be self-conscious. Ana shouldn't fear. Ana should just desire.

Her hips arched against him, a telling movement that was exactly what he wanted. He sucked her harder, loving the way her body responded to his.

Then his hand eased down her body. He kept kissing her breast even as his fingers went between her thighs. He stroked her through the silk, tracing lightly over her sex.

The silk grew damp.

He slid down her body. Locked his hands on her thighs and pushed them even farther apart. Then he put his mouth on her, right through the silk.

She jerked at the touch, but her hands didn't come down.

He enjoyed her for a time that way, kissing and caressing her through the silk. But soon, he wanted more.

His fingers were rougher than he intended, and he heard the silk tear. "Buy you more," he promised. Then his mouth touched her sex.

He'd wondered if she would be sweet.

She was so much better than sweet. One lick, one taste, and Cash knew he was a goner. He meant to be gentle, but soon he was feasting on her. Licking and taking, thrusting his tongue against her, *into* her, and rubbing her clit.

Her hips were arching fast against him now, her body going bow tight. Ana's orgasm was close, and he wanted her to go over that edge. "Do it, Ana," he urged. His tongue thrust inside of her. "Let go." *Don't hold back. Give everything to me.*

His thumb rubbed over her clit, harder, rougher, and then he was licking her, not able to stop, desperate to taste her pleasure as—

She came.

Her cry was muffled, as if she'd tried to bite the sound back, but her body was shuddering and he knew her climax was sweeping over her. Hell, yes.

He savored her a moment longer and she gave another ragged moan.

That moan was it—*can't wait any longer.*

He stripped off his jeans as fast as he could. Cash yanked out his wallet. Grabbed for the condom there and he had his cock covered in less than two seconds' time. Then he was back at the entrance to Ana's body. The head of his dick pushed into her and her hands—

She was reaching for him now. He slammed balls deep into Ana and she pulled him close. Their mouths met, frantic, desperate, and he rolled them on that bed. Ana sat on top of him, straddling him as his fingers locked on her hips.

The thin stream of light fell onto her body.

He urged her up, then down, and Ana moved quickly. He could still feel the contractions of her release, squeezing his cock and driving him wild. His hips arched off the bed as he slammed into her. He couldn't get in Ana deep enough. Couldn't fuck her hard enough. Couldn't give her enough pleasure.

"Cash!" A sharp cry from her, and, hell, yes, she was coming again.

Her orgasm brought on his release. He drove up into her one more time, and the pleasure blasted him, shooting through every nerve and vein in his body. Stars fucking danced behind his eyes, his heartbeat thundered, and he held on to Ana so tightly he was afraid that he was bruising her.

Let go. Let go! That was the small, sane part of his brain screaming at him.

Never. That was his lust, roaring right back.

Ana collapsed onto him. His arms curled around her shoulders and he held her there, her body arching over his, her legs on either side of his hips, his cock still buried in her body. The thunder of his heartbeat slowed, became a distant drumming.

And he still didn't let her go.

Never. This time, it was a whisper deep in his mind. A whisper that seemed to come from his very soul.

Too bad he'd lost his soul long ago.

ANA HAD GONE to sleep in his arms.

Cash lay in bed with her, his arm curled around her shoulders, her hand on his chest. They hadn't talked after the sex. After the best sex he'd had since . . .

The last time I was with her.

He should be sleeping, too. Should have fallen into an exhausted, satisfied slumber with Ana only . . .

Guilt wouldn't let him sleep.

Carefully, he eased from the bed. He listened carefully, trying to hear if Ana's breathing changed. He didn't want to wake her but . . .

Her breathing stayed nice and steady.

Cash crept toward the bathroom. He shut the door, then turned on the light. His hands gripped the chipped sink. He sucked in a long, deep gulp of air, then his head tilted back and he stared into the mirror.

Cash Knox, you are one serious bastard.

Soon enough, Ana was going to hate him. And then what in the hell did he think he would do?

CHAPTER EIGHT

Ana's eyes opened. Her heart was racing, and her brother's broken scream was still echoing in her ears.

"Let my sister go! Stop it! Stop, please! Don't hurt her!"

Had she cried out with the dream? Had Cash heard her? Frantic, she looked to the side.

The bed was empty.

Her fingers reached out and touched the other pillow, then smoothed down over the sheets. Still warm. Cash had been with her, until recently.

Her head turned and she saw the light creeping from beneath the closed bathroom door. She slipped from the bed, but stopped to grab his shirt. She pulled the soft cotton over her—his shirt was huge on her, falling to easily cover her thighs so she didn't have to worry that he might see her scars.

The marks were all on her torso, except for the thin line that sliced over her upper lip. Her abductors had intended to slice her whole face, but they hadn't been given the chance.

She stilled, standing near the bed, her head cocked

as she listened for sounds in that bathroom. Now that she was fully awake, she heard the roar of the water. Part of her was so tempted to go inside, to join him under the spray and get a repeat performance of that awesome pleasure.

Cash Knox knew exactly how to satisfy a woman.

As far as lovers went, he was definitely at the top of her list, even though he'd pushed about the lights.

That's one rule I don't break. No lights.

And no lights also meant . . . no shower. She wished that she could be carefree with her lovers—with him—but that just wasn't in the cards for her.

She'd actually tried, once, when she'd been twenty-one. Twenty-one and convinced that she was falling in love. When you were in love, you were supposed to share everything with your partner, weren't you?

So she'd nervously slipped her clothes off in front of Brian. And then she'd watched the horror fill his eyes.

Horror, then, even worse, pity.

That had been the last time she'd made that particular mistake with a lover. Besides, most men had been totally fine with sex in the dark. Dirty, hot sex . . . why complain?

The shower turned off.

It felt like more than just sex with Cash. The way he'd kissed her, every single scar. The tenderness . . . tenderness that had given way to such fierce desire. Was it any wonder she'd gone back on her vow of no sex with him?

The man was addictive.

And she was still just standing there. What was

wrong with her? Shaking her head, she whirled away just as the bathroom door opened behind her. She glanced back and saw faint tendrils of steam spilling out of the doorway.

Cash stood there, seemingly frozen, his gaze on her. A white towel was wrapped around his hips, and beads of water slipped over his bare chest.

The man was *built*. It looked as if he were sporting twelve-pack abs. So rock hard. Absolutely delectable. Tanned flesh. Strong muscles. And if that towel would just fall a little bit . . .

He cleared his throat. "I didn't mean to wake you."

"You didn't."

His gaze dipped over her. A faint smile curved his lips. "That shirt looks good on you."

Not as good as you look when you're on me. But she held that retort back, for the moment.

"Ana . . ." Her name came out as a sigh. "We need to talk."

That didn't sound good. Her gaze darted around the room and she saw the clock on the nightstand. One a.m. She'd slept longer than she realized. "I didn't mean to stay." She scooped up her clothes. "I'll just change and—"

His hand caught hers. "Is that another of your rules? That you don't stay the night with a lover?"

She looked down at his hand. She could feel the press of calluses on his fingertips. She'd felt that slightly rough touch of his all over her body, and she'd loved every moment of being with him.

"Never mind," he growled. "I really don't want to hear about other lovers." He let her go. "How about

I give a rule? Let's not ever talk about you and other men. I find that shit pisses me off."

He whirled away from her, stalked toward his bag, and grabbed a pair of jeans. He dropped the towel, giving her one fine view of his ass—a *great* ass—and she took a moment to just admire him.

Cash wasn't the shy sort.

She headed toward the bathroom. She'd change fast and then slip to the room next door. Whatever he wanted to *talk* about, well, it could wait until the morning. She felt too vulnerable there with him, in the middle of the night. Vulnerable because—deep inside—Ana swore that she could still feel him. Her inner muscles ached. Her breasts were heavy. And she still . . .

I want more.

She had to get her control back, ASAP. Going in, though, she'd known being with him was risky.

She reached for the bathroom door.

"Don't run away," he said. "Not again."

Her shoulders stiffened. "I'm just going to get dressed." She looked over her shoulder at him. "There's only one exit in this place, Cash." Ana tried to make her voice light. "It's hardly like I'm going to escape."

A furrow appeared between his brows. He glanced toward the motel room's door, and when he looked away, Ana hurried inside the bathroom. She shut the door behind her, locked it, and then, when she knew that she was safe, Ana slowly lifted Cash's shirt. She stared into the mirror, and she saw every single scar. Curving, white lines from the slices—long and twisting. Short, barely one-inch wounds from the stabs. And she'd been stabbed fourteen times. She'd actually lost count after the tenth stab, but a helpful nurse at the hospital had told her about the others.

"Honey, you're lucky. Stabbed fourteen times and you survived."

She turned away from the mirror. Sometimes, she hated her memories. She showered as fast as she could, scrubbing her skin a little too hard. Her hands never lingered on her scars. They weren't as bad now. Not angry and red, as they'd been when she first left the hospital. They'd faded, turned white with time, but the skin was still raised.

She was still marked.

She yanked on the faucet, turning off the water. Ana grabbed for a towel.

A sharp rap sounded on the door. "Ana!"

Jeez. She had been *fast*. "Give me a minute!" She looped the towel around her, making sure she was covered from her breasts to her thighs.

Cash pounded again. "He didn't escape."

Her brow furrowed and she hurried toward the door. The way he was pounding, she expected him to break down the door and burst inside the bathroom at any time.

She flipped the lock. Her fingers curled around the knob and she pulled the door open. "What?"

His gaze dipped over her. Heated.

She snapped her fingers in front of him. "What were you saying?" Though it was definitely flattering the way his mouth had dropped open and his gaze had lingered on her legs. She had good legs, even if she was on the short side.

Unscarred legs.

Cash shook his head. "It was what you said—about not being able to escape because there was only one door."

He'd lost her.

"You said it wasn't like you could escape the motel room."

Okay. Ana waited.

"And the caller said that Forrest didn't escape anything. The guy wasn't bullshitting us. I think he meant those words, literally."

Her toes curled against the old carpet.

"Forrest didn't get out of the psychiatric hospital. He never escaped those walls." Cash's voice was grim. "He's still inside that place. Somewhere . . . deep inside."

THE PSYCHIATRIC HOSPITAL was spooky at night. Ana pulled her battered coat a bit closer and kept her expression blank as she followed Cash past the guards at the entrance to the facility.

Shadows had been thick and heavy on the outside of the building, but inside, the shadows seemed even worse. And there was a terrible stillness about the place, as if it were just waiting for something to happen.

Something bad.

"Didn't expect you back tonight, Agent Knox," the guard said as he checked the clipboard. It was the same guard who'd been on duty when they left. Tall, wide in the middle, with thick, blond hair and light brown eyes. Keegan Johnson. "Thought you were getting some rest."

"We need to search again."

The guard glanced over at Ana. "Ain't the FBI doing manhunts in the area?"

Cash retorted, "The manhunts are no good if Forrest Hutchins never left the hospital."

"What? Course he's gone! We searched every room here—*you* searched earlier today!" Now Keegan seemed insulted as he straightened his spine. "Don't mean to tell you how to do your job . . ."

But he's about to. Ana knew exactly how that sentence would end. She looked over her shoulder. Another guard was to the left, watching silently.

"We missed something," Cash said, voice flat. "You missed something, *I* missed something. And before I spend too much damn federal money on a massive manhunt, I will be taking another look inside this facility."

Keegan pointed to the bank of screens—and video feeds near his desk. "You can look right here. Not like Hutchins is just going to appear, though. He's *gone.*"

Ana stepped forward. "We want to look in the areas that *don't* have video surveillance. We're not here to search any rooms that belong to patients. We're looking at the isolated spots."

Keegan rubbed his chin. "There's a laundry area downstairs. No video cameras there. It's only accessed by staff, so there was never a need." He shook his head. "But there's also no way out from down there. It's one big room that leads nowhere. No windows. Only one door. No escape there."

No escape. The guard's words made unease slither through Ana.

"And what about the top floor?" Cash demanded. "I was there earlier, looked like storage rooms up there, but I saw no surveillance equipment."

"No, none are up there 'cause we don't use that area too often." Keegan was still rubbing his chin. "But, Agent Knox, like you said, you were *there*. Hutchins wasn't just strolling through the place."

Ana's foot tapped on the floor. "And the offices of the doctors on staff? They don't have video surveillance, either, right?"

Now Keegan laughed. "No, ma'am, but it's not like he's holed up in one of their offices. I think they would have noticed a killer sitting in their chair." He gave a little disgusted shake of his head, as if she should have known that.

Keegan was about to get on her last nerve.

"The patients are all locked in for the night," Keegan added, giving Ana a fast, frowning glance. She frowned right back. "You're not going to stir them all up, are you? 'Cause I don't think Dr. Summers will like that."

Hadn't she already told the guy she wasn't interested in patient rooms?

"Don't worry," Cash snapped. "I don't plan to see them at all. And as for Dr. Summers, I'll deal with her. Any other fucking thing you want to say?"

Keegan seemed to finally get that he was about to push Cash too far. Keegan shook his head and stepped back, opening the way for them to go inside and start their search. But before they passed, Keegan handed Cash a keycard. "It's a master," he said, "same as the one you got earlier, Agent Knox. It will open the doors to the laundry area, the storage area, and the administrative offices. It *won't* get you inside any patient wards."

Cash took the card with a brisk nod.

Ana followed him as they left both guards behind. The shadows in the facility stretched like ghostly figures before them.

"What's wrong?" Cash asked her as he came to a stop near a stairwell.

"Nothing."

He stared. "You're nervous."

Yes, so what? "I'm in a psych ward in the middle of the night. Sorry, but this has *scary movie* written all over it."

His head cocked. "Ana, you were recently in a maximum security prison with some of the absolute worst scum in the United States. They were threatening you, taunting you, making me want to kick all of their asses, but you never even broke a sweat."

She rolled one shoulder in a faint shrug. "Everyone has their triggers, okay? Mine is places like this. Psych wards." She couldn't even watch horror movies that took place in insane asylums without having her stomach twist into knots that seemed to last for a week.

And she even knew the reason why, of course.

Not that she'd admit it. But . . .

After my attack, my mind . . . it didn't feel right. Nothing felt right. I was worried I might end up in a place like this.

Her own hell.

"Don't worry," Ana assured him, trying to sound brisk and in control. "I've got this. I won't break down."

"You never do." He swiped the keycard over the panel to the right of the door. "Let's start at the bottom and work our way up."

Sounded like a plan to her. Ana followed him into the stairwell and it was like walking right into a dark, yawning cave. Wonderful. She braced her shoulders, reached for the bannister, and started the trek downstairs.

It wasn't completely dark, after all. A light flickered from the wall, giving a low hum as they passed it. "You really believe he's inside this place?" Ana asked.

Cash was right in front of her. "I do." A pause. "What about you, though? You're the one who said she could figure out how monsters think."

Yes, she had said that, but Ana was hesitant to say what she was really thinking right then.

The first time he contacted me, the caller kept talking about payback.

The Butcher had been butchered, just like his victims. That definitely counted as payback.

And Forrest Hutchins? He'd kept his victims prisoner, starved them.

Would that be his payback, too? She murmured, "I believe if he's inside this place, he's dead."

They'd reached the bottom floor. Cash opened another door, and when they walked into the laundry area, the scent of bleach and detergent burned Ana's nose. One light was on overhead, but Cash hit the switch on the wall and a whole series of lights flashed on, one at a time, lighting up the long hallway. Clothes were tossed into heavy laundry carts on either side of the room. Big, industrial-sized washers waited to the left, while massive dryers were stacked to the right.

No windows. No other doors. The guard had been right about this room. Once you were in, there was only one way back out.

Cash headed toward the dryers. He started opening them, searching inside. So she went for the washers and gave them the same scrutiny.

"A person can go for three weeks without food," Ana said as her hand curved around the side of a washing machine. "Not pretty, not easily, but it can be done."

Cash had finished searching in the dryers. *Not like either of us really expected to see a body curled up in one of them, though.* Ana figured the facility's cleaning staff would have noticed a dead body curled up with the laundry.

"Three weeks for food," she said again, turning to look at the laundry carts. Her gaze narrowed on them. "But not nearly as long without water."

"Three days," Cash said. He'd headed toward the carts. He shoved his hand inside one and pushed around the clothes. "At least, that's the standard. One of Forrest's victims managed to survive ten days. The ME was shocked when he told me that shit. Ten long days . . . his body was attacking itself."

And what had the guy's mind been doing?

Because that had been the true purpose of Forrest's sick experiments—to see what starvation and dehydration did to a person's mind.

Cash's fingers curled around the top of the cart. He pushed against it, then stilled. "Pretty perfect way to transport a body, don't you think?"

She crept closer to him.

"Cover the body with towels or patient clothing, shove him down deep," Cash mused, "and you could just wheel him all through this place without attracting any attention."

Yes, that would be one easy way to take care of a body. "Once you got him down here, though, where would you go?" There *wasn't* any place to go, not that she could see.

Cash headed toward the stone walls. He put his hands on them, pushing, and began to slowly circle the space.

"Um, are you seriously Scooby-Dooing for a secret passage?" Ana asked him.

He stilled. "This room isn't big enough."

"Big enough for what?"

"The space upstairs is massive, but down here, we just have the one room. There's more space. It just must have been closed off a long time ago. Walled up."

A shiver slid over her. "'The Cask of Amontillado.'" She hurried toward the wall and started pressing her fingers to the surface, too. "That was always Asher's favorite Poe story."

She could feel Cash's eyes on her.

Her fingers slid over the surface. Rough stone. Hard, unyielding. "In that story, Poe's protagonist wants to get revenge on the guy who did him wrong . . . so as p-punishment," she stuttered because she'd almost said *payback,* "Poe's lead seals his enemy up inside a wall. And he just leaves him there to die." Slowly.

Her fingers slid over the stone. Rough. Unyielding. And then . . .

Wood.

Wood that had been painted the same color as the stone. At first glance, that segment of the wall blended almost seamlessly with the rest, but Ana could feel a difference. She lifted her hand and knocked on the wood. Sure enough, she heard a hollow sound coming back to her. "Found it," Ana said, voice quiet. "But how the hell would anyone get back there?" It looked as if another room's entrance had been sealed off, boarded up, painted and just left like that.

And this isn't a Poe story. "It's not like our perp could seal someone inside and not leave a trace behind." Hard to miss something like that.

Cash's arm brushed against her side. She tensed, then forced herself to relax. He put his hands on that wooden panel and shoved in, hard.

And the damn thing just swung open. A door, turning on its hinges.

The scent of bleach hit her, stronger, deeper, burning her nose. Her nostrils flared as she stared ahead. It was pitch black inside that new room. And cool air swept out to chill her face.

"Our perp knew his way around this place," Cash muttered. "Very fucking well." He pulled out a small pen flashlight—and he unholstered his gun. His gaze slid toward her. "We don't know what the hell we'll find in there." His voice was low, whisper-soft, reaching only to her ears.

Her gut told her they'd be finding plenty in the darkness.

"Stay behind me," Cash said.

Did he think she was going to argue? Yes, she could take care of herself, but he was the one with the gun.

So, by all means . . . *Go first, Special Agent.* "I'll watch your back," she promised him, her voice barely a breath of sound.

He gave a grim nod and then he was stepping inside. It was a tight space, narrow. His flashlight slid to the left, then to the right. It looked as if they were in the middle of some old hallway. Maybe a hallway that had connected the rooms in the basement? Before they'd gotten walled up?

He shone the light on the floor. Odd. There was no dust on the floor. There were cobwebs and dust coating the walls, but the floor appeared to have been swept clean.

As if someone wanted to hide tracks.

The hallway ended in front of them—it fed first into a smaller room, one that was full of old beds. Very, very old beds. Straps hung from the sides of those beds. *So that patients could be restrained.* A sweep of Cash's light showed a door to the left.

Ana pulled out her phone, and she hit the button for her flashlight app. The air was thick and heavy in that new space. Cloying. Choking her. The scent of bleach was so strong that she had to cover her mouth.

Then they were advancing into the very back room. Cash's light swept slowly across the area—

And stopped.

Just as Ana's breathing seemed to stop for a moment.

She knew why there was so much bleach in the air—someone had tried to use the bleach to mask the scent of death. Of blood and waste.

Cash's light had landed on the body in the middle of that room, the body of a man . . . who looked . . .

Fresh.

God, that was the wrong word. But though his skin had yellowed and his blood had congealed, he hadn't started to decompose, not yet.

He died recently.

Cash rushed forward. She followed, slower. The man's hair was blond and tousled. His eyes were closed. And . . . his mouth was closed . . . closed in . . . a weird way.

"What's wrong with his mouth?" The lips were puckering. Still pressed together so tightly. In death, shouldn't his lips have sagged open? It looked as if he were still pursing them. It looked—

Cash swore. "I think his mouth was glued shut."

Her own lips parted in shock. In disgust.

"That way, he wouldn't be able to scream."

Dear God.

Her gaze slid over the dead man. One of his hands was cuffed to the bed that he'd been strapped on. An old bed, just like the ones they'd passed.

His other hand . . . it was open. And a knife lay on the floor a few feet away.

The blood had come from the wound at his throat. Deep, thick, it looked as if someone had plunged a knife into the man's neck, and Ana remembered her caller's cold words when she'd asked just what the perp had done to Forrest.

"Didn't do a thing. He did it to himself."

Ana took a step forward, then stilled.

Payback? If so . . . payback was hell.

CHAPTER NINE

THE PSYCHIATRIC FACILITY WAS A THREE-RING circus. Patients were flipping out because there were so many cops, FBI agents, and crime scene techs storming the place. Yells and screams echoed through the hospital.

The staff was nearly as bad as the patients. They were all staring at each other with suspicion, everyone swearing they were innocent.

While Dr. Summers just watched the drama with desperate, shocked eyes.

Cash crossed his arms over his chest and studied the scene. The perp had been so very clever. Hiding the victim in the hospital, right beneath the staff's noses. A closer examination *had* shown that Forrest's mouth had been glued shut—freaking super glued shut—so he couldn't call out for help, and even if he had made noise, no one would have heard him. Not with his being hidden so far in the basement. Not with the washers and dryers running to possibly muffle any noise he created.

It had been the perfect kill spot.

Only Forrest wasn't killed right away.

Cash knew he'd have to wait for an official report from an ME, but he was betting Forrest Hutchins had been starved for days. Starved and then . . .

Then what? Given a knife? Given a chance to see just how long it would take before his mind broke and he decided to take the easy way out?

Ana appeared in the doorway. He knew she'd been calling LOST and updating her boss. He'd had to do his own updates with the executive assistant director, and Darius had sure been pissed. Especially when Cash told him . . .

We're dealing with a serial. No other way to look at it. The caller who'd contacted Ana wasn't bullshitting. He'd been behind the murders of Bernie Tate and Forrest Hutchins. And to pull off these crimes, hell, they were looking at one organized, smart killer.

The kind that was the most dangerous.

Ana walked to his side. "Gabe said he can have Sarah on a plane here tomorrow morning. She can work up a profile for you."

He was tempted, but . . . "The executive assistant director doesn't want LOST working on this one."

"What?" Her eyes widened. "You and your boss were the ones who contacted me! You were—"

"I didn't say he doesn't want you, Ana." And this was the part that was going to piss her off. "The EAD definitely wants you to stay involved. After all, the killer is contacting you. Darius isn't about to let you slip away."

He saw the worry flash across her face. "I don't think I like where this is going."

No. "He thinks you're a material witness. He wants me to take you into protective custody."

"That's bullshit!"

Several heads turned at her cry. He winced. "Ana."

"Don't 'Ana' me like that. You know it's bullshit, too. I'm not a material witness. I'm just the one this crazy jerk is deciding to pull into his web. Probably for the same reason *you* pulled me in . . . my connection to Bernie."

"EAD Vail thinks the perp will contact you again." *And so do I.*

Ana looked away.

"You think it, too," he guessed.

"Stands to reason." Her lips thinned. "He called me twice, so I figure if he gets the urge to drop another body, then, yes, I'll be on his speed dial."

"You could be in danger."

"Why? I'm not like his prey." Her laughter held a bitter edge. "I think it's pretty clear this guy has a certain type."

"For the moment. But that doesn't mean he won't change." He wanted to take her hand in his, to pull her close, but there were too many people around. "You are the link to this killer, and EAD Vail wants to know why. He wants you in custody. Hell, Ana, he wants me to bring you back to headquarters in D.C. so that he can personally interview you himself." The executive assistant director also was taking steps to make sure that no call would come through to her phone without the FBI being immediately notified. Cash had already sent in a similar order, but someone had messed up in the chain of command. Cash was pretty sure Darius would be demoting that person and the screwup would *not* happen again.

On the surface, yeah, it looked as if this perp were taking out killers. The worst of the worst. But the EAD had seen things differently . . .

He's proving that he can get to anyone, anywhere, anytime. He's making the prisons look unsafe, making the hospitals out to not be havens. A killer who can attack like this—he's a threat we have to defeat. And as soon as the press makes the connection on what he's been doing . . .

They were going to be crucified in the media. So far, the reporters just knew that Bernie Tate had been killed after an escape. They didn't know about the murderer tied to both Tate and Hutchins.

"Come back to D.C. with me?" Cash said.

"Are you asking me?" Ana eased closer to him. "Or are you giving me an order?"

Both. "Ana, this has to be done."

She nodded. "So an order. Huh. And here I thought I'd been helping you. My mistake." She turned to walk away.

Even with the eyes on him, he couldn't stop. His fingers curled around her shoulder and he swung her back to face him. "You could be a target." He *hated* the thought of her in danger. And, yes, if she was in protective custody, he'd be able to watch over her. Did she have any clue just how important she was to him?

"I'm *not* a killer. I don't fit his MO."

"It's too early to know for certain what his MO is. The guy is calling you. He's making it personal. Even without the executive assistant director's orders . . ." They should be clear on this. "I didn't plan to let you go."

Her eyes widened. "What?"

"I can't have you in danger, Ana."

Dismissively, she shook her head. "My job is about danger. I can handle myself."

She didn't understand. The guilt would never stop for him, and if he didn't do something to help her . . . "Come with me to D.C."

"Still sounds like an order."

Because it was.

She smiled at him. "Cash, you have to be more careful." She rose onto her tiptoes and leaned in toward him. "You can't make love to a woman one night, then take her into custody the next morning. That's not the way things are done. It's just bad form."

He didn't have a choice. *I want you safe, Ana*. And he'd do whatever was necessary to achieve that goal. Bad fucking form and all.

Could Ana kick ass? Hell, yes, he knew she could. But they were dealing with a killer who'd managed to abduct a criminal from a maximum security prison. With a guy who'd hidden Forrest Hutchins in the bowels of the psychiatric hospital, all without leaving a trace of evidence on any camera.

Not amateur hour. Something far, far different.

And the calls to Ana? They chilled him. A bone-deep chill. Because he was afraid the past might be coming back to haunt her.

And him.

"I'm sorry," he told her, and he meant that. He truly wished things had been different for them. "There isn't a choice." Not for either of them.

He looked over Ana's shoulder and saw that Dr.

Summers was watching them. Dark shadows lined her eyes and her hands were fisted at her sides.

She'd been removed from her supervisory position at the facility. And Dr. Summers . . . she definitely had an appointment at the FBI's office, too. There were plenty of things that the executive assistant director wanted to talk with her about.

Her hospital. The fallout.

And it was the kind of fallout that her career wouldn't survive.

THERE WERE INTERVIEWS. Dozens of them that had to be conducted. Ana wasn't allowed to sit in on the interviews, though—oh, no, that just wouldn't be the thing for a *material witness*.

Such bull.

So she had to bide her time at the hospital. Had to stand back and watch the crime scene units come in and search the area.

Cash spent hours closed in with the staff, grilling them all. Trying to find a weak link. Someone who'd seen something.

Someone who *knew* something.

But as more time passed and his expression became grimmer, she knew he was striking out.

So maybe it should be her turn to take a swing. The guards had proven useless. The staff was scared spitless. So that just left . . .

Her gaze slid to the corridor that led to the patient area.

That just left the people that the courts had deemed insane. And she was already cleared to tour the facility, to go wherever she wanted, courtesy of Cash. Time to take advantage of that clearance.

She was sure there were all kinds of rules in place about questioning the patients at River View. She was also sure that she didn't care. After all, she was a civilian, so any FBI regulations or police procedures wouldn't apply to her.

Her steps were soundless as she made her way down the hallway. Everyone was in such a frenzy, no one even glanced twice at her. She knew there were all sorts of patients at River View. Violent offenders like Forrest. And . . .

Less violent offenders. Individuals who had broken minds but spirits that were gentle. She saw a few of those patients right then, in the community room. They weren't cuffed. They weren't strapped down to anything. They were talking with a counselor as they all sat at a circular table.

Drawing.

For just an instant, she remembered the pictures that had been on Bernie's walls, and a shiver slid over her. She pushed open the door that would take her inside. The counselor looked up, but Ana had been with Cash when he interviewed that man earlier.

Dr. Robert Mitchell.

So when Dr. Mitchell saw that it was her, he frowned, but then murmured softly to his patients. She observed them. Three patients. One woman, with long, long blond hair—it fell all the way to her waist in a perfectly straight curtain. She was thin, frail, and her head was bent forward as she diligently drew on her paper.

An African American man was to her right. His hand was moving in slow circles on the page, but he wasn't looking down. He was staring straight ahead, and he seemed a million miles away.

The third patient was an older man. Rough scars—thick, red—twisted the right side of his face. When she'd entered the room, he'd tried to turn away from her, but she'd seen the marks.

He wasn't drawing. A crayon was gripped tightly in his hand, but the tip of the crayon didn't touch the paper in front of him.

As she watched the group, Dr. Mitchell said something low and soothing, then he rose and headed toward her. "I didn't think the FBI was talking to the patients, not yet. Their families need to know—"

"I'm not FBI. And I'm not here to harass them." She could learn plenty without harassing them.

"But . . . you were with Agent Knox."

"I'm a liaison," she said, ever-so-smoothly. "And I just wanted to see how they were doing. I'm sure all these people here can't be good for them."

"No." His jaw clenched. "It's not. It's destroying their sense of security. And when word spreads that one of the patients was killed . . ." His blue eyes glittered behind the lens of his glasses. A dark shade of blue, turbulent. "Their world will shatter. And I worked so hard to bring them peace."

Going on a hunch, she said, "Why are there victims in a place with so many criminals?"

He tensed.

"I know scars from a fire when I see them," she murmured.

"But what makes you think he was the victim?" Dr. Mitchell asked, curious. "Maybe he set the fire."

The scarred man's shoulders were hunched. His chin tucked in low toward his neck. She thought she saw a tear glinting at the corner of his eye. "Because the scars from the fire—those aren't what hurt him the most. He's grieving. It's plain to see." She glanced at the counselor. "Who did he lose in the fire?"

"His wife." Dr. Mitchell paused. "And his son."

Her heart ached for him.

"I can't discuss their treatment but their pasts . . . that's public record."

"Then save me some time," she said quietly, "and tell me about them."

"Henry started the fire when he left a pot on in the kitchen. He'd been drinking, a few beers with the guys, and when he woke up to the smoke alarm shrieking, he tried to get to his family."

As she watched, Henry's hand lifted and stroked his cheek.

"He didn't get to them in time," Dr. Mitchell said, his voice sad. "And he hasn't spoken a single word since that day."

"And the other man?"

"That's Charles. Fifty-two-year-old man, with the mind of a child. When he was seven, his mother became angry with him. So angry that she hit him ten times in the head with a baseball bat."

"Bitch," Ana whispered.

The blonde girl jerked. Ana could see the woman's high forehead, the curve of her cheekbone. *Something oddly familiar . . .*

"Charles needs tranquility. He needs his peace. All of the people here are upsetting him so badly that he can't do his art, and Charles usually loves to draw."

She swallowed. *I'm sorry, Charles.* "And the blonde?"

"Chassity is one of our newer patients. Chassity Pope."

Now her gaze sharpened on the woman.

"Her brother brought her here. And when they walked through the door, she still had stitches in her wrist from when she'd tried to kill herself."

Ana rubbed her chest. Her heart was aching.

"They can't afford any other care, Ms. Young," the counselor told her. "We're a government-funded facility, experimental in many respects."

Because criminals and innocent victims were so close?

Only I'm not supposed to think of them as criminals. The people here—people like Forrest were found not guilty and sentenced to therapy here.

"Dr. Summers tries to innovate with her treatments," he continued, his voice very cautious. "Sometimes she has great success. Sometimes, she doesn't."

"Was Forrest a success?"

His gaze dipped to Chassity. "I'd say no."

Curious, Ana's focus shifted back to the other woman. Chassity had tucked her chin low against her chest and the long curtain of her hair covered most of her face. "How long has she been here?"

"Three months."

"She seems calm." Quiet.

"I can't discuss her care. I told you—"

Her brows climbed. "Come on, don't stop now." Because there was something there . . . she could see it in the guy's body language. He'd tensed up and when he looked at Chassity, guilt kept flashing on his face.

"Chassity had a backslide. There was an . . . incident. That's all I can say." His lips thinned.

An incident? Now she was definitely suspicious. Because hadn't Forrest Hutchins been put in the quiet room because of an *incident* with another patient?

Had that patient been Chassity?

"Dr. Mitchell!"

Uh-oh. Ana recognized the sharp voice of Dr. Summers.

"I need to speak with you, immediately," Dr. Summers ordered.

Dr. Mitchell hurried toward her. And Ana used that opportunity to sidle toward the table. She didn't want to get too close. The last thing she intended to do was stress these patients more but if they knew something . . . if they had seen the killer . . .

It stood to reason that the patients who had more free rein in the facility might have noticed someone with Forrest. Someone who'd stuck out in their minds.

Someone who might have been doing some suspicious shit.

Henry grabbed his chair and scooted it farther away from her, moving so that his scar was totally hidden from her sight.

Ana's heart ached as she stared at him. "I like your circles," she murmured to Charles.

A faint smile curved his lips.

She slipped to the side a bit, looking to see Chassity's drawing. Chassity was using a red marker and she was . . .

It looks like a river of blood.

But it couldn't be. Right? "What are you drawing?" Ana asked her.

Chassity's fingers stilled. She peeked up at Ana. Her pale blue eyes seemed to see right *through* Ana.

"She shouldn't be talking to the patients!" Dr. Summers snapped to Dr. Mitchell. "Get her out of here, now!"

Maybe you should have gotten me out when you came in. Instead, you were too busy chewing out the other doc.

Chassity was still staring at Ana. "My fault," Chassity whispered.

"What was your fault?"

"The blood." She looked down at her wrist, at the raised scars there. Then she turned her gaze to Ana. "You have a scar, too."

Dr. Mitchell was hurrying toward her.

But, at Chassity's words, Henry swung around and looked at Ana. His gaze flew over her face, and his eyes narrowed on her mouth. Then he seemed to dismiss her—

"I have plenty of scars," Ana said softly. "More than I like to count."

Henry's eyes widened.

Dr. Mitchell's hand closed around Ana's shoulder. "You need to go." His voice was low. "I said too much," he mumbled. "I'm in such damn trouble—"

"Summers won't be here long," Ana whispered back. "So don't worry about her. Worry about them." Her gaze slid back to the little group. She wanted to connect with them. She wanted to connect so desperately. Her instincts were screaming at her. Something was happening here, with them.

"Escort her out!" Dr. Summers barked.

Chassity flinched.

Charles stopped drawing his circles.

Ana glared at the doc. "Watch your voice. They need tranquility." Then she jerked away from Mitchell and started stalking toward Dr. Summers.

"I may not have control here much longer," Summers said, "but while I do, I want you *away* from my patients."

"Blood . . ." The whisper came from behind Ana. The one word sent chills over her spine. She looked back.

Chassity had risen to her feet. Her hands were at her sides.

"There was so much blood . . . he came in . . . and he hurt me."

Dr. Mitchell blanched.

Ana stiffened. "Who hurt you?"

Chassity pulled up her hair, dragging it across her face, as if . . . as if she were hiding behind it. "The handsome man. They said he was bad." She pointed to Dr. Mitchell. To Dr. Summers. "And when he hurt me, I knew they were right."

Oh, God, no, don't be what I think.

"They locked him up. And now he's gone for good." Chassity started to hum. "He won't ever hurt anyone again." Then she sat back down at the table and she picked up her crayon.

Ana focused on Dr. Summers. Dark suspicions swirled in her mind. "We need to talk," Ana said.

"Outside." Her hands were shaking. Fury pumped through her.

Without a word, Dr. Summers turned on her heel and headed out of the community room. Ana followed, her blood nearly boiling. As soon as they cleared that room—

Ana grabbed the doctor, probably way harder than necessary but she'd just realized that Dr. Summers had fed her and Cash plenty of bullshit. "The handsome man . . . *tell* me that wasn't Forrest Hutchins."

Dr. Summers had gone deathly pale.

"You said he was in the quiet room because of an *incident*." From the corner of her eye, she saw Cash approaching.

"H-he did have an incident."

"Ana?" Cash called. "Ana, what in the hell are you doing?"

Okay, so maybe it looked as if she'd shoved the good doctor up against the wall. So what? She had.

"She lied to us, Cash." Ana tried to breathe, nice and easy, to get her rage under control. Only she didn't feel controlled. "Forrest was in that quiet room because he'd attacked another patient. Dr. Summers was trying to cover that shit up."

Dr. Summers stared back at her with bulging eyes. "It was one lapse! We were trying to give him more freedom as a test! I had no idea he'd target another patient—"

"No idea?" Ana threw back. "He was a murderer! And you thought some touchy-feely crap was going to fix him?" She looked up, her gaze rising so that she was looking through the glass wall of the community room. Dr. Mitchell had his hand on Chassity's shoulder. "Did you even tell her family about what the hell happened to that poor woman while she was under your care?"

Dr. Summers flinched. "We haven't been able to reach her brother. We've tried again and again, but with no luck."

Cash swore. "Then I suggest you *keep* trying. Or better yet, we'll make sure your replacement handles things. An attack should have been reported immediately and you know that."

But Dr. Summers shook her head. "Really? That's what you're going to say to me?" And her mask fell away. Sadness glinted in her eyes. "Forrest Hutchins wasn't sent to jail after he killed five people. His family was too powerful. They have far too much wealth for him to ever see the inside of a prison." Bitter laughter spilled from her. "So do you really think anything at all was going to happen to him if word got out that he'd roughed up some broken girl?"

Some broken girl. Ana's gaze jerked to Chassity. *I was like her, once.*

"I punished him," Dr. Summers declared. "I put him in the quiet room. I increased his medication and his therapy. I was trying to help him! I was trying to help them both!"

And the doctor was looking incredibly suspicious right then. "Definitely looked to me," Ana murmured, "like Forrest Hutchins got exactly what someone believed he deserved."

Cash gave a grim nod. "He was punished plenty, all right."

"No!" Dr. Summers frantically shook her head. "That wasn't what I meant!"

"Sure would be easy to make sure no one saw Forrest's abduction from the quiet room," Cash continued, "if the head of the facility was the one who'd done that abducting. After all, you knew where every security camera was placed at River View. Just as you'd be one of the few here who knew about the old rooms down below. I mean, you were here when the place was remodeled, right?"

Dr. Summers was starting to sweat. "I want a lawyer."

"Good idea," Cash said. "Very, very good idea."

CHAPTER TEN

D o you think she did it?" Ana asked when they finally left the psychiatric hospital and took refuge for the night at their motel. They were supposed to head out for their trip to the FBI headquarters in D.C. tomorrow, a trip she wasn't anticipating. "Because if she did, I don't think the whole material witness bit really needs to apply to me much longer."

He turned toward her. They were just inside her room, a room that connected to his. They'd barely spoken during the drive back to the motel. She knew he had to be bone weary because she sure was. Crashing seemed like a great idea to Ana.

"I think Dr. Summers had the opportunity to kill Forrest. I think she makes a very compelling suspect."

"And I hear a large *but* in there," Ana said, putting her hand on her hip.

"But I don't see how she could have gotten to Bernie, not yet, anyway. My team is digging through her life now, checking her travel for the last few weeks, and seeing if there is any crossover between her and Bernie Tate."

His team. Right. She'd seen several FBI agents on the scene that day, looking all crisp and business-like in their suits, while she'd still been wearing her faded jeans and her favorite jacket. *Which one of these is not like the other?*

"And I still need you, Ana," he said, voice deepening. "The executive assistant director wants you brought in for questioning. That hasn't changed."

"When you say things like that, it makes me feel a whole lot less like a partner and more like a criminal."

His jaw tightened.

"Does your precious executive assistant director also plan on having a big, heart-to-heart chat with Dr. Summers?" *And her lawyer?*

"Yes. She's supposed to go in tomorrow, too."

Her hand slipped away from her hip. "Then I'll be making that trip, too. Because I really want to see how that goes down." She stepped toward him. "But beyond tomorrow, I'm not promising anything. I'm not about to give up my life so that I can blindly go into federal custody for some extended period of time. You want to tap my phone? Go right ahead. You want to pick my brain—you want the shrinks at the FBI to try and get inside my mind? Go ahead. But I'm not, *not* going to be held captive again. Not by anyone. Even the FBI." *Even my lover.*

He sucked in a sharp breath. "I didn't mean—it wouldn't be like—"

"You don't know what it's like." If possible, she was suddenly even wearier. "You have no idea what it's like to be taken from your home. Tied up. Tortured. You don't know what it's like to think you're dying while you stare into your brother's eyes and see his helpless rage." She rubbed her arms and paced toward the bed. "It gave me issues." Again, her bitter laughter slipped out. "So many issues I'll never get through them all. I can't trust worth shit, not with anyone other than Asher. I can't let down my guard with a lover—with any of them. I can't look at someone and not search for the monster that's hidden inside."

Silence. Heavy, thick, uncomfortable. *I totally know how to stop a man dead in his tracks.*

"What do you see when you look at me?" Cash asked her.

His question surprised her. Ana glanced over her shoulder. She looked at him. Hard. Deep.

He strode toward her, but stopped a few inches away, his body carefully not touching hers. "What do you see when you look at me?" Cash asked again.

"Surface," she barely whispered that word. "An FBI agent. The guy tracking the criminals. The guy trying to stop the darkness in the world."

His lips tightened.

"Surfaces lie," Ana added, sad about that truth. "And your eyes sometimes give you away." It was his eyes that had tempted her to be with him. "The secrets in your eyes show me that you are as screwed up as I am." She saw his nostrils flare, a telling giveaway that she'd just hit the nail right on the head. "You carry plenty of secrets, don't you, Cash? You think you might be up to sharing those secrets with me one day?"

His hand rose, as if he would touch her, but then his fingers clenched as his hand fisted. "I think you've been hurt enough, and the last thing I ever want to do is add to your pain."

"Add to my pain?" Her eyes widened. "Cash, you haven't. You've always been—" She broke off, aware that she'd nearly said the wrong thing. *My release.* But he had been. She lost herself in his arms, in a way that she didn't, couldn't with other lovers. Maybe it was because of the pain she sensed in him, a deep well of hell that matched what she carried inside herself.

If she'd been a different woman, she might have fallen for the sexy agent the first time she met him. Fallen hard and not been able to walk away.

But he scared me then. And he still scares me now.

"I've made so many mistakes," Cash said. The shadows in his eyes deepened. "There are things I wish I could change." He turned around and started marching toward the door. "I can't make those mistakes again."

A chill skated over her. "Am I one of your mistakes?"

He reached for the doorknob, then stopped. "Yes."

That blow went straight to her heart, not that she'd let him see it. "That's not what a woman likes to hear. Just for future reference."

He turned his head, glancing back at her. His eyes glittered. "I wish I hadn't ever taken you to bed, Ana."

Why not just start carving out my heart, Cash? Oh, wait, he was.

"Because if I hadn't been with you, then I wouldn't know what paradise was like. I wouldn't know the pleasure—the fucking drive-me-wild pleasure—that I only get with you. I wouldn't wake up at night, my body in a sweat because I'd been dreaming about you. I wouldn't tense every time I saw a dark-haired woman walking down the street because for just a split second . . . *I thought she might be you.*"

Ana took a step toward him.

"I am no good for you," he muttered darkly. "But I have never wanted anyone more."

That was . . . not carving out her heart. "I happen to think you're pretty good." She didn't want him to leave. Yes, she wanted to crash, but Ana wanted to crash with him. Right there. In his arms.

It was quickly becoming her favorite place to be.

He'd gone statue still, so she did the moving. This time, she was the one who closed the distance between the two of them. She was the one to reach out and touch him. "I have a lot of dreams." She winced. "Okay, I actually have a lot of nightmares, if you want the truth."

His face appeared tortured.

"But sometimes, good dreams slip in. And when they do . . . they're often about you." This whole sharing bit was hard for her, but she wanted to try. With him, she wanted more than just two bodies in the night. There was a deeper connection between them, she knew it. *Or maybe I just want it.* "I don't let people get close, not as a rule. When they get close, they can be hurt. They can be used against you."

His brows pulled low. "I don't know what—"

"You could be used against me." That was a stark truth. "I wouldn't want anyone to hurt you, Cash. If someone tried, it would rip me apart."

And he turned toward her. His hand lifted and this

time, his fingers touched her cheek. Such a tender touch. His hand skimmed down until he was holding her jaw in his palm. "Nothing can hurt you."

If that were only the case. But neither of them were unbreakable, and life was definitely not fair. People were hurt every single day, it was just a fact of life.

His head bent. His lips drew closer to hers.

"I shouldn't do this," he said. "Ana, I shouldn't."

"You absolutely should." They both needed this, needed each other. So why hold back?

"Don't hate me," Cash whispered and then his mouth took hers. Took hers in a deep, hard kiss. Rough, wild, with an edge of desperation that turned her on. She wanted him to be wild and desperate for her. She wanted to ruin him for all other women. Was that wrong? She didn't really care, it was just how she felt.

Always look for me. Always want me. Always dream of me.

Her hands locked around his shoulders as she pulled him closer. Her nails sank into his shirt. She wanted that shirt gone. She wanted them on the bed, clawing at each other's clothes. She wanted the wild release that would come and then . . .

We crash, right into each other. Crash and collapse and start all over again, rising from the ashes.

His hand slid down her body, he caught the edge of her shirt, and his fingers slid underneath it. His touch was hot, electrifying her and—

Someone was pounding on the door. Hard. Hard enough that the wood trembled.

"Ana!"

She pushed against Cash's chest.

He stilled.

"Ana!" The roar that was her name came again. Only it was a familiar roar. Asher?

Why the hell would her brother be at her door?

He pounded once more. "Open up! The clerk said he saw you come in—and that you weren't alone. Open the hell up!"

Cash had reached for his holster—

She caught his hand, not about to let him draw his weapon on Asher. "It's okay. It's my brother." Her brother being seriously insane, but still, her brother. She dodged around Cash and fumbled with the lock on the door. Why was Asher there? Sure, Gabe had asked if she needed backup when she'd called to check in with her boss earlier that day, but she'd told him she was good, for the moment. There hadn't been a need to send in Asher.

And the guy could have called first. Why hadn't Asher just picked up the phone if he was heading her way? Like a normal person?

She yanked open the door. Her brother's fist was still raised, as if he'd been about to pound the hell out of the wood once more. His face was locked in lines of fury, his eyes were dark and stormy. *So much rage.* She hadn't seen that much rage on her twin brother's face since . . .

Ana grabbed his arms. "What's wrong? Did something happen to Bailey?"

Asher had fallen hard and fast for Bailey Jones a few months ago. She'd been a client at LOST one moment, and then Asher's entire life the next. He'd come so close to losing Bailey, and Ana had watched as her brother nearly splintered apart.

"Bailey is fine." Each word was a dark, rough rumble. "Is that bastard with you?"

"What bastard?" She realized the door was only partially open and that he couldn't see into the motel room behind her. "Asher, what's going on? What's wrong?"

Then the door squeaked behind her. Cash was opening it up, about to meet her brother, and this was going to be weird because Asher was obviously out of control and—

"*Cash Knox.*" Asher said the name with fury.

He surged forward, as if he would attack Cash. Ana slammed her hand onto his chest, stopping him. "What in the hell? That's *Special Agent* Cash Knox! And why are you trying to charge at him?"

Cash was silent behind her.

The tension notched up. *There's too much fury in Asher's eyes.*

A chill snaked around her heart.

Cash's hand curled around her shoulder. "Ana, I think I should go."

Asher's face changed. Went even harder, darker. His eyes were narrowed and glittering. "Get your hand off my sister."

Cash's grip tightened. "It's not what you think."

She could feel the tension in Asher's body. She expected him to explode in a fury at any moment, and Asher exploding? Not a good thing. He'd been a Navy SEAL for too long. When he exploded, people got hurt.

People died.

Cash's fingers slid away from her.

Ana sucked in a deep breath. "Look, Asher, whatever has you so messed up . . . we can fix it. Come inside. We'll talk like normal people." They could do that. They could pretend to be normal for just a little while. After all, they'd pretended for years when they were teens. All the way up to the moment when her father had drunk himself to death.

Then, for a time, we both lost it.

"Can't be fixed." He stood in the doorway, a cloud of fury. His gaze went past her and locked on Cash. "What sick game are you playing with my sister?"

"Asher!" She shoved against his chest. Hard. "Are you insane?" Bad question. "There's no game! We're working a case. And you don't say disrespectful crap! You don't—"

"I know who you are," Asher continued darkly.

"Uh, yeah," Ana snapped. "He's Special Agent Cash Knox. He's—"

"He's the sonofabitch's brother." Asher's voice was like a wolf's growl. *"That bastard who took his knife to you? The drugged-out freak who laughed while you bled? He. Was. Cash's. Brother."*

No. No, that was wrong. Asher was wrong. He was *wrong.* "No." The word was too soft, so she said it again, louder, harder. "No." Because saying it louder would make Asher realize how wrong it was. "Louis Griggs didn't have a brother. He . . . his father was dead. His mother long gone. He—"

"He had a half-brother, Ana." Asher spoke grimly. "He had a mother who had a tendency to hook up with losers who left her with kids and didn't look back."

Her ears were ringing. "No."

"Cash is his half-brother. And the sonofabitch . . . Ana, I don't know what kind of game he's playing to get involved with you, but it is over." His gaze was still directed over her shoulder. On Cash. *On Louis's brother?* "You won't hurt my sister again."

Her knees buckled. Stupid, weak reaction. She locked her fingers in Asher's shirtfront so she wouldn't fall.

"Ana!" Asher grabbed her and held tight.

Cash hadn't spoken. He should speak. He should tell Asher to fuck off. Tell her twin that he was wrong. *Wrong, wrong, wrong.* Cash was the good guy.

Cash was . . .

Her head turned. She stared at Cash.

And she knew her brother wasn't wrong.

Cash's face had gone stark white. His eyes—they seemed so bright in his pale face. The lines on either side of his mouth were deeper than before, and in those few precious moments that had passed—moments that were causing her world to collapse—Cash looked as if he'd aged ten years.

Her hand lifted and her fingers touched the scar on her upper lip.

Cash flinched.

"No." Even softer this time. "Cash . . ." Her voice was hoarse, as if she'd been screaming. "Tell Asher he's wrong." A last ditch denial. Because inside, she was screaming. *Wrong. Wrong. Wrong! Wrong!* Cash couldn't be Louis's brother. Cash couldn't have kept that dark, terrible secret from her. He couldn't have lied to her. Couldn't have made love to her and *lied.*

"Ana . . ." Cash whispered her name. "I am so sorry."

We weren't making love. We were screwing. He screwed me and lied.

Nausea twisted her belly and rose in her throat. "I'm going to be sick." Right there—all over him. All over herself. She jerked away from her brother and shoved Cash out of her way.

His brother. His brother. His—

"Ana!" Cash curled his hand around her arms. "Let me explain—"

"I'm going to be sick." Those desperate words were all she could manage and she was afraid that she'd vomit, right then and there. Cash must have realized how close to the edge she was because he freed her and stepped to the side. Ana ran to the bathroom. She slammed the door shut and fell to her knees in front of the commode. She barely had time to lift up the seat before—

His brother. Oh, dear God, his brother.

"ANA!" CASH HEARD her retching in the bathroom and he surged after her. Ana was sick. She needed him. She—

A hard hand closed around his shoulder. "Don't even think of getting near my sister right now."

Cash whirled to confront Asher Young. They'd never met before, but he would have recognized the guy instantly. Asher had Ana's dark hair and her dark eyes, only Asher's gaze was filled with a red-hot fury that promised hell.

I'm in hell. Been there for a while. "Ana is sick," he bit out. "She needs me."

Those words seemed to push Asher over some in-

ternal edge. He swung out, and his fist slammed into
Cash's jaw. Cash didn't try to block the blow because . . . *This is Ana's brother. And I fucking deserve
the hit.*

The blow was strong, powerful, a killer right hook.
Cash stumbled back a step and Asher came at him
again. A fierce left. He took that blow, too.

But when Asher swung again, Cash ducked. Asher's
fist slammed into the wall. "I'm not . . . going to fight
you . . ." Cash grunted.

Asher pulled back his fist, flexed his bruised knuckles and bared his teeth. "Then that will just make kicking your ass so much easier." Asher swung again. This
time, Cash blocked the punch, but he didn't attack.

He couldn't.

*Ana loves this guy. He's her entire world. And . . .
Asher saved Ana.*

"It's not what you think," Cash managed to snap.

Asher laughed. "It's exactly what I think. I had to
dig deep on you—you tried to bury the truth, didn't
you? You and your FBI buddies? Tried to cut all ties.
Not like you want word spreading that you had a sadistic killer in the family, am I right?" He lunged for
Cash.

Cash caught his arms. "I'm not fighting you." His
head turned and he looked toward the bathroom. He
couldn't hear Ana. Was she okay in there? He tore
away from Asher and rushed to the bathroom.

And the asshole tackled him. Asher took him down
with a hard tackle that had them both crashing into
the floor.

Growling, Cash rolled and tossed the guy back. Asher was Ana's brother. He couldn't, *wouldn't* hurt her twin, but he was getting to Ana. She needed him.

"I dug deep and I found out the truth," Asher snarled at him. "As soon as Ana started talking about you, I knew there was trouble. I *knew* it. Ana didn't talk about any other guy the way she did you. And you were just—what? Playing some sick game with her all along?" His own words seemed to enrage Asher even more. *"No one hurts my sister."*

"It wasn't like that. I was never playing a game with Ana."

Asher gave another grim laugh. "Bullshit. You knew who she was the first minute you saw her, didn't you? You knew . . . and you couldn't stay away. Are you as sick in the head as your brother?"

Cash heard a soft click behind him. The bathroom door—opening? He whirled and, yes, the door *was* opening. Ana stood there, her shoulders stooped, dark shadows—almost like bruises—under her eyes. Her skin was pale, making her eyes seem darker, bigger. Sadder.

And she wasn't looking at him. "Ana?" He stepped toward her.

She shook her head.

"Ana, let me explain." He could fix this. Couldn't he? He *had* to fix this. Ana . . . Ana mattered to him. She had, for far longer than she realized. "Please, Ana."

"Asher . . ." Just saying her brother's name seemed to tax her. "Normally, I handle my own business. I kick ass on my own." She looked so small, so delicate in that doorway. "But this time? Do me a favor . . . just . . . get Cash out of here. I don't . . . I don't want to hear anything else right now. I can't."

No. "Ana!"

Asher grabbed him.

And . . . despite Cash's intention to not hurt her brother, he just—he couldn't leave Ana. Asher wasn't going to make him. So when Asher grabbed at him, Cash hit back—just hard enough to stop the guy's attack. Hard enough to show that he wasn't some pushover. Just enough to get Asher to back *off*—

"No!" Ana's cry. Desperate. Hurting. "Not my brother! No!"

Her eyes—her gaze—tore Cash apart. Asher swung at him again, and Cash didn't fight. He did get a black eye. Then Asher locked his hands around him and shoved Cash toward the door. Cash didn't fight. Right then, he couldn't.

Because Ana was crying. Strong, beautiful Ana was crying . . . and it was his fault.

Asher opened the door. Tried to haul him out, but Cash locked in tight. He needed Ana to hear him before he left. "I'm fucking ashamed that bastard was my brother. I don't ever talk about him because it's easier to pretend he wasn't my family."

She flinched.

He was making this so much worse. Hell, was there any way to make it better? "I didn't tell you because I didn't want you to look at me—the way you are now." The way that was ripping his heart right out of his chest. "I'm *not* him. I never meant for you to be hurt. I never meant—"

Tears trickled down her cheeks. "You mean you never meant for me to find out who you were."

He'd actually tried to tell her. Even though he'd known the truth would wreck everything they had. "I wish I'd killed him," he said.

Ana's lips parted, but she didn't speak.

Was she remembering the story he'd told her? About his bastard of a brother? About the time he'd fought back? He'd fought and fought and fought—

Until his mother had pulled him off Louis. Louis, the sick twisted addict who'd made their lives hell.

"If I'd killed him when I had the chance," Cash said grimly, "your life would be so different, Ana. And I am sorry. I'm so sorry for all that you went through. I wish you'd never known a moment's pain."

Asher jerked him close. They were similar in height. Similar in build. And while Asher might have learned plenty of tricks while he'd been a SEAL, Cash damn well knew how to fight, too. He'd been trained at the Academy—Krav Maga was second nature to him, and back in the day, he'd done his time as an army ranger.

After all the abuse he'd taken at his brother's hands . . .

I learned not to let anyone else ever get the better of me.

If he and Asher had really fought, they both would have wound up in the hospital. But with tears in Ana's eyes, that shit wasn't happening. Cash just couldn't hurt her.

Not anymore than he already had.

"She knew plenty of pain, you sonofabitch," Asher rasped. "Two hundred and fourteen stitches. That was the damage your brother did to her. He cut her again and again, and I was tied to my chair, helpless to stop him. He cut her while I *begged* him to stop. While I offered my life. While I offered him anything. And he kept cutting her. *Two hundred and fourteen stitches*."

"Stop it, Asher," Ana pleaded. "Stop!"

But Asher wasn't stopping. "When I got loose, I got his knife."

Cash knew how this story ended. He knew—

"I enjoyed killing him." Asher's voice was ice-cold. And Cash knew Asher was speaking the dead truth. "I dislocated my shoulder so I could get out of those ropes. When Louis came back into the room—still high as a freaking kite—he didn't even look my way. He had the knife in his hand and he was ready to use it on Ana again."

"Asher, *stop*," Ana said, swiping at the tears on her cheeks.

"I took that knife from him. I covered his mouth with my left hand. He didn't even realize what was happening as I slit his throat and his blood poured out. I let him fall and he was jerking and pissing himself on the floor and I was *glad* he was dead."

"Asher!" Ana ran across the room. "Stop it, *stop it! He's an FBI agent! You can't say anything else! Do you understand me?*" Desperate, she shook Asher's shoulders. "Stop it!"

What did she think? That he was going to somehow turn on her and Asher? Try to press charges? No way. No fucking way.

"It was self-defense," Ana cried out. "That's what it was! Not murder! It was *self-defense*."

Cash's heart felt as if she'd just cut it from his chest.

Ana stood in front of her brother, protecting him. "I will swear that to my grave. Louis had his knife—he had to be stopped." She drew in a shuddering breath and her eyelids flickered. "As for his partner . . . same thing with that asshole Wayne. *Same thing.* Self-defense. Self—"

"I waited for him," Asher said.

"No! Asher!" Ana was nearly screaming.

"I knew he'd be back soon. The sonofabitch who'd helped to carve up my sister . . . he'd be back."

Her eyes closed.

Cash couldn't move. He was right in front of the door, but his body was too heavy. His mind too wrecked.

"We could have run," Asher admitted.

Ana swayed.

"But I wasn't leaving that pit of hell while he still lived. I waited, and when I heard him coming . . . I hid behind the door."

Ana was shaking her head. "Self-defense. Asher, stop. *Self-defense.*"

"And I slit his throat, too."

Ana started to crumple. Strong Ana. Falling. Cash grabbed her. "Ana?"

Her lashes covered her dark gaze. He wanted her to look at him. To see him, and not just her attacker's brother.

Cash's hold tightened on Ana. "Ana, no court in the country would ever convict your brother for what he did." Was that what scared her? She feared it hadn't really been self-defense? Because it fucking had been. He'd touched her scars. Kissed every one.

Louis and Wayne—they'd needed to be stopped.

"I just wished I'd killed him first," Cash said. "I will go to my grave wishing that."

Her long lashes lifted. She stared into his eyes. Seemed to be searching for something. *It's me, Ana. I'm the same man. The same man you wanted less than thirty minutes ago. The same man you gave yourself to so beautifully last night. I'm the same. I'm not a monster, Ana. I'm not. I'm—*

"I need you to leave now, Cash," Ana whispered. "Just . . . go, okay?"

His hands slid away from her. He gave a grim nod. "I'll leave now, but we're going to talk in the morning, Ana." They had to talk. This thing between them—it wasn't over. They weren't over. "You still have to go to D.C. You're still a material witness." The case would bind them, for a time. And it would give him a chance to convince Ana that he wasn't the sick bastard she feared. He could explain more.

Try to explain.

I just needed you so much, Ana. I know it sounds crazy but . . . I think I started falling for you when you were just fourteen. I saw you on the news. A beautiful, strong girl. A girl who'd survived so much, and I just wanted to keep you safe. I wanted to take away all of your pain.

But he wasn't going to push her, not then. He didn't want to push to the point that Ana shattered. He wanted Ana strong. He wanted her tough.

He just . . . he'd always want her.

Cash turned away. He opened the door and left Ana.

And even though it ripped his guts out, he didn't look back at her.

Mostly because he'd just realized something important. He couldn't stand to see Ana cry. Her tears tore him apart.

WHEN CASH LEFT, Ana leapt forward. She slammed the door shut. Locked it. Then drove her fist into the wood, over and over again as pain racked her.

Louis's brother. His brother. His damn brother!

Her skin was crawling. The nausea was rising again. And—

I think my heart is breaking.

Because she'd made a terrible, terrible mistake. She'd let Cash Knox get past her guard. She should have known better. Why hadn't she learned? But he'd been so gentle the night before as he kissed her scars. As he told her that she was perfect.

I'm not perfect. His brother made sure of that.

Her fist drove into the wood again and a long crack appeared in the door. She hit it even harder. Again. Again.

And—

Asher's hand curled over hers. "Ana." Concern thickened his voice. He turned her toward him.

She fell into her brother's arms. Her safe place, her anchor. He'd always been there for her, always would be.

"Ana, it's okay," Asher murmured as he stroked her hair. "You're safe."

It wasn't okay. She wasn't safe. She'd never been closer to breaking. Not since—

I woke up in the hospital. That smiling nurse told me that I was lucky, even though I looked like Frankenstein's monster.

A sob broke from her. Asher held her tighter. "He's a bastard, Ana. Forget him. Forget him. You don't—"

"I thought he was different. That I could trust him." But he'd been holding back the biggest secret of all. "I thought that maybe . . . maybe he could be the right one for me." Her eyes squeezed closed as she buried her face against his chest. "I thought he could look past my scars and see *me*." It hurt so much. And all the pain? It seemed to be coming straight from her heart.

The heart that was breaking.

You're perfect, Ana.

His voice was in her head. *Ana, you are the most beautiful woman I've ever seen. Your scars don't matter to me. I want to kiss you, stroke every inch of you. I want you to see yourself the way I see you.*

The way he saw her? Just what way was that? As his brother's victim?

She wasn't just a victim, dammit. She wasn't. She was a survivor. She was a fighter. She was a hunter. She was—

I'm Ana Young. And I'll get through this. Just as I've gotten through everything else.

She let her brother hold her for another moment, then she drew in a deep breath. She didn't have the luxury of a breakdown. No the hell *no*. She didn't want that luxury. "I have to get my bag." The back of her hand flew over her cheeks, swiping away the tears. Her head began to throb. Crying always gave her headaches. Just another reason she hated crying. "Then we're getting the hell out of here." Screw being a material witness. She was getting away from Cash.

She needed some time. She needed some serious space.

And she needed her heart to stop hurting.

CHAPTER ELEVEN

HER WORLD WAS FALLING APART. DR. ELLEN Summers stared around her office, her one-time office, feeling utterly confused. Hopeless. Beaten.

She'd lost her job. The FBI thought she might be behind the killing of one of her patients. The press had already been making calls to her, and they'd been hanging out just beyond the walls of her hospital. They were predators, sharks coming in because they smelled fresh blood.

And that blood is mine.

"Hurry up, Dr. Summers," one of the guards called. "Time for you to leave."

Because she was being escorted out. Like a criminal.

She put her photos in the box. Grabbed her diplomas off the wall. Then her hands curled around the box. She took a few steps toward the guard and—

An FBI agent appeared. One of the agents working with Cash Knox. It was a woman, with dark coffee skin. Her black hair was pulled back, and her no-nonsense stare swept over Ellen. "You don't get to take anything from the facility."

"These are my *personal* items. My diplomas, photographs—"

The woman—earlier, she'd identified herself as Agent Faye Comwell—shook her head. "Evidence. Until I'm told otherwise, everything here is evidence. It's staying."

Ellen's mouth opened, closed. Opened. She didn't know what to say. She—

"Take the box," the agent directed the guard.

Without a word, he took the box and put it back on her desk.

I was giving him orders less than twenty-four hours ago. He'd jump to do whatever I said.

"Now escort the doctor out," the agent said. "Make sure she doesn't get the urge to take anything else with her."

"Yes, ma'am." He reached for Ellen's arm.

She jerked away. "I know my own way out! I know every inch of this facility! I know—"

"Since you knew every inch, it sure would've been easy for you to get Forrest Hutchins down below and lock him in the room," Agent Comwell mused. "Very easy."

Dammit. "You don't need to look at me for this terrible crime." Ellen pulled herself up to her full height, just a sliver under six feet. "I tried to help the people here, never hurt them. I will be vindicated." She believed that. After all, she was innocent.

With her spine straight and her head held high, she left her office. The guard followed her, dogging her steps, and the agent even trailed after them. Ellen's cheeks burned. *I'm not taking anything. Damn them!*

Soon she was leaving the hospital. The reporters were outside, waiting just beyond the perimeter. When they saw her, they immediately started shouting questions.

She ignored them. Tried to ignore them, anyway. They closed in on her, and she once again thought of sharks—in a feeding frenzy. They pushed at her. They shoved cameras toward her face.

She didn't speak. She fought through the crowd. She got her door open. She jumped inside. And then she got the hell out of there.

As fast as she could, Ellen left. Her heart was racing. The dull thudding filled her ears. She'd stayed late—mostly because the FBI kept asking questions and they'd held her there. She'd been grilled, again and again. Her lawyer had been there, and he'd made sure she didn't talk *too* much.

But I didn't do anything wrong. I should have been able to say plenty.

Her lawyer had left just thirty minutes ago. Donovan Langley, IV. He'd been so careful when he talked to the authorities—and to her. He'd kept telling her to toe the fine line between cooperation . . .

And incrimination.

I have done nothing wrong! I always tried to help my patients! Every single one of them. This whole thing was ridiculous. Everything she'd worked so hard to build was about to go up in smoke. She'd lose her hospital, her license. Her freedom?

Her foot pressed down harder on the gas pedal. *Can't lose my freedom. I didn't kill Forrest Hutchins.* But she knew his family would close in for the attack.

They'd try to rip her apart. Everyone always looked for someone to blame.

The road was so damn long. Stretching. Empty. Normally, she didn't mind the isolation. She would listen to a book on tape or she'd mentally review her case files as she drove home, but tonight . . . tonight the situation was different. Tonight, she just wanted to get home and escape this chaos.

Tomorrow would be better. It had to be. She'd have another sit-down with the FBI—they'd ordered her in for more questioning. *Jesus.* She knew that was a big deal. But at least they hadn't forced her into custody.

Because they don't have enough evidence to do that. Not yet, anyway.

She kept a too-tight grip on her steering wheel until she was off that long, lonely road. There was a very small town nearby, Langmire, and when she saw the sign for that little city, some of the tension finally eased from her shoulders. Her car drove beneath the street lights on the town's little strip, and, a few moments later, she turned onto her drive. Her house—a farmhouse that she was renovating—waited for her. Her sanctuary.

She braked and hurried out of her car. Her keys were gripped tightly in her hand. She'd get inside—

"Dr. Summers!"

She stiffened. *Someone followed me.* "I don't have any comments for reporters." She risked a glance over her shoulder but then she realized . . .

I didn't see a car. I didn't hear a car. He didn't follow me.

He'd been there, waiting for her.

"I'm not a reporter." He stepped away from the old fence. Tall, with broad shoulders. He moved with a slow, steady stride. "I need to talk to you."

Fear had dried her mouth. "Who are you?" Because something about him seemed familiar to her. Something that was nagging at the back of her mind.

"I know you didn't kill Forrest Hutchins."

At his words, some of the tension left her shoulders. She still kept her keys gripped tightly in her hand. "Of course, I didn't. My job is to help people, it's—"

"You don't always help." She couldn't see his face. He had a ball cap pulled low over his brow and it was too dark outside for her to make out more than just a general impression of him. "You didn't help Chassity Pope."

"I—I was *trying* to help her."

"She got hurt on your watch."

She backed toward her house.

"And she wasn't the first," he said, sounding sad. "You're supposed to help people. But you don't always care the way you should, do you? Why do you think that is?"

"I—I—" She'd reached her porch steps. Ellen slipped, then climbed up two of the steps. "I want you off my property right now, or I will call the cops."

"The cops are already investigating you. Want me to tell them about George Russell?"

George Russell. The name was from her past, so long ago. Dead and buried. Her skin went ice-cold, then red-hot pinpricks seemed to burst from her cheeks. "I don't . . . he's dead."

"Of course, he is. The man came to you for help. You were supposed to make him better, but after just two session with you—two—he slit his own wrists."

"George Russell was a disturbed individual."

"Eleanore Thomas."

Oh, dear God. She climbed up another stair. "Get off my property."

"You were supposed to help her, too, but you didn't. Another suicide, on *your* watch, Dr. Summers."

"I treat disturbed individuals! Profoundly disturbed! Sometimes, no matter how hard I try, they are beyond my help." Her voice broke at the end. This man—he was frightening her. It was late, and he shouldn't be there. "Get off my property. Now." Then, she didn't wait to see if he listened to her or not because every instinct she possessed was screaming that she was in danger. Ellen spun and ran for her door. She fumbled with her keys, shoving them into the lock. She turned the knob—

He grabbed her from behind. His hands locked around her neck. She screamed, but he laughed. He laughed and his mouth brushed against her ear as he whispered, "Know what I think? I think you're *profoundly* disturbed." Then he slammed her face into the wooden door. The wooden door that she'd just sanded and stained last weekend.

She felt her nose break. Heard the crunch of bones as blood spurted down to cover her lips. Ellen tried to cut him, tried to jab him with her keys, but he just slammed her head into the door a second time.

She didn't feel any crunch then. Actually, she didn't feel anything at all.

THE RINGING PHONE woke Cash the next morning. Squinting, he turned on his side and saw that it was just past seven a.m. His head hurt like a bitch and the ringing phone was just making things worse. He grabbed for it and yanked the phone to his ear. "Agent Knox."

"She's not here."

He rubbed a hand over his face. "Who the fuck is this?" His right cheek was a bit sore to the touch. Courtesy of Asher Young's fist.

Asher. Ana.

Hell.

He'd drunk hard last night, determined to get Ana's tear-filled face out of his mind. He'd gone to a nearby bar—the *only* bar in Langmire. He'd sat at the bar, drinking too much, and he'd seen couples dancing and thought . . .

I want Ana to dance. I want Ana to be happy.

Too bad Ana hated him. With damn good reason.

"This is Donovan Langley. We met yesterday." The man's words came quickly, edged with a faint Boston accent. "I'm the attorney for Dr. Ellen—"

"Summers," Cash cut in. "Yeah, I remember you. Dr. Summers ready for her trip to meet with the FBI?"

"No. That's the problem. That's what I'm trying to—" He broke off, and a heavy sigh slipped over the line. "She isn't here. I'm at her home and I think I see blood on her door."

His hand tightened on the phone. "What?"

"Her car is here. Her keys and her bag are on the porch, and it—it looks like blood."

"Have you called anyone else? Local cops?"

"I called you first." His voice cracked a bit.

"Get back in your vehicle," Cash ordered. "Lock the door. Stay there. Do not touch anything at that scene, got me? I'm on my way."

"Is she . . . is she all right?"

If there was blood at the scene . . . *I'm guessing no.* "Get in your car." He hung up and dressed as fast as he could. It could be a staged scene. Maybe Dr. Summers had panicked and fled or maybe—

Maybe the killer just got a new victim.

Three minutes later, he was in front of Ana's door, pounding damn hard, still feeling like an ass for what he'd done to her, but he needed Ana. She should come with him to the scene. And if Summers *was* a victim, the killer might be planning to make contact with Ana again.

Only . . . Ana wasn't answering the door. "Ana!" Cash called. "Ana, shit, I know you don't want to see me now." *Or probably ever, baby.* "But Dr. Summers is missing! We have a case to work. You wanted to be my partner, remember?" That was the one link they still had. He pounded again. "Ana!"

Wheels groaned as an older lady—dressed in jeans, a T-shirt, and a white apron—came toward him. When she saw him standing there, she stopped, frowning. She had a cleaning cart in front of her, loaded down with towels, garbage bags, and spray bottles. "I thought the room was empty." She started to back away. "Early checkout?"

What? Then he realized just why the room was so

quiet. He rushed past the lady, heading for the motel office. The clerk was inside, watching the news, but when he saw Cash, he straightened quickly.

"My partner," Cash snapped. "Room 109. She's gone?"

The guy's Adam's apple bobbed. "L-last night. Left around midnight."

When he'd been drinking his ass into a stupor. Shit. Ana had run from him. And he didn't blame her. Not even a little bit but . . .

I can't let you go, Ana. He turned away from the clerk and headed outside. He had a crime scene waiting, so he couldn't chase after Ana. He couldn't run to her and get her to try to understand—

I was a bastard, baby. I should have stayed away from you, but I didn't. I wanted you too much. I needed you too much. And I still do.

After their one night together, two years ago, he'd known he was screwed. Ana deserved only good things in her life. Total honesty from her partner. She'd left him, and it had hurt like hell, but he hadn't followed. Because he'd known she deserved someone so much better than him.

Then the damn Bernie Tate mess had brought them back together and he'd realized his feelings for Ana Young had never gone away.

He'd been living in hell for a very long time. Being with Ana again . . . it had seemed like he'd finally gotten to glimpse a bit of heaven.

Rain started to fall on him.

Fuck me . . . right back to hell. He pulled up his collar and ran for his rental. He'd take care of the scene at Dr. Summers's place, and then he'd go after Ana. Things weren't over between them, not yet. He just . . . he couldn't let it end this way.

Not with Ana hating me.

"I'M SORRY, ANA."

She was back home. Safe and sound . . . *such bull.*

Asher stood in her living room, shifting from foot to foot, looking nervous as all hell, and Asher wasn't the nervous type.

They'd driven through the darkness. She'd stumbled into her house, showered for far too long, hidden in her bedroom, then realized . . .

I won't hide. I won't. She hadn't done anything wrong. She hadn't lied. She hadn't screwed with someone's life. That had all been Cash. "What tipped you off about him?" Her bare toes pressed onto her hardwood floor. She was wearing an old T-shirt and her sweats. Her comfort clothes. She wanted as much comfort as she could get right then.

"You were different when you talked about him."

She frowned at her twin. "I don't even know what that means."

"I think you were falling for him."

She looked away. "No, I wasn't." *I'd already fallen. Too fast. Too hard. And now I'm paying the price for my mistake.*

"I was a bastard, okay? An interfering bastard. But you softened when you said his name. You slipped up. Didn't call him Agent Knox. You said, 'Cash' like he was a friend. A lover."

She flinched. "We aren't going there." She grabbed

for a cup of coffee. Straight black. She needed that caffeine hit hard right then.

"You never seemed . . . interested in other men like that."

She'd been interested in plenty of men.

"There was emotion when you talked about him. I saw it. And I . . ." He raked a hand through his hair. "I checked him out because I wanted to make sure the guy wouldn't be a threat to you. I just wanted to make sure he was everything you needed. You deserve the damn best, and I wanted to make sure you got it."

Everything you needed. Her palm pressed to the mug of coffee, letting it warm her skin. "What do you think I need?" She was curious about that.

"Someone who will always put you first. Someone who would walk through fire for you. Someone who looks at you and knows just how wonderful you are. A guy who can't be bought, can't be threatened, a guy who won't back down from anything or anyone, not when it comes to you. Because *you* are his everything."

She had to laugh at that. "Oh, Asher, a guy like that doesn't exist."

"I want him to exist, for you. I want you happy."

His guilt. It was always there between them, no matter how many times she told him that *nothing* had been his fault. "Look, just because you fell in love and you get the whole white picket fence deal with Bailey, it doesn't mean that's happening for me." She took another long sip of the coffee. "And now I have to ask . . . do you investigate every guy I meet?"

"No." He held her stare. "I only did it this time because you were different."

"Something made those alarm bells of yours ring, and I don't think it was because my voice went soft when I said Ca—when I said his name." She didn't want to say his name right then. It hurt too much. "So spill."

"Before I joined the Navy, I did more checking on Louis and his twisted bastard friend Wayne. Call it sick curiosity, call it unfinished business, call it whatever the hell you want . . . I needed to know more about them."

She waited.

"I found out that Louis had a mom who was still alive. A mom who—at the time—had just divorced some deadbeat named Curtis Knox. Don't know why it took her so long to divorce him. Court papers said he'd abandoned her and their kid long ago."

Knox.

"The name stuck with me. So when you mentioned your Agent Knox—"

"He *isn't* mine."

Asher nodded. "No, of course not." His voice was gentle, but then he cleared his throat and said, "When I heard Cash's last name, the bells rang, and I had to dig deeper, just in case. And sure enough, I learned that Cash was the only son of one Curtis Knox. Cash's mother, Sonya, had three husbands before she passed away of cancer at the age of sixty-two. Her current husband—well, the husband when she died—was Jason Gates, and from all accounts, he was a decent sort. Ex–school teacher, church member. You know, all the regular 'decent' indicators."

The coffee wasn't working. Maybe she needed something stronger. Whiskey?

"Husband number two . . . that would have been Curtis Knox. The guy who abandoned her. Cash's dad."

Ana exhaled. "So that brings us to husband number one." Louis's father.

Asher nodded. "Gerald Griggs."

She flinched and a few drops of coffee spilled onto her fingers. She barely felt the burn. Her knuckles were lightly bruised, courtesy of her punches against the wood in her motel room.

"Seems Gerald got killed in a drug deal gone wrong. Louis was five at the time. Sonya remarried pretty fast, but then Sonya found herself saddled with two kids and—"

"And as time went by," Ana said, feeling incredibly sad for the other woman, "her son Louis decided to turn her into a punching bag." Because he'd gotten on drugs . . . the same drugs that had hooked his father?

"When I checked them out," Asher continued quietly, "I found out that Louis left the house when Cash was thirteen."

Because that was when he fought back. Cash had told her . . .

"Any idea why?" Asher asked, tilting his head.

"Yes, I know exactly why." She turned away from him. "Because Cash said he'd kill him if the guy ever lifted a hand to their mother again."

Silence. The kind of rough, raw silence that seemed to flay open her skin. "What else do you have?" Ana asked. "If you've got more secrets, spill them now."

"Cash joined the military and served four years in the army so Uncle Sam would pay for his school. He studied criminal justice, then was recruited straight away by the FBI."

"Then he shot up through the ranks and decided to what? Play some sick-ass mind game with me?" She put down the coffee and paced toward her window. She stared outside and wrapped her arms around her stomach. "Why? Why did he do it?"

"I don't know. Maybe he's as twisted inside as his brother."

She shook her head, an instinctive denial because . . . *He's not.*

·"Ana, you can't trust this guy, okay? I know you have a soft heart."

Her spine stiffened. "Since when?" She schooled her expression as she looked back at him. "I'm the big, bad bounty hunter, remember? I can track anyone down, anywhere, anytime. I've brought in the worst of the worst and I never hesitated." Hell, no, she hadn't. "I've—"

He shook his head. "This is me, Ana."

And he could always see through her lies.

"You went after those criminals because you didn't want them to hurt anyone else. You saw the victims, the broken families that were left in their wake, and you wanted to help them. *That's* why you tracked down those bastards. That's the same reason you joined LOST. You care—you care so much about the victims. About helping people." He walked to her side. "That's just one of the many things that makes you so special. Your big heart. No matter what happens, you try to keep finding good out there in the world." But his lips pulled down. "Don't try to find good in Agent

Knox. There's only going to be pain for you with him. Your pasts—they're too messed up. There will *always* be pain between the two of you."

Because there was no escaping the past.

"He lied to you. You *can't* trust him."

Her phone rang, vibrating on her kitchen counter. Exhaling, she brushed past Asher and went to pick up the phone. Then she saw Cash's name on the screen. She'd programmed it—well, before everything had gone to shit between them.

Ana stilled. *I knew he'd call. After all, I ran. I'm supposed to be in D.C., not in Atlanta. I ran and—*

Screw it. She picked up the phone. "What?"

"Ana, are you safe?" There was a frantic edge to his voice.

"Yes, I'm safe." She looked back over at Asher. His eyes had turned to angry slits. Oh, yes, he suspected the identity of her caller.

"Thank Christ."

"Don't call me again—"

"Don't hang up! Dammit, don't!"

She wanted to, but the ragged intensity in his voice stopped her.

"Dr. Ellen Summers is missing, Ana. I'm at her place now, and from the look of things, Dr. Summers was attacked. There's blood at the scene, her bag and her keys were abandoned—"

"You think our perp took her?" She shook her head, even though he couldn't see that motion. "That doesn't make sense. I mean, look at the people he's been targeting. Bernie Tate killed three people. Forrest Hutchins murdered five. Dr. Summers has never been convicted of anything—she was the head of the psychiatric facility!" Hardly fitting the victim profile that seemed to have emerged.

"All I know right now is that she's gone. We're going to check to see if this blood belongs to her or to someone else. The FBI is still monitoring your phone—"

He thinks the killer will be contacting me again.

"And you are still needed in D.C., Ana."

The breath she sucked in felt cold as ice.

"I get that you're pissed at me." His voice had dropped.

"Pissed doesn't even come close." It wasn't so much the fury that was fueling her. It was the pain. *I didn't realize he could hurt me this much.* Because she hadn't realized how vulnerable to him she'd become.

"But I have a job to do," he continued doggedly. "And you *are* a material witness in this case. I'll be coming for you, Ana."

"Cash—"

"I should have told you sooner. I'm sorry. But I am *not* my brother. I would never hurt you."

"You already have, Cash." Pain slipped into her voice. The very fact that he *had* been able to hurt her, well, that told Ana just how far and how fast she'd let herself fall for the special agent.

"I'm coming for you, Ana," Cash said once more. His words almost sounded like a warning.

She hung up the phone. Ana glanced back at her brother.

"What happened?" Asher demanded.

"Someone else may have been taken." Someone who didn't fit the profile. She rubbed the back of her neck.

"I want to go into the office." Because she could use LOST's resources to dig into the life of Ellen Summers. The woman shouldn't have fit the victim profile, so maybe something else was at work. Maybe she'd staged the scene to make it appear that she'd been taken—or maybe the woman had known too much.

These abductions have been so big. Maybe it's not just one person we're looking at. Two people could have been involved.

Dr. Summers and . . . someone else? And that *someone* had turned on the doctor?

She had no clue, just too many suspicions, so it was time that Ana got to work.

CHAPTER TWELVE

A LIGHT KNOCK SOUNDED ON ANA'S OFFICE door. It took a moment for that sound to penetrate because Ana was focused so intently on the material before her.

The knock came again, and she blinked, a bit blearily, and straightened in her chair. "Come in!"

The door opened, revealing Dr. Sarah Jacobs. Sarah's long, dark hair was pulled back, secured at her nape, accenting her features. "Ana, can we talk?"

Ana blinked again. She liked Sarah—the woman was smart, savvy beyond belief when it came to killers, and she had survived her own hell. She and Sarah even favored each other a bit, dark hair and eyes, though Sarah had a classy vibe about her that Ana had never been able to emulate.

Sarah looked like she belonged in a ball room, high society, and Ana . . .

Give me my jeans and battered coat, put me on a motorcycle, and let me ride away.

"Ana?" Sarah said again.

Ana cleared her throat and waved toward the empty

chair that sat on the other side of her desk. "Of course, come in."

Sarah flashed her a relieved smile and stepped inside. She shut the door and then hurried forward.

Some people at LOST were intimidated by Sarah— Ana got that. They worried that Sarah would profile *them*. And since everyone there was hiding their own pain and secrets, most folks didn't want to be put under Sarah's microscope.

I don't care. I almost want to know . . . will the darkness inside of me ever stop growing?

Sarah eased into the chair across from Ana.

"I thought you were working on a case in Colorado," Ana said.

"I was." And another smile spread across Sarah's face. This time, the smile lit her eyes, too. "We found her, Ana. We found Ginger Day. Missing for three years . . . *three years.* And we found her."

Ana's heart jerked in her chest. "That's wonderful!"

Sarah nodded. "Yes . . . she's . . . she's going to need a lot of counseling." Her smile dimmed. "A lot," she said, softer. "She'd been held in a cabin that whole time, a chain around her ankle keeping her prisoner."

Ginger Day. The name clicked for Ana because she'd been looking at Ginger's file recently. An eighteen-year-old girl who'd vanished during a cross-country trip. She'd made it as far as Denver, but then never been seen again.

"Our team went in, with the local cops," Sarah said. "The man holding her—he didn't survive the confrontation. He made it clear he would rather die than surrender. And dying . . ." Sarah exhaled. "That's what he did. But he *didn't* take Ginger with him."

Ana's heart raced a little faster. This was the work that mattered—helping victims like Ginger. Finding them, ending their hell. Giving them a new chance. No, the road ahead for Ginger Day would not be easy, but she was alive. She was free.

You have to take things one step at a time, Ginger. Go slowly. Don't rush. Don't—

"I was just wrapping things up," Sarah murmured, "when I got the call from Gabe about your case." Sarah seemed hesitant now, and that was odd. Sarah wasn't usually hesitant about anything. "Gabe thought I might be able to help create a profile for the perp."

Ana leaned back in her chair. "Yes, well, I wish." She pinched the bridge of her nose. "But the FBI is closing ranks. They want to use their own profiler." And she also didn't want to talk too much about the FBI. Because when she did . . .

It hurts. I think of Cash.

She was trying to shove him into the deepest, darkest part of her mind.

"Just because they're using their own resources," Sarah said smoothly, "it doesn't mean we can't still go forward. Sometimes, it's best if two profilers work a case. You can look for similarities in the profiles. Differences."

Ana's hand lowered. "Don't you want time to decompress after your case?" Something was off. Now that she looked closer at Sarah, she could see that the woman's hands were clenched, her posture too tight. Sarah was sitting on the edge of her seat, and a fine tension seemed to grip her. "Sarah?" Now Ana was worried. "Is something wrong?"

Sarah glanced back toward the shut door, and then her stare returned to Ana. "Gabe sent me everything he had on your case so far. I—I studied the material during the flight home."

Sarah had just stuttered. Sarah never stuttered.

"I think there could be more victims out there."

Ana felt shock rush through her body. "What?"

"The killer . . . he's so brazen. Taking these high-profile victims. That isn't the way it works. That's not the way it *starts*. You don't go right for the top of the food chain, not if you don't know how to kill. You start small. You build your confidence. You *learn* how to kill. How to not leave mistakes. Forensic evidence."

Ana forced herself to take a slow breath. Everything that Sarah was saying made sense. "How long do you think our killer has been honing his craft?"

"A very, very long time." Sarah's voice roughened. "Killers always accelerate, it's what they do. Start small, gain confidence, *learn* from their mistakes."

"This guy isn't making mistakes." That scared Ana. "He's not leaving evidence, he's getting victims from maximum security prisons and psych hospitals and—"

"That tells me that he's been doing this a long time. And since he's perfected his craft, you can bet he has plenty of other victims out there."

Her stomach twisted. "But he only started calling me when Bernie Tate was killed. If there are other victims, why not contact me about them? Why now?"

"I don't think he knew about you, not until Bernie." Sarah leaned forward a bit more in her chair. "I think we are looking at a very skilled predator, one who makes a point of learning everything that he can about his victims. When he selected Bernie as prey, the perp learned about you. Something he learned piqued his curiosity. No . . ." She shook her head. "Something he learned made him think that you would understand him. That you were a kindred spirit."

Ana jumped to her feet. "He's a murderer. I'm *nothing* like him."

And for an instant, she saw Cash's tortured face in front of her. *I'm nothing like my brother.*

Her eyes squeezed shut. Did he think she didn't know that? *Cash isn't a killer.* Cash wasn't a sick freak who took pleasure in carving up his prey. He was . . .

I think of him, and I hurt.

He was the man who got to me. Who made me realize how vulnerable I truly was.

"He thinks you are like him. He thinks you understand," Sarah said again.

"Payback," Ana whispered. "He told me they would all get payback." Her eyes opened. "Is it because I was a victim? He thinks that I'd understand the need for vengeance?"

"Perhaps." But Sarah seemed to be hesitating. "I also think . . . it may be due to your previous job."

"Bounty hunting?"

"You tracked down criminals. You made them pay. Isn't that what this guy is doing?"

"I didn't kill anyone," Ana snapped. There was a big difference between being a bounty hunter and a murderer.

"No. And perhaps he thinks that you should have.

Perhaps he thinks these people that he's stopping—the only punishment that is fitting is death."

Ana started to pace. Sarah's profiles—jeez, she'd been right when she told Cash that no one could get into the mind of a killer like Sarah.

Don't think about Cash now. Don't. The problem was that she *always* seemed to be thinking about him. She'd hightailed it back to Atlanta because she'd thought some distance would help her. But was there any distance when he was always in her thoughts?

"If he had other victims," Ana began, "wouldn't we know? I mean, we should—"

"You know how many missing cases we get each year," Sarah cut in, her voice sad. "People vanish every day. Could be that he just made them vanish."

"But now he's calling attention to his work."

"He's perfected his art," Sarah said simply. "I think he wants the world to know what he's doing. After a while, most serial killers feel the urge for recognition. Fame. They've gotten away with their crimes. Proved they're smarter than everyone else. Real apex predators."

Ana's mind was spinning. "If there are other victims, we can find them. I mean, he has a type, right? Killers. People who've—"

"Did I ever tell you how my father picked his victims?" *Murphy the Monster.*

Sarah didn't normally talk about her father, not with anyone at LOST. When your father was an infamous serial killer—one who'd escaped federal custody and was currently MIA—well, that wasn't a general topic for conversation.

Especially since our whole job is to find the missing. And no one here has turned up Murphy. Ana knew that Gabe had been searching for the killer, diligently, quietly. Did Sarah know about that hunt?

"Murphy thought . . . he believed he was taking out individuals who'd committed offenses. Offenses in his mind, anyway." Sadness flashed on her face. "One of his victims—Ryan Klein—he was just a high school boy. A normal kid. He'd never broken any laws. He just—he made a joke in PE about me. Just some stupid joke. He laughed at me and gave me this dumb nickname." Sarah licked her lips. "That was the only thing he did. Just that. And I found him in my basement. My father had killed him."

Ana wasn't pacing any longer. She'd frozen.

"My father researched his prey, you see. Much like this killer. And he'd found out that Ryan picked on kids a lot. Those who were weaker. He said that Ryan would become trouble, so he'd stopped him before that could happen. Murphy judged Ryan, found him wanting, and he killed him."

"Sarah, I'm so sorry."

Sarah stiffened, as if the words of sympathy had hurt her in some way. "My father had a victim type. People he found wanting. This killer—he's judging people, too. So maybe his judgements started small. Maybe he wasn't judging murderers, maybe he was judging everyday, average people. They did things that he saw as wrong and he punished them. Gradually, he worked up to where he is now."

That was a terrifying scenario.

Sarah continued, "We can create a victim profile

based on that information and then use NamUs to pull up the missing persons' database and do some cross-referencing. If other victims are out there, we *will* find them."

Ana moved closer to Sarah. She propped her hip on the desk and studied the other woman. "You're holding back on me." She could see it.

Sarah's lips thinned.

"Is it . . ." And a suspicion had formed in Ana's mind. "Is it because you think Murphy could be the killer we're after?" *This killer—he's judging people, too.* Just like Murphy. Because he *was* Murphy? "Maybe the killer is attacking so high up the food chain because he *has* been killing a long time. We both know Murphy had plenty of victims."

Sarah shivered.

"And Murphy managed to escape from a federal prison. He *knows* prisons. Their weak spots. It's not a stretch to think that he could have gotten to Bernie Tate." Actually, the more she thought about this, Ana began to wonder . . .

Is it him?

"Maybe he's even contacting me because I work with you. Because I'm a link to *you.*"

"No." Sarah was adamant on this. "This isn't the way my father works. It's too elaborate for him. Too showy, if that makes sense."

Ana waited.

"Murphy is smart, he is cruel, and he . . . he fits the victim profile."

Victim? Surprise pushed through Ana. "You think your dad could be one of this guy's kills?"

"Yes." Sarah rose to her feet. She brushed off the front of her shirt, though nothing was there. "Murphy has been dark for some time now. I do think—if he were able—he would have contacted me. You see, Murphy always had one weakness." Her chin lifted and she stared straight at Ana. "Me. He didn't love me the way a father would normally love his child, but . . . I supposed he loved me the only way he could."

"Okay, Sarah, seriously, you're creeping me out."

"I know. I tend to creep out most people." She said this simply. "Murphy risked his life to save me a while back. He put himself on the line because I matter to him. But since then, he's completely vanished. I know the press thinks he either slipped out of the country or he's holed up in some mountain retreat someplace, planning his next kill, but in light of what's happening, in light of this particular perp's kills . . . I have to wonder . . . could Murphy be another victim? That would make it all the more logical for *this* killer to contact you. You were connected to Bernie, and, through me, you were connected to Murphy."

Sarah thinks her father is dead. What was Ana supposed to say? *Sorry? I hope your serial-killing dad wasn't tortured to death?*

"He's doing an-eye-for-an-eye type attacks." Sarah smoothed back her hair. Not that a single hair was out of place. *She's still nervous.*

"Yes." Ana knew this. "The butcher was butchered, Forrest was starved until his mind broke . . ."

"And Murphy made his victims vanish. Maybe that's what happened to him. Maybe that's why LOST hasn't been able to find so much as a single trace of my father."

So Sarah *did* know that Gabe was searching.

"This perp has perfected his technique—he's created an MO that is fluid, depending upon his victim. The person we're after is highly dangerous, incredibly organized, and utterly determined to complete the mission that he has created for himself. If he's not stopped, the killings *will* continue."

That was what Ana feared. "He may already have a new victim." She headed back to her desk and passed the file she'd been working on to Sarah. "Dr. Ellen Summers vanished sometime last night."

Sarah opened the file and began to flip through the notes.

"I looked for a record on her. No laws broken, not even any speeding tickets," Ana said. "But during the course of her career, six different patients—all under her direct supervision—killed themselves."

Sarah looked up. "A psychiatrist has a great deal of influence over her patients. Especially individuals that have vulnerable psyches."

"That's what I was thinking. Maybe our killer did his research—just as you said he likes to do—and he found out that Dr. Summers wasn't as helpful as she wanted the world to believe." Or, another alternative . . . "Or maybe Dr. Summers just had patients who were in so much pain, *they* chose to end their lives. Tragic events—tragedies, nothing more, but our perp, who thinks punishments must be delivered—"

"Has decided she's guilty, no matter what."

Yes.

Sarah tilted her head to the side as she studied Ana. "You know, you'd make one hell of a profiler."

Ana shook her head. "What can I say? I'm just good with monsters."

DR. ELLEN SUMMERS opened her eyes. The room was dark. Quiet. Far too quiet. She tried to sit up, but found that—

My arms are trapped. They're pinned against my body. I can't move them. She flopped, twisting like a fish on a line. She screamed, "Help me! Help me!"

And lights flashed on. Blinding lights that had her blinking frantically and then looking around.

Blue walls. Painted such a soft blue. Soothing blue. No windows. Only one door.

And . . .

I'm on a twin bed. No sheets, just a mattress.

The reason her arms were pinned to her—*oh, my God, I'm in a straitjacket.*

The door opened.

He was there. Only she could see him clearly now. There were no shadows, just the bright light shining on him. And he didn't look like a monster. In fact . . . he looked . . .

"I know you," she whispered.

"And I know you." He took another step toward her. "I know you're lying to the world. I can see through the lies. I can see what you really are."

"No." She shook her head. Again and again and again. "No, you're wrong. I'm a doctor. A psychiatrist. I help people." She rolled her body toward the edge of the bed. "I can help you, if you give me the chance. I can—"

His laughter cut through her words. "You want to help me? Why? Because you think I'm disturbed?"

"You kidnapped me. You have me—you have me in a *straitjacket!*" Her voice rose to a shriek on those last words and Ellen sucked in a deep breath. *You have to stay calm, Ellen. Panic won't help you. Stay calm. Get control. Treat him like a patient on the edge.*

Because the guy *was* on the edge—no, he'd gone over it. And he needed to be one of her patients because he was obviously insane.

Obviously.

"I put you where you belong." He waved his hand to indicate the room. "Painted this recently, just for you. Thought you'd find it fitting."

And she could smell the fresh paint fumes making her a bit light-headed.

"Tell me, Dr. Summers . . . do you feel *calm?*"

No, she felt as if she were about to splinter apart. "Let me out of the jacket."

Again, he laughed. "Don't you just love it? I had to find that on one of the online bidding sites. Totally worth the fifty bucks I paid for it."

"Stop this." Her voice came out calm. Quiet. "You don't want to hurt me. You came to me for *help.*"

He shook his head. "I came to you because I needed to access a target. I got that access and along the way, I found out what you really are."

No, no, no.

He walked toward her, and she saw that he had a water bottle in his hand. She hadn't realized it but, suddenly, she was dying of thirst.

"How's the head feel?" he asked her.

It ached, just like her nose did. She'd been aware of the constant, throbbing pain from the moment her eyes opened. She'd just tried to ignore it and focus on staying alive. A very important goal.

Get his trust. Get the fuck out of here.

"It hurts," she admitted weakly.

"Um, yeah, probably does. You've got a concussion and a broken nose." He didn't sound overly concerned, but he did come a bit closer, with the water bottle in his hand. "You want a drink?"

Forrest Hutchins had been starved, dehydrated. She'd heard some of the crime scene techs talking about his condition. Apparently, she wasn't going to share the same fate as him. She also wasn't going to be a fool. "You could have drugged the water."

"The bottle has never been opened. Here. Watch." And he twisted the top, distinctly breaking it open.

Her mouth began to salivate.

He gripped the bottom of the bottle tightly. "My intent isn't to starve you or have you dying from dehydration."

She'd figured that out.

"So drink."

She opened her mouth. He poured the liquid in, still gripping the bottle tightly at the bottom. She drank and drank, guzzling that water. She needed her strength. She needed to get strong. She needed—

"That's enough." He stepped back. He was smiling. A smug, satisfied grin. His fingers moved up the side of that water bottle and . . .

A stream of water began to pour out from the bottom side. She blinked, wondering if she was imagining that stream but—

"I didn't open the cap," he told her, appearing incredibly pleased with himself. "But I did use a syringe to pump a few drugs of choice into the water."

She twisted on the bed.

"You had so many interesting drugs at your hospital. You know . . . some of those drugs can actually make patients worse. They can *cause* hallucinations. Depression. Intense anxiety." He made a sad, *tsk, tsk,* kind of sound. "Wonder what that brew will do to you?"

"No!"

He turned away from her. "I can't wait to find out."

He was leaving her. And he'd *drugged* her. "No!" Frantic, she rolled her body off the bed. She hit the floor hard, a jarring impact that rattled her teeth. But she didn't let the pain stop her. Her legs weren't bound, so she shot up to her feet. She ran forward—

He'd already slammed the door shut, locking her in.

Sealing her in the blue room.

The quiet room?

"No!" Ellen screamed. "I don't belong here! *No!*"

CHAPTER THIRTEEN

W HEN HE WALKED THROUGH THE DOORS OF LOST, Cash knew he'd find trouble waiting for him. And he didn't really give a damn. He had an assignment, a mission, and he wasn't going to let anyone stand in his way.

The receptionist saw him first. She stared at him with only vague recognition on her face. Then she seemed to place him. "Agent Knox?" She looked down at the planner before her. "I didn't realize you were coming in today. Did you need to see Gabe—"

"No, I'm here for Ana."

"She's in her office." The woman hesitated. "But I think Dr. Jacobs went in with her a few moments ago and—"

"I remember where her office is, thanks." So Ana hadn't told the others at LOST about him yet. Good. That would buy him a little time. But if Asher appeared . . .

All bets are off.

He still didn't want to fight her brother, but he was getting to Ana. He wouldn't be leaving Atlanta without her. LOST wasn't the only one with a jet. The FBI had sent him to retrieve Ana with the private plane they used for special operations because she was deemed to be a priority witness.

No more running. No more evading.

He reached her door and didn't stop. It wasn't as if knocking politely would help his cause. Once she knew he was there, Ana would just tell him to screw off. So he grabbed the knob and threw the door open. "Ana, you have to come with me."

The receptionist had been right. Ana wasn't alone. She also wasn't just with Sarah Jacobs.

Gabe Spencer was in her office.

So was Asher Young.

Fuck, it looked as if he wasn't getting out of that place without a fight. Fine by him. There were some things in the world worth fighting for.

Ana was one of them. Actually, as far as he was concerned, she *was* the one thing. He'd fight hell and heaven for a chance to prove himself to Ana.

But before he could say another word, Asher had lunged out of his chair.

"Asher, *stop*." Ana's voice snapped like a whip.

And . . . her brother froze. But his glittering, dark gaze promised hell.

"Uh, yeah," Gabe said slowly, glancing between Asher and Cash. "Someone want to tell me what the hell is happening? Though, Asher, the fact that your knuckles are cut and bruised to hell and back and Agent Knox is sporting some interesting colors on his jaw and eye . . . well, I do have a few guesses about what's happening here."

"No," Cash said flatly. "You don't." His shoulders

were tense, his body battle ready. "I'm taking Ana to D.C. The executive assistant director wants to talk with her personally. She's a material witness, and I don't really care who I have to go through"—he stared straight at Asher as he said this—"but I will be taking her with me when I leave. The EAD thinks Ana may be in danger, and we want her in federal protection, immediately."

"We know how to protect our own here," Gabe replied, voice mild. "So if Ana doesn't want to leave with you—"

"You don't want a war with the Feds," Cash snapped back.

"Actually, it wouldn't be my first time tangling with them." Gabe gave him a hard smile, one that showed plenty of teeth. "And I don't believe in throwing my employees to the wolves. So if Ana doesn't want to leave, well, then I'm afraid you *won't* be taking her, Agent Knox."

Fucking hell. All of these people were trying to drive him crazy.

"Let's all calm down." It was Sarah who spoke, her voice low and soothing. "Everyone, *breathe*. We all want the same thing, right? For this guy to be caught? For the murders to stop?" She nodded toward Cash. "Agent Knox, it's been a long time."

Yes, it had. He'd crossed paths with Sarah a few times in the past, on cases that had been dark and twisted as all hell.

There were always cases like those. Always killers waiting in the dark. He hadn't told Sarah about his past, but he'd felt a kinship with her. After all, she understood what it was like to have a monster in the family.

"You didn't tell me that you'd worked with Sarah," Ana murmured. Her lips twisted. "But then, there were lots of things you failed to mention."

He took that jab right on the chin, and it seemed like a far harder hit than any delivered by Asher.

"Agent Knox worked with me a few years ago," Sarah said smoothly. "I've always respected him." Her gaze swept the room and lingered on Asher. "Though I'm getting the feeling that others may not feel the same way."

Ana hadn't told them. Not Sarah and not Gabe, judging by their expressions.

But Cash wasn't going to keep secrets any longer. He wanted to show Ana that he could be different. He *would* be different. "Ana and Asher both want to kick my ass because they found out a secret I'd kept, something that shamed me straight to my core." He exhaled slowly. "My half-brother, Louis . . . he was one of the men who abducted them. He was one of the bastards who hurt Ana."

Gabe swore. Sympathy flashed in his eyes when he looked at Ana, and then rage lit his blue stare when he focused on Cash once more. "And you dared to come into my office, asking to work with her?"

"Yes, I dared." For Ana, he would fucking dare anything. Time for the world to see that. He was going to fight for what he wanted. And the first thing—the *main* thing that mattered to him?

Keeping Ana safe.

She will be leaving with me.

"You've got some serious balls," Gabe snapped.

I do. Thanks for noticing.

"No, maybe he's just screwed in the head," Asher threw out. "Like his brother. Like—"

"Stop." Ana's voice, quiet. Firm. "He's not like Louis, and we both know that."

Surprise rolled through Cash.

"*Stop.*" Sarah's voice—a little louder. Angrier than Ana's had been. "Cash Knox isn't some hyped-up drug addict. He's not a sadist who enjoys doling out pain. He doesn't torture. He doesn't kill." She marched to his side. "Just as I don't hunt down people who've pissed me off. I don't wait for their weak moments so that I can go in and torture them. I don't kill them. Don't dismember them. I'm not my father." Her voice was shaking as her shoulder brushed his. "And Cash isn't his brother."

But Asher wasn't backing down. He glared at Cash. "Why did you lie for so long? Why not tell Ana the truth?"

Cash focused on the only person who mattered in that room. Ana. She was standing in front of her desk, her body tense, her arms at her sides, and her chin tipped up.

Ana . . .

Asher wanted to know why? Ana wanted to know why? Then he'd tell them. "Shame."

She flinched. Her hand rose, started to touch the scar on her upper lip—

"*My* shame," Cash said quickly. "Mine. I didn't tell Ana the truth because I knew I wasn't good enough to be around her. I knew I didn't deserve anything from her. But there is something about Ana . . ." And he found he was moving closer to her, helplessly. *A moth to the flame.* Ana was his flame. Ana—she was becoming his everything. When she'd left, he'd been gutted. She didn't get how much she mattered to him.

Maybe it was time to start showing her. Just as it was time to stop pretending to be something he wasn't.

"I knew the instant Ana found out the truth, she'd never look at me the same way. I would be forever tainted. *His* brother. That knowledge would always be there."

Asher started to step into his path. *Be fucking clear here.* "I let you have your swings last time because you're *her* brother. I know you matter to her. So I took that shit, but swing at me now, and you'll regret it. I'm talking to Ana. I'm having my chance to say my piece." His jaw locked. "You don't want to get in my way right now."

Asher's lips parted.

"Everyone—just *stop*." Ana's voice. Still calm. Still quiet. Still firm. She'd locked her arms around her stomach, as if she were hugging herself. "I need some privacy with Cash. Can you all—can you give me that?"

"Of course." Sarah immediately headed for the door.

Gabe hesitated, but then he gave a tight nod.

"Ana . . ." Asher wasn't moving. He was too busy glaring at Cash. Cash glared back. He was furious at her brother, but he also understood the guy. Asher blamed himself for the pain Ana had experienced. *Oh, man, you have no clue. I blame myself every single day. If I'd killed Louis when I had the chance . . .*

Ana heaved out a frustrated breath. "Asher, I can take care of myself. And really, what do you think he's going to do to me, here, at LOST?"

Asher's nostrils flared.

"You're her twin," Cash said flatly. "She loves you. I get that. I don't want to hurt someone she loves."

Asher looked smugly satisfied.

"But what's happening here—it's between me and Ana, and if you get in my way, I will lay your ass out on the floor."

That smug satisfaction slipped a bit.

"You might have been a SEAL," Cash added darkly. "But I was a Ranger. And I'm not your punching bag."

Asher stepped toward him.

"Leave, Asher." Her voice wasn't as calm now. "I can take care of myself. Just go outside. Help Sarah run the check on NamUs like we discussed. I can handle this."

And Asher headed for the door. His steps were dragging and he sure looked unhappy, but the guy left. The door closed behind him with a soft click.

He was alone with Ana.

Beautiful, perfect Ana.

And he didn't know what the hell to say or do.

"Why'd you let him get all those punches in last night? You didn't even try to defend yourself. And you kind of look like hell right now."

He shrugged. "Figured I was due those hits."

Her gaze darted to the floor, then back up to crash with his. "Because you slept with me?"

He shook his head and closed in on her. She tensed, but he kept walking. Cash only stopped when he was about a foot away from Ana, and he made sure not to touch her. He'd only touch her when she asked for his touch. Hopefully, if he was a very lucky bastard, one day, she *would* ask. One day. "I was due . . . because I hurt you."

"Cash . . ."

"I didn't want to hurt you. You've been hurt more than enough."

Ana flinched.

"Shit. I'm sorry." He was. He felt clumsy and awkward around her. She stared at him with those dark, soulful eyes, and he wished he could make things better for her. "Do you think that I haven't wanted to go back in time? To go back and kill him when I had the chance? Every day, I have that wish. If I'd just stopped him then, you never would have been hurt."

"Why do I matter so much?"

Because you're you. He cleared his throat. "I saw a news video of you—hell, Ana, I think I was eighteen. Just getting ready to go into the army. I was supposed to ship out the next day. And there you were—on the news, all dark eyes, pale skin. Pain and strength. The reporter was saying that Louis Griggs had hurt you. *My* brother. He'd done that. You were so vulnerable, I didn't know why anyone would ever hurt you. I saw the pain in your eyes. The grief. And I wanted to help you. Something seemed to—to just give way in me right then. I wanted you better. I wanted you whole. I wanted to take away every single moment of pain that you'd ever had."

But he hadn't. Instead, he'd just made her hurt all over again.

"Fate brought you into my office two years ago. I

couldn't believe my eyes. Ana Young, all grown up. So beautiful it almost hurt to look at you. And your eyes—still as dark and deep. But there wasn't grief in your gaze any longer. There was pride. Power. You'd saved yourself. You hadn't needed anyone else to do the job."

"Asher stopped your brother." She shook her head. "Asher—"

"I'm not talking about who killed those bastards. I'm talking about *you*. About how you came back from the darkness and made yourself strong, day by day. You did that. You came back."

Her throat moved as she swallowed.

"I was drawn to you, and when you asked me to go out and have a drink, there was no way on earth I could have said no. I knew the whole time, I should have told you who I was. *Tell her. Tell her. Tell her.* Those words beat at me, never stopping." He wanted to touch her so badly. His hands clenched as he kept them at his sides. "Then I kissed you and the only thing I knew was need. I had you in my bed, and my control shredded. I couldn't get close enough to you. Couldn't touch you enough." He expelled a ragged breath. "Then dawn came. You left without a word, and I—I couldn't chase you down. Because then you'd know who I was. And I'd hurt you."

Ana's gaze searched his. "But you came to LOST, looking for me."

"And I was just going to work the case." That had been his plan, anyway. "My boss *did* want your co-operation because I told him how amazing you were. You truly can track down criminals like no one's business. You know your shit, and I realized what an asset you would be on the investigation. I came to find you because the FBI needed your help tracking Bernie."

"You should have stopped me. Stopped us before we went too far."

She thought he actually could have done that? Did the woman not realize just how much he wanted her? "Try living in hell for two years and then getting a glimpse of paradise. You won't turn away from that. You hold as tightly to it as you can." Just as he'd held tight to her. "And everything I said to you the other night? It was true. You are beautiful, Ana. You are perfect. You need to understand that. Know it in your soul."

Her gaze cut away from his. Her hand rose, trembling fingers reaching to trace the scar on her lip.

Cash caught her hand in his. "You are perfect." He hadn't meant to touch her—he hadn't—

Her dark stare came back to him.

"I'm the one who's twisted up. That's why I told you, I wasn't the good guy you thought I was. I wish I could have been. I wish I could have been the guy you wanted, Ana. The one who'd never let you down. The one who could protect you from every threat out there." Pain roughened his voice. "I wish I were anyone but the man who hurt you so much. Just by being his brother, I hurt you."

"Cash . . ." Ana shook her head. "No secrets, do you understand me? You can't keep secrets. All they do is rip people apart. Secrets come out and they destroy."

She was talking to him. That was progress, right? Actual progress.

"What other secrets are you holding back?" Ana asked him. "What other things have you—" She stopped her eyes widening. "He knew."

"What?"

"The killer—the caller—he told me not to trust you. Said you weren't the man I thought. He *knew* about you."

Cash considered that, and realized . . . *shit, she's right*. But if the guy had been digging into Cash's past . . .

Why?

Ana's breath hitched. "Sarah thinks he researches his prey. That he digs into their lives, finding out all he can about them."

"You think I could be one of his targets?" *Bring it, asshole. Come and get me.*

"I don't know." Those dark eyes of hers seemed to see straight through him. "Have you crossed lines, Cash? Done things that he would think you needed to be punished for?"

He was still holding her hand. His fingers were lightly stroking against her inner wrist. "I was a soldier, Ana. I killed on missions, yes, I won't deny that. And while I've been an FBI agent, I've had to shoot two perps. I didn't want to do it, but I had no choice. The first man, he was about to shoot my partner. I had a split second to fire, and I did." No, he didn't like remembering that moment. He tracked the most violent criminals in the United States, the ones who were dark, disturbed predators, and those predators often did not surrender easily. They'd rather kill, go out in a blaze of glory, and not spend the rest of their lives locked in a cage. "For the second man, he had a teen in front of him, a hostage. The bastard was a sick freak who'd kidnapped the boy years ago. We'd tracked them down on a tip, and when we went in, the guy put his gun to the boy's head. Said if we didn't get the hell out of there, he'd blow the kid's brains out."

He could see that terrible scene. The trailer that had reeked of human waste. The boy's too thin, emaciated frame. Kenneth "Kenny" Barn had been eleven when he went missing. He'd just vanished while walking home from school. Four years later, he'd been found, in that dank trailer. "I wasn't going to leave the boy. So I shot the perp—right in the head." His blood had gone on the boy, the kid had been screaming but . . .

He was alive. He made it out alive.

"So yeah, I've spilled blood. I've killed. And if the bastard out there thinks I need to get some payback for that, then he can come the hell on." Cash would be waiting. His fingers slid over her wrist once more. He was in Atlanta for one reason, to get Ana. To take her back. He was supposed to follow orders. Supposed to get this job done.

He was holding her hand. Her guard was down. It would be so easy to yank out his cuffs. To lock one around her delicate wrist. To lock the other around his. They'd be bound together. He could force her to leave with him.

Instead, his hand slid away from hers. He wasn't going to damage the fragile truce that seemed to be forming with her. He wasn't going to do anything to damage *her,* not ever again. Maybe they'd never get back to the place where they'd been. Maybe she'd never look at him the same way.

But . . .

He could try.

"I want you to help me, Ana. I want you safe." He nodded. "I appreciate you giving me the chance to tell you my side of things." He would never forget the way she'd looked last night. Hearing the truth about him had made Ana physically sick.

I did that to her. I never want to hurt her again.

"This guy is out there, hunting." He needed to push the difference between their relationship and the job that they both had to do. "Ellen Summers could still be alive. We need to find her."

Her hand had fallen back to her side.

"The perp contacted you before, it's only a matter of time until he does it again." Cash believed that with every fiber of his being. "Come with me. Come to D.C. Talk to the executive assistant director. Let's get this bastard. Let's stop him before he kills again."

Then he waited.

Ana, choose me. Choose to come with me.

"I may never hear from him again, Cash."

He shook his head. "That's not true." He glanced back at the closed door. "What did Sarah have to say about him? About why he's contacting you?"

"She thinks he believes I'm . . . like him. That I can understand him. Because of my past."

That was exactly what Cash feared, too. "He wants to share what he's doing. Wants recognition. You give him that. Ana, he *will* be contacting you again. Only this time, he might not just call you. He may try to make face-to-face contact. He's dangerous. And he's closing in on you."

"I can handle myself."

"I know." He did. "But why do you have to be alone? We can help each other. I actually thought . . . I thought we made pretty good partners."

She didn't speak.

"Help me stop him, Ana. Help me—"

Her phone rang.

Ana tensed.

So did Cash. Ana pulled out her phone and he saw the words *Unknown Caller* on her screen.

"Speak of the devil," Cash said grimly.

Ana flinched and then her finger swiped across the screen, taking the call and then tapping the button to turn on the speaker.

"I DON'T LIKE this shit." Asher paced in the conference room at LOST, anger humming in his blood. "We should have thrown that guy out into the street."

"Man, you need to breathe. And stop pacing like that—you're making me dizzy."

When Asher stopped to glare, Gabe smiled at him. "Look, I get that you think LOST is all-powerful, but even we would run into some issues if we started throwing federal agents off the premises."

Asher growled. "He's—"

"Not his brother," Sarah said, her voice cold. She was sitting in the seat to the right of Gabe, not surprising really, because when it came to LOST, Sarah *was* Gabe's right hand. She was also the agent who would be opening up the West Coast division of LOST soon. "Cash Knox isn't Louis. He's not responsible for the things that Louis did, so you need to get that straight in your head. I get that this is personal for you, believe me, I do. But you can't put his brother's sins at Cash's door."

"He hurt Ana."

"He didn't want to—don't you see? That's what this was all about. He never wanted her to be hurt, so he didn't tell her the full truth about himself. Not that I blame him. It's not like I enjoy leading with the fact that my father is a killer." She began to fiddle with the gleaming diamond ring on her left hand. Sarah didn't normally fiddle. She was still. *Still waters run deep.* The very fact that she was showing a small crack in her façade had him feeling like shit.

"Sarah." He forced his back teeth to unclench. "You know I'm not meaning anything against you. You're nothing like your father."

"And when your rage cools, you'll realize that Cash is not at all like his brother. He certainly seems different to me." She stared down at her diamond, then looked up at him. "You probably don't know this, but my father hurt Jax."

Jax . . . he knew the name. Jax Fontaine had certainly captured plenty of attention for his exploits in New Orleans. The guy had been thought to be the leader of the criminal underworld there, but then . . .

Then Jax met Sarah.

The guy had been obsessed since that meeting. And Sarah had agreed to marry him. The shiny ring on her finger? It had come courtesy of Jax.

"My father did things to Jax . . . to Jax's family . . . things that can never be forgiven." Her chin lifted. "But Jax doesn't blame me for what happened. When he looks at me, I know Jax only sees me. Not my father. Not the river of blood Murphy left in his wake. Jax sees me, nothing more. And he loves me."

Ana doesn't love Cash.

But, fuck, wasn't that the whole reason he'd launched the investigation into the guy's past in the first place? Because Ana had been different when she mentioned him? Small slips that Asher had noticed because he and Ana were so close. "I just want to protect her."

"I understand." Sarah's voice was soft and he knew she truly did understand what he meant.

I failed Ana once. I never want to fail her again.

"But you need to realize," Sarah continued, her voice still soft, "Ana isn't fourteen any longer. She knows how to fight her own battles. How to make her own choices. And sometimes, she'll make choices you don't agree with, and when she does that . . . there's not a damn thing you can do about it."

Sarah thinks Ana is going to choose Cash. He shook his head. No way. No—

"You can't control your heart. That's a lesson I learned the hard way. Wrong time, wrong place, wrong man. Sometimes, you find a connection to someone and you never realize the danger, not until it's too late." Her shoulders rolled back. "And by then, you don't even care that you're walking into fire. The flames feel too good."

THE CALLER DIDN'T have to be the killer. It could be a telemarketer. It could be a wrong number. It could be—

"Why did you leave, Ana?"

It was him. Same robotic voice. Same app. Same game.

"I have a job to do," Ana said, fighting to keep her voice flat. A hard task considering the way her emotions were nearly ripping her apart. "You were the one who reminded me of that, remember? There are people who need me in Atlanta. People who are missing."

Robotic laughter crackled over the line. "But someone's missing here . . ."

Cash had his phone out. He was texting fast and furiously. No doubt, trying to get his agents to get a lock on the caller.

"You have Dr. Summers," Ana said. She knew she was supposed to keep the perp on the line as long as possible. If she did that, then Cash's team would be better able to find the guy. She'd do her job.

More robotic laugher. "I do."

"Why? Why'd you take her? She's not like Bernie Tate or Forrest Hutchins—"

"Don't be too sure of that."

"She's not a convicted killer!"

"Not all killers wind up in jail. Special Agent Knox knows that truth. And so do you."

Ana looked over at Cash. He was still texting, his face grim. She pressed her lips together, then said, "Let Dr. Summers go."

"Why?"

"Stop it." The words came out angry but her control was just gone. "Stop that stupid voice. Why are you hiding behind it? You're making the bad guys pay, right? You're doing some kind of revenge hunting? If everything you're doing is so damn justified, why hide?"

Cash's gaze had jerked up to meet hers.

I went too far.

There was silence on the line. Oh, God, he'd hung up. Too soon. They wouldn't be able to find him. They—

"You're right, Ana." The robotic voice was gone. This was a man's voice. Low, deep, smooth. No accent. "I shouldn't hide, not from you. After all, you understand, don't you?"

Sarah had said the killer believed she understood him. That she could relate to his kills. "I do. Sometimes the only punishment that works is an eye for an eye."

"Bernie Tate was a big player in prison. All of the other inmates feared *him*. And he was just in there, making plans to hurt you. Sitting in his cell, jerking off to pictures of you. He thought I'd help him. That we'd take you out, but he was wrong."

Cash's eyes had gone flat and cold.

"Thank you," Ana said, realizing the role she needed to play with this man. If he thought she understood him . . . *then I will.* "Tate needed to be stopped."

"The Butcher isn't going to hurt anyone else." Pride deepened his voice. "I did that."

"Yes, you did . . . just as you stopped Forrest, didn't you?" Getting his confession was step one. She'd heard it. A federal agent had heard it.

"Forrest wasn't being *rehabilitated*. There is no such thing. He was in there, and he was hurting people. Summers should have stopped that. Should have stopped him. She let it happen, and now she's paying for her crime."

"Hurting other people . . . you're talking about what he did to Chassity, aren't you? He hurt her, and that's how he wound up in the quiet room."

"It's nice and quiet for Dr. Summers now. She's getting the treatment she needs." Again, pride rang in his voice.

"How did you know he was hurting Chassity?" Ana asked him.

Silence.

That question made him uncomfortable.

"Did someone at the hospital tell you? And how did you know what Bernie was planning?"

"So many questions, Ana, but you don't get the answers. It's my turn."

Cash mouthed the words, *"We've got him."*

Yes! "Your turn for what?"

"To ask you . . . you want payback, too, don't you?"

"No. No, the men who hurt me are dead."

"But Cash Knox isn't. He's tied to your past, Ana. Don't trust him. He's one of the monsters."

The perp didn't know that Ana had already learned the truth. "What are you talking about?"

"We'll be meeting soon, Ana. I'll tell you everything then." His voice dropped. "It's nice . . . not to be alone."

Then he disconnected the call. Ana stood there a moment, staring at Cash.

"Not going to happen," he said grimly. "He is *not* getting you."

But it had certainly sounded as if that was what the perp meant. He planned to meet her. So far, when people met the perp, they wound up dead.

Ana curled her trembling fingers around the phone. "He said that Dr. Summers was paying—*was paying*. Not that she'd paid. It sounds like she's still alive." Ana hoped so, anyway.

And it also sounded as if Dr. Summers was definitely *not* an accomplice, but a victim.

"Tell me your team got his location."

Cash nodded. "FBI agents are moving in on the spot now."

Hell, yes.

"I need you to come with me, Ana." Cash said. "Stay with me. Work with me. My team could have the bastard in custody within the hour. And if that's the case—"

"If that's the case, then he'll want to talk to someone. And that someone isn't going to be you." *He's one of the monsters.* "Sarah thinks there were more victims. A lot more. We'll need him to share everything that he's done. He won't share that with you." *But I think he will share it with me.* Ana knew what she had to do. Determined now, she nodded. "I can get him to talk, I just proved that."

"Does that mean we're partners again?"

"It means I'll come with you, I'll stay until we have this guy pinned to the wall." She'd just gotten him to confess directly to Bernie's murder. She would get more. "And that's all I'm promising."

Cash nodded. "That's all I want. You make the rules."

She'd made rules before, and then instantly broken them, with him. For him. "Fine. Rule one, don't touch me, Cash." Because when he touched her . . . it hurt.

In her heart. His touch made her want things that she shouldn't. His touch confused her. It . . . "Just don't."

He nodded. "Not until you ask."

Confident bastard.

"This time, we'll be taking the FBI's jet when we head to Virginia. It's waiting at the airport. Let's get the hell out there. This SOB isn't going to play any more games. No more revenge."

"No more payback," Ana murmured.

If only it were true.

They rushed out of her office with Ana pausing only long enough to grab her jacket. But once they were outside, Asher was just walking out of the conference room. He saw them together and stiffened.

"I don't have time for a fight," Ana said flatly. Cash was in front of her, his pose protective. As if she needed protecting from her own brother. "The perp just called—again. I am in this, Asher. Whether I want to be or not. The FBI was able to get a lock on his signal, and Cash's team is closing in. When they bring the guy into custody, I'm going to be there."

Sarah appeared just behind Cash.

"If there were more victims," Ana said, determined, "I will get him to tell us about them. That's what LOST does, right? We find the missing. If he took people, if he made them vanish without a trace, I will find the truth." She didn't want to reveal too much about what Sarah had told her, so Ana hoped the other woman understood . . . *If he killed Murphy, I swear, I will find out for you. I'll give you the closure that you need.*

Last night, she'd been hurting and she'd run, her

only instinct to flee and protect herself. But that wasn't who she was. She didn't hide.

She stood her ground. She fought.

That would be exactly what she did now.

"My agents tracked his cell signal," Cash said. "By the time we touch down in Virginia, they will have already closed in. They know time is of the essence, particularly if we've still got a live victim. They're moving, and so are we."

Asher looked like he wanted to argue—typical Asher—and he strode forward.

She saw Cash tense but . . .

"Do you need backup?" Asher asked. "Because LOST provides one hell of a backup team."

Her breath eased out.

Cash nodded. "Don't see why we can't work together." His head turned as he looked at Sarah. "Ana already told me I should get you to work up a profile. On the way here, I convinced my boss that two profilers are better than one. Especially when one of those profilers is Sarah Jacobs." He nodded toward Sarah. "I'd be real interested in hearing what you have to say."

Sarah flashed a quick smile. "Consider it done."

"And as far as boots on the ground are concerned . . ." Cash glanced back at Asher, then said, "We have that covered now. But if anything changes, I'll be sure to let your team know." Then he hesitated. "Nothing will happen to Ana on my watch. I can assure you, I'm willing to do anything necessary to keep her safe."

Asher laughed at Cash's words. "You've got things all wrong, man. Ana is the one who will be watching your ass on this mission, and consider yourself very lucky for that fact. She'll make sure that nothing happens to *you*."

And that was precisely Ana's plan. Because she might be pissed as all hell at Cash. She might be hurt. But no one else was taking a shot at him. And when the killer had said that Cash was a monster, that he had payback coming . . .

No. You won't hurt him. Guess again.

FBI Agent Faye Comwell lifted her hand, giving the signal that it was time to approach the little cabin that sat at the end of Juniper Lane. It was the *only* cabin on that lane, nestled in Virginia's Blue Ridge Mountains. Isolated, the perfect spot for a killer to use as his base. Her heart was pounding frantically in her chest, but her hand was dead steady. This was her first lead on a charge, and she wasn't about to let Cash down. He trusted her to do this job, and she was absolutely going to do it.

The team was in place. They had backup from the local authorities. *Let's do this.*

The techs had traced the call Ana Young received—they'd pinged towers and done all the weird tech-y stuff that the crew loved to do. And now they had their perp.

Her hand slid back to her side as the agents—all wearing bulletproof vests—kicked in the front door. They were going in hard and fast, a real blitz attack. That had been their plan all along.

To go in. To destroy. To wreck this guy's carefully laid plans.

The little cabin was about ninety miles from River

View Psychiatric Hospital. And eighty miles from Wingate Penitentiary. Nearly dead center of the guy's kill zone.

She swept in behind the team, her gun up, her body battle ready. There were no lights on inside—a check of the property had shown that the lights and water had been disconnected years ago. The place was abandoned, foreclosed. Forgotten.

Again, perfect for their killer.

When she went inside, a stale scent hit her. As if the cabin had been closed up for too long. A little rancid. *Bad food?* There wasn't any furniture inside. Just plenty of dust. Cobwebs.

The agents were fanning out. Property records had shown that the place was just over fifteen hundred square feet. They had studied the layout of the property before moving in, and each agent had been assigned a room to search.

Those same property records had told Faye about the previous owner . . . Jonathan Bright, a former construction worked who'd retired to the area, then passed away thirteen years ago.

One of the agents called out, "Clear!" It was the first word to be spoken in that house.

Faye paced in the small living room. Old newspapers were on the floor. Everything had been cleared out—who'd done the clearing after Jonathan Bright died? She hadn't been able to find any next of kin. And why were newspapers left behind? Yellowed, old newspapers.

Another agent echoed, "Clear!"

Dammit. Their perp wasn't there. She'd just spotted

a phone, tossed on the floor, near one of those yellowed pieces of paper.

"Nothing, Agent Comwell!" said a third agent. "No victim, no perp."

Not anymore. She holstered her weapon. She put on her gloves and bent to pick up the phone. It would be bagged and tagged as evidence. "He *was* here," she muttered. But he was gone now.

Gone . . . with Dr. Summers?

She rose and looked around that dark place. "Get a crime scene team in here, right away." Maybe the perp had been a real dumbass and left prints or even DNA—just a little spit on that phone—for them to find. Cash had always told her that criminals had a habit of getting too cocky. Too assured.

And then they messed up. Had this guy messed up? They would be finding out soon.

Her gaze lingered on the yellowed newspaper. Curiosity drove her to bend down and her gloved fingers touched the paper.

It wasn't a full sheet, though. More like a clipping.

Area girl disappears . . . family desperate for her return.

A clipping from fifteen years before.

CHAPTER FOURTEEN

"YOU'RE SURE?" CASH ASKED AS HE HELD HIS phone close. They were currently in the middle of their flight, a private flight on the FBI's dime, and Ana tensed because she knew the news he was getting wasn't good.

"Dammit, yes, I think he wanted us at that location for a reason. This guy is smart, we know that. Every single move he makes is calculated for maximum impact. That cabin matters. Get the crime scene team to do a thorough sweep and dig up every bit of information that you can find on the property's previous owner." He listened for a moment, his eyes narrowed. "Ana is with me. I'll call you back when we touch down."

He ended the call a few moments later and stared at her.

"Let me guess," Ana murmured. "Our perp wasn't at the location?"

"His phone was. Obviously, he wanted us to find the place. Why—well, that remains to be seen."

She glanced away from him, staring out the window. "I seem to be flying a lot with you lately."

"Ana, thank you for coming back with me."

"I'm doing this for me, Cash, not for you. I want to see this case through to the end." *I don't want him hurting you.* "I've been thinking about what he said before, on the phone. He's so deliberate. I wonder . . . he may have been telling us exactly where Dr. Summers was being kept." She looked back at him. "He told us that Dr. Summers was paying for her crime."

"He thinks she's done something wrong."

"Whether she has or not . . . he said it was quiet for her now."

His eyes widened. "The quiet room. Forrest was in the quiet room right before he was taken."

Ana nodded. "And he told us that Summers was getting treatment." She bit her lower lip. "You get treatment in a mental hospital."

Cash shook his head. "You're saying they're back in that place? Hell, the guards have been doubled at River View. No way can they be—"

"He couldn't get Forrest out of there, so I don't know that he'd be able to get Dr. Summers back in." Her mind turned over the possibilities. The options. "Are there any other facilities like that in the area? Some place that would be easier for him to access?"

"Let's find out." Cash pulled out his laptop and his fingers flew over the keyboard.

Just what pain did the killer think Dr. Summers had doled out? *Treatment.* Had her treatment itself been the crime?

Cash's fingers tapped quickly on the keys. Her gaze slid over his features. So tense. So determined. Looking at him last night had hurt her but now the shock was wearing off. When she looked at him, she just saw Cash.

Her heart hurt for what could have been.

He's one of the monsters.

Cash gave a low whistle. "I think we've got something." He looked up at her. "There's a facility—way smaller scale—about an hour away from River View. It actually closed down when River View opened, and the place has been vacant for years."

A chill slid over her body. "Wonder if they have a quiet room there."

He looked back at his laptop, tapped some more. His eyes narrowed. "The place was called Bellhaven, and I swear, that name is familiar to me. It's—" His jaw clenched. "Fuck, I think Dr. Summers used to work there. When I was researching her bio, I came across the place."

"We need to get there," Ana said. "Or if your team can get there faster—*get them to her.*"

He was shoving his laptop onto the nearby seat and rising. "I can get the pilot to reroute us. There's a small airstrip near Bellhaven, one that the FBI has used before. *And* I'll damn well be calling in the team. We'll all swarm that place."

But we have to do it fast. Because they didn't know if Dr. Summers was still alive.

Or if she'd already received her full payback.

BELLHAVEN LOOKED LIKE an old church, one that had slowly begun to wither and die over time. Cash stared up at the heavy stone building. There was even a steeple right in the middle of that building, shooting toward the sky. Maybe it *had* been a church, once upon a time. Now, well, the place was just—

"Creepy," Ana said from beside him.

She was right. It was.

"Got to say, Cash," Ana murmured. "You're bringing me to the most interesting places."

No, he was bringing her to hell, but he wasn't sending her in unarmed. They'd arrived at the old facility just moments before—and a black SUV was currently heading down the pothole-laden lane toward them. That was his team—he'd talked to Faye just moments before.

He reached into his duffel bag and pulled out a Glock. He offered it to Ana. "It's loaded and ready to go."

Her fingers closed over the weapon.

"If this bastard comes at you, Ana, don't hesitate, understand? You fire."

She nodded. "Don't worry. I can—"

"Take care of yourself. Yeah, I know." He stared at her as the SUV braked a few feet away. "Doesn't mean I'm not scared as hell."

One dark brow lifted. "Then I'm surprised that you're letting me go inside at all."

"Better to have you with me, at my side, than out here alone. The guy has been smart all along, playing his game, leading us on a chase. I don't want to risk him coming after you while we're in there searching the damn place for him." Leaving her on her own? Hell, no, that wasn't happening. Not now. "You stay with me, got it? Every step of the way."

"I got it." She checked the weapon with quick competent movements. "And I'll watch your back."

She was so gorgeous. "Ana—"

The other agents were climbing from their SUV. Faye had extra bulletproof vests that she was carrying in her arms.

Cash cleared his throat. "Okay, we're breaking into teams. We want to search this place, top to bottom." They'd all come in quietly, hoping to have the element of surprise on their hands. But since the facility was so isolated, the perp could still have easily seen their vehicles if he'd been watching. Cash's gaze slid to the sky. The sun was starting to set. There would be no power in that place, so they needed to get the hell in there and get moving as fast as he could. "Make sure you're all carrying flashlights, got it? Stay together, teams of two every moment. Ana will be with me." He handed Ana a flashlight that had been in his duffel bag. "We could have a victim in there. So let's get the hell inside and get her out."

His team was a well-oiled machine. They knew how to storm a building and he backed up, letting Faye take the lead. She was a damn good agent, one of the best he'd worked with, and he had total confidence in her—and in every member of his team.

They raced quickly toward Bellhaven. Cash had thought they'd need to break down the main doors but when he got close enough, he saw that the doors were already open. A heavy chain lay on the ground, cut in the middle.

Sonofabitch . . . he's here.

He knew the others were thinking the same thing. A heavy tension swept over their group, and they filed in fast, taking up ready positions with their guns.

The walls inside were a dirty yellow, with hanging chunks of wallpaper and peeling paint everywhere. A staircase led up to the next floor, and a thick coat of grime covered what had once been white steps. Faye motioned, indicating that half of the group—there were eight of them in all, counting him and Ana— would go upstairs. Cash stayed below, and when the other ground-level team went left, he and Ana went right. The doors to the patient rooms were open, and he looked inside, doing a sweep with his gun at the ready. He saw the old beds that had been left behind. Just the bed railings, the springs—no mattresses.

Ana was quiet as she followed right with him, staying close just as she'd promised. One after the other, they searched those rooms—all were empty.

"We need an isolation room," he whispered, bending close to her, but making sure not to touch Ana. He wouldn't break that vow, and one day, she *would* ask for his touch. "Not a normal patient room. That's where he'd keep her." Because the quiet room at River View had been isolated from the others.

They turned down another hallway, a narrower one this time. A look inside the room on his right showed him four bathtubs, big, heavy tubs that were bolted into the floor. Like the stairs, those tubs were filled with a heavy layer of grime.

And there was still no sign of Dr. Summers or their perp.

Who in the hell was the guy? And now, since Ana had convinced him to drop the voice modulator, they knew they *were* dealing with a man. Cocky, taunting. The perp thought he had total control.

He was wrong.

As they walked in that hallway, shadows drifted through the windows. The sun was going down fast, and they needed to find Dr. Summers before they were plunged into darkness. He looked in the next room— saw a table, old straps. An overturned surgical tray.

"I can't believe all of this is still here," Ana whispered.

He could. The facility had shut down seemingly overnight. The staff had been transferred over to River View, and no one had exactly been given the time to come back for a cleanup. They'd taken all of the major equipment, but the other things . . . they'd probably figured they would sell with the building. Go for scrap.

Only the building hadn't sold.

He opened another door. It gave a long, low squeak. Cash realized he was looking into . . . "What in the hell?"

"It's a padded cell," Ana said. "Feel the wall, Cash. It's soft. We are talking serious old-school here."

No, they were talking serious trouble. Because those padded cells had been soundproofed. If there was another one of them at Bellhaven, Dr. Summers could be in there, screaming her heart out, and they wouldn't hear her.

He backed out of that room and retreated to the hall. "Let's keep going."

A few more empty rooms and then . . .

"Dolls?" Ana whispered. "What the hell?"

And there were dolls there. A whole line of dolls, with missing eyes. The dolls were set up in a nice, neat group, right beside another door.

His gaze swept over that door. It wasn't made of wood—it was different. Thicker. Just like the door to the padded room they'd seen moments before. He reached for the knob, but it wouldn't turn.

Every other door had opened easily. This one didn't.

Because it was getting so dim in there, he let his flashlight beam hit the doorknob.

That's a new knob. With a brand-freaking-new lock. It gleamed beneath his flashlight.

"Step back, Ana," Cash said.

She slid back.

He kicked at the lock. Once, twice, three times and the thing gave way. It busted beneath his kicks and the door swung open. Just as before, he saw a cavernous darkness waiting for him inside. No windows, no other door.

Just the dark.

He stepped inside and began swinging his light from the left side of the room. *Left to right, do a full sweep and then we'll go—*

A growl came from the darkness. Instantly, he jerked his flashlight in the direction of that growl. The light hit a figure hunched on the floor. A woman, with her dirty hair falling over her face, her upper body locked in what looked like a straitjacket.

"That's Dr. Summers!" Ana said and she started to rush toward the other woman.

In that moment, Dr. Summers let out a high, desperate scream. She threw her head back and Cash's light hit her directly in the face. Her eyes were wide, wild, and she flew to her feet, still screaming as she charged at him.

Shit.

He didn't want to risk shooting her, so Cash shoved his gun into his holster two seconds before they collided. They hit the floor hard, with him on the bottom, taking most of the impact. She kept snarling and screaming, her whole body thrashing. And she was trying to *bite* him.

He grabbed her shoulders and rolled with her, trapping her beneath his body and holding her down. "Dr. Summers! Dr. Summers, calm down! I'm Agent Cash Knox with the FBI. Do you remember me?"

She stopped screaming. Her body went limp beneath his and she let out a low, mewling cry.

What in the hell did he do to her?

"You're safe," Cash told her. "My team is here. We're going to get you out of this place, understand?"

Tears leaked from her eyes. "Quiet . . ."

"Is the man who took you—is he still here, Dr. Summers?"

"Quiet . . ."

Shit. Was she saying she was in the quiet room or that they needed to be quiet because the guy was still around? Either way, he needed to get her out of there. The victim's safety always came first. Always.

"I'm going to let go of you," he explained softly, aware of Ana edging closer to them. "And you're not going to attack again, right? I need you to stay calm, Doctor. You're safe now."

Ana had her light shining down on him. He didn't know where his light had gone—he'd dropped the flashlight when he and Dr. Summers collided. Very slowly, he eased back and his fingers slid away from Dr. Summers's shoulders. She didn't attack.

She just kept crying.

"He put her in a straitjacket," Ana murmured. "And he left her in the dark?"

He'd done more than that. The way the woman had attacked, the way her body shuddered . . . Cash figured the perp had drugged the doctor, too. *The better to keep her controlled? Or the better to drive her out of her mind?*

"We need to get her out of that jacket."

Cash helped the doctor rise to her feet. She trembled against him. "It's okay," he said again and he reached for his phone. He needed to call the other agents and let them know she'd been located. He put the phone to his ear as Ana crept closer to the doctor.

Ana put her hand on the other woman's shoulder. "He's not going to hurt you any longer."

The doctor's shoulders fell. "P-please . . ." Her voice was far more subdued now. "Get me out—out of this thing!" Her body heaved as she fought against the jacket.

His lips tightened. The call he'd made was answered and Faye said, "You found him?"

"No, I found her. Ana and I are getting Dr. Summers out of here. You keep the teams searching."

Ana had moved behind the doctor. She was fumbling, pulling the twists and ties on the straitjacket.

"Thank you," Dr. Summers whispered.

No more screams. No more attacks.

"Did she say if he was still here?" Faye demanded.

He slid the phone away from his mouth. "Dr. Summers." He said her name, fast and hard, wanting to reach her while she seemed relatively calm.

Relatively sane.

Her head turned toward him.

"The person who took you—is he still here?"

Her gaze darted around the dark interior of the room. "I—I don't know . . ."

Ana pushed the jacket off the doctor's shoulders. It hit the floor with a heavy thud.

"How long has it been since you've seen him?"

"I—I don't . . . I don't know. It's just been d-dark . . . so d-dark . . ."

He put the phone back to his mouth. "She doesn't know. We're getting her out, securing her. Keep searching every inch of this place."

He shoved the phone back into his pocket. His fallen flashlight cast a bright glow on the far wall. He bent, intending to scoop up that flashlight. But he bent in front of that flashlight, and his shadow swept behind him, big and dark on the wall.

And then Dr. Summers screamed. High, wild, desperate.

He spun back to face her, but—

She was curled on the ground. Her knees were tucked under her and her hands were sliding on the cold floor. "Find it . . . f-find it . . . have to f-find it . . ."

"Cash, let's get her out of here," Ana said, voice shaking. "Now." She reached out and put her hand on Dr. Summers. Ana's hand curled around the doctor's shoulder. "You're safe."

"F-found it!" A gleeful cry.

And Dr. Summers lurched to her feet.

Cash had his flashlight in his hand, and the glow glinted off the object she held. *Oh, fuck.* "Ana, get away from her!"

But Dr. Summers had moved so fast—and she'd caught Ana off guard. *Because Ana just saw a victim, not a threat.*

Now Dr. Summers was behind Ana, the knife cutting into Ana's throat. Ana wasn't holding the gun he'd given her—Cash could see that she'd tucked it into her waistband. *Because she didn't see a fucking threat.*

He kept his light shining straight on Dr. Summers, and Cash aimed his gun at the woman's head. The instant she'd grabbed Ana, he'd yanked his gun from the holster. "Let her go," he snarled at Dr. Summers.

"Monster, monster, m-monster," Dr. Summers chanted. "He came . . . told me . . . monster coming. Have to stop . . . m-monster . . ."

"I'm not a monster," Ana said softly. Cash could see the blood dripping down her neck, but no emotion was in her voice. No pain. No fear. She was calm.

A whole lot calmer than he was.

I have a shot. If she doesn't let Ana go, I will take it.

"Monster . . . m-monster . . ."

Because Dr. Summers was so much taller than Ana, he had a clear headshot. *But she's the victim!*

"Cash, don't." Ana's voice. Quiet. Calm.

What did she think? That he was just going to stand there and watch her die? Watch the crazed doctor slit her throat? The hell, no, he wasn't. "I'm the monster."

He made his voice sound angry. *An easy task because I'm fucking furious!* "You grabbed the wrong person. You want me."

Dr. Summers whimpered.

"Let her go. Come and attack me. I'm the one you want. Not her. She's a victim." Then, because the doctor was staring right at him, Cash made a show of slowly lowering his gun. "I'm the monster," he said once more.

"Uh, Cash, what are you doing?" Ana wasn't so calm any longer. He could hear her worry. Fear.

Fear for him?

And what was he doing? *I'm trying to save your sweet ass, baby.* And if he got cut along the way, big damn deal.

He didn't drop his weapon, though, not yet. He just looked as if he were about to place it on the floor. "Let her go," he said. "Come for me. Come *at* me. You want the monster? Then here I am."

Dr. Summers gave a wild cry. She shoved Ana to the side and ran at Cash, with her knife up, her hand tight, claw-like around the handle. He lifted his gun. He could shoot her. Stop her.

But . . .

She's a victim, dammit. A victim.

The knife sliced down at him. He lifted his forearm, intending to block that slice and then disarm her. The blade flew over his skin. He felt the cut burn into him and then—

Thud.

Dr. Summers crumpled to the ground. Ana stood behind her, the flashlight gripped in one hand, and the weapon he'd given her in the other.

"Dammit," Ana swore. "I bet I gave her a concussion."

Because she'd just driven the butt of her weapon into the back of the doctor's head.

"Had to stop her, though," Ana said with a sad shake of her head. "You were working hard on some hero complex and I was afraid you were about to let her carve you into pieces. Jeez, you're bleeding." She reached out and touched him.

Cash stilled. "Ana . . ."

"What was that all about? Offering yourself up like that? Why have you gone crazy?" She yanked at his shirt, ripping some of the material and starting to wrap it around his arm. "You're going to need stitches. You're going to scar from that—"

"I didn't want her to hurt you." He wanted to touch Ana, so badly, but he didn't move.

She stilled. "Don't risk your life for me again, got it?" Then she was backing away and bending over the doctor. "She's breathing. Hell, I didn't want to hurt her, but she wasn't stopping! And you weren't fighting back."

He would have fought back. He just hadn't planned to kill the doctor. He bent over her, felt for her pulse. Far too fast. "She is on something." And that would make her dangerous until they got her to safety. He scooped the doctor in his arms, barely feeling the throb from the slice she'd given him. "Let's get her the hell out of here." They needed an ambulance.

"I'm going first." Ana hurried in front of him, her gun at the ready. "Just in case there are any more surprises waiting, I'll make certain you're covered."

Dr. Summers moaned. "M-monster . . ."

"Don't worry, Doc, this monster is getting your ass out of here. You *will* be okay."

A SWIRL OF lights illuminated the exterior of Bellhaven. An ambulance roared away from the scene, taking Dr. Ellen Summers to safety. Another ambulance waited nearby, and Cash was in the back of it, growling at the tech who was trying to tend to his arm.

Cop cars were spread out, their lights so bright. Crime teams were running into the facility, desperately searching for evidence.

The FBI agents had finished their sweep of Bellhaven. The perp hadn't been there, he'd obviously fled before they arrived. He'd left his victim, pumped full of who the hell knew what . . . and he'd put a knife in her cell.

Why? Did he want Dr. Summers to use that knife on herself? Or on the people who came to save her?

Ana breathed out slowly. In her mind, she could still see the doctor charging for Cash. And Cash—he'd had his gun lowered. He'd just been waiting for the attack. *He told her to come at him. To leave me alone.*

Playing the hero.

Or actually *being* a hero?

Her hands shoved into her pockets as she strode toward the ambulance. The EMT was just finishing up with Cash's stitches.

"When was your last tetanus shot?" the EMT demanded.

"I'm good," Cash growled. "Just slap a bandage on me and I'll get back to work."

The woman frowned at him, but she did roll a bandage over his wound.

"Difficult patient," Ana said softly.

Cash's gaze jumped toward her. "It's just a scratch."

"A scratch that needed seven stitches," the EMT muttered.

Cash sighed. The EMT finished up and then he was climbing from the back of the ambulance. Ana tensed, then forced herself to relax. His blood had been on her fingers, warm and wet and terrifying her. She'd known the wound wasn't life threatening, of course, but . . .

His blood. Something inside of her had seemed to break as she felt his blood dripping through her fingers.

"Thanks for the backup, Ana," Cash said, voice a rumble.

She shook her head. "You're the one who made her let me go."

He shrugged. All of the lights in the lot let her easily see his expression. His gaze was sharp as he studied her neck.

That wound *had* just been a scratch. Not deep enough for any stitches, it already stopped bleeding by the time the ambulances screeched up to the scene.

"You put yourself at risk," Ana said, "to protect me."

Once more, he shrugged.

Her eyes narrowed. In a flash, she'd grabbed his shirt front and fisted it in her hand. "Don't do that crap again."

"What?"

"I had it handled. I would have disarmed her. You

didn't need to put yourself at risk. You didn't need to hurt yourself for me."

But he laughed. A tired, rough sound. "Oh, Ana, when are you going to get it? I'd damn well do anything for you."

She jerked back as if she'd been burned. "What? No, no, you—"

"Anything, Ana. With you, it's that simple for me." Another agent called his name. Cash sighed. "Excuse me. I'll be right back."

She stood there, the lights swirling around her, her head shaking in denial. *No, no, no.* Why would Cash say that? Why would she matter so much to him?

Why does he matter so much to me? So much that I nearly broke apart when I found out how much he'd been hiding from me.

Ana backed away. The cops and the FBI agents were swarming inside, and a K-9 unit had just arrived. She knew the dogs would be checking inside Bellhaven, and they'd be searching the surrounding woods, hoping to catch the killer's scent.

Was the killer long gone? Were they wasting their time?

Maybe—once Dr. Summers was stabilized—she would be the key. She could tell them everything she knew about the perp who'd abducted her.

But if we've taken Dr. Summers, then won't the killer move on to his next victim?

Her gaze returned to Cash. He was talking with the female agent she liked so much—Faye Comwell. Their heads were together as they chatted and a shiver slid down Ana's spine. She pulled out her phone, just—just needing to look and make sure the killer hadn't tried to call her again.

Was she actually expecting his call now? Yes, she was, and Ana knew that was twisted.

But we followed your clues. We came here, just where you wanted us. So now what happens?

Her eyes closed, just for a moment, as she tried to think like the killer. She'd been so cocky when she told Cash that she understood monsters, but this particular perp, he was different.

Why pull us out here? Did you want us to save Dr. Summers?

It was all about payback. Vengeance. Hurting those who'd hurt others.

Her eyes opened. She turned, staring into the darkness of the woods that surrounded Bellhaven. *So who hurt you?* Who had created this monster? Maybe they'd been looking at the case wrong all along. It wasn't about who the victims were. It was about why this guy wanted to punish them so much.

Because he'd been hurt. He'd been a victim, too.

Bellhaven. River View. Wingate Penitentiary.

Places picked by chance? Or places that might mean something to the killer?

We don't need to look at his victims, we need to look at these places. At him. Cash was striding toward her. "The cabin," Ana said, excitement sharpening her voice. "The one where your agents found the ditched phone . . . who did you say owned it?"

"A guy named Jonathan Bright." Cash tilted his head. "But he'd been dead for years and—"

"The places aren't random."

"Uh, no, I agree. He's picking them specifically for his victims—"

"I think he's picking them for him. Because they have meaning . . . *for him*." Her heart was racing faster now. "We need to learn everything we can about Jonathan Bright. Every single thing." Her gaze slid back to the imposing structure of Bellhaven. "What if he was here?"

"Ana?"

"What if Jonathan Bright was a patient at Bellhaven? Think about it, Cash. You find the perp's phone at Jonathan's old cabin. We find the victim we were looking for here. It's like we're following a map. One place at a time. We started in the prison. Then we went to the cabin where we found Bernie. Next stop . . . a psych ward, River View. And River View took us to another cabin." She licked her lips. "Then here. It's a map. The places—they mean something, I know they do."

He was silent. "We have to see what connects them all."

She nodded. "We find that connection, and we have our killer."

THEY'D GOTTEN DR. Summers out of her quiet room. Had the doctor had time to think, to consider her actions, to quiet her demons?

The ambulance had roared away, taking her from the scene of the crime.

The cops were still there. The FBI agents. The scene was so chaotic, no one even noticed him. A stolen cop uniform, a badge pinned to his chest, and he blended right in.

He saw Ana. And Agent Knox. Huddled close together.

"It's a map. The places—they mean something, I know they do."

Ana's voice was so determined. He smiled as he turned away from her. She was right, of course. The places he'd selected did mean something. Ana understood because she understood *him*. She had, from the very beginning.

After all, Ana had been to hell, just like he had. She knew what the fire felt like as it burned.

"We have to see what connects them all." That was Knox talking.

His smile vanished. Knox wasn't like Ana. Knox wasn't there to stop the darkness. He was the darkness.

And he's next.

He would take Agent Knox and give the man his own punishment to face. Knox wouldn't have a chance.

"Officer!" Someone was pointing at him. A woman in a suit, with a badge pinned to her hip. "They need backup on the south perimeter. Get over there!"

South perimeter. Right. He started running that way only . . .

He stopped after a few moments and glanced back. Ana was still huddled close to Knox. Their bodies were leaning together, almost . . . intimately. It was wrong. Ana wouldn't want someone like him.

At that moment, Ana looked up. Her gaze focused right on him. He couldn't move. She was looking dead at him. Seeing him.

It was the first time he felt as if someone had really seen him in a very, very long time.

He smiled at her.

She stiffened.

His smile vanished.

Ana took a step toward him. No, no, this was not the place for their meeting. Not the time. He wasn't ready.

He turned, running for the woods as panic hit him. A panic he hadn't felt in so long.

He ran . . . and he remembered . . .

Fleeing. Bare feet on the ground. My heart racing. He's coming after me. He's so close. Coming . . . coming . . . have to get away. He's going to hurt me. He'll kill me . . .

Running.

Running.

CHAPTER FIFTEEN

"C ASH!" ANA'S VOICE WAS SHARP. HER HAND flew out, locking around his arm. "That cop there . . ."

He turned his head, following her stare.

"Something is wrong." She took a step toward the cop. "The way he was watching me . . . it's . . . something is *wrong*."

The guy had turned and started running toward the woods.

Ana shoved away from Cash, heading after him. "Stop!" Ana yelled. "Wait!"

Agent Faye Comwell turned to look at Ana's cry. "I told that officer to search the perimeter. Why do you need him?"

The guy was heading toward that perimeter. But . . .

Shouldn't he have stopped at Ana's cry?

He hadn't. He'd just seemed to run faster.

Cash gave chase, too, pulling out his weapon. If Ana's instincts were screaming at her, then he was going to listen to her. Their feet pounded over the earth as they darted into the woods. Behind him, he could hear the cry of the barking dogs.

And ahead of him—he could hear the officer, running hard and fast.

He shouldn't be running from us. Not if he's just some local cop.

Ana pushed through a heavy patch of bushes and then—she stopped.

Cash stopped.

He didn't hear the thunder of the other man's footsteps. The area was suddenly far too quiet.

"Where did he go?" Ana spun around. "Where the hell is he?"

He was out there. Waiting. Watching.

Cash stepped in front of Ana. "Hey, you sonofabitch," he called out. "Is this what you do? You hide? You sneak your ass back to the scene of a crime and then at the first sign of trouble, you panic? Is that what you are—a fucking coward?"

Ana grabbed his arm. "Cash . . ."

"I think you are a coward. I saw what you did to Dr. Summers. Left her in that straitjacket. Drugged her. Locked her in the dark. What kind of man does that? What kind of—"

"The bitch deserved it!"

The roar had come from the left. And it was just what Cash had been hoping to hear—he'd taunted the perp deliberately, knowing what his weakness would be. In classic style, the guy had taken the bait.

Cash lunged to the left. He heard the frantic thud of footsteps, rushing away.

You won't get away. We have you. You're done. Done now.

Others were behind him, alerted by Cash's frantic

race into the woods. Was the perp running wildly? Or had he mapped out some kind of exit strategy? He's always seemed so prepared, but maybe he'd slipped up this time.

Ana was right at Cash's side, running so fast. She'd been the one to spot the bastard with instincts he would never doubt. Ana. She was—

A gunshot blasted.

Cash threw his body against Ana's, sending them both tumbling to the ground. He felt the burn of a bullet blaze across his shoulder. *Hell*. The guy wasn't going down without a fight.

Ana was quiet beneath him, her body tense.

Footsteps thudded away once more.

"Stay behind me," Cash ordered Ana. Because if that guy fired again, he didn't want that bullet hitting her. Then they were off, rushing after the perp as they dove through the thick woods.

An engine's growl reached them, revving.

Shit. Cash ran faster. He burst out of the clearing just as a motorcycle roared away. He lifted his gun. "Stop!" he roared.

The driver didn't stop. Cash fired. He saw the driver spasm when the bullet hit him, the motorcycle swerved but the guy got his control back. Cash fired again—

But the motorcycle had disappeared around a winding curve.

Sonofabitch.

He yanked out his phone. "All points bulletin!" Cash snarled into it. "Get an all points bulletin out right away! We've got a perp on a Harley-Davidson Softail heading east on Dunlay Road. The driver is armed and dangerous. Contain him," he barked, giving the order directly to the local dispatch unit. *"Now."* He whirled back around, intending to get back to that parking lot and get the cops searching for him.

They could still catch the guy, if they moved fast enough.

HE'D BEEN HIT. The bullet was still in him, burning, tearing into his flesh. The bastard had shot him.

Agent Knox had been far too close.

He fought to maintain control of his bike, knowing that he had to hurry. Knox would send agents after him, local cops. They'd all be searching frantically for his motorcycle.

Good thing he planned to ditch it.

Another curve, and then he saw the run-down gas station. It waited for him, just a few yards away. And as soon as his headlight hit it . . .

Two headlights flashed on, signaling him.

His partner was there. Waiting with another ride, just as he'd planned.

Always be careful. Always be two steps ahead of the law. That was a lesson he'd been taught so long ago. A lesson that had stayed with him, as so much of the brutal instruction had.

He drove his bike to the back of the station. Hid it behind some old piles of wood. It would be found, eventually, but by then, he'd be long gone. He started walking and realized . . . his back was soaked with blood.

He was dripping blood, leaving a trail in his wake. Leaving evidence behind, for the first time.

They get your DNA. They get you. Don't fucking let that ever happen. Another lesson. Another memory. He kicked up the dirt there, trying to hide the blood trail. Maybe they wouldn't see it. Maybe—

"Hurry up!" The yell had him jerking to attention. "I just heard on the police scanner—they're looking for you!"

He stopped kicking the dirt and ran toward the VW Beetle that waited. An unassuming ride, selected for just that reason. He jumped in the passenger side and groaned when his right shoulder hit the seat.

"What's wrong?" his partner demanded.

He yanked the door closed behind him, gritting his teeth against the pain. "Nothing."

"That's a lie. We aren't supposed to lie to each other."

He turned to look at his partner, squinting to see her in the darkness. No, they weren't supposed to lie, not to each other. That had been part of their plan. Part of their pact, all along.

"You're bleeding," she whispered. Her head turned and she looked toward the old station. "Your blood could be on the bike. You know the rule—"

"Drive." The pain was becoming excruciating. He leaned forward, thinking it might not be as bad if he didn't let his shoulder touch the seat. "Knox shot me, okay? Just *go.*"

She floored the gas pedal and the car shot from the station.

"Slow down, dammit," he growled. "You don't want to look like you're running! They're trying to find a motorcycle, not this car!"

And if they could just take it slow and steady and not panic, they'd get out of there safely.

One step at a time.

"How did he know?" she asked. "How did he realize it was you? I thought you were going to stay away from him—"

"Ana saw me."

From the corner of his eye, he saw her stiffen.

"Ana called out to me. I—I didn't stop." Because he'd panicked. Dammit, panicked. He'd slipped back in time and became someone else as he ran through the woods. "I ran and Knox shot me." Though he'd tried to shoot that bastard first.

But that wasn't the way I wanted it to end.

"The bullet . . . it's still in my back." Sweat was coating his skin. "You're going to have to . . . get it out . . ."

She was silent. Her hands were tight on the wheel, her gaze directed straight ahead.

"We'll get to our . . . safe house . . ." He felt dizzy. "I'll . . . be okay . . ."

"You weren't supposed to get shot. I told you that going up there was risky. Stupid. Risky." Her voice hardened with each word. "But you did it because she was there. You almost got caught because of her."

"Just . . . drive . . ." She was right, but he didn't want to hear it, not right then.

"You know the rules . . . you know what happens if you break the rules."

He stiffened. "Everything is . . . okay." Nausea twisted in his gut. He hadn't been in this much pain in so long . . .

Running through the woods. Bare feet pounding. Have to get help. Have to—

"I don't think it's okay," she replied, her voice cold. "I don't think anything is going to be okay."

AT THREE A.M., Ana stood in the middle of her motel room—another no-tell, motel—her body too tense for sleep, and her mind in chaos.

Agent Faye Comwell had brought Ana back to the motel just over an hour ago. Cash had stayed out on the hunt, desperately looking for a perp who seemed to have vanished into thin air.

No one was supposed to vanish that way.

Tell that to all the victims that LOST seeks.

She heard footsteps outside. Heavy, hard. She tensed, but they went past her door and a few moments later, she heard rustles from the room beside hers.

Cash's room.

He'd been so grim as he continued the search. Determined as all hell to find the perp.

He hadn't come to her, so she guessed that meant he hadn't turned up anything.

But it would still be nice to hear that straight from him. Ana grabbed her coat and her room key. She hurried next door and knocked lightly on the door. The parking lot was dark and quiet behind her. "Cash? Cash, it's me."

The door opened. He stood there, one hand gripping the frame, the other on the doorknob. He'd taken off his shirt and his shoes and he looked dark and dangerous and . . .

Sexy.

Don't. Don't go there. You aren't supposed to find him sexy. You're done with that, remember?

Ana cleared her throat. "May I come in?"

He didn't move. "We didn't find him, Ana. The bastard slipped right through our fingers. When we get daylight, we'll start the search again."

Okay, right. That was what she'd wanted to know. She turned away, but then . . .

Ana looked back at him. The bandage was still around his forearm and a second white bandage covered his shoulder. "I didn't realize you'd been hit." He'd been shot? And he hadn't said anything?

Cash shrugged. "It was just a graze." Once again, his voice was so deep and dark.

Her breasts tightened.

No, do not do this. "I want to come inside. We need to—to talk."

"Ana . . ." His body tensed. "It's been a real long day. My mind . . . my control . . . it's not what it needs to be with you."

"What does that mean?"

He swore. "It means it's late. It means you need to walk away from me."

"But I thought I could trust you." She just had the need to keep pushing him. Weird. Wrong. But still there. "Isn't that what you've been telling me?"

"Only you don't believe me."

That was before you risked your life for me. Twice.

"Come inside, Ana. If it's what you really want." He took a step back.

She crossed the threshold.

He had a few lights on in his room, the lamp beside

the bed. The overhead light near the door. The bathroom light . . .

She suddenly wished it were darker. It was easier to bare her soul in the dark. *I've been hiding in the dark for so long, I'm almost afraid to be in the light.* And that was a scary truth.

He paced away from her and kept his hands at his sides. "You did really well today, Ana. I don't know what tipped you off about the man in the cop uniform—"

"He was smiling." A cold, chilling smile. "We were in the middle of chaos, Dr. Summers had just been rushed away in an ambulance, and he was just—staring at me and smiling." She shook her head. "So, yeah, you could say that made alarm bells go off."

"I know you described him before . . ."

Yes, she had. "The lights hit him just right. He was about your size, big shoulders. Square chin. He had dark hair, cut a little short." *Nothing that stood out. Nothing that made him any different from anyone else.*

"You're still talking to the sketch artist tomorrow?"

"Yes, yes, I am." She ran her hand over the back of her neck. "Cash, look, I need to know . . . why did you do it?"

His shoulders tensed. "I've already been over why I didn't tell you the truth about—"

"No." She gave a short, hard shake of her head. "I mean, why do you keep risking your life for me? *Twice* you did that tonight. You deliberately provoked Summers to attack you, and when that perp fired, you put yourself in front of me."

He stared down at his clenched hands. "I said I'd look out for you."

"And I said I didn't want you to lie to me again."

His head whipped up. His eyes glittered at her.

Ana sucked in a deep breath—one for courage—and she took a step toward him. "It's just you and me here right now. So don't lie. Don't tell me that you were just doing your job."

"I was."

"Don't tell me you'd do the same for anyone."

He swallowed. "I wouldn't let an innocent be harmed."

She took another step toward him. "No, you probably wouldn't. Because I was right about you all along, wasn't I?" *The good guy. The one you were supposed to be able to count on.* "You want to know why it hit me so hard when Asher told me the truth?"

"Because you thought I'd betrayed you. That I was playing some sick game with you." His hands were tight fists. "I wasn't. I *wouldn't*. No games, not with you. Never with you."

"No. You don't understand." Another step brought her even closer to him. His knuckles had gone white. Why? Why hold them so tightly? "I was sick because I was hearing the truth—dark and twisted and seemingly so ugly—and I looked at you, and . . ." Her voice fell to a whisper. "And I still wanted you."

He backed up. His shoulders hit the wall. "Ana."

"Why are your fists so tight, Cash?"

"So I won't touch you."

Because he'd told her that she would have to ask for his touch.

"I ran away from you," Ana said. "Because I was scared to death."

"I would never hurt you."

No, she didn't think he would. "I was scared that I needed you too much. That I couldn't see you clearly enough." A soft laugh escaped her. "My instincts have usually served me well. Like tonight, I knew something was off. That guy, he didn't fit . . ." Her head tilted as she studied Cash. "You know what my instincts always said about you?"

"No."

"They said you were the kind of man I should want. The kind I needed. The kind who wouldn't let me down." Sadness pulled at her.

"But I did."

She stared at his hands. "How long are you going to let guilt eat you alive?"

"Considering that you just found out—"

"I'm talking about your brother. How long are you going to blame yourself for the things that he did?"

A muscle jerked in his jaw. "Don't you blame me?"

Ana considered that, long and hard. "No, I don't."

Surprise had his eyes flaring. "Ana—"

"I'm mad as hell that you weren't honest with me from the beginning. Would I have gotten involved with you? Probably not so fast, but the connection is there between us—we both know it. I look at you, Cash, and I ache. It's something basic, elemental." Lust. An attraction that went beyond reason but . . . "I read your files, you know."

"What files?"

"The files that LOST emailed me tonight. I got Gabe to dig up every bit of intel he could find on you—and trust me, Gabe has plenty of strings that he can pull. So for the last hour, while I waited for you to return, I tried to learn every secret you had. *Not* just your FBI cases. Your military career. Even what you were like as a kid."

"Ana . . ."

"For the record, though, you're a damn good agent. Fair and tough. You don't back off from cases, and you don't give up on your victims."

"Neither do you."

She gave him a faint smile. "Perhaps we're more alike than I realized."

"Ana . . ."

She put her hand on his chest, right over his heart. His skin was warm, his muscles strong beneath her fingers. "When the case is over, I could run again. I could go back to Atlanta. You could go back to the Bureau. We could both go back to our lives. That would probably be easier for us both." Easier than dealing with the train wrecks of their past.

"Easier," he repeated. His hands were still at his sides. He wasn't touching her. He—

"I don't want easy. I don't know if I think easy things are worth having. I'd rather fight for what I have. Fight as hard as I can." She rose onto her toes and brought her mouth close to his. "So this is me, Cash. This is me, fighting for what I want. Fighting for *us*. I want a chance to be with you." To not always hide in the dark. "Maybe we'll crash and burn. Implode. But maybe . . ."

"Maybe we won't," Cash said.

She shook her head. "Maybe we won't." Her stomach was in knots. She hadn't been this afraid in—

No. Ana shut down the thought. This wasn't the

time for fear. For this moment, she was going to hope. "I want you to kiss me, Cash."

Immediately, his head lowered. His lips pressed to hers. Soft. Gentle. So very careful.

"I want you to touch me, Cash."

A shudder ran the length of his body. His hands lifted and curled around her hips. Again, he was so very gentle. Careful. Not holding her too tightly. Not using his strength.

"Kiss me harder," she whispered against his mouth.

And he did. He gave her the passion that she needed. That desperate, wild rush. Her hand still pressed to his chest. Her tongue licked over his bottom lip and Ana loved the rough, ragged groan that he gave to her.

"I want you," Ana murmured the words as her lips pulled from his. "I want you to make love to me, Cash."

"Ana, be sure."

She'd never been more sure of anything.

"Shut out the lights," Ana told him. She backed away. Turned and headed for the bed.

"One day," he said from behind her, his voice rough with desire and a need that barely seemed to be in check. "One day, you'll want the light with me."

Ana laughed and looked back at him. "Oh, Cash, I already do. I'm just not brave enough for that yet."

HE DIDN'T CRY out when she removed the bullet from him. His hands grabbed tightly to the table before him. He was curled over that table as she worked. She had tweezers in her hand and every poke had him swearing.

She'd had to cut him with a knife, to make the wound big enough for her to get inside. Now she was pulling out the bullet.

Get it the fuck out.

"There." She dropped the bullet on the table beside him and started trying to disinfect his wound. He didn't know what the hell she was pouring onto him, but it hurt like a bitch and he held even tighter to that table as spittle burst from his mouth. The pain reminded him—

You don't cry, you hear me? You never cry. You take what I give you. You be a man.

"I think you need stitches. Can you stay still while I stitch you up?"

He'd gone still already. "Yes."

She moved behind him, her steps fast. "You're not going to pass out on me, are you?"

He almost laughed at the question. She should know better. After all, he'd survived pain so much worse than this. They both had.

She came back to the table. He knew she'd heated her needle. They'd learned to tend wounds long ago.

Learned to tend them. Learned to give them.

"I think we should leave," she said. The needle sank into his skin and his eyes closed. "They're going to find your bike. They'll find your blood."

He wasn't so sure of that. "If we leave . . . if we run . . . no one will understand our work."

The needle pulled at his skin. Or maybe that was the thread she was using.

"I don't understand it," she whispered.

His eyes opened. No, she didn't understand. That was the problem. She should have—but . . .

She's not like Ana.

"And why are you risking everything for Ana Young? She's not our target."

No, she wasn't. She was so much more.

"You could have been killed because of her." Now anger roughened her voice. "I don't like that."

He wanted to say that it hadn't been Ana's fault, but that would be a lie. Ana had called out. Ana had sent the other cops after him.

Because Ana had tried to do the right thing.

Wrong, Ana. Wrong.

"I don't like her," she continued grimly.

Her words made alarm bells ring in his mind. He turned his head, looking back at her. She'd stopped stitching him up. Her fingers were covered with his blood. Her shirt stained by it. Her beautiful eyes were glassy and her face—*still so lovely.*

He knew he had to handle her carefully. He always did. "I have something for you."

Her brows lifted.

"Brought it here . . . earlier for you." He rose, wincing a bit. He was dizzy—probably from the blood loss. The dizziness and the nausea would fade, soon enough. And he could deal with the pain. "Look in my bag."

She turned away, but not before he saw the smile on her face. She'd always liked presents.

That's how she came into my life in the beginning. Going after a present . . .

I have something for you . . .

Words that had sent them both to hell. The guilt he carried would never end. He'd been the one to go to her. She hadn't suspected that he was a threat. She'd smiled and she'd come with him and, before their hell had been over, the girl she'd been had died.

And someone else had come to take her place. Someone who liked pain and blood far too much.

She opened his bag and gave a quick cry. Her fingers curled around the doll as she lifted it up.

"Another one for your collection," he told her, giving her a quick smile.

She'd always loved the dolls even though . . .

She'd gone through a darker period, when she'd cut out the eyes of her dolls. It had worried him, and he'd known he had to steer her in the right direction. He had, of course. As long as they were together, she was strong. She was fine.

"Thank you." A smile made her lovely face absolutely gorgeous.

He grinned back at her and strode to the sink. He washed his hands, watching the blood slide down the sink. "I'm the one who should thank you. You saved my ass tonight."

"Because you let Ana Young hurt you . . ."

He tensed, then forced himself to relax. The red water swirled down the drain.

"She shouldn't have hurt you."

"She didn't—" he began, but broke off. He sucked in a deep breath. He knew how to handle her. Always. Voice softer, he said, "Ana is like us. She's a survivor. She understands."

"No, I don't think she understands anything."

He turned off the sink and spun back to face her.

And that was when he realized she'd jammed the tweezers into the doll's eye. She was twisting those tweezers in deep, harder and harder. "She doesn't understand anything at all," she murmured.

CASH TURNED OFF all the lights. Part of him was afraid that he was dreaming. That in a moment, he was going to wake in a hot sweat, and Ana wouldn't be there.

He'd be alone, and she'd be gone.

He leaned over the bed and his fingers slid over her skin. "Just making sure," he rasped.

"Sure of what?" Her voice was a husky temptation in the dark. She'd stripped—he'd heard the rustle of her clothes—and as his fingers rose to her shoulder, he just touched more soft skin.

"Sure that you weren't going to vanish."

"I don't plan on going anywhere."

That was good. His fingers slid over her collarbone. Lightly, carefully.

Ana laughed. "I'm not going to break apart, you know. I promise, I'm quite strong."

He knew that with utter certainty.

But he also knew just how precious she was. He didn't want to rush her or scare her. He just wanted her. "Tell me how to not fuck this up."

She laughed again and his heart felt a little lighter. "You generally know how to do this part well."

In the dark, he smiled. "Good to know."

"But if you really want to know what I want . . ."

Her hand rose and curled around his wrist. "I'll show you." She pulled him onto the bed with her, and Ana moved fast—straddling his hips so that her legs were on either side of his jean-clad thighs. Her hands were on his chest, her bare sex right over his cock. Just his jeans separated him from that hot paradise, and he wanted those damn jeans gone.

She bent and her mouth pressed to his nipple. Cash hissed out a hard breath and when he felt the edge of her teeth on him, a ragged groan broke from him. He grabbed the sheets, fisting them in his hands as his body tensed. He knew what she was going to do even as her hands began to slide down his chest. Oh, fuck, yes, he knew.

He just wasn't sure his control was going to last. "Ana . . ." Cash tried to warn her.

But her hands were fumbling with his fly, opening the jeans and pulling down his zipper. He wasn't an underwear kind of guy, so his eager cock jumped toward her. Did she realize he'd been hard the minute he saw her standing in his doorway, with the light falling behind her? Her eyes had been so dark. Her lips so red.

She'd been so beautiful.

He'd tried to send her away. Tried to stand firm, but he suspected that when it came to Ana, he'd always be weak.

Her fingers closed around his cock as she kissed her way down his stomach. "You're so strong," she whispered, her breath blowing over him. "Just so you know, that's really hot."

A choked laugh came from him.

Then her fist pumped his cock, from base to tip, and he sure as hell stopped laughing. "*Ana*."

"It's about trust," she said, her voice pure temptation in the dark. "I want to know that you trust me completely."

He did. No hesitation.

"I want to know that you'd let me do anything with you that I wanted."

Baby, have at me. Did she think he'd argue? What man in his right mind would argue with her?

"And maybe . . . one day . . . I'll let you have anything you want."

His eyes widened. He wished he could see her.

Because that's the thing I want. To have Ana, to see her completely in the light. He wanted Ana to stop hiding. To know just how perfect she was to him.

Her hand pumped him again, base to tip, and then he felt her breath stirring over the head of his cock. "Ana . . ." *Baby, I am so close to the edge.*

Her lips closed around him. She licked him, she kissed him, she sucked him, she nearly drove him right out of his freaking mind. He felt the sheets start to tear beneath his grip, but he couldn't let go. Lust and need built ever higher in him, clawing his insides as he fought to hold back. He wasn't going to come, not until he was inside of Ana and she was climaxing all around him. Because when it came to Ana, he'd always have one rule.

Ladies fucking first.

"I like the way you taste."

His eyes squeezed shut. "Trust me, baby, I *love* the way you taste."

"Do you? Then give me your hand."

His hand flew toward her. She pushed it down, between her thighs, and she was wet for him. Wet and ready and so perfect. He thrust his fingers into her, wanting to push her toward the edge of desire, that rough precipice that he was already on.

Ana gave a low moan—beautiful music.

His fingers slid out of her, gliding over her clit, then he brought his hand to his mouth.

Tasted her. Just a taste. Not enough.

He needed a whole lot more.

But she was licking him again. Taking him in deeper, driving him nearly mad. He'd never wanted any woman the way he wanted her. Never would again. Only Ana.

She was seared into his soul. So deep inside, he'd never be free of her. Did she realize it?

Did she think it was just sex? Or did she know . . . with her, it was so much more.

His hands slid down and locked around her shoulders. "Ana . . . enough." Because he was too close to coming. He pulled her up and then she was taking over—sliding back into position with her legs straddling his hips. His cock shoved toward her sex, only this time, nothing was between them.

Nothing at all. Flesh to flesh.

Fuck. "Protection. I need—" He needed to thrust deep and hard into her, to explode when he was buried inside of her, but he'd made a vow to always protect Ana. He locked his hands on her hips and rolled them, putting her beneath him on the bed. Then he yanked out his wallet and the condom there. Good thing he'd had a backup. He ripped open the packet with his teeth and rolled on the condom. *Get more condoms, ASAP.*

Then he was pushing her legs apart. Catching her hands in his and pinning them to the bed. He thrust into her, long, hard, sinking as deep as he could go.

She arched against him, and he was lost. Control shot to hell and he didn't care. Faster, harder, deeper, he thrust into her. The bed pounded into the wall—and he didn't care.

Nothing mattered to him right then but Ana. Having her. Giving her as much pleasure as she could stand.

Again and again.

Her legs wrapped around his hips. Her body heaved up to meet him, perfectly matching his wild thrusts. Over and over. His hands slid from hers so that he could clasp her hips. He lifted her up even more, sinking deeper, claiming her fully—

She cried out his name and he felt her sex spasm around him.

He'd been waiting for her. Only then did he erupt, pumping into her on a release that never seemed to end. Pleasure flooded through him and he held her too tightly.

Slowly he became aware of his pounding heartbeat. Of the ragged rasp of his breath, of Ana's. He leaned down and kissed her once more. Soft. Light. Then he eased from her body. When she gave a little gasp, he realized that she was still riding aftershocks of release.

So sexy.

He went into the bathroom, ditched the condom, then came back with a warm cloth that he pressed between her legs. Ana didn't speak. He'd left the light on in the bathroom, and a faint glow spilled out—but only as far as the foot of the bed.

Cash headed back to the bathroom. He left the cloth, then paced toward the bed. "I don't want you to leave," Cash said. Simple. True. "I don't want you going back to your room. I want you to stay here, with me." That night would be the start. They could take things one day at a time. One night at a time.

And see where they wound up.

Ana's hand lifted and her fingers curled around his. "I'll stay."

Relief swept through him. He climbed into the bed and she slid toward him. His arms wrapped around her and he held her close. She seemed to fit, perfectly, as no one else had before.

"You should know," Ana murmured. "I have nightmares. So if I wake up screaming . . ."

His chest burned. "Then I'll just kiss you and tell you that no one will hurt you. That you're safe."

She snuggled closer against him. "That will be nice. No one's ever done that before."

That burn grew worse. He kissed her temple. "I'm here now." *And I'll tell you every night. And maybe, maybe one day, the nightmares will stop.*

THE KNIFE SLICED into her skin. It cut deep, and the pain was white-hot. Ana locked her teeth together and stared straight ahead . . . straight into her brother's horrified eyes. He was tied in the chair across from her, yanking and twisting as he tried to break free.

But he couldn't escape. Neither could she.

But she could stay silent.

Asher . . . her twin wasn't silent. He was screaming. *"Let my sister go! Stop it! Stop, please! Don't hurt her!"*

Asher didn't get it. The man with the knife enjoyed hurting her.

Another slice. Even deeper this time. Ana licked her lip and tasted blood. The first slice had been to her face. Only her attacker had stopped after that.

"Let's save her pretty face for later."

And the knife had gone into her body, again and again. She tried to keep her eyes open. Tried to keep looking at Asher. When the end came, she wanted *his* face to be the last thing that she saw. She wanted Asher to know that she hadn't been afraid. That she was strong.

Another slice of that knife and she could feel tears sliding down her cheeks. The pain was wrecking her. Destroying the girl she'd been. Leaving someone else—some*thing* else in her place.

Don't fear the pain. Don't tense when the knife hits you. Look at Asher. Look at him.

"Let my sister go, you fucking bastard! You want to hurt someone? Hurt me, not Ana! Let her go!"

Ana's eyes were sagging shut. Asher's voice was fading.

Was she dying? Ana didn't want to go out like this. Tied up, trapped. Some sick bastard's toy.

She didn't want to go out like this . . .

Her eyes closed.

And part of her—

"Ana, baby, wake up. You're having a nightmare."

Her eyes flew open. It was dark, only a thin stream

of light coming in from the open bathroom door, and he was there with her.

Cash. Holding her tight. Pressing a kiss to her temple.

"You're safe," he whispered. "No one is going to hurt you here. You're safe."

Her drumming heartbeat slowly returned to normal. She was in bed with him, his arms around her. He was lightly stroking her shoulder.

"You're safe."

Her eyes began to drift closed. The nightmare—the memory—was blessedly fading away. Maybe she would be able to sleep the rest of the night without the dark images haunting her. Maybe she'd be okay now.

"You're safe . . ." His voice followed her as she slipped back into sleep.

CHAPTER SIXTEEN

HER PHONE RANG, MAKING ANA JERK AWAKE. She blinked a moment, getting her bearings, and she realized she was still in bed with Cash. Naked, wrapped in his arms. And sunlight was pouring through the blinds.

She grabbed for the covers, yanking them over her body just as his eyes blinked open. "Ana?"

She clutched those covers tightly and crawled over him. Her phone was on the floor—somewhere. "It's my boss." She recognized the country music beat on the phone—it was a beat she'd picked out just for Gabe. She snagged the phone and answered, voice a bit breathless, "Ana."

"I've got the information you needed."

Cash was sitting up in bed. Only he wasn't covering his nudity.

And he looked way too good first thing in the morning.

"Our team started with Jonathan Bright. Just like you said, he was our key. We started with him and worked backward, and damn, but you were right on target."

Cash was staring at her, his expression tense.

"Cash is here," Ana said. "I'm going to put you on speaker so he can hear what you have to say, too, okay?"

There was a beat of silence.

Yes, so it's just after six a.m. and my voice was thick from sleep, and I just said that Cash was with me. Didn't take a rocket scientist to connect those dots.

Her finger swiped over the phone as she edged back toward the bed.

"Jonathan Bright." Gabe's voice carried easily. "Died at age sixty-two. He was in town, making what appeared to be his weekly shopping trip, when he was struck by a sudden heart attack. That was thirteen years ago."

Thirteen years.

"Before that attack, Jonathan led an . . . interesting life. When he was fifteen years old, his mother sent him to Bellhaven."

First piece of the puzzle, sliding into place. "You know why he went there?"

"No. Can't find anything other than an old admission log for him in the state system. No details on why or even how long he was admitted. But I did get another blip on my radar. Jonathan's father? Marcus Bright? He was an inmate at Wingate Penitentiary."

Cash climbed from the bed and yanked on his jeans.

"He'd murdered a coworker, stabbed him seventeen times in what court records described as a 'fit of rage'—and Marcus died a year after going to Wingate."

Wingate. Bellhaven. "Jonathan Bright sure has some powerful connections to our kill spots."

Cash nodded grimly. "The perp wanted us to see these connections. That's why he left the phone at Bright's cabin."

"Maybe the phone wasn't the only thing we were supposed to find out there," Ana said, trying to figure out what was happening. "Maybe we need to go back to that cabin and look again." Because if she just took the puzzle pieces on the surface . . .

Jonathan's father was incarcerated for a violent murder.

Jonathan was institutionalized by his mother when he was a teen.

Jonathan lived alone, in a secluded cabin, limiting his contact with the outside world.

She licked her lips. "If you look at his life, the guy would sure start to fit the profile for a killer."

Cash's brows lowered. "Faye told me about a news clipping she found at the cabin—for a girl who'd gone missing."

"What girl?" Ana demanded.

Cash brushed by her and pulled out his phone. He scrolled through the photos. "Got her to send me a pic before the guys took it in for evidence. It was an abduction that happened years ago . . ." His shoulder brushed her arm and she squinted as she stared at his phone.

Area girl disappears . . . family desperate for her return.

She scanned the article. A thirteen-year-old girl named Jenny Love had vanished while walking home from her bus stop. Her parents were pleading for any information that might lead to her return . . .

"Maybe Jonathan knew what happened to that girl." *Because maybe he was the reason she went missing.*

Gabe cleared his throat, the sound drifting over the line. "Did some research on that end, too. Seems that while Jonathan was living in that cabin . . . three boys and two girls all went missing, never to be seen again. One of them is a cold case file that you were working, Ana. Cathy Wise."

Cathy Wise. The first time that Cash had appeared at LOST, Ana had been looking at Cathy's file. "She was thirteen when she vanished. Blond hair, blue eyes. She'd gone to visit her grandmother in Virginia. The girl went out one day for a walk and never came back."

"All the vics that vanished in the area had a similar story—all were twelve or thirteen, right at the age where the cops first thought maybe they were runaways, so valuable damn time was wasted. The kids weren't taken too close together—looked like the abductions spanned ten years. A boy named William Marshall—Billy—he was taken first. Cathy was taken last. She was taken . . ." Gabe's sigh filled the line, "Four months before Jonathan Bright died. After his death, there were no more missing kids who fit the age profile or abduction style."

Cash's eyes glittered. "We need to get cadaver dogs out to his cabin."

Ana nodded. "We're . . . we're sure Jonathan's death was from natural causes? A heart attack, that's what you said?"

"No autopsy was performed. No records of one. Local coroner just called it on the scene based on evidence."

She clutched the covers a bit tighter. "Thank you, Gabe."

"You need anything else, Ana?"

"Sarah's profile," Cash said. "I want her take on this case."

"She should be finishing up with that soon." Gabe paused. "Sarah's actually on her way up there."

And Ana knew exactly why—Sarah was afraid their perp had killed her father. Whatever she'd determined in her profile so far, well, it had apparently just reaffirmed that belief.

"I gave her the jet. After what Ana told me happened last night"—*because, yes, Ana had called in to brief her boss*—"I didn't want to take any chances. LOST will be helping the FBI, whether your boss wants that assistance or not."

They talked for a few more moments, then Ana hung up the phone. She hurried into the bathroom, dressing quickly, and she heard Cash talking in the other room.

Ordering the cadaver dogs.

If bodies were at the cabin, they would find them.

THE HOSPITAL WAS quiet. Nurses bustled in and out of the rooms, and machines beeped softly. Cash glanced down at the gleaming floor, seeing his reflection beam back at him. Ana was at his side, her steps sure, confident.

A search team and cadaver dogs would be meeting them at Jonathan Bright's old cabin. But before Cash and Ana joined that team . . .

He wanted to talk with Dr. Summers.

"She's not quite herself yet," the doctor to Cash's right

said. Dr. Anthony Paul. He'd been treating Dr. Summers. "Blood tests showed a very, very high amount of drugs in her system."

"What kind of drugs?" Ana asked.

"A real cocktail," he said, shaking his head. "Antipsychotic drugs, depressants, stimulants. You name it, and it was probably in that blend. Those drugs should *never, never* be mixed that way. Hallucinations—both visual and auditory—as well as depression and aggression result from that combination. When Dr. Summers was first brought in, we had to strap her down on the exam table, both for her safety and for the safety of the hospital staff treating her."

Cash felt the faint pull of his stitches. "Definitely a good idea," he muttered.

They turned left and entered another corridor. A security guard gave him a nod.

"We took your concern about the patient's safety very seriously," Dr. Paul said. "A guard has been on this floor every moment."

Good to know.

Dr. Paul opened the door to room 604. There was a slow, steady beat from inside.

Cash started to cross the threshold, but Dr. Paul held up his hand, stopping him. "The patient is much more stable, but I would caution you . . . because of the drugs, her memory is going to be skewed. The things she says may not be accurate."

He was sure the perp had been counting on that fact. *If* Dr. Summers had survived, nothing she said would be admissible in court because she would be deemed an unreliable witness.

Smart bastard.

The doctor's hand dropped and they all entered the room.

"She's still strapped down," Ana said.

At her words, Dr. Summers's eyes flew open.

"For her safety," Dr. Paul murmured. "And ours."

Dr. Summers squinted as she looked at Ana. Then her stare slowly trekked to Cash. When she saw him, she stiffened.

"Hello, Dr. Summers," Cash said, keeping his voice soft and nonthreatening. "I was hoping you could answer some questions for me." Just because her testimony might not hold up in court, well, that didn't mean he wasn't curious about what she had to say.

A shudder went over the length of her body. The machine beside her beeped faster.

"Dr. Summers, do you remember what happened to you?" Cash's voice was still soft. Her gaze darted around the room.

"It's okay," Dr. Paul said. "You're safe here, remember?"

But her hands were twisting against the straps. "Monsters."

Ana eased closer. "What about the monsters?"

"They were everywhere." Her voice was husky, thick. "He told me . . . he told me that I should kill the monsters. They had to be st-stopped."

Dr. Paul shook his head. "I'm sorry. She's still suffering the effects of the medication—"

"Then he said . . . I *was* a monster." Dr. Summers twisted her bound wrist. "He . . . he put the knife on the floor and he left me there."

Oh, Jesus. Cash realized just what the perp had intended. *For Dr. Summers to take her own life, the same way her patients had.*

"Did you see his face?" Ana asked her.

Dr. Summers gave a jerky nod. "I . . . think so."

Excitement pulsed in Cash's blood. "What did he look like?"

Dr. Summers smiled. "I have no idea." She started to whistle.

Fuck.

"Maybe try coming back again in a few hours." Dr. Paul scanned her chart. "Or tomorrow. Her mind will be clearer then—"

She stopped whistling. "He was so nice the first time we met."

Cash heard Ana's sharply indrawn breath. "The first time?" Cash pressed.

"When he brought his sister to me," Dr. Summers said, nodding. "He had to commit her, for her protection." For an instant, she sounded like her old self. "She was a danger to herself and to others. She'd attacked him just the week before, he showed me the healing wounds. Attacked him. Tried to kill herself. He was just devastated." She sighed. "But after a month with us, she'd shown such progress. She didn't seem violent at all. That's how we were able to move her to be with a more general population in the facility." But then sadness chased across her face. "I didn't know what was going to happen to her. That wasn't my fault. She should have never even been in the violent offender area. She snuck past the guards and went in there . . . Luckily, I stopped him before he hurt her too much."

"Chassity Pope," Ana said. "You're talking about her, aren't you?"

Dr. Summers started to whistle again.

"Dr. Summers?" Cash prompted. "Tell us—"

"I would like ice cream." A broad smile split her lips. "Ice cream and lemonade and no monsters." She shook her head. "No monsters for me. Not today . . ."

Dr. Paul sighed. "She's going in and out as the drugs flush from her system. And you have to keep in mind, even the things she's saying . . . she could be making them up. Twisting real events with the shadows in her mind."

"I think she knows exactly what she's saying," Ana retorted. She inclined her head toward Dr. Paul. "And you should damn well get that woman some ice cream. I think she's earned it."

Cash and Ana exited the room. Their steps were fast as they headed down the hallway. As soon as they cleared the hospital, he turned to face off with her.

"We need to talk with Chassity Pope," Ana said.

Hell, yeah, they did. They also needed to talk with her brother. And he wasn't quite convinced that Chassity was crazy. Maybe that had just been a ruse to get her inside the psychiatric facility. *To get access to Forrest? And to Summers?* Had they both been targets all along?

He pulled out his phone. "I'll get Faye to head the search at Bright's property. Then you and I will be heading to River View."

BUT CHASSITY POPE wasn't at River View.

"I'm sorry," the temporary administrator-in-charge said, wringing her hands. "Her brother came in right after Dr. Summers was—was taken. He insisted on re-moving his sister from the facility. Said she had been endangered here and if we didn't want the press to hear about their story, we would expedite her paper-work." Her wide-eyed gaze darted between them. "I gave approval for her dismissal. I mean . . . a family member was there for her. He was the one who'd first admitted her, so it was his choice to take her out. He had the legal right—all of his papers were in order."

"I want those papers," Cash barked. "Now."

With this damn case, they went . . . *two fucking steps forward.*

Three steps back.

The administrator hurried away.

"Her work was done here," Ana said. "So there was no need for her to stay in the hospital."

He swore. "Do you think she was faking all along?"

Ana's gaze turned distant. "I saw her in the com-munity room. She *looked* hurt. Looked like a victim. I just . . . I don't know."

"I didn't think two of them were working together." But he should have considered that shit. The crimes were so big, so elaborate…hell, yes, they would be easier to pull off with two people. "Should've seen it sooner."

"Here!" The administrator was back, clutching the file before her. When Cash reached for it, though, she hesitated. "Do you have a court order?"

Cash growled. "What I have is Dr. Summers lying in a hospital bed. I have her telling me that Chas-sity Pope's brother put her there. And I need to know where I can find him."

Ana pointed to the surveillance camera. "And if that

thing was on when he came to get his sister, we need his picture."

The administrator nodded. "It was . . . I—I can get the image for you."

Hell, yes. Hell, *yes*. Now they were talking.

HIS EYES OPENED. He stared at the wooden beams above him, his heart pounding as the nightmare slowly faded.

Running. Running.

He heard laughter from the other room. High, mocking. Shit. He jumped from the bed and hurried toward the kitchen. "Chassity!"

She spun around, a knife in her hand. "Don't call me that."

But he'd grown used to that name. They'd used it for the longest.

"It's not my name." She smiled at him. The knife was still in her hand. She brought it down, hard, slicing into a melon. "I don't have to pretend any longer." And again, she laughed.

He breathed, slow, deep. "Be careful. I don't want you to cut yourself."

Her smile stretched a bit. "You always take such good care of me."

He tried. Unfortunately, he was failing.

He could see that she was starting to slip away again. *She wasn't strong enough for River View. I should have seen that.*

"THESE ARE HER drawings," Ana said. They were in Chassity Pope's old room at River View. A fast call to the FBI executive assistant director and they'd gotten full access to every bit of data that River View had on their former patient. Court order? More like a court demand . . . one that had come with a push from the EAD.

"I saw her doing this one the other day." Ana held up a piece of paper. Shit, it looked like a river of blood.

"Guess she likes dolls," Ana added. She offered Cash other images.

Sketches of dolls with round faces and dark eyes.

And a red river was behind them all.

"She seemed so fragile that day. I looked at her and I saw a victim."

"Maybe that was what she wanted you to see." What she'd wanted them all to see. Talk about the perfect disguise. He hadn't heard from Faye yet, but he knew the cadaver dogs should be arriving at Bright's cabin any moment. Would they find bodies out there? Bodies that were linked to Bright and to Chassity Pope?

Chassity Pope had appeared to be a victim. Was she really a killer?

"WE NEED TO get out of town, Chassity. Lie low for a while."

Her shoulders tensed. "I've asked you to stop calling me that. I'm done with her." She tapped her chin. "I want to be someone new."

He knew this game. They'd certainly played it often enough. And fine, if they were going to hide out for a time and plan their next move, they'd both need new identities. It was a good thing he knew who to hit up to get all that paperwork to go with a new identity. But forgeries cost a pretty penny, though. "Who do you want to be?"

She twirled her long blond hair. "I think I want to be . . . Ana."

He stiffened. "Ana?"

She looked at him from beneath her lashes. "You like that name, don't you? Because you seem to like her." She came around the counter and touched his shoulder. "You like her so much you have a permanent reminder of her now."

"I like you."

"And you like her." She pouted. "That wasn't part of our plan."

"She's like us, Chas—" He cut himself off before he said her name. He'd just gotten into the habit of calling her that. "She's not bad. She wants to stop the monsters."

"I think she is a monster. I think *she* needs to be stopped."

His hands flattened on the table. "I want you to stay away from her."

"Why? So you can get close to her?" And she suddenly seemed very, very sane. "Isn't that *your* plan? To find someone who understands you? Someone who gets you? You think you can connect with her?" Anger darkened her eyes. "I've been with you all this time and you're going to throw me away for her."

He rose, shoving back his chair. The legs screeched as they skidded across the floor. "I wouldn't throw you away for anyone. You know that." But he also knew . . .

Sweetheart, you didn't come out sane. I tried to stop

*him. I tried to help you. But I was too late. He broke
you. With his torture and his pain, he made sure you
were shattered into a million different pieces.*

He'd tried to put those pieces back together, but they
hadn't fit just right, her mind had been different.

And each day, he feared that she was slipping further and further away from him.

One day, would she become one of the monsters?
And if she did . . .

Was he really going to be able to stop her?

"THE NAMES ARE FAKE," Cash said as he paced in the
local sheriff's office. He'd made the place their base of
command, needing a spot where all the law enforcement personnel could congregate. "Just got a hit back
from the FBI . . ." He turned and met Ana's gaze. "The
real Chassity Pope died when she was four years old.
Her brother Kurt died with her. Their whole family
was killed in a car accident."

He'd put up an evidence board behind him. And
right in the middle of that board, he had a picture of
Chassity Pope and her "brother" Kurt. The picture of
Kurt was grainy, but they could see that he was a tall
male, fit, with dark hair swept back from his forehead.

As soon as she'd seen the photo of Kurt at River
View, Ana had tensed.

He'd known they were looking at the same "cop"
she'd seen the night before. Ana had met with a sketch
artist, and she'd talked to that guy, giving him all of
the details she could on the cop she'd seen.

The sketch was beside the grainy image. *We can see
you now, asshole.*

"A killing team," Sarah Jacobs said. She'd arrived an hour before, and they'd quickly brought her up to speed. "You don't see them often, not in cases like this. Most serials are territorial. Dominant. They don't exactly play well with others."

"I don't think these two are playing," Ana said. "And what they're doing . . . do you think they even consider it killing?"

Sarah's lips thinned. "I think they consider it justice."

Yeah, that was what Cash had feared, too.

Sarah rose from her chair and walked toward the pictures. "My profile will change again—I didn't have them working together, so everything I have . . . it's flawed. And I don't like making mistakes." She squared her shoulders. "So let me just take a step back and tell you what I *do* know about killing teams." She pointed to the photos. "One of them is dominant. One plans the acts. The other follows. Maybe the other is even bait."

"Chassity could have been the bait," Ana decided. "We were buying the idea that Forrest attacked her—maybe that wasn't what happened at all. Maybe she was playing a role, and that role involved getting him punished, getting him sent to the quiet room so he'd be away from everyone else."

Sarah inclined her head. "And I think Bernie Tate would have opened up much more quickly to a woman. After all, he never saw women as threats. Just prey."

Ana stared at Chassity's picture. "So she's the perfect prey?"

"Perhaps." Sarah was still hesitant. "It's so hard to say yet. Two killers. That means twice as much danger."

"All the agents and local authorities have pictures of

these two," Cash said, tapping his fingers on the conference table. "APBs are out for them. I know I hit the bastard when I fired last night, but no hospital has reported treating anyone who matches his description."

Sarah shook her head. "I don't think he'd go in for treatment. That would expose him too much and he knows it. That would—"

The door flew open. A young deputy stood there, cheeks flushed. "We just found the motorcycle," he said, beaming. "Turned up behind an old service station on Highway 18."

Excitement heated in Cash's blood. "Get a crime scene team out there right away. I want every inch of that motorcycle and the area around it checked. The bastard might have left prints, DNA—*something* that can lead us to his true identity."

"Yes, sir!" The guy snapped to attention then hurried away.

Cash started to pace. "The pieces are coming together." They had suspects. They had the abandoned ride. They had—

His phone rang. Cash pulled it from his pocket and saw Faye's image on the screen. He answered the call and put the phone to his ear. "How are the dogs working out?"

There was a beat of silence. "Sir . . ." Faye said, her voice very formal. "I think you're going to want to come out here."

"Some deputies just found the motorcycle. I need to—"

"We've got three bodies so far."

He stiffened.

"Not bodies, sorry." She sounded flustered. "Remains. Bones. That's all that's left. And they're . . . they're small bodies, sir. Like kids." Her voice thickened. "They're all lined up in a row. The dogs found them about twenty yards from the cabin. He planted them underneath a willow tree. Left them in shallow graves. We'd barely broken the surface when we saw them."

A weeping willow.

Sonofabitch. "I'll be right there." He hung up the phone. Ana and Sarah were both watching him, their eyes wide. Cash cleared his throat. "Ana, you were right."

She frowned.

"Jonathan Bright's cabin was picked for a reason. The dogs just found three kids out there—the crew dug up their bones."

CHAPTER SEVENTEEN

THE LOCAL ME'S EXAM LAB WAS SO COLD. ANA shivered as she stared at the three black bags that had been brought in to the facility just moments before.

Bones were in those bags. Children.

"I'm betting they'll match up with the missing kids that disappeared from the area," Cash said, his arm brushing against her. "The ones Gabe told us about? Jonathan Bright . . . fuck, he must have taken them. Taken them and buried them out at his cabin so they could never leave him."

"We're missing two." Two little bodies. Because Gabe had said that five children went missing. Three boys. Two girls. Nausea rose in her stomach as she stared at those bags. The kids were always the hardest for her to handle. So young, so innocent.

So helpless.

Ana's finger slid across her upper lip. "Do you think one of them is Cathy?" Little Cathy Wise. "Her mom is still looking for her. She's the one who hired LOST. But there was so little evidence to go on with Cathy's case. No witnesses. No clues. She'd just vanished."

Because she was in the ground? Under Jonathan Bright's willow tree?

God, but she hated the darkness out there.

The ME, a tall, distinguished, African American man with silver at his temples, cleared his throat. "It's going to take me a while for these exams. I have the list of missing children that Gabe Spencer sent over, but we'll need to compare dental records. DNA. It's not going to be a fast process."

No, Ana knew it wouldn't.

"There's no point in you staying here tonight," he continued. *Dr. Thaddeus Cole.* He was the only ME around for miles—the one that several counties had to use. He had a small lab just outside of Langmire. "I'll call you as soon as I know anything, but the positive IDs . . . just be prepared that those could take days."

Or weeks.

"We know," Sarah said softly. She'd come with them to see the scene for herself. "It's not the first time we've found remains this way. On TV shows, they identify them fast. Within hours, minutes." Her smile was sad. "Real life doesn't always work that way."

No, it didn't.

"Was any clothing found with them?" Ana asked. "Any personal possessions at all?"

The ME shook his head.

"Agent Comwell is still at the scene," Cash said. "If she finds anything else, we'll know right away."

Ana rocked forward onto the balls of her feet. "Can you at least tell us . . . are the victims male? Female?"

Dr. Cole hesitated. "It's harder to tell with children's

bones. You can see small differences, but most signs don't become more defined until puberty."

The kids had been twelve and thirteen when they vanished.

"I don't want to rush," he said quietly. "I want to take my time and do things right. I think they deserve that."

Yes, yes, they did. She shoved back her hair. "I understand."

"As soon as I know," he said again. "I'll contact you. Until then, why don't you all get some sleep?" Dr. Cole nodded. "I'll be the one burning the midnight oil."

Ana turned and followed Sarah to the door, shuffling along slowly. It had been a bitch of a day. After they'd left the psychiatric hospital, they'd rushed out to Bright's cabin.

And they'd seen the evidence tape and flag rows, organized so carefully by the crime scene techs. Seen the bones peeking up from the black dirt.

Small bones.

Lives cut too short.

She heard the rumble of Cash's voice as he spoke to the ME, but Ana didn't glance back. She followed Sarah outside, needing to get some fresh air.

As soon as they cleared the building, Sarah put her hands on her knees and leaned forward. "I hate it when kids are hurt." Her hair fell over her face. "Kids are the most innocent. We're supposed to protect them."

Ana tried to get the scent of the ME's lab out of her nose. Antiseptic. Bleach. Death.

"When we get the files on the kids at LOST," Sarah continued grimly, "and we see the age progression photos that are created . . . the way they *could* look . . . I always hope that maybe they are still out there. Maybe they don't even know who they are. A mind is such a fragile thing. So easily broken."

"Especially when it has help," Ana finished. The night air was cold and she needed that chill. Ana exhaled. She was bone tired but more than that . . .

Her heart hurt.

Three little bodies. Lives lost too soon. Parents who had looked and looked. Their kids would finally be coming home, and it broke Ana's heart. "I didn't think we'd come home."

Sarah straightened.

Behind Ana, the door creaked open.

"When Asher and I were taken . . . those bastards had already killed our mom. They were using their knives on me. I was sure we were going to die." And she'd been so close in age to those who'd gone missing in Virginia.

I was fourteen. Still a child, until that day.

Her childhood had died with each slice of the knife.

"I was tied up and hurting and I was sure I'd never be free again. There were things I'd wanted to do." Her lips curled. "Dance. Be on a stage. Graduate high school. Go to Mexico. Fall in love." Ana shook her head. "And when I was under the knife, I said goodbye to all of that. Death was coming, and it hurt so much—not because of the knife—but because I knew what I would miss." She had to blink away tears. "Knowing what you lose . . . it nearly rips you apart."

"I'm sorry, Ana."

"You shouldn't be sorry for me. I made it out. I have

my chance at life." Even as she said those words, Ana stiffened. They were true. She *did* have her chance, but she kept living in fear. Fear of killers that were only ghosts now.

Ghosts in her mind.

"I have my chance," she said again. Her thumb jerked toward the building behind her. "They don't." They just had black body bags. The tattered remains of families that were still waiting for them.

The families that would finally get to say good-bye.

She looked over her shoulder and saw Cash standing in the shadows, watching her.

Sarah coughed—a very delicate, very fake cough. "I think I'll go do some work in my motel room. You two . . . I'll see you in the morning."

Yes. The morning. The bright day.

The victims.

Ana offered her hand to Cash. He came forward and his fingers curled around hers. "Let's get out of here, Cash," Ana said. Because her chest felt too tight. Her eyes burned. And she couldn't stop seeing those three black bags.

He nodded.

THE BODIES HAD been found. Dug up. Brought into the light. When he'd swung by the cabin, he'd seen the buzz of activity. He'd made sure not to get too close, not this time.

He'd wanted those bodies to be found. He'd wanted the parents to know what had happened to their kids. So many times he'd thought about picking up a phone and calling them. Telling them what had happened.

He'd studied carefully, learning how to make a call like that without being traced. He hadn't wanted anyone to come find him.

But . . . in the end . . . Chassity had convinced him not to make the calls. She'd said there was another way. A better way.

He stared at the ME's office. The dead were in there. They'd been brought into that building in zipped black bags. Those bags didn't seem like such a better way to him. But he'd given in to Chassity, the way he usually did.

Guilt could make a man do so many things.

Ana was there now, walking away from the squat building. She was holding hands with Agent Knox, like they were tra-la-la-ing off into the sunset or some shit. Kids were dead—bones were waiting in that building—and she was just walking away.

He'd expected better from her.

Knox was rubbing off on her. Obviously.

The media was blasting about the case. So many news vans were in town, lining up and filling the small main street. It was a feeding frenzy, and he had to be careful.

Knox had gotten a grainy picture of him from River View. The agent had posted that picture and one of Chassity. Said they were "persons of interest" in the investigation. Bull. Knox wanted to lock them both up, but that wasn't happening.

He pulled his ball cap low and turned away. A few moments later, he was in Chassity's Beetle and driving away. He had supplies on the seat next to him—hair dye that he'd swiped from the drug store for Chassity.

They'd cut her long hair, dye it, and she'd be able to pass for a new person.

She'd specifically requested the dark dye.

Her dark hair will be same shade as Ana's.

His hand tightened around the wheel.

He'd go darker with his hair, too. Maybe black or brown. Or he could shave it. Something different. Throw on some glasses, and he'd be good, good enough to fool most people. That was the thing about folks . . .

People don't pay attention to the shit around them. They barely give anyone a second glance. Don't look too hard at them and they never look too hard at you.

Another lesson. One he'd never wanted. He hadn't wanted any of the lessons, dammit. He hadn't wanted this life. This pain. But his choices had all been taken away from him.

The things that sick bastard made me do. He ensured that I'd always be tainted. A killer, just like him. He made me . . .

The engine vibrated and he hit a hole in the road as he turned on the path that would take him to Chassity. The lights were off, the cabin was dark. Another holdover from long ago.

When night falls, shut off the lights. No one will ever see you.

He parked the car. Grabbed their supplies and headed inside.

This particular cabin had been their base, on and off, for quite a while. He knew with certainty that the owner wasn't coming back. The dead never came back.

The cabin was pitch black inside and for a moment he tensed. *Too quiet.* "Chassity?" Had she left? How—on foot? She—

She turned on a flashlight, holding it just below her chin. "Boo."

He slammed the door shut. "Trying to be funny? 'Cause that's not—" He broke off. She'd already cut her hair. Cut it . . .

In the same style that Ana had.

"Didn't I tell you not to call me Chassity?" She plucked the supplies from his hand. "That's not who I am any longer. I'm Ana."

"No, you're not."

She was walking ahead of him, the flashlight bobbing in one hand.

"You're *not* Ana." Anger roughened his voice.

She swung back toward him.

"You're Cathy." Maybe she needed that reminder to yank her back. "You are—"

She hit him, slamming that flashlight into his face. *"Cathy is dead!"*

He backed up a step. It had been a long time since she'd attacked him. So long that he'd thought she was better.

But she was swinging the flashlight again. "Dead, dead, dead!"

He hadn't lied when he'd gone to see Dr. Summers the first time. Cathy was violent. She had attacked before.

It was just hard to blame her. She'd been hurt so much. Hurt while he could only stand there and watch her pain. She'd been a victim back then.

Only I'm afraid she's gone too far now. I think she's becoming one of the monsters.

She swung the light at him again, but he caught her wrist. Hating it, he ground her bones together. She screamed, and the flashlight fell from her fingers.

"Don't be like him," he whispered to her. "Please, don't." *That's what he wanted. He wanted to make us both freaks like him.*

She started crying. He kept his tight grip on her wrist. He didn't want to break it.

He didn't want to break her.

"Don't be," he warned.

CASH SHUT AND locked the motel room door. *His* room. Just where Ana wanted to be.

I don't want to miss my chance.

He turned off the light just inside the door.

She stood near the bed, watching him. Her heartbeat seemed too fast in her chest.

Cash headed toward the bathroom and turned off the light in there. Now the only illumination came from the lamp on the side of the bed. He reached for the lamp—

"Cash." His name came from her—a little rough, a little shaky but that was only to be expected. She was terrified. "Leave the light on."

She saw the tremble in his fingers.

Then he clenched his hand into a fist. "You want to talk?" He turned toward her. "Ana, we'll do anything you want. We'll—"

"I want to make love with you." She wanted to stop thinking about death and pain and killers that escaped justice for too long. And . . . "I want to take a chance with you."

"Baby . . ."

"Leave the light on." Her stomach was in knots. "Though at any moment, be warned, I may tell you to turn it off. I may lose my nerve."

"Not you. You're the strongest woman I've ever met."

She didn't always feel strong. Sometimes she felt scared and confused. Hurt.

Damaged, deep on the inside.

Warped.

"Will you . . . will you sit on the bed?" It would be easier if he wasn't standing up, all big and strong and watchful. She needed a position of power. He had to sit and—

"Anything you want, Ana. Always." The bed groaned beneath his weight.

"Don't touch me, not until I'm done, okay?" Because if he touched her she might not be able to get through this. His touch always did strange things to her.

Just as he did.

"I won't."

Good. Okay. The lamp was still on. The light was oddly soft. She eased out a low breath.

This won't be taken away from me. Not anymore.

Because she realized that it was something she'd given to the bastards who'd hurt her. Simple joy in her own body. Confidence.

Her fingers curled over the hem of her shirt. She lifted it up and tossed the shirt behind her. Goose bumps rose on her stomach.

She kicked off her shoes. Ditched her socks. Realized this was probably the unsexist strip tease ever—

"Don't stop," Cash rasped.

She swallowed and her hands went to her waistband. She unhooked her jeans. Slid down the zipper. The hiss seemed incredibly loud to her, nearly as loud as her racing heart.

Ana pushed the jeans over her hips. She let them fall to the floor, then stepped out of them, clad just in her bra and her boy shorts underwear.

The scars sliced across her stomach and her sides.

His gaze was slowly traveling over her body. Seeing all of those scars.

For just a second, she closed her eyes, almost feeling dizzy.

I won't let them take this from me.

Her shoulders straightened. Her eyes opened. She lifted her hands, putting them behind her back, and she undid the clasp of her bra. Then she let the soft material slide over her arms as she dropped the bra, too.

Cash was silent, but his jaw had hardened.

He hadn't touched her. He'd followed the rules. But . . .

She wasn't done. Not yet.

Her hands were toying with the sides of her underwear. Not a sexy tease, just . . . a fear movement. A delaying action.

No more delaying.

She shoved the underwear down her legs and then she stepped closer to the bed. Closer to the light. There was nowhere to hide now, and she didn't want to hide. She was sick of the dark.

I want the light.

His gaze slid over her, from the top of her head all the way down to her feet. He didn't miss anything. His green eyes darkened. Gleamed. And—

"Do I get to touch you yet?"

She barely managed a nod.

"Thank Christ." His hands curled around her hips and he pulled her between his spread thighs. "Ana Young, you have the most gorgeous breasts that I've ever seen in my life."

She blinked. He was—he was talking about her breasts?

"Knew they tasted like heaven. Now I see they look like heaven, too." And he put his mouth on her nipple. He licked and sucked and her fingers sank into the thickness of his hair.

Heat began to pool. Her sex ached.

"So sexy." He kissed his way to her other breast. His tongue slid over her nipple and she moaned. His fingers tightened on her waist. "You are the most gorgeous woman I've ever seen."

Ana started to shake her head.

"Stop." His voice snapped out, hard. Angry.

She stared down at him.

"You. Are. Gorgeous." He gave a rough laugh. "Ana, I am so turned on by you right now that my dick is going to have a permanent impression from my zipper. I look at you, and I nearly explode. You're the sexiest thing I've ever seen." And once more, he licked her nipple. "Sweet pink nipples." He sucked. Nipped.

She moaned.

He kissed a hot path down her stomach. "Pure temptation."

Her knees wanted to buckle. It was a good thing he had a grip on her waist.

"And your sex . . . fucking hell, woman, I think you might drive me insane." His hand slid around and pressed to the front of her sex. "Sweet . . . hot."

She was getting hotter with every moment that passed. *Wetter.*

He lifted her up, pulling her toward his body and then sitting her on top of him. Her legs curled around him.

"Ana, you are beautiful."

Her heart drummed faster.

"You are sexy. You are gorgeous. You've been starring in my wet dreams for about two years."

Her lips parted in surprise.

"But I swear, the reality of you is so much better than any dream. So much better." He kissed her, driving his tongue inside of her mouth.

Something inside of her seemed to break open. The last of her fear vanished and she kissed him back with a wild ferocity. She could feel his arousal pressing against her. Thick and hard and long. He hadn't been lying. He did want her. He did think she was sexy. Scars and all, he was touching her, caressing her, rocking his cock against her.

The scars don't matter.

So she just . . . she let them go. Her hand curled around his shoulders. "I want you right now." In her. Deep. Driving them both to oblivion. "I want you, Cash." Only him.

Always . . . him.

His hand slid down between them. She arched her hips, making room for him to unzip his fly. His cock

shoved toward her, she felt the hard length against her
sex. She wanted him in—

"Condom," Cash gritted. "I'll get—"

"Are you clean?"

"Yes."

"So am I. And there is no risk of pregnancy. I'm
covered. This time, I want to be this way with you. I
need to be this way." Flesh to flesh. She'd never been
this way with another man. She wanted to give everything she had to him.

Just as she wanted to take everything that he had.

He positioned his cock. Their gazes held. Then his
hands were curling tightly around her hips once more
as he jerked her down onto him.

Her breath heaved out. He filled her so completely.
Skin to skin.

"I love you, Ana."

She shook her head. No, he hadn't said—

"I love you."

Then he was lifting her up and down, making her
move faster, his cock driving deep. The angle of her
body, the way she pressed against him . . .

There was no restraint. There was no holding back.
It was just them. Giving everything. Surrendering.

Igniting.

Her climax hit her, stealing her breath, shaking her
body. Her sex clamped around his cock, so greedy for
more, and he growled out her name. She felt the hot
splash of his release inside of her. And it just made her
pleasure last and last. It made her need *grow*.

Not enough. Her breath was heaving out. Sweat covering her body. She should be fulfilled but . . .

"Baby, I'm not stopping."

He rolled her on the bed, positioning her beneath him. His cock was swelling inside of her, hardening again as she stared up at him with wide eyes.

"You *are* the sexiest woman I've ever seen. But for that . . ." He gave her a wicked grin. "There are consequences."

Consequences?

He thrust into her.

Her sex—already wet from their releases and so very sensitive—quivered.

"I don't think I can ever get enough of you. I could have you forever." He withdrew, then thrust deep. "And it wouldn't be enough."

Her legs rose, her hips arched.

"I'm going to let go this time," Cash said. "I'm going to—"

"Hard," Ana panted. "Fast. Make me come again."

"Hell, yes, baby. Anything." He bent and kissed her. "For you."

Make me come. Make the darkness fade. Make me feel alive.

Taking a chance . . . with him.

Living . . . with him.

He tossed away his shirt. Her nails sank into his skin. He drove into her, fierce and wild and rough, and she laughed, nearly feeling high with the pleasure. Pleasure. Power.

Life.

Again and again, he thrust into her. Strong, deep thrusts that lifted her off the bed. That had her head tipping back.

He kissed her breasts. Teased her nipples. Then he caught her legs and lifted them up, pushing them over his shoulders so that he could get into her even deeper.

She moaned and jerked beneath him. Every thrust had the length of his cock gliding over her clit as he plunged into her.

The second climax hit her even harder than the first. She gasped out his name as the pleasure pulsed through her, seeming to charge every nerve ending in her body.

He stilled as the orgasm left her trembling. He was full and so thick inside of her, and her sex was squeezing him with the contractions of her release. Squeezing—

He came. Another hot release inside of her as he growled her name.

In the aftermath, their breath panted out. They fell together on that bed, and his arms just seemed to go naturally around her. Ana didn't rush to pull the covers over her. She didn't move at all, except to snuggle a little closer to Cash.

I love you, Ana. His words whispered through her mind once more.

"Do you want me to turn off the light?" His voice rumbled against her.

But she gave a slight shake of her head. "No, I want to leave it on. I want to stay in the light for a while, with you."

It would be the first time she'd fallen asleep in the light in so very long.

He pressed his lips to her temple, and Ana had never felt safer.

THE KNIFE SLICED into her skin. It cut deep, and the pain was white-hot. Ana locked her teeth together and stared straight ahead . . . straight into her brother's horrified eyes. He was tied in the chair across from her, yanking and twisting as he tried to break free.

But he couldn't escape. Neither could she.

But she could stay silent.

Asher . . . her twin wasn't silent. He was screaming. *Let my sister go! Stop it! Stop, please! Don't hurt her!*

Asher didn't get it. The man with the knife . . . he enjoyed hurting her.

Another slice. Even deeper this time. Ana licked her lip and tasted blood. The first slice had been to her face. Only her attacker had stopped after that.

"Let's save her pretty face for later."

And the knife had gone into her body, again and again. She tried to keep her eyes open. Tried to keep looking at Asher. When the end came, she wanted his face to be the last thing that she saw. She wanted Asher to know that she hadn't been afraid. That she was strong.

Another slice of that knife and she could feel tears sliding down her cheeks. The pain was wrecking her. Destroying the girl she'd been. Leaving someone else—some*thing* else in her place.

Don't fear the pain. Don't tense when the knife hits you. Look at Asher. Look at him.

"Let my sister go, you fucking bastard! You want to hurt someone? Hurt me, not Ana! Let her go!"

Ana's eyes were sagging shut. Asher's voice was fading.

Was she dying? Ana didn't want to go out like this. Tied up, trapped. Some sick bastard's toy.

She didn't want to go out like this—

"Ana." Her eyes opened. The light still spilled from the lamp. Cash's arms were around her. "You're safe, Ana."

Her breath slipped out as the memories faded. "Tell me again."

"You're safe, Ana."

She shook her head. "Not that. Tell me that you love me again."

And he did. No hesitation. "I love you, Ana."

She was smiling when she fell back into her dreams.

CHAPTER EIGHTEEN

ANA'S PHONE WOKE HER, THE LOUD CRY JAR-ring. Her eyes flew open and she glanced around.

There was plenty of light in the room, but the light still spilled from the lamp. The clock on the nightstand showed her that it was just a little past five a.m.

"Ana?" Cash's voice was a deep rumble.

Her phone rang again. Was it the ME, calling with news?

Or is the killer?

She hopped over Cash and scooped up her phone. It had been in the pocket of her jeans so it took her a frustrating moment to get it out. "Hello?"

"Ana." The robotic voice was back.

She didn't hesitate. Her fingers instantly flew over the phone's screen, hitting the button to activate her speakerphone.

"Ana, I know you found the bodies."

"I did." *Keep him talking. The FBI can get another trace.* Where would that trace lead them this time? Cash was already texting on his phone, so she knew he was alerting his team. The FBI agents weren't at this motel—there hadn't been enough room for them all, so they'd been given a house to use near the sheriff's office. "You wanted me to find them."

"I wanted the world to know what a twisted fuck Jonathan Bright was. He liked to hurt children. Liked to torture them. Liked to try to turn them into little monsters." The grating voice blasted from the speaker.

"We only found three bodies." *Not bodies. Remains.* "Are there more?"

"Two more victims."

That would equal the original five that Gabe had mentioned. "Where are they?"

"You come to me, and I'll show them to you."

Cash gave a frantic shake of his head.

"Tell me where you are," Ana responded quietly. "And I will."

Cash's gaze flashed his fury.

"Right now, I'm standing in front of the ME's building. He's working so hard for you, isn't he? Trying to find out whose bodies are on his table. But I can tell you their names. I can tell you who they are."

"Do it then. Say it."

"Christopher Hey. Little Christopher. I think he was . . . twelve?" The robotic voice laughed. "Cute kid, before."

Nausea rose in her throat.

"Jenny Love. She was thirteen. She lasted longer."

Longer than what?

"Peter Francis. Twelve. He cried so much for his mother. Cried and cried . . ."

Ana's breath heaved out. "And the other two victims? Who were they?"

Silence.

"Who were—"

"I'll tell you who they were. I'll show them to you . . . when you come to meet me."

Cash was texting frantically on his phone.

"I lied, Ana. I'm sorry." Suddenly, the robotic voice seemed repentant. "I'm not outside the ME's office. I'm *in* his lab. With him. I have him on his exam table and he's tied down."

Ana staggered back a step.

"He cuts open everybody that comes across his table. If you call the cops and tell them that I'm here . . . if you tell your FBI lover . . . I'll cut him open, too."

"But—but Dr. Cole doesn't fit your profile!" The words burst from her. "He hasn't done anything wrong!"

"Hasn't he?"

Frantic, her gaze focused on Cash. Had he texted his team already, telling them to rush to the ME's lab? She shook her head, again and again. "Don't hurt him!"

"Come to me, and I won't. Tell no one . . . just come. And I'll answer all your questions. I'll finally see if you understand me."

"Okay, okay, fine, I will be there."

Cash took an aggressive step toward her.

She threw up her hand to stop him. "Why are you using the voice modulator again?"

Silence.

"I thought we were past that. You let me hear you before. Why not now? *Why not now?*"

But she saw that he'd hung up on her. Shit. Ana grabbed her clothes, yanking them on as fast as she could. "Make sure your people don't go storming into that lab! Keep them back, Cash! Keep them back!"

She nearly stumbled as she tried to grab her shoes.

Cash caught her arm. "Keep them back? While you run straight into death? Oh, hell, no, baby, that's not happening. Not on my watch."

"Cash, you heard him! He will kill—"

"He will kill you if you go in there alone. The guy is unhinged, Ana. He's not some victim. He's a killer. You aren't going in alone."

"Cash . . ."

"We go in together. We're partners, remember? Damn good partners. You'll watch my back. I'll watch yours. *That's what we do.*"

"If he sees you, he might kill Dr. Cole."

Cash's lips thinned. "And if you go in there alone, you could die before I get to you. I can't let that happen, Ana. I won't." He released her arm and jerked on his clothes. He checked his weapon, then shoved it into his holster. "My backup weapon is in the car. Let's get moving."

So that was it? "Cash—"

He was already yanking open the door to their motel room. "No, Ana. No arguments. Your life means too much to—"

Boom.

The gunshot seemed to come from nowhere. One moment, Cash was looking back at her, he was standing in the doorway, and in the next instant, he'd fallen back and blood soaked his shirt.

"Cash!" Ana screamed his name and ran toward him.

Boom.

The shot hit her, not in the chest, but high in the shoulder. She staggered, nearly going down—

"I will shoot you again, this time in the head, if you don't come with me right now."

Ana's head whipped toward the doorway. A woman stood there, a woman . . .

Her hair is like mine. She . . . she almost looks like—

The woman's gun was aimed at Ana, but then she jerked the weapon down, suddenly aiming it at Cash once again. "Better plan. He's still alive, but not for long. If you don't get your ass over here, I'll make sure his brains are all over the floor. *Bang, bang.* Just like he's done to the suspects he takes down."

Ana lunged forward. Her whole arm felt numb. "No! Don't shoot him!"

The woman grabbed her. She was taller than Ana, and far stronger than she looked. She shoved the gun to Ana's temple. "Walk with me. Now. You stop, you stumble, and my finger pulls the trigger." She gave a little laugh. Light. Twisted. "And you'll be dead. Then I'll be the only Ana."

What?

Ana glanced down at Cash, desperate. His eyes were opening. He stared blearily up at her. "Ana?"

But the woman was yanking her out. Pulling her away.

This bitch is crazy if she thinks I'll let her over-power me. I just needed to get her away from Cash so she wouldn't shoot him again. And now—

"Ana?" That was Sarah's voice. Sarah had run out of her motel room—one a few doors down from Cash's.

She was racing toward Ana and the crazy bitch who held Ana. "Ana, what's happening?"

The gun jerked away from Ana's head. Ana's attacker aimed it at Sarah.

"Get down, Sarah!" Ana yelled as she struck her assailant with her elbow, driving hard into the other woman's stomach. The woman grunted and stumbled even as she fired.

Ana grabbed for the woman's wrist. She twisted it hard—

"Ow!" A frantic scream, but the woman didn't let go of her weapon.

Fine. Ana drew back her fist, ready to break the woman's face—

And then she felt someone grab her from behind.

"I'm sorry, Ana." It was *his* voice. The man she'd heard the other night, when he'd finally ditched the voice changer. "I can't let you hurt her anymore."

She hadn't even heard him sneak up on her, but now his right arm was locked around her throat.

Because he's the real threat. The woman was the bait. The distraction.

"We're leaving, now," he snapped. Then he yanked Ana against him. "Don't make me hurt you."

Was he freaking kidding? She head butted him. "Sarah, get help!" Ana screamed. "Get—"

"I'm sorry, Ana." Then he stabbed a needle into the side of her neck. "I'm sorry."

Screw sorry. Cash had been shot. Cash needed help. Cash—

"Ana!" That was Cash's roar.

Her head turned toward him, but everything seemed

to be happening in super slow motion. She saw Cash standing in the doorway of his motel room. His shirt—it seemed red because there was so much blood. He was lifting his gun. Aiming it at the bastard who held her.

And—

The man who'd just stabbed Ana with the needle jerked her in front of him. "You think you can make the shot? Injured, bleeding out like that? You think you can be the hero again? I fucking don't." And he laughed.

The woman—*crazy bitch bait*—ran away, heading toward a VW Beetle. She revved the engine even as the bastard who held Ana began to haul her in the direction of that car.

She wanted to fight him, but Ana felt too sluggish. She couldn't even lift her arm. Her body was weighted down, down . . .

"See you around, *hero*," the perp taunted as he scooped Ana into his arms and ran for the car.

His mistake. He'd just given Cash a target. Cash needed to . . . "Sh-shoot . . ." Ana tried to yell. But her voice just came out as a whisper. "Sh-shoot . . ."

"He won't," her abductor muttered. "Because you're not a stranger. Your life matters to him." He jumped into the back of the Beetle with her still held tightly to him.

The tires squealed as they raced away.

THEY'D TAKEN ANA. His blood-covered hand still gripped the gun as that Beetle rushed away. Cash lurched after them, and fell on his face.

"Cash!" Sarah grabbed him and rolled him over. Her eyes widened as she saw the damage. "Lie still," she ordered him. "I'm going to help you."

Screw him. He didn't matter. "Go . . . after them." He pushed his gun into her hands. His chest burned— that bullet had torn into him, and his whole body had gone weak. "Help Ana . . . get APB . . ." Just talking took every bit of strength that he had.

The wound was bad. He knew it. He'd tried to turn at the last moment, but the hit had been so close to his heart.

His heartbeat was slow. Erratic. He could feel it, as if his heart were struggling . . .

Sarah put the gun down next to her. She ripped open his shirt and her breath hissed out. "Dammit, Cash, do not *die*." Then she was putting her hands on his wound, applying pressure.

"No!" The word tore from him. "Get . . . Ana . . . can't lose her . . ." Didn't Sarah see who the priority was? *Not me.* "Get on the ph-phone . . . APB . . . can stop . . . can stop . . . car . . ." Everything was getting darker.

And his chest didn't hurt now. It felt numb.

He felt numb.

"Cash!" Sarah's voice was sharp. Demanding. "Dammit, do not do this! Do you understand? I don't like it when people die on me!"

Only fair. He didn't like dying.

Not when there was so much to live for.

Like Ana.

Ana . . . "Save . . . her . . ."

"Cash!"

Her voice wasn't loud any longer. And he wasn't even sure if his heart was still beating.

IT WAS BRIGHT. Too fucking bright. A light shone down on him and Cash squinted, trying to figure out where the hell he was.

People were around him. Wearing masks. Leaning in too damn close. He tried to swipe out at them, but some dick had strapped down his arms.

"He's awake," a woman said, sounding surprised.

"Shit . . . Ron, check his anesthesia . . ."

Cash yanked on the straps.

"Agent Knox, you just have to stay calm." It was the woman again. He had no clue who she was. "You're safe. We're going to take good care of you."

But when he looked over at her, he saw that her gloved fingers were stained with blood.

His blood.

They were cutting him open.

They were all wearing green scrubs. White face masks. *Doctors. Hospital.*

Not dead. Not dead . . . yet. He tried to talk but couldn't. Some damn tube was in his mouth. He needed to ask, had to find out . . .

Ana. Where's Ana? Is she safe? Did they find her? Where. Is. Ana?

But his eyes were closing again and the too-bright light turned to darkness.

IT WAS TOO bright. Ana squinted against the light. It was shining right into her face. She tried to lift her hand, wanting to shield her eyes, but someone had bound her hands behind her. Tied them tight with thick, rough rope.

"She's awake," a woman said, giving a quick, light laugh. "I didn't think I'd be able to play so soon."

Ana couldn't see her—she couldn't see beyond the light. She tried to speak, but her lips were taped shut. Bound and gagged.

But alive. I'm still alive.

Was Cash? The last time she'd seen him, he'd been covered in blood. She blinked against the light and the tears that were filling her eyes.

"She's not supposed to be awake yet." It was a man's voice. Angry. Then he was leaning over her, a big, menacing shadow behind the light. "Sorry, Ana. It's not time yet." And a pinprick of pain whispered along her neck. That pinprick and then . . .

Her veins seemed to turn cold.

He drugged me again.

He backed away. "Glad we switched rides when we did."

The bright light fell away from her.

She was on her side, her legs curled up, her feet tied just like her hands.

He stared down at her. "See you again soon, Ana."

And he—he slammed a door shut. No, not a door. Too small for a door.

A few moments later, the surface beneath her—around her—above her—began to vibrate. She smelled exhaust and Ana realized—

Not a door. A trunk. He locked me in a trunk.

And it was so dark, her veins were so cold, and she was afraid. So very afraid.

But not for herself. For Cash.

Was he alive?

Cash . . .

God, she hoped so. Because Ana didn't really want to think of a world without him.

CHAPTER NINETEEN

CASH OPENED HIS EYES. HE COULD HEAR A steady beep, could smell the light scent of antiseptic, and slightly starchy sheets were beneath him.

The walls were white, and a wipe-off board was positioned on the wall at the foot of his bed. The words *Nurse: Suzy* were written in big, swirling letters on that board.

He was alone in the room. Not surprising, he was usually alone. He'd gotten used to being that way except . . .

With Ana.

The fingers of his left hand reached for the IV that fed into him. He yanked it out, barely feeling the pain, and a little spurt of blood shot into the air. Cash sat up in the bed, feeling weak and hating that weakness. He looked down at his chest and saw the bandage that covered him.

He'd survived. He didn't know how bad his injuries were, and right then, he didn't care.

The only thing he cared about was Ana.

Cash swung his legs to the side of the bed. The machines near him were beeping like crazy, probably because he'd yanked out that IV. The noise they made grated on his ears and caused his temples to throb. He pushed to his feet, then stood a moment, swaying.

The door to his room flew open. A pretty blonde stood there, staring at him in shock. "What are you doing?"

"Leaving." He was stark naked. "Clothes would . . . help." His voice sounded like a frog's croak.

"You can't leave!" she cried, obviously shocked. "You had surgery two days ago! You need to rest. You need—"

"Two . . . days ago?" He shook his head, sure that he had misheard her. Probably because of all the damn machines. "Not . . . possible."

"What's not possible is you—leaving. You're going to mess up all of Dr. Brown's fine work. I mean, you cheat death and that's great, but you don't get to go out and start running marathons the next day!" She bustled toward him and put her hand on his shoulder. "You need to get back in bed and—"

"Give me something to wear . . . or I'll be walking out of this hospital naked."

Her jaw dropped. But then she rallied. Her big smile came back. "You're a little confused. You—"

"Naked. That works." He took a step away from the bed.

But once more, the door opened. Only this time, an older man in a finely cut suit stood there.

FBI Executive Assistant Director Darius Vail.

Vail sighed. "For the love of God, Suzy, get that man some clothes."

The nurse obviously knew who the new visitor was because she snapped to attention. She ran to the bathroom and came back out with a robe. She tried to help Cash put it on, but he took it from her and struggled into it himself.

"Your stitches—" she began.

He just grunted. "They'll pop or they won't."

The executive assistant director shook his head. "Told you he'd be a terrible patient. Suzy, will you give us a moment?"

She flashed her big smile at the executive assistant director. "Of course, sir." She hurried past him but tossed Cash one last, warning look on her way out.

Darius paced toward Cash. "Knew you'd be chomping at the bit to get out of here. That's why I came by so early today."

"Two days." His voice was still raspy. Probably because he'd had tubes jammed down his throat. "She said I'd been out for two days."

Darius nodded. A tall, distinguished African American in his late fifties, Darius was a no-nonsense player. He got the job done, with minimum risk for his agents. He valued his personnel, and he never shied away from a challenge. Normally Cash admired the guy, but when Darius said, "Yeah, two days have passed"—well, Cash wanted to shove his boss out of the way and go charging out of the hospital.

"Two days," Darius said again as he settled himself directly in Cash's path. "And, no, I'm sorry to say, there has been no sign of Ana Young during that time."

Cash locked his muscles. "It was a black VW Beetle, older model, license plate—" Shit, what had the license plate been? His hand lifted and he rubbed his temple. "License plate—"

"Dr. Jacobs gave us the license plate. And we found the car abandoned at a rest stop. Only there was no sign of Ana, and the car had been wiped clean."

Cash shook his head. "I have to find her. I need to—"

"The FBI is working in conjunction with Ana's team at LOST. I know this is personal for them, so when Gabe Spencer showed up, I wasn't about to close him out of the investigation. I figure we could certainly use his help. After all, when it comes to finding the missing, LOST knows their shit."

Cash tried to step around the executive assistant director, but Darius caught his arm. "You're not strong enough for this. Do you know how close that bullet was to your heart? You were in surgery for four and a half hours."

"I'm strong enough." He was alive. And he didn't care about the bullet, not then. Ana. *Ana.*

"Cash . . ." Darius exhaled heavily. His hold tightened. "It's been over forty-eight hours. You know the odds—"

Cash knocked his hand away. "Don't talk to me about odds." He didn't need to hear them. Didn't need to know that with every moment that passed, the chances of finding Ana were supposed to dwindle. "Screw those odds. Ana survived before and she'll do it again. She's the strongest woman I've ever met. The smartest. She'll get in the perp's head . . . Ana understands monsters. She won't be killed. She *won't.* She'll stay alive and I'll find her, and Ana will be *safe.*"

That was the only option. The only way he could think. Because if he imagined Ana hurt, dead . . . then Cash's world would rip apart—*he* would rip apart. It couldn't happen.

Ana. I have to find Ana.

"You'll be a liability out there," Darius said grimly. "You're too weak for this."

Liability. "I would die if it meant Ana could come back. They took her on my watch. *Mine.*"

The door squeaked open. Asher Young stood there, his face locked in hard, angry lines. Had the guy been outside the whole time, eavesdropping?

"I said I'd always keep her safe," Cash continued, voice grating. "I failed Ana. I have to get her back."

Darius didn't turn to see who'd slipped into the room. "Even if you kill your damn fool self?"

Even then. "Don't plan on dying," Cash rasped. "Plan on catching the perps who took my Ana. Plan on getting her back, no matter . . . the cost."

"You're letting your personal feelings get in the way. You'll be a detriment—"

A detriment. A weakness. Fuck, no. "My feelings will help me find her. My feelings . . ." And, yeah, he looked straight at Asher as he said this. "My feelings make me need to search, they will make sure I *never* stop looking. I will bring Ana home." Now he glanced back at Darius. "And either I'll be . . . working with you . . . or on my own . . ." But he wasn't staying in that hospital. He was going to find Ana.

"Told you he'd say that," Asher drawled. He lifted his hand, and a black duffel bag hung from his fingers.

"Sorry I'm a little late. Got his clothes." Asher strode into the room. The faint lines near his mouth were deeper and he had dark shadows under his eyes.

Ana's eyes.

It was the first time that it had actually hurt to look at Asher.

"I'm getting my sister back," Asher said. "I don't think she's dead. Not Ana. She's waiting for us, she's staying alive for us, and I think it's time we stopped making her wait."

"Cash . . ." Darius began.

Cash took the duffel bag from Asher. "I'm sorry. I didn't stop them, I didn't—"

"Didn't shoot because you were afraid you'd hit my sister?" Asher shook his head. "Save the apologies. I already know what happened. Sarah told me. Told me all about how you dragged your bleeding ass out of the motel room and tried to crawl after my sister."

He'd crawled? Cash didn't—

"Do you love her?" Asher asked.

"Yes." He stared straight into Asher's dark gaze. "I love her and I will do *anything* to get her back. Those perps—they said I was a monster. They're about to see just how much of a monster I can truly be."

Because for Ana . . . he would unleash hell. All of the darkness he'd kept chained so carefully inside of himself, it would come out. For her.

No one hurt Ana.

No one took Ana.

And no one fucking had better kill her.

"Get your ass dressed," Asher said. "We have work to do." He turned away, then stopped. He waved his hand toward Cash. "But maybe get some extra bandages from Suzy. You're already bleeding."

Cash looked down and saw the blood soaking through the heavy white bandage that covered his chest.

THERE WAS A little doll in front of her. Ana turned her head, staring at the doll. It was a pretty doll, with short, dark hair, a wide smile . . .

And no eyes.

She remembered the dolls she'd seen, all lined up in a little row at Bellhaven. Those dolls had been positioned right in front of the room that housed Dr. Summers.

"You left them there," Ana said, her voice soft and low. Not because she'd been screaming and she'd broken her voice. Not because she'd gone days without water.

She'd had plenty to drink.

And she hadn't screamed. Why? There would be no point. They'd driven her far and fast, and from what Ana could determine, they were in the middle of nowhere.

Her ropes had been traded for a chain—a long one that circled her left ankle. The other end of the chain was secured around the bedpost. A very massive bedpost. One that didn't break easily. Ana knew because she'd been trying to break it ever since the drugs had finally worn off and she could stay awake for more than five minutes at a time.

"You left the dolls," Ana said as she glanced up at the woman who'd come into her room. Before, the door would only open for a brief moment. Food and water would be shoved inside, and then Ana would be left alone.

This time, though, the scene was different.

This time, the bitch who'd shot Cash had crept into Ana's room and she'd put down the little doll.

The woman—with her dark hair cut just like Ana's—lifted a finger to her lips. "That's a secret," she said, "you aren't supposed to tell."

Where was the man? The one who'd drugged her? The one who'd started this whole mess?

Ana stared at her, hard, trying to see past the dark hair and perhaps look back in time. What had this woman looked like years before? When she'd been a teen . . . or . . . maybe just a kid? Something Sarah had said to Ana a few days before nagged at her mind.

When we get the files on the kids, and we see the age progression photos that are created. The way they could look . . . I always hope . . . maybe they are still out there. Maybe they don't even know who they are. A mind is such a fragile thing. So easily broken.

Ana swallowed the lump in her throat. "I'm so sorry."

The other woman shuffled a little closer.

"I didn't see it the first time I saw you, back at River View. I was so intent on searching for a killer, I missed the victim right in front of me." She kept her voice low, easy, knowing that she had to be very careful with the woman in front of her. The woman she'd first met as Chassity Pope but now . . . now Ana realized who the woman really was. "I'm sorry," Ana said again.

The woman jerked. "Don't say that." Her voice was sharp.

"Your mother . . . she's still looking for you."

All of the color left the face of Ana's abductor.

"You're not Chassity—"

"No, no, I'm—"

"You're Cathy, aren't you?" And she could see the faint signs there. The shape of her chin, a little more defined, but the dimple was still there. Her eyes were still wide, tipping up a bit at the corners. Her nose was different, broken, twisted a little. "You're Cathy Wise."

"No!" This time, her retort was a scream.

"You were abducted when you were thirteen." Ana still kept her voice soft. "Did Jonathan Bright take you? Is that what happened? He took you while you were walking—"

"My grandmother *gave* me away!" she screamed. "She gave me to him! And my mother didn't care! No one ever cared!" Again, she shuffled a bit closer. She was wearing a big, dark jacket, one that swallowed her slender frame.

"Is that what he told you?" Ana stood in front of the bed, her hands at her sides. "Jonathan lied. He wanted you to feel alone. Isolated. No one gave you away. He took you, just as he took the others."

Cathy—*she has to be Cathy*—gave a frantic shake of her head. "No, no, no!"

"I work for an organization called LOST." She eased out a quick breath. Her palms were wet with sweat. "We find people like you, Cathy. People who've gone missing. Your mother came to LOST. She brought pictures of you. She wants to find you and bring you home—"

"My mother was a bitch who never cared about

me! She dumped me with my grandmother so she could spend the summer driving the roads with some dumbass truck driver she met at a bar! I was in the way, so she dumped me!" Spittle flew from Cathy's lips. Her voice lowered a bit as she said, "I was in my grandmother's way, too. Always in the way." Her hand lifted, sweeping up from the cover of that thick jacket. "Only now, you're the one in the way."

She had a gun in her hand. The same gun that she'd used on Cash.

Pain cracked inside of Ana's heart.

Cash is okay. Cash is alive. Cash will come. That was all she could allow herself to think about him. Nine little words. A mantra that held her sanity in check.

"You're messing things up," Cathy told Ana. "You're messing him up!"

The man who'd drugged me. Ana knew exactly who Cathy was talking about. "Who is he to you?"

"My friend. My brother." A wide smile spread. "Maybe more."

Oh, hell.

"He likes you, so I'll be you and you'll be gone." Cathy aimed her gun at Ana. "I had to wait until he was away." Now she sounded as if she were making a dark confession. "He was watching me, too close. I think he was mad because I killed your lover."

Cash is okay. Cash is alive. Cash will come.

"He wanted to kill him, you see. Because your lover—Knox—he was a bad man."

"No, he's not." The denial burst from her.

But Cathy shook her head. "He's bad. We know . . .

Knox . . . it was his brother who scarred you." And curiosity glinted in her eyes. "I want to see the scars."

What?

"I can see the one on your lip, but it's small." Cathy took another step forward. "I read that you have a whole lot more. When you were at River View, you said—"

"I have plenty of scars," Ana said. *And I'm betting you do, too, Cathy.* Maybe they weren't scars on the skin, but Ana knew they would go so much deeper.

All the way to Cathy's battered soul.

"Show them to me." Cathy motioned with the gun.

Ana slowly lifted up the hem of her shirt.

"Oh, they're ugly." Cathy seemed happy. "You're ugly, Ana."

And you're sick, Cathy. I'm so sorry. You need help.

"I don't like ugly," Cathy said. "I don't like you."

"Cathy, I want to help you."

"No, you don't. You want to stop me." Suddenly, Cathy's gaze seemed very, very focused. "But I don't want to be stopped. I like what I'm doing. I've been doing it for a very long time, and it feels good."

Goose bumps rose onto Ana's arms. "How many people have you killed?"

Cathy sucked in a deep breath, then exhaled on a robust sigh. "I don't really remember." She tapped her chin with the gun, tapping right on the little dimple there. "I remember the first. It was Daddy Jon. We killed him slowly. Watching him go, day by day . . . getting weaker and he had no clue. Put it in his drink. Didn't even know what was happening."

They poisoned Jonathan Bright. Only, she wanted

to be sure about the *they* part. "You were the one who called me on the phone at the motel." *That* was why the caller had used the voice distortion. It hadn't been the man who'd made contact with Ana that time. It had been Cathy. "You told me the names of the victims. You mentioned Jenny Love. Peter Francis. Christopher Hey." Ana pressed her sweaty palms to her stomach. "But according to all the newspaper reports back then . . . another boy went missing, too. A—a boy named William Marshall."

Cathy tensed.

"Did William help you kill Jon? Is that what happened? Did the two of you kill Jon so that you could be free?"

Cathy shook her head. "We killed him . . . because he was a monster. Monsters have to be killed."

Monsters like Bernie. Like Forrest. Like Dr. Summers?

"How do you decide who's a monster?" Ana asked her softly.

"Billy decides. Billy knows."

Billy. *William.* Okay, she could work with this. "Billy doesn't think I'm a monster, Cathy."

"He thought Agent Knox was." She gave a little laugh. "So I killed him."

Cash is okay. Cash is alive. Cash is coming.

"But now Billy is mad." A furrow appeared between Cathy's brows. "He's watching me too much. Looking at me . . . like I'm a monster."

"You're not," Ana said quickly. "You're a victim. I can help you, Cathy. We'll leave this place together and I'll take you back to your mom and—"

Wrong thing to say.

"I'm not going back," Cathy said, the gun trembling in her hand. "I'm staying with him, forever, just like he promised. I'll never go back." Her eyes glinted. "And you won't stop me. You don't *understand* anything!"

The woman was going to fire. Ana knew it. And there was nowhere to run. So Ana didn't run.

She lunged forward. She'd spent too much time alone in that room and she'd realized just how far she could reach, chained as she was. She'd just needed Cathy to come a little bit closer. To get within range . . .

So I kept talking. And she kept coming toward me.

Cathy was starting to smile—

But Ana grabbed Cathy's wrist and twisted hard, hard enough to break bones this time. *I'm sorry, I'm sorry—*

The gun fell from Cathy's fingers as she let out a pain-filled scream. Ana drew back her fist and delivered a hard right hook to the woman's jaw. Cathy stumbled back. Ana scrambled for the gun, but when Cathy had dropped it, it had slid across the floor and it was—

Just out of my reach.

"You're going to pay for that!" Cathy yelled. "I'm going to cut out your eyes! Cut them out! Naughty girl, naughty! You're going to pay!"

But the door opened behind Cathy.

He was there.

The man she'd seen at the motel. Tall, with wide shoulders. Bright blue eyes. A handsome man.

A very, very dangerous man.

William Marshall?

He bent and scooped up the gun.

"Shoot her!" Cathy screamed. "She was trying to escape! She attacked me!" Cathy whirled toward the man. "I told you she was bad. She's a monster. She has to be stopped."

Ana tensed. If he fired on her from such close range, she'd be dead.

Think, Ana. Think.

He'd said she understood him. She'd boasted to Cash that she understood monsters and . . . "Hello, Billy," Ana said, and her voice only cracked a little bit.

He blinked. Then he inclined his head toward her. "Hello, Ana."

SWEAT COVERED CASH's forehead. Drenched his back. He'd headed to the base that had been set up for Ana's search, and after a twenty minute briefing, he realized—

"You all have jack shit."

Gabe's jaw tightened. "No one saw anything at the rest stop. It was too early in the day. They stole the vehicle that belonged to one of the cleaning crew members—and the old sedan hasn't turned up anywhere. The Beetle they left behind was also a stolen ride. It had been wiped clean. The only thing we found inside it was some blood in the trunk. Blood that was a match for Ana."

Cash stared at the map that had been tacked to the evidence board. All of the crime sites were marked on that map.

Jonathan Bright's cabin.

River View.

Bellhaven.

Wingate Penitentiary.

And even the little cabin that had been the Butcher's final resting place.

"The sedan hasn't turned up," Cash said, his gaze trekking over that map. "Because they took it off road. They're lying low and making their plans."

"So who do we think those two bozos are?" Darius demanded.

Cash looked back to see that the executive assistant director had crossed his arms over his chest as he leaned against the conference room table.

"I think they're victims," Sarah said, clearing her throat. "We found the remains of three children at Jonathan Bright's cabin, but five children were abducted during that time—five children who all fit his victim pattern."

Cash yanked the list of those suspected victims off the wall. "I heard the caller tell Ana . . . he said the bones belonged to Christopher Hey." He crossed off that name. "Jenny Love." Another name to cross off. "And Peter Francis." He drew a line through that boy's name.

"We don't have confirmation of their identities from the ME yet," Faye said.

Their whole group was assembled in that room. Darius, Faye, Gabe, Asher, and Sarah. The FBI and LOST—working together.

"The caller could have been lying," Faye continued as she pursed her lips in thought. "To throw you and Ana off the track."

True. It was certainly possible but . . . "Two names remain. Cathy Wise and William Marshall."

Sarah opened the manila folder she held. "LOST was hired to find Cathy six months ago. Ana had taken over the case. There were no leads, nothing that could put us in a new direction, but I had our assistant send over a copy of the age progression photo that was made of the victim." She tacked that picture on the evidence board, putting it right next to the photo that had been taken of Chassity Pope at River View. "Am I the only one who sees a similarity?"

"No," Cash gritted. "You aren't." His gaze lingered on the photo. "So if one of our perps is Cathy Wise . . ." His gaze slid to the photo of Chassity's "brother" that they'd taken. "Then maybe we're looking at William Marshall, too."

Asher swore. "They were just kids. Taken. Hurt—"

Just as Asher and Ana had been taken. Only the results of those abductions had been far different. Asher and Ana had escaped. They'd killed their abductors. They'd gone on to try to help people, to help victims.

Cathy and William . . . "They're trying to stop monsters."

"Ana isn't a monster." Asher's voice was furious.

"No." Cash narrowed his gaze on those photos. "But they think I am."

"That's why you wound up with a bullet in your chest," Sarah said.

Gabe grunted. "But that wasn't their usual style. I mean, Cash hadn't shot anyone—"

"Yes, I have. I've killed two perps in the line of duty. So maybe they thought that was the way to end me." Only he wasn't out, not yet. He turned to face Darius, sucking in a quick breath at the stab of pain.

Another stitch, giving way. "We know they took her some place isolated. Some place where they felt they'd be safe. They moved fast with Ana, and they're going to lie low, so they'd need supplies. They'd need to be sure no nosy cops would be coming around too soon."

Darius inclined his head. "All of that is true only *if* they plan to keep Ana alive for a while."

The room got very quiet.

"If they're intending to kill her, if she's already dead, then they could be in the wind. That's something all of you . . ." Darius's gaze swept the assembled group. Sympathy flashed in his dark eyes as his stare lingered a moment on Asher. "It's something all of you need to accept."

The drumming of Cash's heartbeat filled his ears. "Ana isn't dead."

"How can you be so sure?"

"Because, like I said, she isn't a monster."

Darius just shook his head.

"So where is she?" Faye asked. "Where do they have her? There are a million spots where she could be. Do you *know* how many cabins are in the Blue Ridge Mountains? Cabins, houses, motels . . ."

Searching them all would take forever, he knew that. But maybe they didn't need to search. Maybe they were the ones who just had to use the right bait. "They wanted the world to know what they were doing," Cash said. He lifted his brows as he looked at Sarah. "Killers want recognition, right?"

She nodded. "Fame. They want to show the world just how good they are."

Right. "So they were paying attention. Watching the

reporters. They wanted people to see who they were."
He nodded. "That means they're still watching. Especially since they just attacked a federal agent."

"They'll be waiting to see if you died," Darius said.

Waiting to see if he was dead and waiting for their crimes to get the attention they felt they deserved. "If they're watching, then I'm damn well going to give them a show they won't forget. Get a crew of reporters ready right now." Because he was ready to go live.

And be the perfect bait.

CATHY GAVE A wild cry and started to charge at Ana. Ana tensed her hands and came up as she prepared to attack—

But Billy caught the other woman around her waist. He jerked her back, holding her against his body. "Cathy, you have to calm down."

"She has to die!"

Ana flinched.

"She hurt me!" Cathy yelled. "She has to die! Punish her! Payback! Payback!"

This time, Billy was the one to flinch, but his voice was gentle as he said, "It's going to be okay. Didn't I say that I'd always protect you? Everything is okay."

Slowly, some of the bright red color faded from Cathy's cheeks.

Billy led her to the door. "Why don't you fix lunch for us? I'll be right out."

Cathy nodded. She didn't look at Ana as she left the room.

And Ana didn't take a breath until Cathy was gone. "She's dangerous."

Billy stared at the floor. "She wasn't always this way. Once she was just a girl, but then he took her." A stark pause. "No, he made *me* take her. Got me to lure her away . . ."

She stepped closer to him and the chain dragged on the floor. Billy had tucked the gun in the waistband of his jeans. "You mean Jonathan Bright?"

"He was a bastard. A sick, sadistic killer, and I enjoyed watching him slowly die. He had no clue—no fucking clue—that I was putting drops of poison in his drink. But what choice did I have? I couldn't let him keep taking kids. Hurting them. That was what he did. He got us kids. If we did *exactly* what he wanted, he let us live, but one screwup"—he shook his head—"and we had to drink the black water."

The black water.

Poison.

"I was careful. Not too much, not enough that he could taste it. I drank it myself to make sure, just sips for me. And I waited and waited . . . and the day he finally didn't come back, I knew we were safe. He was dead."

"You killed your first monster."

Billy looked up and smiled at her, as if pleased. "I did."

"Why didn't you go to the cops then? Go back to your families?"

His smile dimmed. "Cathy was my family."

"You—"

"He made me hurt them, Ana."

Goose bumps rose on her arms.

"He made me . . . poison them. Even got Cathy to do

it. See, he never killed the kids right away. He hurt his victims. Kept them. Made them suffer."

"Wh-why didn't he kill you?"

His breath whispered out. "Because I did just what he wanted. I was his bait. I went to the other kids, got them to walk away with me. Walk away so that he could grab them and then . . . when we were at his cabin . . . he . . ." His words trailed away.

Ana waited, knowing how very important this was. She needed to hear his story so that she could understand him.

"He said I could never go home again because I'd killed. The first time I did it, I—I didn't even know, I swear!" His eyes blazed. "I thought I was giving Jenny something to drink. She'd been bad, tried to get away, and he'd punished her." Billy swallowed. "He beat her with his belt for hours, and she was on the floor, crying. When he told me to give her the drink, I thought I was helping her. Then he started to laugh . . ."

"And Jenny died," Ana said, her heart twisting.

"The black drink. I knew what it was then. And he made me use it on the others. He *made* me do it."

But he's not here any longer. You don't have to hurt anyone now.

"I never disobeyed. I always followed the rules." His voice was flat. "And because of that, they all died."

"Cathy didn't die. You saved her. You—"

"I didn't do it soon enough." Sadly, he shook his head. "You just saw her, Ana." His voice roughened. "He'd already broken her by then. And Cathy—he liked to get her to do things. Bad things. Not just give the others the drink. He made her *punish* them."

The bastard had kept those kids alive for that long?
For an instant, sadness flashed on his face. "I think she still likes those bad things, despite all I've done."

"Her mother is still looking for her."

"I know. I watch her mom, from time to time. I knew when she went to LOST." He gave her a quick smile. "That was how I found you."

Ana shivered.

"Found you." A furrow appeared between his brows. "And Bernie. Checked you out, learned his story and knew that he couldn't just *stay* in prison. That wasn't right. That wasn't the end for him."

He killed Bernie because of me? Ana tried to keep her breathing nice and easy as she schooled her expression. "Cathy's mom," she said deliberately, trying to steer the conversation back to her. "If you keep tabs on her, then you want to help her. Let's give that woman her daughter back. Let's—"

But he was shaking his head. "The daughter she lost is long gone. Cathy can't live in a normal world any longer, don't you see that?"

"You tried to get her help," Ana said, the words tumbling out. "You sent her to River View—"

"It wasn't for help. It was so she could kill Forrest Hutchins."

Cathy killed him?

"I told you. She likes bad things now. After Jonathan was gone. I had two choices. I could have gone to the cops. They would have thrown me in jail—"

"No, you were a child! A victim!"

"I was a killer."

That's what you are now. You weren't then. But if

he'd been a boy at the time, he might not have understood that. He would have known only fear. Pain. Desperation. And desperation could drive a person to dangerous extremes.

"My other choice was . . . I could try to help Cathy. I could try to fix the things that he'd done to her. That *I'd* done by tempting her to walk with me that day."

"You never let her go."

He stiffened. "What would have happened to her without me? *I protected her!* She wanted to hurt herself! To hurt other people! She was sweet and kind the day I met her on that walk." His words came faster. "Four months with Jonathan changed that. Four months *broke* her. She was asking him to take another girl. She was asking to help *hurt* that girl. I had to stop Jonathan before he did that. I had to stop—"

"Cathy."

Silence. She wondered if she'd pushed too far.

When he spoke again, his words were wooden. "I had to find a way for her to . . . to follow her urges but not become a monster."

OhmyGod. "She was the one who shot Cash."

"I knew she was getting the—the urge again."

The urge to kill?

"I could tell by the way she was talking. So I thought . . . if I gave her a target, it would calm her down." His lips thinned. "And get him out of the way."

Out of the way. "I-is he dead?"

He looked away.

Cash is okay. Cash is safe. Cash is coming.

Billy paced, but didn't come closer to Ana. "She killed Bernie, too. He didn't think a pretty girl like her could be dangerous. She was his type, you know? He liked to hurt the pretty girls."

Pinpricks of heat filled Ana's cheeks. "Bernie had all of those pictures of me. One was a sketch of me in my jacket—someone had been watching me . . . reporting to Bernie."

"I—I'm sorry, Ana. I did that. Like I said, I found out about Bernie by researching *you*. When I first contacted him, I had to prove that I would be a good partner for him—" He glanced quickly at her. "It was a lie, of course. I would never be his partner. I would never hurt someone like you."

"Like me . . . ?"

"You want to stop them, too. You want to help people. That's what I'm doing. You see that, right? I'm stopping the killers."

Bernie Tate was in jail. He was already stopped.

"I gave Bernie information about you to show that he could trust me. I convinced him that Cathy and I—we wanted to help him. The fool believed everything. When that transport broke down, he *ran* to us. See, we'd done that. We *made* it break down. It was all part of the plan. And Bernie came so willingly. It was too easy for Cathy to kill him."

Cathy kills a lot of people. Ana was getting that truth, and it terrified her.

"I'm stopping monsters." Billy's voice held the distinct ring of pride. "And I'm making sure that Cathy . . ." His gaze darted to the closed door. "I'm making sure she doesn't cross any lines."

Cross lines? They were way past the line-crossing point. "How many people has she killed?"

He didn't speak.

Maybe that was the answer—a horrifying one. And Ana knew that the only way out was to break the bond between Billy and Cathy. To drive a wedge between their deadly partnership. "She was going to kill me. That's why I hit her. She had the gun aimed at me, and she was going to shoot."

He pulled the gun from his waistband and stared at it. "After she . . . after we got here, I took the bullets out of the gun." He focused on Ana. "She wouldn't have killed you. See, I'm a step ahead. I always have to be." He turned away. "Get some rest. I'll bring some lunch in for you soon—"

"What if you're not a step ahead next time? I don't want to die."

His shoulders stiffened.

"I have a brother. Asher. He's my twin." *Make it personal. Make him see you as a victim.* "I want to see my brother."

But Billy didn't look back. He opened the door.

"I want to see my brother!" Ana yelled.

The door closed softly and the lock turned.

"I *will* see my brother," Ana vowed.

BILLY EASED OUT a long deep breath and he schooled his features before he headed into the kitchen. He could hear the sound of a TV blaring. Cathy liked the TV.

She hated silence. Another leftover trait from their time with Jonathan Bright.

He'd lock us in the closet. It would be dark. We couldn't make a sound. The first to make a sound would be punished.

She had a knife in her hand when he went into the kitchen. Her left hand. Her right was cradled against her body. A melon was in front of her, but she wasn't cutting the melon. She was staring at the knife. "I saw her scars. So many scars. Made with a knife just like this one."

Unease slithered through Billy. "What are you watching?" He pointed to the TV but then saw—

"He's still alive," Cathy said, sounding sad. Disappointed. "I should have shot him again. If you hadn't been so determined to get her, I could have finished."

I wanted Ana. I finally wanted to have something— someone—for me. Because Ana understood.

And, unlike Cathy . . .

She's not crazy. Yes, he knew Cathy was insane. Another reason why he'd had to keep her close. Her family wouldn't have been able to take care of her, not the way she was now. They wouldn't have understood.

They wouldn't have let her kill. And Cathy liked to kill. She liked to make people bleed.

"Now he's on the TV," Cathy murmured, "and he's saying bad things about us."

Billy stalked closer to the TV and he turned the volume up. Sure enough, there was Special Agent Cash Knox, filling the screen, saying . . .

"Our two suspects are highly disturbed individuals . . ."

Cathy laughed. "Does that mean he thinks we're crazy?"

"They are suspected in the abduction of Ana Young . . ."

"He doesn't look very hurt." Cathy put her hand on

his shoulders as she peered harder at the screen. "I was aiming for his heart. How did I miss?"

Two images flashed on the screen—a shot of him and a shot of Cathy. They were grainy, but clear enough, and he knew they'd come from River View—he could tell, based on the background of the shots. *Video security footage.* He'd known that was a risk but he'd needed to get her out of that place.

Besides, we've both already dyed our hair. Changed the cuts. We look different, just enough to fool most—

"They took Ana Young," the FBI agent continued, staring straight out of that TV set. *"But they made a mistake. I'm the one who should be with them. I'm the monster."*

Cathy dropped the knife. It hit the floor and she clapped. Then she moaned and brought her right wrist close to her body again. Had Ana broken her wrist?

"I will gladly trade myself for Ana," Cash continued. *"All they have to do is call me. Tell me when. Tell me where to be. They want me dead? So be it. But let Ana go."* His eyes glittered. *"Let her go. Ana is good. She doesn't deserve this, and you know it. Take me. I've got Ana's phone. You have her number. Call it—talk to me."*

And, standing just behind Cash . . . Billy saw another man. Tall, with dark hair like Ana. Dark eyes. He'd seen pictures of that man before. Ana's brother.

Her twin.

The guy's face was grim and dark.

Billy turned off the TV, hitting the remote with a hard stab of his finger.

"Let's do it!" Cathy said happily. "I want to finish! Let's call him!"

"No, Cathy, it's a setup. We call him and he just brings the whole damn FBI down on us."

Her lower lip poked out. "But I didn't finish."

Sometimes, she was so much like a child. Had her mind frozen when she was thirteen? When Jonathan had hurt her so much? "We stay low. We let the heat die away. That was our plan, remember?" They had this great cabin, on five private acres. No one was close by—no one cared about what they were doing. "We stay low. They aren't going to find us." He picked up the knife.

"When are we going to get rid of her?"

His fingers tightened on the handle of the knife.

"We can't . . . keep her." Now Cathy was adamant. "We have to get rid of her."

He spun to face her. "We *aren't* killing her!" The words emerged as a shout. The first time he'd shouted at her in—

Cathy started to cry.

Shit. He had to be so careful with her. Always so careful.

"I don't like her," Cathy said. She lifted her wrist. "She hurt me, and I want her dead."

"No. She's not—"

"I want her dead." Then Cathy spun away from him and ran for her bedroom.

He stood there, holding the knife. He'd tried so hard with Cathy. Tried so hard to make everything right. To make all of the pain up to her.

But it was his fault. He looked back at the hallway . . . the hallway that led to Ana . . . and, still holding the knife, he headed back to her.

"You sure that was wise?" Asher asked Cash when they backed away from the reporters. "Offering yourself up like that?"

"I want her back."

"And you're really ready to trade your life for my sister?"

"I would trade anything for her. I would—"

His phone rang. *Not my phone. Ana's.* Cash stilled. So soon? He yanked the phone to his ear. "Cash Knox."

"I want to kill her." It was a woman's voice. Soft. Oddly gentle.

"Don't." He nearly shattered the phone in his grip.

"I want her gone. And I also want to finish you. You're bad. He told me you were bad, so it's okay for me to kill you."

"I am bad. You should kill me, not her."

"I want to kill you both."

Fuck. "Tell me where you are," Cash said quickly, "and I'll come to you."

"Just you? No one else?"

Cash stared straight at Asher. "Tell me where you are."

"Can't do that . . ." Her voice had dropped even more. "But I bet you can come and find me . . ."

The lock turned, the door opened, and when Ana saw the knife in Billy's hands, she slid back on the bed, moving until her shoulders bumped into the wood of the wall. "Don't!"

He stopped, frowned, then looked down at the knife. "I'm not here to kill you."

Could have fooled me. "Then why do you have a knife?"

His lips thinned. "Because I didn't want to leave it out there with Cathy. She's not her best right now."

When the hell is she her best?

"I came to tell you . . ." He exhaled. "Cash is still alive. I just saw him on the news."

Cash is okay. Cash is safe. Cash is—

"You know what his brother did, don't you?" Billy asked her.

"I know."

"Then how can you let him touch you? How can you let him—"

"He isn't his brother."

"He *killed* two men—"

And you killed Jonathan. "Cash killed in order to save people. You and I? We've both seen evil up close, haven't we?"

He didn't respond.

"Cash isn't evil." She paused then said, "He's the man I love."

Billy fell back a step. "You . . . can't." He lifted the knife and pointed it at her. "You're not supposed to love him. You were like me!"

No, I wasn't.

"No. No. You're confused. It's the drugs. They're still in your system." He turned away. "You'll be better later. I'll come back—"

"Why didn't you kill Dr. Summers?"

He looked back.

"Or rather, why didn't you let Cathy kill her?"

"Because Dr. Summers hadn't killed anyone, not directly. I thought there might still be hope for her."

That was what she'd figured out, but Ana had needed him to say the words. "I think there's still hope for you, too, Billy. Let me go. Help me and show me that I'm right."

He shuffled from the room.

And Ana didn't call out after him.

BILLY STAYED OUTSIDE the cabin, running scenarios and plans through his head, over and over again. Shadows slid from the trees that surrounded the cabin. So many trees.

Perfect privacy.

He'd gotten that place years ago. It had actually belonged to another victim. No one had noticed when that fellow disappeared.

Cathy had enjoyed him.

Cathy.

She was outside, too. Walking through the woods. Talking softly to herself. She seemed happy again, and that was good. As long as Cathy was happy, she was controllable.

It wasn't her fault. Bright had just hurt her too much. *And I watched. The way I watched him hurt all the others.* Because Billy had known if he fought back, if he tried to help Cathy, then he'd pay.

The black drink.

He hadn't wanted to die. So he'd played by the rules. Done what he was supposed to do.

He'd survived.

But now I stop the monsters. Why can't Ana see how that's good? I stop them and I help Cathy.

Cathy gave a little laugh and she ran toward him. She had something in her hand. He started to smile.

And then he realized it was a dead bird.

Cathy ran her fingertips over the bird's still body. "So pretty . . ."

"Cathy . . ." He kept his voice calm. "The bird is dead. Put it down."

She put it down. "It's pretty." She looked up at him. "Ana isn't pretty. She's scarred."

"That's not her fault."

But Cathy had turned around and gone back to the woods, leaving that dead bird at his feet.

He backed into the house, worry gnawing at him. He'd hidden the bullets in his room, and he wanted to make sure she hadn't found them. He headed into his bedroom, checked in the bottom of his closet—

Still there.

Relief had him feeling a little light-headed. He hurried out of his room but found himself pausing near Cathy's closed bedroom door. She was outside, so it would be okay to glance in, just to make sure . . .

Make sure of what? That Cathy doesn't have more weapons?

He'd taken the gun. Taken the knife. And . . .

I need to be sure.

He opened her bedroom door. Its hinges squeaked.

He'd have to oil them soon. He stepped inside, his gaze sweeping around. Cathy liked to keep things clean. Even when she got bloody in a kill, she liked to clean up fast. She—

A phone was on Cathy's bed. One of *his* phones.

Billy ran toward that phone and saw—

It's still on . . . a call is connected. Hell, no! He grabbed the phone as rage washed over him. He slammed it onto Cathy's nightstand again and again and again.

"What are you doing?" Cathy cried out from behind him.

He whirled around. "What did *you* do?" But he knew, in his gut, he knew . . .

Just as he knew they were both lost.

She smiled. "I took him up on his offer." Then she clapped. "I get to kill the monster!" She looked so pleased with herself.

She—

Whoop. Whoop. Whoop.

He could hear the sound of a helicopter, approaching quickly.

Coming for them.

Sad now, he walked toward Cathy. "You won't kill any monster."

"But—"

"You just killed *us*." Because the FBI had tracked them through that call. The helicopter was too close. And Billy didn't think there was any way to escape.

Not this time.

CHAPTER TWENTY

WHAT'S THE PLAN?" ASHER DEMANDED AS he lowered the helicopter.

"I go in alone and I bring Ana out." Cash spoke into the microphone. They were both wearing pilot headsets so they could communicate easily. They were right above the cabin. *Hold on, Ana. I'm almost there.* Cash saw no sign of anyone out there. Were they all holed up inside?

"Negative," Asher snapped back. "You're injured. You're not up to par. We go in together—and you don't do any dumbass shit like trying to get yourself killed. Ana will be pissed if something happens to you."

They heard a grunt from the backseat. Faye and Sarah were back there—and both were armed.

"Faye," Cash said into the headset because she was linked up, too. "You and Sarah guard the perimeter. If you see the perps come out, then do whatever it takes to stop them."

"Understood."

Sarah was silent.

The helicopter began to lower to the ground.

"You love my sister, don't you?" Asher said.

"Enough to die for her."

"Yeah, well, like I said, let's *try* not to do that shit."

Whoop. Whoop. Whoop.

Ana jumped from the bed when she heard that distinct *whoop* sound. A helicopter. One that was coming closer.

Whoop. Whoop. Whoop.

Cash. *Cash is okay. Cash is—*

The door to her prison flew open. Cathy was there, with wild eyes and a big smile on her lips. "I get to kill him! He's coming for you and I get to kill him! He's going to trade and you're going to die! You're going to—"

"Cathy, *stop!*"

Billy yanked Cathy around to face him. He had the gleaming knife in his hand. The butcher knife.

Is he going to use that on her . . . or me?

"We have to think of a way out of this, Cathy," Billy said. "Maybe we can make a deal. We can buy some time, we can—"

In a flash, Cathy had grabbed his hand. She twisted his wrist—the same way that Ana had twisted hers earlier. And the knife sliced into Billy's side. Blood spurted out, soaking Cathy, and she laughed.

Billy staggered, then fell to the floor.

Cathy stood there, still holding the knife in her left hand. "Look what you made me do!" She pointed a finger at Billy.

Oh, hell.

He was shoving his hands against the wound and blood was seeping through his fingers.

"Get up," Cathy told him. "Come on, come on, let's go make the trade . . . Get up!"

But Billy had gone pale. He was bleeding so much.

"I don't think he can get up," Ana said softly. "I think you cut him too deeply."

Cathy whirled toward her.

"You . . . like hurting people, don't you, Cathy?"

The woman smiled. She looked far, far from innocent then.

"You hurt Billy too much, though." Ana picked up a pillow that had been on her bed. She was afraid Cathy would stab her any moment and if she did—

Like the pillow will be much protection. But it was all she had.

"Billy needs help," Ana said. "That helicopter outside? Those people on it will help him. Go get them. Bring them to Billy. Get their help."

Cathy nodded quickly. "I will! I will!" Her finger swiped over the bloody knife. "But I have to do one thing first . . ."

"What?"

"Kill you. You're ugly, Ana. *Ugly.*" Then Cathy ran across the room, slashing with her knife. "And I don't like ugly things. Daddy Jon was ugly. Monsters are *ugly. You're ugly.*"

CASH RAN TOWARD the cabin, his gun drawn. Asher was right on his six. There was still no sign of the perps and the house was dead silent. It was—

A woman's scream pierced that silence.

Asher kicked in the front door.

Cash rushed inside, following the sound of that dying scream. Following it and—

He burst into a smaller room. Ana was on the floor, fighting with a woman who had dark brown hair. The woman who'd shot him before. The woman was swinging her knife. She'd already cut Ana—he could see too much blood.

"Freeze!" Cash roared.

The dark-haired woman looked over at him. She laughed for just a second. "Monster. I'll get you next—"

No, you won't.

She started to lunge at Ana with her knife. Swiping down hard in an arc that would send that blade into Ana's chest.

He fired. The bullet hit the dark-haired woman right between the eyes, a shot that went straight through her head and had her brains—

Don't think about it. Ana. Ana is what matters.

Asher beat him to Ana. Asher pulled his sister off the floor and held her tight. Ana was bleeding. It looked like the knife had sliced her on her hands and arms, defensive wounds.

Cash pulled her from Asher's arms and his gaze frantically flew over her. No deep wounds, despite the blood that had terrified him. She was—

"You're okay," Ana said, smiling up at him as her body swayed a bit. "You're alive." Her smile trembled. "And you came."

He yanked her closer. He held her so tight and didn't even care about the pain radiating through him. Ana was alive. Ana, his Ana was okay. "I love you," he rasped. "Ana, I love you. Love you . . ." He kissed her. Desperate. Frantic. So happy she was alive. So—

"You killed her!"

Cash whirled at the roar.

A man stood in the doorway, swaying. Bloody. Tall with dark hair and wild blue eyes.

"You killed Cathy!"

Cash made sure he was blocking Ana with his body. That joker hadn't been there moments before. He'd checked the room. He'd—

The guy lifted his gun. Cash had holstered his when he grabbed Ana. He'd been so desperate to get to her.

"You're going to die now," the man promised him.

Cash squared his shoulders.

And Asher stepped in front of him.

What? What the fuck?

Asher had his gun out and aimed. "The only other person who is dying today . . . that would be you, hoss, unless you put that gun down right the hell now. You kidnapped my sister. That means I already want to send your ass to hell. You *know* what I did to the last two men who tried to hurt us."

"Y-you killed them . . ." His voice stammered out, but the man didn't lower his gun.

Cash pulled his weapon from his holster. Asher might think he got to play the hero, but he was wrong. Cash wasn't about to let anything happen to Ana's brother. *That would hurt her too much.*

"That's right," Asher snarled back. "I did. So drop the weapon or I'll be shooting *you*."

"I can't—won't go to jail . . . I've . . . already

been . . . in prison . . ." The guy mumbled. "My . . . whole life . . . was prison . . . ever since . . . I was . . . kid . . ."

"Drop your weapon," Asher said again.

But Cash knew the guy wasn't going to do it. He'd just said he wouldn't go to prison. *I've seen this shit before. Men pushed too far. Men who won't give up because they'd rather die than face justice.*

This guy has already lost everything. There is nothing else for him to lose. Nothing—

Cash shoved Asher out of the way. The perp wasn't aiming at Asher, though, and not at Cash, either. He was putting the gun to his own temple.

"I'm sorry, Ana . . ." the guy said.

"No!" she screamed.

He was about to pull the trigger.

Shit.

Cash fired, aiming for the guy's leg. The bullet hit him, tearing into bone and flesh and the man fell, slamming into the floor. Cash rushed forward and kicked the guy's weapon away from him. "You're not going out that way."

The perp was howling in pain now, bleeding from some wound in his gut and trying to reach for his wounded leg.

"Cash!" Ana called after him.

Asher eased closer to Cash. "I'll keep watch. You take care of Ana."

He looked back at her. She'd tried to rush after him, but a damn chain was around her ankle, holding her back. Her eyes were wide and desperate. And she was so beautiful.

Cash went to Ana. His hand was trembling when he lifted it to touch her cheek. Her head turned and she pressed a quick kiss to his palm.

"Ana . . ."

Her lashes lifted. "Get me the hell out of this cabin, Cash."

He nodded.

"And . . . Cash?"

He waited.

"I love you." She threw her arms around him, holding him tight. Her body shook against his. "I love you so much."

His arms curled around her. He just . . . held her.

He heard the thunder of footsteps behind him and Faye's quick voice—he knew she'd come running at the sound of gunfire. She was on her phone now, trying to get the ETA for the rest of the team.

Cops and EMTs would be coming soon. "Tell them to bring a fucking blowtorch," Cash rasped. "A blowtorch, a crow bar, whatever the hell we can use on this chain."

Ana squeezed him tighter. She was alive. She was—

Ana tilted back her head and stared up at him.

She was his whole world.

"I KNEW YOU'D find me," Ana said, rolling on the bed so that she faced Cash. It had been twenty-four hours since she'd been airlifted out of that cabin. Twenty-four hours of madness—reporters, police interviews, and even that long denied one-on-one chat with FBI Exective Assistant Director Darius Vail. "I just figured I had to stay alive until you found out where I was."

His gaze slid slowly over her face. They weren't making love. She wanted to, oh, she definitely did, but he was injured—injured far more seriously than she'd realized. When she'd seen him storm into that cabin bedroom, she'd thought he was fine . . .

Then she'd hugged him and felt the blood soaking his shirt.

He'd had to go back to the hospital. Had to get more stitches.

But now he was in bed with her. They were both safe.

"If you'd died, Ana, I don't know what I would have done." His voice was so gruff.

Her head tilted as her finger trailed lightly over his hand. "You would have been okay, Cash. You're strong. You would have—"

He shook his head. "I don't think you understand how important you are. You keep me sane. You keep me grounded. You give me hope—and when I look into your eyes, Ana, I think the world might not be such a bad place. Because *you're* in it. You make it better. You make me better. Without you . . ." He shook his head. "I'd be the one who was lost."

Her heartbeat quickened. "Well, don't worry, I'm not planning on going anyplace."

His gaze slid over her, like a tender touch. "I know we moved fast."

She gave him a little smile. "I don't know. Some would say our relationship started two years ago."

"I want to marry you, Ana. I want to spend every day and every night with you. I want to be at your side. I want to see you smile. I want to see you happy."

She had to blink quickly. "That's funny . . . because all of those things? I want them for you. I want to be at your side." She leaned forward and kissed him. "I want to see you smile. I want you happy. So happy, Cash." He deserved to be happy. He needed to let go of his guilt. Let go of his past.

They both needed to bury the past.

And to start a future. Together.

"Your brother hates me," Cash said.

She waved that away. "He's coming around." She knew this, with certainty. "After all, you're just the kind of man he wanted for me."

Cash began to shake his head again, but she kissed him once more.

Her brother had already told her the type of man he wanted to see her with . . . *Someone who will always put you first. Someone who would walk through fire for you. Someone who looks at you and knows just how wonderful you are. A guy who can't be bought, can't be threatened, a guy who won't back down from anything or anyone, not when it comes to you. Because you are his everything.*

Yes, Asher was coming around because he'd seen for himself just what Cash would risk for her.

His life.

"I love you, Ana."

She would never get tired of hearing that.

Ana snuggled close to him. The light from the nearby lamp spilled onto them. Sleep was tugging at her, a bone deep exhaustion, and she wanted to slip away cradled in his arms. "I love you." Saying the words felt right, just as he felt right.

Finally, someone just for her. Someone who filled all of her dark spaces. Someone who held her in the night and in the light.

Someone to trust.

Not just a lover.

So much more.

"I love you," Ana said once more, then she closed her eyes, knowing she was safe. Always safe.

In Cash's arms.

EPILOGUE

D R. SARAH JACOBS STARED AT THE MAN ACROSS
from her. His hair was longer, his blue eyes
were wide, a bit confused. He wore an orange
inmate uniform, though she doubted he'd see the
inside of a prison for much longer.

No . . . William "Billy" Marshall had recently been
evaluated by not one but two court-appointed psychiatrists and those guys both had thought that he was,
well . . . insane. Though they'd used other words, of
course. Nicer, more clinical words.

*Suffering severe posttraumatic stress as a result of
his abduction.*

Dissociative personality disorder.

Intense psychological trauma.

"Hello," Sarah said softly after too much time had
passed and Billy remained silent. "Do you know who
I am?"

He shook his head.

"My name is Sarah Jacobs." She waited, trying to
see if her name would ring any bells for Billy, but he
just stared back at her. "I work with Ana at LOST."

He straightened. His hands were cuffed in front of him. "Ana?" He leaned toward Sarah. "Is Ana okay? Is Ana—"

"She's all right." Sarah stared at him. "She wants you to answer some questions for me." Actually, Ana didn't know about this little talk, not yet. Gabe had pulled strings to get Sarah this one-on-one conversation, an off-the-books type of chat. "She wants to know . . . she wants to know about all the people you and Cathy killed."

He stared down at the table. "They weren't people. They were monsters."

Right. That would be the dissociative aspect of his condition. He'd distanced himself from the crimes by dehumanizing the victims.

"Was one of those monsters . . . Murphy?" Her father. A serial killer. A man who'd slaughtered so—

Billy's gaze sharpened on her. A faint smile curved his lips.

Sarah went very, very still.

He knows who I am. He knew all along. He's playing a game with me.

"Tell Ana . . . come see me . . . I'll tell Ana . . ." His shoulders fell, as if he were exhausted.

But Sarah was already on high alert. This man—he was smart. He and Cathy Wise had killed God only knew how many people.

Once upon a time, he'd been the victim of a horrible crime. After Jonathan Bright's death, though, Billy had managed to live, to thrive on his own off the grid for years, and to keep Cathy Wise in check. He'd *handled* her, brilliantly, for so long.

"They're wrong about you," Sarah said as she studied him.

He kept looking down at his hands.

"I know my killers," Sarah said.

He still didn't look up.

"You wanted Cathy to kill them all, didn't you? Did you help Cathy to break apart? You and Jonathan? Did you work together on her?"

His head slowly lifted.

Her mind was spinning. "You were the first one he took. The one he kept the longest. What happened during that time?"

The other psychiatrists thought that Billy's mind had fragmented during that time but she . . .

I think he became a killer. "You were the bait, weren't you? That's how he got the others. You brought them to him."

Once more, a faint smile curled his lips.

"You brought them in and then you watched while he hurt them. Until . . . Cathy." How old would Billy have been then? Seventeen? "You were a man then, so you decided that it was time for you to take charge. To stop following *his* orders."

He blinked. His face had gone blank.

"You killed him and you kept Cathy because you liked the power you had with her. Did she always do whatever you said?"

He looked around the room. They were alone. No cameras. No guards. He pulled on the handcuffs— they were linked to a chain that had been secured around the leg of the table. "Always," he whispered to Sarah. "Right until the end . . ."

And that was when she'd died.

He stared into Sarah's eyes. "I won't be locked away behind bars."

No, because he'd convinced the other shrinks that he was crazy, but she could see the truth. "You weren't going to kill yourself at that cabin, were you? You *knew* Cash would stop you."

He laughed. "He's such a good shot. If he'd thought I was the cold-blooded killer, he would have shot me right between the eyes, too."

"Cathy was about to kill Ana," she said, feeling goose bumps rise on her arms. "Cash had no choice but to shoot her."

He shrugged. "So I gave him a choice, with me."

Instead of appearing as a killer, you turned yourself into a victim before him.

Smart. Clever bastard.

"You aren't supposed to be here," he whispered. "You snuck in. Naughty girl . . ."

Sarah stiffened.

"That's why I can talk to you. No one will ever know what I say."

And he was saying plenty.

"No cameras are running. No witnesses. Just us," he whispered. "There will never be any proof of what I say here."

"You think people wouldn't believe me?" Now she was angry. "I'm a respected profiler, I'm—"

"I'm the boy who was taken and tortured. I'm the one who is so very . . ." He smiled. "Lost."

Sarah's heartbeat drummed steadily in her chest. "What were you like before he took you?" Because

William Marshall's parents were dead. He had no
living family. No one who could tell her about the boy
that Billy had been so long ago.

"Trying to see if I was already . . . different?" His
laughter was rough. "Jonathan did like the different
ones. The kids who enjoyed hurting themselves. Or
their pets. He'd watch the kids for a while. Make sure
they were just right."

Right . . . like you'd been right?

"Said kids like us were easier to take. A bit of trouble, so the cops and the parents always waited longer
to start looking for us. Thought we'd left on our own.
Made it so much simpler for him." Billy inclined his
head. "He liked to bring out the darkness inside. Some
people, they just have a lot of darkness, you know
what I mean?" He paused. "Betting you have plenty of
darkness, being Murphy's daughter and all."

She licked her lips. "Yes. I do." A very true answer.
"The kids who died . . . I guess they weren't dark
enough?"

"They didn't follow the rules." Said without any
emotion. Did he have any emotion left inside of him?
Sarah wasn't so sure. "Sometimes, those rules meant
we had to do very, very bad things."

A new picture was emerging in her mind. That was
the thing about a profile. The more information you
had, the more the profile would twist and turn.

If Jonathan Bright had truly picked a certain "type"
of child . . . one that was already striking out by hurting others, perhaps he'd honed his own monsters.

Nature versus nurture. Kids that *could* have grown
up to be perfectly normal had been altered. Their

darkest urges pulled out, they'd been tormented until they either broke . . .

Or they changed.

Sarah stared at the man before her, and she saw a monster gazing back. "How many people did you and Cathy kill?"

"Twenty . . ."

Surprise had her heartbeat kicking to double-time speed, but she didn't let her expression alter. "Did you murder my father? Did you kill Murphy?"

The door opened behind her. She looked back and saw a guard slide inside the room. She'd only been promised five minutes. Five minutes with the prisoner completely secured. She needed longer. So much longer.

"Time's up," the guard said, his voice brisk.

Dammit. Sarah looked back at Billy.

"I didn't have the pleasure of meeting Murphy." Billy blinked innocently at her. "But maybe one day . . . when I get cured . . . I'll be able to go back in society. I'll be sure to look for him then."

The guard came around the table. He unlocked the chain that bound Billy to the table and he led him out of the room. Billy's steps were slow as he shuffled away.

Sarah sat there a moment, a dull ringing in her ears.

After a moment, she gathered her bag and hurried outside. She'd just left the secure holding area when—

The FBI executive assistant director stepped into her path. "Judging by your face, Dr. Jacobs, that little meeting went as I feared it would."

She drew up short.

Darius inclined his head toward her. "I had to give my approval to get you in there. Who do you think Gabe contacted? Lucky for him, I had already agreed to provide LOST with a favor."

"Billy Marshall might have been a victim once," she said clearly, "but he's a killer now." Something she believed with utter certainty.

"I know." He sighed. "But no jury is going to convict that guy. They'll see him as damaged. Broken. The defense will show pictures of a boy who was taken from his family. The jury will look at those images and they'll never see him for the predator that he is today. They'll find him not guilty. Probably by reason of mental defect or maybe they'll just straight up pull jury nullification. I've seen shit happen like that before."

"He said . . . twenty victims. That he'd killed *twenty* people."

"Do you believe him?"

"No." She shook her head. "I think there are more."

His eyes closed. "Hell." Sadness and rage blended on his face. "Sometimes, I think it won't ever end."

"If he gets out, Billy will just kill again."

Darius nodded. "Then I guess I have to make sure he doesn't get out."

Easier said than done.

He turned away from her, but stopped. "Did you find out about your father?"

"He said . . . he said he hasn't killed Murphy."

"And did you believe *that?*"

She had. "I think he would have bragged about the crime."

Darius seemed to absorb that for a moment. "I

agree." His head tilted as he studied her. "Did you know that there are about two hundred and fifty serial killers on the loose . . . at any given time?"

"Yes." Her stomach clenched. "Yes, I did know that."

"Course you knew." He offered her a tight smile. "Well, we just knocked that number down, didn't we? Consider this a win. He won't get out, not for a long time, and when he does . . . we'll be ready for him."

Right. They had time to fight this battle.

She nodded and her grip tightened on her bag.

"Besides, until then, he'll be staying at River View Psychiatric Hospital." His lips twisted. "Dr. Summers won't be supervising his care, but she had friends at that place. Friends who I am sure . . . well, they'll give dear Billy extra special treatment." His laughter was mocking. "*Extra* special. Bet he didn't count on that . . ."

Chill bumps skated down her spine.

"Payback can be a real bitch," Darius said. Then he headed down the narrow hallway.

Sarah stood there a moment, heart racing.

And she knew he was right.

People paid for their crimes, in one way or another. No one ever escaped justice.

Not really.

Not forever.